STRANGLEHOLD

Margie Lee Schlinker

Copyright © 2017 by Margie Lee Schlinker

Designer Book Template © 2017 Renee Fisher
https://www.reneefisher.com

Cover Design: Stephanie Bernotas
Cover Photo: Kai Dorner
Author Photo: Steve Trupiano

ISBN-13: 978-1975842291
ISBN-10: 1975842294

Endorsements

"This book was gripping. It took my breath away—a really great read! Thanks for sharing. I loved the characters, all very realistic and intriguing. The pace is fantastic—it moves quickly but fills in a lot of interesting details...there was never a dull moment."

Paul Schult, Senior Pastor, Redeemer Lutheran Church, Redwood City, California

"This book is a slam dunk—very well done! Very interesting. An awesome read. I thoroughly enjoyed it!"

Chuck Schlie, Senior Pastor, Messiah Lutheran Church, Weldon Spring, Missouri

"*Stranglehold* weaves together life in a small town with a crime spree that shocks the community. As the mystery unfolds, the characters come to life. You won't want to put this book down until the murderer is caught!"

Judy Besancenez, retired elementary teacher/librarian

Margie masterfully wove together my favorite story elements in this stirring narrative. Likable characters, mystery lurking everywhere, interesting setting, and exciting climax. I loved *Stranglehold*!

Laura Fleetwood, Author of Seekingthestill.com and I Heart Mom.

"This was my first introduction to reading a "whodunit" mystery, and boy I have experienced the hook of it! I couldn't put it down—even at 3 a.m. When I reached the end, I wanted more. I need the sequel now!"

Deborah Lein, Telecom EDI QA

Dedication

Many people have helped me during this exciting journey to write a mystery novel. They have read drafts, given me insight, really good advice, and most of all, encouragement. I am grateful to all of them.

However, from the beginning there has been one constant, encouraging voice, pushing me to continue my work, to fight self-doubt, and to press on to complete my goal. That very special person is my dear friend, **Judith Louise Besancenez.** *Judy is a retired teacher and elementary school librarian whose love of teaching did not stop when she left her library full of books. In her kind and gentle manner, she read my copy, made valuable suggestions, and forced me to get out of my comfort zone. Her actions are a constant reminder to me that teachers are amazing people. Because of them, we can read, write, and earn a living! They are truly a precious gift from God!*

Table of Contents

Prologue

The elderly woman knew she was going to die. She was not strong enough to loosen the rope that her attacker held tightly around her neck.

"Why would someone want to kill me?" she asked herself as the pounding in her chest beat harder and harder, her heart desperately demanding the flow of oxygen. In the waning light of consciousness, she did a quick assessment of her life to find the answer to her question.

"Did I offend someone? Did I cut off a driver who followed me home? Did I interrupt a burglar?"

With one last determined ounce of energy, she jerked her head around to see her killer. Her fear turned to confusion as she looked into the face of someone she knew, loved and trusted…and saw the smile on that person's face.

Chapter 1

No one would ever call Bill Tom Bradley a handsome man, least of all Bill Tom Bradley. Yet, with a rugged, angular face, an easy smile over perfect teeth, and honey brown eyes that sparkled when he laughed, Bill Tom got more than a second glance from most women with any working hormones. The fact that he was oblivious to their admiration made him even more appealing.

As police chief of Hillside, Missouri, Bill Tom was a familiar presence around town. The way he filled out his blue jeans and long-sleeved, light blue shirts had even the community's younger women fanaticizing about the well-toned hard body that resided beneath the disturbingly thin layer of fabric. Not a bad accomplishment for a man of 50. Many of the unattached women in town brought baked goods to his office, invited him to dinner, or contrived an "emergency" to gain his attention, but all their efforts were in vain. Bill Tom was a one-woman man.

He had built his life around Sarah Louise Fischer, the young woman he met and married while he was in the Marine Corps. When Sarah died from ovarian cancer, Bill Tom buried his heart with her on the slopes of the cemetery in Hillside, and focused all his love and attention on their daughter, Kayla, who was just ten years old when she lost her mother.

On a pre-dawn Tuesday morning in August, Bill Tom was looking forward to his daily breakfast date with Sarah. He drove slowly up the steep gravel road that led to Trinity Lutheran Cemetery, hopped out of his truck, sat down and leaned against a tree next to Sarah's gravesite. He sipped his steaming hot coffee and tore into a fresh hot sausage biscuit.

"Here's to you, Sarah," he said. He raised the Styrofoam cup toward her gravestone. "Good mornin', darlin'."

He looked forward to these quiet mornings alone with Sarah. Just being close to the place where she was buried gave him comfort and a sense of peace. He used this time to mull over life's problems and challenges and plan his path forward.

Bill Tom loved the town of Hillside in the early morning. The sun, rising slowing over the ridge behind him, cast golden rays of light across the pale sky. The vast steeples of the Catholic and Lutheran churches, sitting like fortresses on the facing hill, created a stark, black outline against the ocean of blue.

Hillside had grown up sporadically on and between three hills that formed a triangle, with the busiest street in town--Highway 24-- meandering through the valley. Visitors who crossed the rickety old Missouri River Bridge into the town were instantly swept up in a time warp that took them back to Germany in the 1800s.

Settled by German grape growers in the 1830s, Hillside was rich in red brick houses with green shuttered windows, an equal number of churches and taverns, and more wineries than anything else. It was the kind of town where everybody knew everybody else's business, and at the end of a hot summer day, members of each household went to bed with no more security than a thin metal latch on a screen door and a prayer to God for safekeeping.

Relaxing under a tree in Trinity Lutheran Cemetery, Bill Tom could look over to "church hill," follow it to the left along the ridge to the Grand Mountain Winery hill, and observe all points in between. He watched as, one by one, the lights in the houses of Hillside began to twinkle in the dark valley below. He heard a dog barking on the winery hill and knew that Clyde Voss, the owner and master vintner, had arrived at work with Goldie, his Golden Retriever.

Bill Tom leaned his head against the tree, closed his eyes and sucked in a full load of invigorating fresh air. As he finished his last bite of breakfast he could see that the town below was quickly coming to life. Highway 24--called Market Street--was picking up some traffic.

He laughed to himself. In the town of Hillside, when four cars pulled up to the four-way stop sign at one time, the unusual event was called a traffic jam.

He had just finished his last sip of coffee and stuffed the biscuit wrapper into the empty Styrofoam cup when he noticed something strange. Amos Pruitt's red pickup truck was speeding along Market Street, weaving in and out of traffic.

"*What in the world is wrong with that man?*" Bill Tom jumped to his feet.

He watched the speeding truck until it made a reckless left turn in front of an oncoming car, sped up a hill and stopped with a jerk in front of a red brick house. Bill Tom knew it was the home of Esther Gaines, Amos's sister. He climbed into his truck and headed off to see what was going on.

As he pulled up behind Amos's pickup he saw that his deputy, Randy James, was already there, standing just inside Esther's front door. Trudy Brinkmeyer, Esther's neighbor, was talking to him. Bill Tom jumped out of his truck and ran up the steps that led to the house.

"Bill, it's just awful," Trudy said as he stepped onto the porch. "Esther is dead." She hurled her small body against Bill Tom and cried into his shoulder.

"What happened?" he asked his deputy. He put his arm around Trudy and patted her back. His own voice cracked. Esther Gaines was a good friend. And she was his daughter's Godmother.

"It's true, BT," Randy said. His eyes were wide with shock. "Mrs. Gaines is dead. Trudy found her this morning. I heard her screaming clear down on Market Street by our office."

"I can't believe it. I just can't believe it," Trudy sobbed. She tried to wipe her tears off of Bill Tom's soggy shoulder. "I talked to her yesterday morning before she left to go to that book fair in St. Louis. She felt fine. I didn't see her when she got home. I was at the high school, mending the football uniforms. What happened to her?"

"Trudy, I'll go in and try to find out. Did you call an ambulance? How do you know she's dead?"

"I'll show you." She grabbed him by the hand and he followed her through the foyer into the kitchen at the back of the house. Bill Tom took one look at Esther's body lying on the floor and froze in place.

Lying on her back in an awkward position with her knees bent to the side and her feet touching her backside, Esther Gaines had the unmistakable look of death. Her body had a bluish cast and her eyes were wide open, staring blankly at the ceiling. Her elbows were bent and her hands were clenched into fists. Her face held an expression of terror. Her brother Amos sat next to her on the floor holding his head in his hands.

Esther had been a teacher at Hillside High for over forty years. As far as Bill Tom knew she had no enemies.

"I called an ambulance, BT," Randy said. He walked briskly into the room and stopped talking the instant he saw Amos.

"She was my precious little sister," the grieving man said. His voice was shaky; tears rolled down his flushed cheeks. "When she was born I was six years old. I was disappointed that she wasn't a boy, but she turned out to be the best thing for me. Until I met Aggie, she was my best friend."

"I know," Bill Tom said. He walked over to Amos and patted him on the shoulder. "Why don't you go into the living room so you can sit down? There's nothing more you can do for Esther, and I need to get some things done in here before the ambulance comes."

At Bill Tom's gentle persuasion, Amos rose to his feet, swiped his hand across his tear-stained face and walked into Esther's living room.

"Go with him, Randy, and see what you can do to help," Bill Tom whispered. "Has anybody besides you, Amos, and Trudy been in the house since Trudy found her?"

"I don't think so." Randy shook his head, put his arm around Amos and led him into the living room.

"I came over this morning to bring Esther some blueberry muffins," Trudy said. "When she didn't answer the door, I just came on in and called her name. You know Esther sometimes forgets to lock her door. That's when I found her. It was about 15 minutes ago. I called Amos first thing. I didn't see anybody else in the house."

Bill Tom nodded his head. "Trudy, would you go outside and wait for the ambulance to get here? I noticed some neighbors standing in their front yards looking toward the house. No doubt they'll be down here in a minute. Will you try to keep them outside for me?"

Trudy nodded, her face red as a beet, and went to wait for the ambulance.

Bill Tom waited until she left the room, then knelt beside Esther's cold, lifeless body.

"What happened to you, Esther?" he whispered, his voice thick with emotion. He felt his own eyes well up with tears as he looked at the dead woman who had been such a good friend. Through the tears, he stared at the one element of the scene that made no sense at all, the one that had aroused his curiosity the minute he walked into the room.

Esther was wearing a short-sleeved pink tee shirt, pink and white checked Capri pants and white sandals, typical summer clothes for a hot and humid August day in Missouri. Why then, did she have a white wool scarf wrapped around her neck?

Bill Tom leaned forward and carefully lifted the scarf to get a look at her neck. A deep purple rope burn confirmed his suspicions: somebody strangled her.

He laid the scarf back in place and gently reached up to close the dead woman's eyes. Suddenly he jumped up, turned toward the sink and threw cold water in his face. For a second he thought he was going to be sick.

His head was pounding and his heart was racing. Esther Gaines was like an older sister to him and now he had to find her killer. It had been a long time since he had to solve a murder.

As an ex-Marine, he had worked in the Secret Service, and then as a detective on the St. Louis County police force. When a bullet from a fleeing suspect's gun grazed his shoulder, Sarah begged him to quit the force. So he became a security director for a local manufacturing company until he took the job as police chief of Hillside. In his seventeen years in the small town of 2,000 people, there hadn't been one murder. In fact, according to town folklore, the closest thing to a murder happened on April 10, 1872 when Eldo Morgan got drunk, tried to shoot the mayor over a disagreement about Eminent Domain, and shot the mayor's horse instead.

Randy walked back into the room and looked at his boss. "Amos is going to call Aggie. She's in Kansas City visiting her cousin."

"Come over here for a second," Bill Tom motioned for Randy to join him by the sink. "She was strangled, Randy," he whispered. "She didn't die of natural causes. Did you look through the house before I got here?"

Randy nodded his head and backed away from Bill Tom so he could look at Esther's body.

"The minute I saw the scarf I told Trudy to stay here in the kitchen and I searched all the other rooms. I looked downstairs, too, but I didn't see anything unusual. I can't believe someone would want to hurt Mrs. Gaines. We've got to get to the bottom of this real quick."

"What I want you to do first, Randy, is go back to the office and call Walter Beacham. He's a buddy of mine from the Marines and he's a crime scene investigator with the St. Louis County Police Department. Mary Ann knows his number. Ask him if he can get a crew together and bring them out here to scour over this place. Tell him we need him this morning, if at all possible. And then find the crime scene tape, wherever that is, and get this place roped off."

Just as Bill Tom was about to go tell Amos what happened to Esther, he heard the ambulance sirens and headed for the front door instead. The ambulance pulled up in front of Esther's house and Dr. Woodrow Schrader jumped out of the passenger side before it came to a complete stop. He ran up the front steps, ignoring the crowd of neighbors that had gathered in the yard, and met Bill Tom at the front door.

"What happened to Mrs. Gaines?" he asked. "I heard the emergency call come in, so I came along with the guys." He nodded his head toward the two men dressed in white scrubs carrying a gurney up the steps.

"Come inside and I'll fill you in," Bill Tom said. He gave the doctor a grim look.

"Somebody strangled her, Woody," he said when they were beyond hearing distance from the crowd outside.

"What? Who would want to kill Mrs. Gaines? Was it a burglary or something?"

"Randy's checking it out," Bill Tom sighed. "I have to go tell Amos that his sister was murdered. I'm pretty sure he thinks she had a stroke or a heart attack. He took that hard enough. When I tell him the truth I don't know what he'll do.

"I'd like you to examine her body, but try not to disturb anything. I have a crime scene investigation team on the way from St. Louis."

Woody and Bill Tom looked up as the paramedics reached the kitchen door.

"I'll tell them what's going on before I examine her," Woody said.

"Ask them to watch the front door and not let anybody in," Bill Tom said. "I don't want more traffic in this house until the crime scene investigators get here."

Bill Tom squared his shoulders and took a deep breath. He walked into Esther's living room and stared at the grieving man sitting on the couch. It was 7:15 according to the clock on Esther's mantle. Rubbing his fingers across his tired eyes, Bill Tom felt like he'd been up for hours.

He sat down on the couch next to Amos. As he prepared to speak, he shot a brief glance heavenward for divine guidance.

"Would you like a glass of water or something, Amos?" He put his arm around the man's shoulders.

"Thanks, but I'm okay," Amos answered, slowly turning to meet Bill Tom's gaze. "Look around this room," he said, referring to Esther's tastefully decorated sage green and cream-colored living room. "Think of how many happy Sunday afternoons we've spent in this house, playing cards or singing funny songs at the piano--and waiting for a great dinner."

Bill Tom nodded in silence, swallowed hard and took a deep breath.

"Amos," he began, "there's just no easy way to say this, so I'm just gonna have to give it to you straight. I'm sorry to have to tell you this, but it looks very much like Esther was strangled."

He bowed his head and tightened the grip he had on the old gentleman's shoulders. The room was eerily silent except for the steady ticking of the clock on the mantle and the soft hum of central air conditioning. Bill Tom's words hung in the room like a dark cloud.

Amos was quiet, but Bill Tom could feel him begin to shake.

He moaned slightly at first and then more loudly as the reality of Bill Tom's words sunk in, and his grief was coupled with growing rage.

"Who would want to hurt Esther?" he shouted. He stood up, clenching his fists. "I'll kill the son-of-a-bitch with my bare hands," Amos yelled between sobs. He punched his right fist into his left palm.

Bill Tom jumped up and again put his arm around the guy's shoulders.

"Don't talk like that, Amos," he said. "It won't do any good for you to take the law into your own hands. You'll just make matters worse. I promise you I'll find out who did this and you'll get your day in court. But you've got to let us handle it. Why don't you go lie down in the guest room for a while? Were you able to get in touch with Aggie?"

"Her cousin is driving her back to Hillside," Amos answered. His voice was a bit calmer now, but he was still shaking.

Bill Tom helped Amos into the guest room and made sure the man was comfortable before he closed the door and headed for the kitchen.

He was about to ask Doc Schrader for an estimated time of death when he heard Trudy call to him for help. She was fighting the paramedics' perilous efforts to keep her from entering Esther's home.

"What do you mean, I can't come in?" Trudy yelled. "Esther was my best friend, and I need to get this food into her house before all her relatives get here."

Bill Tom and Woody reached the scene just in time to see Trudy--holding a crock pot--give one of the drivers a left hip push that almost sent him sailing over Esther's front porch wall.

"Trudy, what in the world are you doing?" Bill Tom asked. He was shocked at her behavior, but he tried to keep his voice low. The scene in front of Esther's house was drawing a large crowd of friends, neighbors and curiosity seekers.

"Esther is dead," Trudy said, fighting back tears. "I put some left-over pot roast in my crock pot to warm it up. I want to plug it in on her countertop and this dim-wit won't let me in the door!" She nodded toward the startled ambulance driver.

Bill Tom looked down at the frazzled, curly-headed blond woman and let out a deep sigh. Usually she was a level-headed person. She and her husband Bud had been good friends to him and Sarah. Trudy's son Brian and his daughter Kayla were in the same class at school and had gone to the junior prom together. Bud died just six months after Sarah, so Bill Tom knew the grief she had to endure. They had become good friends, but, under the circumstances, she was testing his patience.

"Trudy, don't you have electricity?" he whispered. "Plug the damn thing into the wall in your kitchen."

"Bill Tom, everyone knows that when a family suffers the death of a loved one, food becomes a very soothing and healing medicine." She returned Bill Tom's stare with a defiant one of her own. "The aroma of a nice pot roast in this house will bring comfort and healing to poor Amos and Aggie and their kids. This is the only way I know how to help them. Please let me through."

"Just give me the pot, Trudy," Bill Tom whispered. "I'll plug it in myself. Will you please go over there on the lawn and wait for me?" He nodded to a place in Esther's yard where a group of ladies had gathered. "I need to talk to you about something. But you have to give me a minute. And don't go stirrin' up the neighbors to support your food theory. I don't want more pots of food in this house, okay?"

Trudy sighed, nodded her head, and hurried down the porch steps to join a group of women standing by Esther's colorful flower bed.

Bill Tom and Woody exchanged an amused glance and headed back into Esther's kitchen. As he plugged Trudy's crock pot into the wall socket and carefully set it to "low"--Trudy would be furious if he let the damn thing burn--he realized that he was getting a giant-sized headache.

He tried to ignore the pain as he turned to Woody, who was back on his knees examining Esther's body.

"She was definitely strangled, Bill," the doctor said. "We'll do a thorough exam, of course, but it certainly looks like that was the cause of her death. We need to wait for the crime scene people to get here before we take her body to the morgue."

Just then, Randy walked back into the room.

"I called your friend, Mr. Beacham," he said, looking at Bill Tom. "He said he'd get a crew out here in an hour. And I looked for the crime scene tape, but I couldn't find any. All we have is this yellow ribbon we used to tie on the trees when Eddie Maxwell came home from Afghanistan last year."

"Randy, we're not gonna secure a crime scene with yellow ribbon." Bill Tom shook his head in frustration. "You're gonna have to find that tape."

"We've got some in the ambulance," Dr. Schrader interrupted.

"Thanks," Bill Tom said. "I've got to leave for a little while but I have to go talk to Trudy first."

"Go get 'er, boss," Randy said. He punched Bill Tom on the shoulder. "I just saw her standing by the flower bed--a snap dragon among the petunias."

"Are snap dragons carnivorous?" Bill Tom raised his eyebrows.

"Not usually. But in your case I think she'd make an exception. She looks like she's ready to bite somebody."

Bill Tom wrinkled his face and headed for the front door.

"Stay here and watch over things while I go look for Kayla, okay? She went horseback riding with Brian this morning."

"Yeah, I'll do that boss," Randy said. "I hope you find her quickly. I know you don't want her to hear about this from somebody else."

"You're right," Bill Tom said as he headed for the door. "I'm glad Kayla's cell phone is broken. I hope Brian has his turned off."

From Esther's front porch he could see that the news about her death was traveling at lightning speed across the small community. That made his meeting with Trudy very important.

He ran down the steps and hurried over to interrupt her conversation with three other women.

"Trudy, I need to talk to you," he said. He nodded politely to the ladies standing by her.

"We're so upset about this, Chief Bradley," they said, almost in unison. "Was it her heart?"

"It's a sad day for all of us, ladies," he said. "We're still trying to find out what happened."

He put his hand on Trudy's back and pushed her gently toward the corner of the yard where they could talk privately.

"Trudy, when I got up this morning Kayla was fixing a basket of food for herself and Brian. She said they were going on an all-day ride. Do you know where they were going? Did Brian take his cell phone?"

Trudy shook her head. "He forgot it. I saw it on the kitchen table this morning. If I were you I'd go up to Bud's old cabin--you remember where it is, right? Off of that old road at the end of Grand Mountain Skyway. When Brian was a little boy, he and Bud went riding a lot and they'd always stop at the cabin for breakfast. I think you guys went with them once in a while."

"I hope you're right, Trudy." He stopped for a second and looked over his shoulder to make sure no one else was within hearing distance.

"Before I go look for the kids, I need to tell you something, and I need you to keep calm and not lose it in front of all these people. Okay?" Bill Tom gave her a stern look.

"What? What do you need to tell me?" He had Trudy's full attention.

"It looks like Esther was strangled," Bill Tom whispered into her ear. "She didn't die of natural causes."

Trudy's eyes grew wide as the blood drained quickly from her face. She clamped her hand over her mouth and started to shake. He grabbed her arm.

"Trudy," he whispered, "you've got to hold it together. You can't let anyone else know what I just told you. Do you hear me?"

Trudy nodded, her hand still over her mouth. Bill Tom put his arms around the tiny women and gave her a tight hug.

"We'll get through this, Trudy, but right now I've got to go find our kids. Do you understand?

Trudy squeezed Bill Tom's hand and bowed her head.

He patted her on the back and ran down to his truck. All he could think about as he headed up the hill to Grand Mountain Skyway was how Kayla would take this news. His heart ached when he thought about his beautiful daughter who'd had to endure the pain of losing her mother at the age of ten. Would she be able to bear another huge loss in her life? If it would help, he'd cut out his own heart to spare that girl any pain.

Chapter 2

Bill Tom's truck stirred up dust as he turned off Grand Mountain Skyway onto the dirt road that led to Bud Brinkmeyer's rustic three-room log cabin. Sure enough, he saw the cabin and two horses tied up outside. Trudy had been right.

He brought the truck to a screeching halt, jumped out of the cab, ignored the horses, took the cabin steps in two giant strides to get to the porch, and pounded on the door.

"Chief Bradley," Brian Brinkmeyer acknowledged him with surprise in his voice, "come on in. Is something wrong?"

Bill Tom gave Brian a weak smile and a pat on the shoulder as he walked into the room.

Kayla was just getting up from the kitchen table to greet him. It was obvious the two had been eating their breakfast.

"Hi, Daddy," she said, "want something to eat? It's not all healthy stuff," she teased. She gave her dad a big smile. "I'm sure there's some high calorie, high cholesterol sweet roll we can find for you."

He looked at her, his heart aching, and tried to smile.

"Honey," he said, putting his arm around Kayla and looking back to find Brian, "come over here and sit down with me. Something's happened and you kids need to know about it."

Bill Tom sat down on an old worn couch with Brian on one side and Kayla on the other.

"Dad, what is it?" Kayla asked, her green eyes growing narrow with concern. "What's happened?"

Bill Tom looked at her, then at Brian and pulled them closer to his side.

"Kids, I have some bad news," he began. He swallowed hard, struggling to keep his composure. "Brian, after you guys left on your ride this morning, your mom took some muffins over to Mrs. Gaines' house for breakfast. She found Mrs. Gaines on the kitchen floor. She was dead."

"What?" Kayla's hand flew to her mouth. "We just went riding with her on Sunday--just two days ago, Dad. She was fine. What happened?"

Bill Tom ached with pain as he watched Kayla's face grow white with shock. To his surprise, her eyes remained dry and she was keeping her composure.

"It looks like she was strangled," he answered, glancing over at Brian who appeared to be in a daze. Instinctively he gave the boy an extra hard squeeze as he continued. "Doc Schrader is doing a medical exam. I came up here because I wanted the two of you to hear it from me before you heard it from someone else."

"Is my mom, okay?" Brian asked.

"She's upset, but she's holding it together," Bill Tom said. He looked at the boy with genuine affection. "She started cooking for Amos and Aggie. You know your mom, she gets through things like this in her own way." Bill Tom had to smile slightly as he thought of Trudy trying to get into Esther's house with that pot roast.

"That's an understatement," Brian said. "I'd better ride back right away so I can be with her. You ride back with your dad, Kayla. I'll get both the horses back to the barn."

"Why don't you both come with me?" Bill Tom suggested. "We'll tie Hank and Ernie to the back of my truck and head on down the hill."

"Dad, I can't even imagine our lives without Miss Esther," Kayla said. She looked very pale and Bill Tom thought she might faint.

"Honey, do you need to sit here for a while before we leave?" Bill Tom asked.

Kayla nodded her head and started to cry. Much to Bill Tom's disappointment, she reached in front of him and put her arms around Brian for comfort.

"Well this is awkward," he thought as the two teenagers hugged each other across his chest. "Why don't I just get out of the middle here?" he suggested to the two grieving teens.

"Oh, Daddy, I know this hurts you, too," Kayla said. She pulled him into a three-way hug.

They sat on the couch in this uncomfortable position, trying to give each other comfort. Bill Tom pushed his face into his daughter's shiny red hair and let himself cry, if only for a moment.

Gently, he tried to disengage himself from the embrace so he could get a grip on his own emotions and get back to work.

"You guys just sit here for a few minutes," he choked. "I need to make a phone call."

As Bill Tom stood up, the teenagers wasted no time lunging into a tight embrace. Bill Tom had always known that Kayla and Brian were close--they had grown up together. Now he found himself wondering just how close. They seemed to be very familiar and comfortable with each other's bodies.

He walked into the kitchen to make his phone call and get away from the kids. Seeing Kayla and Brian embrace like that made him wish that he could go home to the soft, warm comfort of a loving woman.

"It's Bill Tom," he said into his cell phone at the sound of his deputy's voice. "Did Beach and his crew get there yet?"

"Yeah, they're here, BT," Randy said. "And you should see 'em. They're dissecting this place. Your friend Beach is something else. He's always smoking a cigar and barking orders at the crew. And he keeps lifting the lid on that pot roast. Doc Schrader told me Trudy brought it over. I hope he doesn't get ashes in it."

"Tell him I'm on my way, Randy," Bill Tom said. The mental image of Beach made him smile.

Walter Beacham, III was one of St. Louis' top crime scene investigators. Long-time friends from the Marine Corps, Bill Tom had once called on Beach for help when the company he worked for--a steel manufacturer in St. Louis--had a break-in. Some sensitive government documents had been stolen and Beach found the evidence and solved the crime.

Beach was built like a Sumo wrestler, but his personality wasn't as charming--until people got to know him. Underneath the huge mass of humanity, the big, round, red face and his crass remarks about the way dead people looked, lived a heart of gold and a man who would do anything in his power to stop a killer.

As Bill Tom headed back into the cabin's living room, he thought he should announce himself.

"Are you guys ready to go?" he called out as he rounded the corner. He looked at them, now sitting side-by-side, holding hands on the couch. Pale faces. Red eyes. Two kids who just lost a trusted teacher and friend.

"We're ready, Chief," Brian said, looking at Kayla for affirmation.

Bill Tom dropped Brian off at Cooper's barn where they boarded their horses. Then he drove Kayla to their house.

"I'm coming in with you, Sweetie," he said as she started to get out of the truck.

"Oh, Dad, you don't have to do that. I know you've got work to do. You've got your hands full. You don't have to worry about me."

He pulled his keys out of the ignition and opened the door.

"Just the same," he said with a smile, "a gentleman always escorts his lady to the door."

He looked at his daughter and gently stroked his hand across her cheek.

"I love you more than anything in the world, Kayla," he said, his eyes moistening again. "I'd do anything I could to keep you from feeling any pain."

She leaned over, gave him a quick kiss and a hug and they both got out of the truck and walked to the house. They could hear Moonshine, their three-year-old Yellow Lab, howling in delight as she sensed their presence.

Bill Tom looked around the outside of their house and up and down the street. When he opened the back door he examined the lock carefully.

"You think the killer is still around here, don't you, Dad?" Kayla asked, bending down to pet Moonshine.

"I'm just checking things out, that's all." Bill Tom walked through their kitchen, down the hall and to the front door.

Kayla followed him.

"Dad, the last time you checked the locks on all our doors was when I saw that scary movie on TV when I was eight years old and you had to convince me that nobody could get into this house. Now what's up? Do you think the killer is still around here?" she asked again, her eyes challenging him to tell her the truth.

He looked down into his daughter's beautiful face and realized that she was no longer a little girl. She deserved and needed to know the truth.

The sudden ring of his cell phone saved him from trying to answer her questions.

"BT, I need you to get over here as soon as possible," Randy yelled into the phone. He sounded out of breath and very frustrated. "Somehow Trudy got back into the house and she and Beach got into it over that silly pot roast."

"I'm on my way," Bill Tom said. He shoved his phone back in his pocket and looked at Kayla.

"I've got to go now, Honey" he said. "Randy's got some problems over at Miss Esther's. You stay here and keep the doors locked, okay?"

"Do you think the killer is still around here?" she repeated her question.

"I don't know. Just stay inside, keep the doors locked and call me immediately if you need me."

"Okay, Dad," Kayla promised. "I know this is a hard day for you. I just want you to know that I love you and we'll get through this together, just like we always do."

She smiled at him, crossed her fingers and touched her heart.

Chapter 3

When Bill Tom arrived at Esther's house he could hear the ruckus before he could actually see it. And once he walked into Esther's kitchen he couldn't believe his eyes. There was his friend, Beach, eating what appeared to be a roast beef sandwich, with Trudy Brinkmeyer slapping his arm with a potholder.

"Hey, Bill Tom, good to see ya," Beach yelled to his friend. He was grinning from ear to ear. A petite five-foot-two lady hitting him with a potholder was just no match for the big, burly, good-natured guy.

"Trudy, what in the world has gotten into you?" Bill Tom rushed over to rescue Beach. "Have you gone absolutely nuts?"

"He just helped himself to the pot roast I was heating up for Esther's family, Bill Tom. Without even asking," she said, her voice high-pitched in excitement. Her face was red and her hair was a mess.

"Trudy, calm down!" Bill Tom pulled the potholder from her hands and grabbed her shoulders. He was shocked that the normally rational woman would exhibit such bizarre behavior.

"I tried to help Amos and Aggie and now the family isn't going to get to enjoy it," Trudy said, looking at Bill Tom with her teary, bloodshot eyes. "He's eating the family's comfort food."

"Trudy, he just ate one sandwich…I think. Now you get out of here, go home and don't cause any more trouble." Bill Tom gave Trudy a stern look.

Suddenly Brian ran into the room.

"Mom, what are you doing? I could hear you screaming all the way down the street."

"Brian, take your mom home and try to calm her down," Bill Tom said. He could tell the boy was shaken up at the sight of Esther lying on the kitchen floor.

He handed Trudy over to Brian, patting the boy on the back. She calmed down quickly in the presence of her son.

"Make her some hot tea or something," Bill Tom suggested. "Try to get her to relax. And Brian, even if you have to tie her up, don't let her come back over here, okay?"

"Okay, Chief," Brian said. He put his arm around his mother's shoulders. "I'll try."

"Do the best you can," he said.

"How did she get back in here?" Bill Tom asked Randy after Brian and Trudy left the room.

"She just ignored the crime scene tape, BT," Randy said, totally exasperated. "I tried to keep her from coming in, but she kicked my leg and I fell down the porch steps. I think my knee is bleeding."

Randy left the room in search of a bandage while Beach leaned against the kitchen wall finishing his sandwich and watching the scene with an amused grin.

"I'm sorry, Beach," Bill Tom said. He shook his head in disbelief as he extended his hand to greet his good friend.

"Billy, I'm an ex-Marine and a retired FBI profiler. I've been a crime scene investigator for over twenty years and nothing like this has ever happened to me before," Beach said. He shook his friend's hand enthusiastically.

"I'm sorry," Bill Tom said. "Trudy's just not herself today."

"She's a wild one, huh? Is she your girlfriend?"

Bill tom shook his head,

"Normally, she's very level-headed. But Esther was her good friend and neighbor, and they were very close. So what do you think about this situation?" he asked, eager to get the focus back on Esther Gaines.

"My crew is lifting fingerprints all over the place, Billy," Beach said. "What'd you do, sell tickets to the crime scene?"

"Esther Gaines was a well-loved woman, Beach. Taught English at the high school for over forty years. She had a lot of traffic in this house. Trudy found her this morning and called her brother, Amos. Randy heard Trudy screaming and came to see what was wrong. I got here after Amos arrived. Doc Schrader has been in here, too, plus the paramedics. I guess any other prints you find could belong to the one who strangled her," Bill Tom said. He shrugged his shoulders in frustration.

"I think we've got everything we need for now," Beach said.

"How soon can we take her to the hospital morgue, Beach?" Bill Tom asked. He sank into one of Esther's kitchen chairs and rubbed his eyes.

"I told your doctor friend he could take her at any time. He wanted to wait for you, said you would want to walk with him to escort her body to the ambulance," Beach said. "We'll finish up here and meet up with the Doc over at the morgue. We're gonna really want to look at that scarf and the rope burns."

Bill Tom nodded in silence. He was looking at Esther's body.

"I think Esther's brother is still resting in her guest bedroom," he said. "I'm going to get him so he can walk out with us."

The neighbors who had been standing in the yard all morning formed a line of respect along Esther's sidewalk as Bill Tom, Dr. Schrader and Amos walked alongside the gurney that carried her body. Some of the people reached out to pat Amos's arm as the men walked by.

After the ambulance was out of sight, Randy drove Amos home, Beach and his crew took off for the morgue, and Bill Tom drove to his office.

As he pulled his truck into the parking lot, he wasn't too surprised to see so many cars parked around the building.

Inside, the place was a madhouse, everyone wanting to know what happened to Esther. Mary Ann Crawford, Bill Tom's secretary, was trying to maintain some degree of order.

"If you'll all be quiet for just a second, I'll try to respond to your questions one at a time," she said in her usual efficient manner.

"We heard that someone might have killed Esther, is that true?" one man asked from the back of the room. Everyone else agreed that they had heard the same rumor.

"Here's Chief Bradley now," Mary Ann said, nodding toward the door. "Maybe he can answer your questions."

Everyone turned to him in silent expectation.

"We haven't completed our investigation yet," he addressed the group. "We're working as fast as we can to determine the cause of death. If you all will just go on about your business, I promise you we'll work as fast as we can to find out what happened. As soon as we know, we'll let you know."

Bill Tom tried to be as kind and patient as his frazzled nerves would allow.

"I heard this was a robbery? Do you think she was murdered?" a number of people asked.

"We're still gathering all the facts," he said. "What I need for all of you to do is go home, or back to work and just go on about your daily business. I promise you I'll let you know what happened as quickly as I can."

One by one the people left Bill Tom's office. He shook hands with many of them as they walked by. He hoped they knew that when he had accurate information he could share with them, he would do it.

When the office had cleared out, he looked at Mary Ann, and walked over to give her a big hug.

"Esther and I went to school together," was all she could get out before she leaned her head against Bill Tom's shoulder and cried.

"I know you've had a tough morning, too, Mary Ann," he said, patting her on the back. "Are you going to be able to stick it out with me? I'm gonna need someone to field the phone calls."

"I'll stay as long as you need me, Chief," Mary Ann nodded. "I'll call George and tell him he's on his own for supper if you need me to stay late."

"At this point let's just take one hour at a time, okay?" He tried to give her a reassuring smile.

She nodded and both of them went to work, she answering the phone calls that were coming in every few minutes and he trying to put together a plausible motive for murder and a list of suspects.

When news reporters from St. Louis and Jefferson City called to get his comments--bad news traveled fast--he confirmed that Esther had been found dead but refused to give any other details of what he described as an ongoing and intense investigation.

He was just finishing up his paperwork at six p.m. when the phone in his office rang for about the fiftieth time.

Instead of transferring the call into Bill Tom, Mary Ann walked into his office.

"It's Mr. Beacham," she said. "He has some news about Esther."

Bill Tom took a deep breath and picked up the phone.

"We've got tiny green fibers on her neck and fifteen sets of fingerprints from the house," Beach said. "We'll be working here through the night."

"Is there anything I can do to help you," Bill Tom asked?

"No, Billy, I think you'd just be hangin' around for nothing. I'll call you if something comes up. I think you should go home and try to get some rest. You're gonna need it."

"You're right about that, Beach. Call me on my cell if you need me."

Bill Tom walked Mary Ann to her car and drove home to what he knew would be a restless night with very little sleep.

Chapter 4

In the northern suburbs of Baltimore, Maryland, the mid-August evening breezes were blowing gently through the tall hickory trees that lined most of the streets. Brook Jennings stood on her back deck, surveying her well-manicured yard for the last time. Silently she said a dry-eyed farewell to the rose bushes she had patiently pruned, the colorful back flower bed of perennials, and the pots of annuals that sat around her deck. The young couple who had bought her house promised they would take good care of all the flowers.

Twisting her shoulder-length curly red hair with her fingers, Brook turned suddenly, bit her bottom lip hard, and walked back into her house for a last inspection before she left it for good.

The day had been challenging. The movers came early and Brook agonized every time the three burly men took a piece of furniture from her house.

"Don't worry now, lady," the burliest one of them said, "we do this for a living. Twenty years now we been workin' as a team. Ain't hurt nobody's furniture so far!"

She had smiled and nodded at them, but she still had her doubts.

She walked slowly through the brick two-story that had been her home for sixteen years. She knew the creative names of the paint on all the walls...names like Honeydew, Mushroom, and Golden Harvest. All picked out to blend perfectly in her tastefully decorated home.

It looked so odd now, empty and sparse. As she headed up the stairs to her bedroom, her footsteps on the hardwood echoed throughout the house. She had carefully filled every nail hole with spackle and touched up the paint. There wasn't a speck of dirt anywhere. The place was pristine.

Suddenly she shivered as a cold chill rippled down her spine.

"I've got to get out of here before I lose it," she mumbled, looking at herself in one of the mirrored closet doors in her bedroom.

She stared at her reflection. Khaki jeans, a white tee-shirt and a black cardigan sweater. If this had been any other Tuesday night she would join her neighbors to drink margaritas and chitchat on someone's deck, or go out to dinner with friends. Instead, she was going to get into her car, leave her home and her friends and head west, to Missouri.

"What in the world were you thinking?" she asked the reflection in the mirror. "You've got to be crazy to be doing this."

Then she remembered why she was going and tried to regain her firm resolve.

Her thoughts were interrupted by the gentle sound of door chimes.

When she opened her front door she was immediately greeted with a tight hug from six-year-old Madelyn, whose parents, Lisa and Mike, had come from next door to say good-bye.

"I know you're about ready to take off, but Madelyn insisted on coming over one more time before you go," Lisa said apologetically. She and Brook had exchanged many tearful good-byes over the past few weeks and they each vowed there would be no tears at the final hour.

"It's okay, I'm glad you came," Brook said, bending down to hug the little girl with straight brown hair who was tugging at her leg.

"I don't want you to go, Mama Brook," Madelyn said, tears streaming down her cheeks. "We haven't finished that puzzle yet and who's gonna put my hair up for my next dance recital?"

"Oh, Sweetie," Brook began, fighting hard to hold back her own tears, "your dad is great with puzzles and your mom can fix your hair in a bun."

Madelyn looked back to see if her mom was listening and then whispered into Brook's ear.

"It always comes out right away after she fixes it," she said.

"Tell her to use more Bobby pins," Brook whispered back.

Some other neighbors had come up to Brook's gigantic porch that ran the whole width of the front of the house, all waiting for their turn to say good-bye.

"Now I want to know something, Madelyn," Brook said, trying to use a stern tone and looking squarely into the child's enormous brown eyes. "Did you make up with Joey Drews? You know he only teases you because he likes you. Boys are funny that way."

"Mommy helped me make him some cookies," Madelyn said seriously, and once again looking around to find her mother, she added in a whisper "but when she wasn't looking I spit in the dough!" She looked up at Brook with a triumphant grin on her face.

Brook let out a laugh and then forced her voice to sound serious.

"Maddy, grudges are a really heavy thing to carry around," she began. "If you don't let go of those bad feelings they'll bring you down. You'll be unhappy all the time and you won't enjoy your life. Will you promise me that you'll try to get along with him?"

"Okay, Mama Brook," Madelyn said, looking sad again. "I'll try. But if he tries anything funny, I'm gonna deck him," she said, holding up her fist.

"If you're gonna hit somebody with your fist, keep your thumb on TOP of your fingers," Brook said, showing the little girl how to make a fist fit for battle. "And only use it in self-defense!

"Now give me a big hug. Mama Brook's gotta get on the road." The little girl wrapped her arms around Brook's neck and gave her a sloppy wet kiss on the cheek.

"I'll miss you, Mama Brook," she said, and ran down the steps to cry on her dad's shoulder.

"Are you sure you don't want to wait until morning?" Lisa asked, walking over to Brook. "You know we have plenty of room for you to spend the night, and Maddie would be delighted."

"No thanks, I like driving at night," Brook said, wiping tears from her eyes as she stood up. "Besides, the sooner I get this trip going the sooner it'll be over. I'm anxious to see my new house in Hillside and make sure all my furniture fits. I want to be settled in before school starts next week. It's gonna be hard enough getting to know all new students and my fellow teachers."

Brook thought for a moment about one particular student who was going to be very important to her.

"Call us as soon as you get there," Lisa said, her voice cracking, "and call us on the road in the middle of the night if you get sleepy or have trouble, okay? You have your cell phone charger, right?"

"Yes, I do," Brook said, forcing a smile, "and yes, I will call you from the road if I need to. Now, I've got to get in that car before I lose my nerve."

Brook gave the young woman another hug, said good-bye to all the other neighbors and made her way to her white Camry sitting in the driveway. The tan leather felt cold against her skin as she settled into the driver's seat.

"Fall's coming quickly," she thought, turning the key in the ignition.

She backed the car out of the driveway, waved a final good-bye to her neighbors and turned her attention to the road ahead. She forced herself not to look into the rear-view mirror.

Brook had planned her entertainment for the trip…a couple of books on tape and her favorite CDs. She threw a bottle of No Doze into her purse just in case.

As she passed through the northern edge of the city into the beautiful Maryland farm country with its gentle rolling hills, the pain of leaving her friends began to ease up a bit.

It was such a beautiful evening. Farms with white fences and horses lined the two-lane highway she had chosen to take to get to the Pennsylvania Turnpike near Harrisburg. In the almost eighteen years she had lived in Maryland she had grown to love the state for its beauty and its convenient location between Washington, DC, Philadelphia and New York. It was easy to enjoy the best of country and city living.

Brook thought about the first time she came to Maryland. She hadn't had a plan. She just left her apartment in St. Louis, headed her car east on I-70 and drove as fast as possible. Almost no worldly possessions--just her car, the money from her savings account and the clothes she had stuffed into her old college trunk.

It was divine providence that led Brook to Baltimore. As she was traveling on the Pennsylvania Turnpike her car began making a funny sound and the temperature gauge indicated that the motor was running hot.

She pulled off at the turnpike's Breezewood, PA exit to have the car fixed. As she was leaving, she misunderstood the mechanic's directions to get back on the turnpike and found herself headed for the Baltimore/Washington, D.C. area.

"What the heck," she thought, and kept on driving. Since she had visited Washington, DC on her high school senior trip, she chose to go to Baltimore--a place she had never seen.

Chapter 5

Armed with an undergraduate degree in English and some impressive experience as a corporate communications director, Brook found a job working at Baltimore's largest real estate association.

The president of the association was Jim Jennings--a guy with a kind heart, a keen mind, and a weakness for attractive red heads. The two were married a year after Brook arrived in Baltimore.

As Brook turned onto the Pennsylvania Turnpike at Harrisburg, the sky had grown dark and the moon was full. She couldn't help thinking about the man she had shared her life with in a picturesque setting in northern Baltimore.

Their marriage had been a happy one--not steamy, but warm and comfortable. After what she had been through when she lived in St. Louis, Brook thanked her lucky stars every night that she had found a man who would love her for who she was--faults and everything.

The sadness that existed between the two was Brook's inability to conceive a child.

"We've got the kids in this neighborhood," he'd said. "You know, it takes a whole village to raise a child. We'll be helpers."

Brook nodded in silent agreement and enrolled in the University of Maryland to get her teaching certificate. If she couldn't have children of her own, she'd enjoy the company of the neighbors' kids and teach English to adolescents.

Their comfortable lifestyle was shattered suddenly when a drunk driver hit Jim's car as he was coming home from a late-night meeting, killing him instantly.

Friends and neighbors surrounded Brook and supported her through the first grim weeks and months as shock gave way to anger and anger was replaced by grief.

Finally, the bitter pain of grief subsided and she found herself able to think about other things and once again find joy in living.

In the three years since Jim's death, Brook tried to rebuild her life and surprisingly, to do that, she found herself thinking more and more about her previous life in St. Louis and the incident that made her run away so abruptly.

Brook waited until she got off the turnpike and into West Virginia before she stopped for a break in driving. The brightly lit truck stop hurt her eyes as she steered the Camry into a parking place.

Once she threw water on her face, popped a No Doze and gulped down a cup of coffee she felt refreshed enough to keep on driving.

"I've got to keep going or I'll lose my nerve," she thought as she merged her way onto I-70 West. "Maybe it's time for some music."

She reached for her pile of CDs without looking and ended up listening to the Righteous Brothers. The seductive sounds of *Unchained Melody* brought back memories of her life in St. Louis.

Brook had worked in the communications department of a local steel manufacturer. Known as a party girl with no particular interest in settling down, Brook was a regular at every happy hour planned by her co-workers, and she had more than her share of brief romantic escapades. In her mind's eye, she had a blueprint, a perfect image of the man of her dreams.

During a short business trip with three male co-workers, Brook spent the night with one of the guys--a guy she'd had her eye on for a long time. It wasn't until three weeks later, when she woke up barfing for the third morning in a row, that she realized she might be pregnant. When her doctor confirmed her suspicions, Brook felt like she had hit a brick wall. Thank goodness her parents were dead; the shock of a pregnancy out of wedlock would have killed them.

Brook had to swallow her pride and tell her boss, who took the news better than she had expected.

"I'll help you as much as I can," the kind man had said. "Now, don't take this the wrong way, Brook, but do you know who the father is?" He was well aware of her party-girl reputation.

"I'm not sure," she lied, protecting the guy's identity.

She spent lots of time wondering how she would raise a baby by herself. She loved children and always wanted to have a big family. Through long talks with her friend Sarah Bradley, Brook knew that Sarah and her husband, Bill Tom, had been trying to have a baby. Nothing had worked, not even *in vitro* fertilization.

A week after Brook's doctor confirmed that she was pregnant, she called Sarah and invited her to lunch.

Wasting no time, the minute the two were seated at a table in the restaurant, Brook sprung the news on Sarah.

"Sarah, I'm pregnant," she began, reaching across the table to grab her friend's hands, "and I want you and Bill Tom to adopt my baby."

"What?" Sarah was speechless.

"I'm in no position to raise a child, Sarah," Brook continued. "The father is married and I don't want him to know. You and your husband would make wonderful parents. Please say you'll do this for me."

"I can't take your baby from you, Brook," Sarah objected. "A baby is the greatest gift in the world. Don't you want to at least give it a try? I can help you."

"I'm single. I have a career. I wouldn't be a good mother," Brook insisted. "And Sarah, I would stay out of your lives. Once the baby comes, I'll move out of town and you'll never see me again. Just promise me that you'll take my baby, love it and raise it as your own." Brook looked pleadingly into her friend's eyes.

Sarah's eyes filled with tears. "Well, I'll have to talk to Bill Tom about it," she said. "But if you're sure about this, I'll do it," she said, taking a deep breath.

Whatever Sarah had to do to convince her husband to accept Brook's offer no one knew for sure. But in the end he agreed. The legal papers prepared by Brook's attorney made it official that William Thomas and Sarah Louise Fischer Bradley would adopt the baby born to Mary Brooklyn Turner.

Brook shivered as she remembered Bill Tom's icy stare as they sat around the table in the attorney's office. She knew he had a bad opinion of her.

Chapter 6

The next seven months were like hell for Brook. She constantly dealt with the gossip and cold stares from co-workers, especially since word got around that she didn't know who the father was. She felt like the devil, always on the verge of throwing up, and her ordinarily slim body was getting stretched way out of proportion.

No longer the happy hour party girl, she drove straight home after work and welcomed the quiet solitude of her apartment. She was very careful to take good care of herself. She got enough rest; took the necessary vitamins; walked every day--all for the sake of the child that grew within her, and the child's expectant parents.

For Brook, there were no exciting shopping trips to pick out things for the baby; no plans to decorate a nursery; and no friends secretly organizing a baby shower. The word had spread that she was going to give her baby to her best friend, Sarah Bradley.

After twelve hours of hard labor and a problematic delivery that left her unable to conceive another child, Brook gave birth to an eight pound, four ounce baby girl. She asked the nurses to take the baby out of the room quickly, glancing at the child for only a brief moment.

A month later, Brook turned in her resignation and left St. Louis for the east coast.

She heard later that Bill Tom Bradley had surprised everyone by accepting a position as police chief of Hillside, Missouri about eight weeks after she left.

Wooosh!!!! A speeding pickup passing too close to Brook's Camry brought her back into the present. She was driving through the eastern part of Illinois by the time the sky was getting light.

"I'm making good time," she thought, rubbing her tired eyes. She decided to stop at the next reasonably big town for a quick breakfast.

The Pancake Pantry in Effingham, Illinois, was already packed at seven a.m. when Brook settled into a booth by the window.

"Eggs, scrambled, bacon, toast and coffee," she said to the young waitress who greeted her. "Make it heavy on the coffee, please."

"Would you like some juice or water with that?" the girl asked.

"Both." Brook said, smiling. "Orange juice, if you have it."

As she watched the young girl walk away, Brook couldn't help but wonder about the baby girl she had given away almost eighteen years ago.

After Jim died, Brook subscribed to the *Hillside Herald*, the small town's weekly newspaper. She hoped that, from time to time, she might get some information about her daughter.

Sure enough. The small town paper listed the names of all the grade school and high school kids who had made the honor roll and Kayla Bradley's name was always there.

One week the paper ran a story about the Lutheran church youth group's mission project and there was Kayla Bradley, right in the middle of the group.

Brook had cut out the photo of the girl's face so she could carry it in her wallet.

The paper carried other stories too, about Bill Tom. Headlines like "Police Chief Bradley to Serve as Parade Grand Marshall," and "Police Chief Bradley Leads Crime Prevention Seminar" still made her heart pound and her stomach churn. She hated to admit it, but there was a part of her that was intimidated by Bill Tom Bradley.

The waitress interrupted Brook's thoughts when she delivered her breakfast. Brook dove into it with reckless abandon. She was surprised at how hungry she was.

She thought again about the paper and how shocked she had been when she read an article about Bill Tom, and the reporter made a reference to his *"late wife, Sarah, who died following a year-long battle with ovarian cancer."*

Brook had fought the temptation to try to contact Bill Tom. She had loved and trusted Sarah as a close friend and, indeed, she had entrusted her with the life of her child. She felt the need to talk to someone about it, but in the end she decided that Bill Tom would not be happy to hear from her.

But it was the news about Sarah's death that made Brook think about moving back to Missouri. If she could get to know her daughter--and maybe even become friends, or at least on friendly terms, with Bill Tom--it would be like a dream come true.

"Sarah's gone now," Brook reasoned with herself, "and my teenage daughter does not have a mother. I just need to know that she is okay."

Brook had tried to imagine what it would be like for Kayla, growing up with only a father, and a father in the very person of Bill Tom Bradley. Brook thought that he might be a great father, but there was that dark, brooding side of him that often made him difficult to be around. What if Sarah's death put him in that frame of mind for good? How was her daughter ever going to survive that? Brook decided that she had to find out for herself.

She returned to school, took the necessary steps to earn a teaching certificate in the State of Missouri and started corresponding with Hillside High's English Department Head, Esther Gaines.

Through a year's worth of correspondence, Brook and Esther discovered that they had a number of things in common. They had both wanted children; they had both lost their husbands; and they were both dedicated English teachers. Esther offered Brook a position on the teaching staff at Hillside High.

As Brook finished her coffee, she suddenly felt excited. She had less than two hundred miles to go and she was eager to meet Esther Gaines…the only person in Hillside who would be happy to see her.

Brook paid for her breakfast, got into her car and turned back onto the interstate headed for St. Louis. As she took the outer belt around the city she ignored the temptation to drive by the old familiar neighborhoods.

Instead, she kept driving, stopping only for gas and a bathroom break.

Chapter 7

Brook's hands were shaking as she crossed the Missouri River Bridge into Hillside. As a young adult, she'd often come to the town with her parents to visit the wineries and enjoy the charming little restaurants along Market Street. Surprisingly, the town looked pretty much the same. She was happy about that.

Reading the directions Esther had given her, Brook drove slowly along the main drag looking for West Fourth Street. She turned the corner and pulled up in front of Number 1217. The house had crime scene tape all around it.

Puzzled, Brook climbed out of her car slowly and stood at the bottom of the steps leading to Esther's porch.

"Hello, there. May I help you?"

Brook looked up to see a tiny woman with a head full of curly blond hair walking quickly across the grass in front of the house next door. She was waving her hand in the air.

"What happened?" Brook asked as the woman got close to her.

"It's just terrible," the woman began. "That's Esther Gaines' home and yesterday morning I went to take her some muffins and I found her on the floor, dead! She was strangled!" The woman looked at Brook with curiosity. "I noticed your license plates are from Maryland. Are you the new English teacher?"

"Yes," Brook answered in shocked disbelief. "I'm Brook Jennings. I was supposed to come to Esther's house the minute I got into town."

"Oh, Mrs. Jennings, I'm so sorry to be the one to give you the bad news. I'm Trudy Brinkmeyer, Esther's neighbor," Trudy said, wiping her hands on her apron and extending her hand to Brook.

Brook shook the woman's damp right hand.

"Esther had an envelope full of information to give you," Trudy said, smiling at Brook. "She also dropped by the realtor's office and managed to get the keys to your house so she could turn on the air conditioning. I guess you two had worked that out."

"Yes, we did," Brook responded. "Do you know where the envelope is now?"

Trudy sucked in a deep breath of air, looking exasperated.

"Esther told me you were going to come to her house first thing, so I told Chief Bradley that I needed to keep that envelope for you, but he insisted that his deputy take it to his office."

At the mention of Bill Tom, Brook's heartbeat quickened. She hadn't planned on meeting him face to face until after she'd had a chance to freshen up from her trip.

"I guess I'd better go retrieve it from him," Brook said, forcing a casual smile. "Could you direct me to his office?"

"Sure," Trudy said. "Just go back out to Market Street — that's the main drag--make a right, go down two blocks and make a left turn at the four-way stop. His office is on the left-hand side, midway down the block."

"Thanks." Brook smiled at the friendly woman and headed for her car.

Chapter 8

The Hillside Police Department office was located in one of the oldest buildings in town. Mary Ann Crawford, wife, mother of two, and grandmother of seven, was Bill Tom's secretary, friend and sometime surrogate mother. She tried to do her best to add homey touches to the musty old office building.

After some bribery with orange-cranberry muffins and other baked goods, she convinced Bill Tom and her husband, George, to paint the walls of the dingy old office with a creamy off-white color. Then she hung pictures of Hillside on the walls and set lush green plants on the filing cabinets. Every few hours she sprayed air freshener around the outer office to eliminate the musty odor. A large bulletin board with seasonal decorations held fax copies of the national register's list of missing children and a couple of index cards from local citizens describing lost pets or advertising sale items.

Most of the time Bill Tom was grateful for Mary Ann's motherly touches, especially when they included homemade baked goods. But on this day, after hardly any sleep, he found that the smell of strawberry-scented air freshener was making him sick.

Although he'd gone to bed before midnight, he couldn't sleep. After tossing and turning for a few hours he finally got up, took a long shower and drove back to his office.

Now, in mid-afternoon, he couldn't concentrate because his stomach was churning and his head was pounding.

"May I help you?" Bill Tom heard Mary Ann ask someone who had just come into the office.

"My name is Brook Jennings. I'm the new English teacher at Hillside High. Trudy Brinkmeyer told me that Chief Bradley has the keys to my house."

"Oh, Mrs. Jennings, I'm Mary Ann Crawford, the chief's secretary. Esther was so eager to meet you. I guess you've heard about our tragedy?"

"Yes, I was shocked," Brook said. "I just got into town and I stopped by Esther's house to get my keys. Her neighbor --Trudy Brinkmeyer--told me what happened."

"I'm sure the chief will want to talk to you," Mary Ann said.

"Come in," Bill Tom called from his desk when Mary Ann knocked at the door.

"Mrs. Jennings, the new English teacher, is here to get the keys to her house," Mary Ann announced.

"Send her in," Bill Tom said. He continued to stare at the papers scattered all over his desk.

Mary Ann closed the door as Bill Tom looked at up at the woman and nearly passed out.

"Hi, Bill Tom," Brook said, with a tentative smile.

"Please don't tell me that you're the new English teacher," he said after a moment's hesitation. He made sure his face showed no emotion.

"Well, gosh, Bill Tom, we haven't seen each other in almost eighteen years, I thought you might at least say hello before making me feel unwelcome," Brook said.

"Why are you here?" he asked. He had no intention of showing any signs of hospitality.

"I am the new English teacher at Hillside High," Brook said. "I understand that you have the keys to my house. If you give them to me, I'll get out of your office right away."

"Not so fast," he said, "you didn't answer my question. Why are you *here*? There are plenty of other places where you could teach high school English."

"I read about Sarah's death in Hillside's weekly newspaper," she said, slowly approaching his desk.

At the sound of Sarah's name, Bill Tom let out a heavy sigh and turned to look out the window.

"I was worried about Kayla growing up without Sarah," Brook continued. "I just came here to see her, to get to know her. I promise you I have no intention of telling her that I'm her mother."

"You're not her mother," Bill Tom snapped. "Her mother is dead and buried in the cemetery at the top of the hill."

"I meant her birth mother," Brook corrected herself. "You have told her that she's adopted, haven't you?"

"You gave that kid up without so much as even looking at her," Bill Tom ignored her question and continued his anger-driven verbal attack. "You didn't give a damn about that baby. How dare you pretend to care about her now?"

"I didn't look at her because it would have been too painful," Brook said, fighting back tears. "Sarah was my best friend. I knew the two of you couldn't have children of your own and I also knew you would be great parents to my baby."

"You stay away from her," Bill Tom warned. He pointed his index finger at her. "I don't want you to have anything to do with her."

He threw Esther's envelope of notes and the house keys at Brook, who caught it before it hit her in the face.

"Well, thanks for such a warm welcome," Brook said. "I should have known I could count on you to be a jerk…some things never change."

Brook turned to leave when, suddenly, Bill Tom's door opened and in popped a teenage girl with long red hair and facial features similar to Brook's.

"I'm so sorry, I didn't know anyone was in here," Kayla said. "Mary Ann's not at her desk and I just thought my dad was alone."

The pretty young girl looked at Brook with a big smile.

"I'm Kayla Bradley," she said. She extended her hand to Brook.

"I'm Brook Jennings, the new English teacher," Brook said, grasping the girl's hand with both of hers.

"Oh wow!" Kayla exclaimed. "Miss Esther--Mrs. Gaines-- told me so much about you." Then in a more serious tone she asked, "You heard about Mrs. Gaines, didn't you?"

"Yes, I did," Brook said, still holding the girl's hand. "I'm so sorry you lost such a good teacher."

"Since Sarah died, Esther has been like a mother to Kayla," Bill Tom interjected.

"Well, I need to go find my house," Brook said. With some effort she let go of the girl's hands. "I guess I go back out to Market, turn left and follow the street up to Maple Drive?"

"You're going to live on Maple Drive?" Kayla asked. "That's where we live! I was going to get a ride home with Dad, but if you're going that way I could ride with you and direct you to your new house."

"Oh, I'm sure your dad would be happier if you stayed here and rode home with him, Kayla," Brook said. She glanced at Bill Tom for affirmation.

He gave her an icy stare and remained silent.

"Are you kidding?" Kayla asked. "He hates it when I stick around here, bugging him. Besides, he'll probably be here for hours. It's okay with you, isn't it, Dad?" She looked at him for approval.

"I really want you to stay here, Kayla," Bill Tom said.

"Oh, Dad, I don't want to stay here. I was going to walk home if you weren't ready to leave now. And since your desk is such a mess I know you'll stay here forever. Please let me go!"

"Then show her where her house is and go straight home," Bill Tom said. "Mrs. Jennings probably wants some time to be alone."

Brook looked at Bill Tom helplessly as Kayla insisted on going with her. "I'll send her home right away."

"We'll have to move all my CDs from the front seat." Brook turned to look at Kayla, as they walked across the parking lot. "I wasn't expecting to have a personal guide take me to my new home."

"I may as well warn you," Kayla said with a laugh, "a CD player in a car in Hillside is a wasted luxury."

"Why do you say that?" Brook asked, smiling at the girl. "Because Hillside is a two-song trip of a town," Kayla explained. "If you start at the bridge and drive all the way through town to the high school, you only get to hear two songs. If you want to listen to a whole CD in your car you have to get out of town. Or go parking on Grand Mountain Skyway," she added with a laugh.

Chapter 9

Bill Tom watched Brook and Kayla through the blinds covering his office window as they walked to Brook's car. It was an incredible sight! From the back they could have been twins, except that Kayla's red hair was straight and Brook's hair was curly.

With a heavy sigh, he sat back down at his desk. The encounter with Brook had made his upset stomach even worse. Yesterday Trudy had found Esther Gaines dead on her kitchen floor, and now he had to face a woman he'd prayed he'd never have to see again. His greatest fear was that she would someday come back for her daughter. In just a little over twenty-four hours, his quiet and peaceful life had been turned upside down.

"Yesterday was hell and today the devil walked in," he thought, holding his head in his hands.

"You look like you could use some coffee." Mary Ann interrupted his thoughts as she walked into his office with a freshly brewed pot of premium roast. "I just ran next door to the store to get some regular. I've been secretly giving you decaf, but after yesterday I thought you might need something stronger."

"Does it have any whiskey in it?" he asked, managing a weak smile.

"You come over to my house after work and George will have a whiskey with you," she said, setting the steaming pot on Bill Tom's desk. "Right now I'm going to get back to work. If you need me, give a holler."

The thoughtful woman patted Bill Tom's hand and left his office, quietly closing the door.

As he poured coffee into his big black mug that said "I'm a Texas coffee drinker," Bill Tom's thoughts were about as far away from Esther Gaines as possible.

Seeing Brook Turner--or what was she now--Brook Jennings again after so many years had shaken him to the core. He felt like his whole body had taken a ride in a blender on chop mode.

He told himself that he was upset because he was worried about what she wanted regarding Kayla, but in his gut he knew there was more to it.

He had a history with the woman that he spent a big part of his life trying to forget. She was his wife's best friend, but when she got pregnant out of wedlock, Bill Tom knew she was trouble. Through the gossip in the office he heard that Brook had no idea who the father was. He asked Sarah to quit hanging around with her and that's when Sarah gave him the shock of his life. Since Brook knew they could not have children of their own, she wanted them to adopt her baby.

"What is it about her?" he thought, angry at himself for letting her get to him so easily. He couldn't stand the sight of this woman and yet he couldn't get her image out of his head. The years had been kind to her. She had always been attractive, and now she had a soft glow about her as well. Time had smoothed out the rough edges; her light green eyes were warm and kind and, even though he knew he had hurt her by the way he had treated her and she had become defensive, her expression was one of sadness and remorse, not hate. She had not reduced herself to letting go with the cheap shots like he had done. He was ashamed of himself.

The thing that stuck in his mind the most was the way she had looked at Kayla…an expression co-mingled with love and amazement. But she handled the situation well, he had to admit.

If he was going to be honest with himself--and he rarely was regarding his feelings—-judging from this brief encounter with her, it seemed like Brook might not be such a bad person, after all. It was his guilt that was causing the problem. He couldn't stand the sight of her because he had always enjoyed the sight of her, and those deeply buried feelings made him feel guilty.

Ever since he'd met Brook she'd been a thorn in his side. He had a natural attraction to her that he could not explain. How could he think that way about another woman when he was married to the sweetest woman on earth?

Sweet. Maybe that was the issue. With Sarah, sex had been sweet, minus the heat. No variety; no take-me-now-or-I'll-die kind of urgency. No surprises. In short, sex had been dull and life had been predictable. He had loved Sarah, but in his heart of hearts, he was not in love with Sarah.

"You've got yourself one helluva case here, Bill," Beach interrupted the chief's trip down memory lane. "Were you asleep or something? When you didn't answer my knock, Mary Ann told me to come on in."

Bill Tom shook his head to clear his thoughts.

"No, I was just resting my eyes for a second," he lied. "I didn't get much sleep last night."

"Are you okay?" Beach asked with concern. "You look like hell."

"Right now I feel like I'm livin' there," Bill Tom said.

Beach stuffed his oversized body into one of Bill Tom's chairs.

"You know, Billy," he began, "this isn't the first murder case you've ever tackled. I know you were friends with this woman, but you've got to set those feelings aside for now and focus on the issue at hand."

Bill Tom looked across the desk at his friend--who also looked pretty tired after staying up most of the night--and thought about telling him what was really wrong. But he decided to talk about the case instead.

"Did Woody release her body to the funeral home?" he asked.

"Yeah, about an hour ago," Beach said. "She's over at Meyer's Mortuary. Her brother and his family are there making the final arrangements now. And some other relatives came in from Jeff City."

"Who would want to kill Esther?" Bill Tom asked. "I can't begin to imagine..."

"I know you don't want to hear this, Bill, but it's probably someone she knew. That's the most likely scenario," Beach said, trying to stretch his cramped body into the uncomfortable chair. "The best clue we have is the trace of tiny green fibers we found in her neck. We know she wasn't strangled with a regular rope or with someone's hands. From my experience it seems like it could be the kind of thing women use as drape tie-backs. You know what I mean?

"We spent the morning finger-printing the people who were in her house over the last two days so we can match them with the prints we got yesterday," Beach continued. "Everyone was real cooperative. Now they're all scared that some random-killing madman is on the loose. I heard Trudy Brinkmeyer sent her son to Spader's Hardware to get more locks for the doors. Poor kid. She made him sleep on the floor in her bedroom last night."

Bill Tom shook his head and ran his fingers through his hair. He wondered how many other people in town were taking similar precautions.

"What kind of clues do you guys have for me, Beach?"

"Very few," Beach said. "We think the killer was tall because the rope marks curve up in the back. We checked her kitchen chairs and the vinyl floor for shoe marks and came up with nothing. There were no traces of skin under her fingernails. So far, the fingerprints we found have matched those of the people we know were there. She had some kind of cookie-baking party with some of her friends last Saturday, so that's why there were so many sets of prints. Here's a list of the women who were there," Beach handed Bill Tom a sheet of paper. "One guy was there, too. A kid named Todd Mack. I think he's Esther's niece's boyfriend.

"There's no doubt in my mind that this was a premeditated murder--death by strangulation--not much evidence to go on except for the dead body and the rope fibers," he continued. "She didn't interrupt a burglar. Her purse was right there and it had over a hundred bucks in it. As far as we know, nothing else was taken. Amos and Aggie are going to do a more thorough search tomorrow. I'm sorry," Beach concluded. He looked at his friend and shook his head.

Bill Tom pushed himself away from his desk, stood up and walked over to the window that looked out at the parking lot. On this mid-August evening he could see that some of the tree leaves looked slightly brown--the result of a scorching hot summer with little rain for relief.

"Green rope fibers. That's our clue?" he asked, looking around at Beach.

"That'd be the one," Beach responded. "The only significant one."

Bill Tom turned back to the window, his mind busily running through the facts of the case. Then he turned back to face Beach.

"I guess I'll be looking for a green rope drapery tie-back, then," he said. "Can I take the crime scene tape down and open up her house again? Her relatives are already coming into town and Amos will need to get in there."

"Yeah, you can release the site," Beach said, pushing himself out of the wooden chair. "I'm gonna head back to St. Louis with the team and the evidence. When we come up with more information I'll give you a call right away."

"Thanks for your help, Beach," Bill Tom said, shaking hands with his friend. "I know you have other things on your plate. I appreciate you taking the time to help me."

"No problem, Bill." Beach patted his buddy on the back. "Always glad to help. Sorry we couldn't come up with anything else, but keep in touch, we'll help if we can."

Bill Tom walked his friend to his car, came back into the office, called Randy, who was patrolling the streets, and asked him to remove the crime scene tape from Esther's house. Then he leaned back in his chair and looked at the list of people whose fingerprints had been found in Esther's house.

Besides the people he already knew had been there, he counted eight names--names of silver-haired grandmothers who were

Esther's friends, and her great niece, Mindy, who had just graduated from Hillside High in June and was one of Kayla's best friends. The last set of prints belonged to Todd Mack, Mindy's boyfriend.

"Why was he there? And when?" Bill Tom asked himself, writing a question mark next to the boy's name.

"Mary Ann, would you come in here for a second, please?" he called out to her. "I want you to get some phone numbers for me.

"Just leave them on my desk when you get them," he said, handing the sheet of paper to her as she walked into his office. "Right now, I'm going to go home to my daughter," Bill Tom said, thinking again about Kayla and Brook. He wondered if Kayla would be there or if she'd found a way to hang out with Brook. Kayla was a friendly girl. Nothing would make her happier than making the new English teacher feel welcome.

Chapter 10

For their part, Brook and Kayla followed Bill Tom's instructions to the letter after they left his office. Brook showed Kayla the outside of her new house and then drove her straight home. Kayla offered to help Brook unpack when all her belongings arrived from Baltimore.

At Bill Tom's house, Brook waited for Kayla to get inside, then she headed back down the street toward her new home. When she had purchased the house from Emil and Anna Monroe, she had no idea she would end up living just ten houses away from Bill Tom. She hoped he didn't think that was a deliberate plan on her part.

The house in Hillside was smaller than the house she left in Baltimore. This one was also a two-story brick, but it had two small dormer windows. Instead of a big front porch, it just had a concrete slab with one step up from the sidewalk. There was no roof over the slab.

Brook took a deep breath and opened the front door. Once inside, she was pleasantly surprised. Someone had been there to turn the air conditioning on for her. Obviously it had not been Esther Gaines. She'd have to remember to thank whoever did it.

At first glance, Brook fell in love with the house. A hardwood entry foyer separated the dining room, which was on the left, from the living room, on the right. The front hallway led back to the "TV" room and the kitchen. The stairs leading to the upper level were just off-center from the front door. The walls were painted an eggshell white and the carpeting going up the stairs and in the three ground level rooms she could see was beige. To her delight, there was a screened-in porch off the dining room, accessible through French doors. A door off the back wall of the dining room obviously led to the kitchen.

She walked down the hallway, already planning where she would place some of her furniture. The "TV" room was small but cozy, with a corner gas fireplace--for a "chick fire," her husband, Jim, had always said. She walked through the open doorway into the kitchen and caught her breath in amazement. The kitchen had been totally redone, with painted beige cabinets, a center island, and a small alcove that would serve nicely as a breakfast nook. Just as the description had said in the sale document, there was a microwave oven above the stove and a huge pantry for food storage.

There was also a tiny half bath that had been tucked neatly into the area underneath the stairwell in the front hall, sink facing toilet, no extra space.

The upstairs had three bedrooms and one full bath, all looking the same with beige carpet and eggshell paint. The master bedroom was at the front of the house. It had the two dormer windows. Brook was happy to see that each window had a window seat with storage space. The closets were big, but not as big as the ones she had in her old house.

Once she'd had a chance to inspect the place from top to bottom she walked back out to her car to bring in her luggage. Her movers had promised to be in Hillside the morning after she arrived. She guessed she'd spend the night in one of the hotels on the river bluff. For the time being, though, she just wanted to sit in her new home and relax.

She called her friend, Lisa, back in Baltimore, to let her know that she had arrived safely, after an all-night fourteen-hour drive. Then she walked into her living room, sat down on the soft carpet, leaned against the back wall and thought about the events of the day.

She couldn't believe that Esther Gaines had been killed. She hadn't had a lot of time to think about it, but when she did it made her sad and gave her the creeps, too. With that thought she jumped up to make sure her doors were locked.

When she sat down again, this time on the brick floor of her screened-in porch, she finally let her mind go to the place it wanted to go--ten doors up the block to the house where her daughter lived.

Over and over again she relived the moment when Kayla had burst into Bill Tom's office and they had met for the first time. And then the girl had actually ridden in her car. They could have been any regular mother and daughter, just out for a while to run errands and enjoy each other's company. Brook's eyes welled up with tears as she realized it had been the happiest moment of her life.

Lost in thought, and exhausted from her long drive and challenging day, Brook walked back into her living room and curled up in the corner on the carpet for a short nap.

Sometime later, she woke up with a start. Judging from the dim light in the house, she guessed it was close to 6 o'clock. Brook glanced around the room and froze. As she looked into the dining room she saw someone's shadow through the sheer curtains over the front window. She jumped up and ran to see who was there. It was Bill Tom. She opened the door to confront him.

"Is there something you wanted, Bill Tom?"

"Geez! You scared me! What the hell are you doing in there with no lights on?"

Brook looked at him, wishing that she'd had the time to fix her hair and freshen up before she had to see him again.

"I live here," she said, trying to calm down. "I saw your shadow in the window. I thought someone was trying to break in. What are you doing here?"

"I was on my way home. I saw your car. It's very cloudy and I didn't see any lights on in your house. I thought I should check it out," Bill Tom said.

"There are no overhead lights in the two front rooms," Brook said. She brushed her curly hair from her face to get a better look at him. "The Monroes took their dining room chandelier when they moved…it was some kind of family heirloom or something.

"I'm sorry I yelled at you," she said. "But you scared me."

They stood looking at each other in the dusk of the evening-- Bill Tom, standing by her front window, she on the concrete slab that served as her front porch.

She tried to access Bill Tom's demeanor. His facial features no longer had that harsh, angry look.

"I'd invite you in for some coffee, but my coffee pot's somewhere on the road between here and Baltimore," she said, trying to make a joke.

"You can't stay here all night without lights and without a bed," he said, avoiding eye contact with her. "Do you have a place to stay tonight?"

"I thought I'd go check out one of the hotels on the river bluff," Brook answered. "Do you have any suggestions?"

"The Cliffside Inn is the nicest, I hear," Bill Tom said. "Go get your stuff. I'll wait till you lock up and get in your car."

She nodded her head and turned to grab her overnight bag. "He was concerned about me," she thought, feeling slightly amused. Then she decided that he was just a cop, doing his job.

"I'm all set," she said, locking the front door of her new home.

"Be careful on that step," he said. He took her overnight bag and put his free hand on her elbow as she stepped off the porch.

She settled into the leather seat of her Camry and turned to him to take her overnight bag.

For the first time, she looked at him without anger or defiance. She thought he looked tired…and very handsome.

"Thanks for checking up on me, Bill Tom, I'd have slept there all night and not been able to move in the morning," she said. She offered him a tentative smile.

"Welcome to Hillside, Brook," he said, without expression. He stepped back, she closed the car door and backed out of her driveway. In her rearview mirror, she could see him watching her as she drove down Maple Drive toward Market.

Chapter 11

As she approached the business part of town she saw several restaurants and realized that she was hungry. She pulled into one of the parking spaces in front of a small building with red and white curtains in the windows.

"Good evening, Ma'am. My name is Doug. Welcome to the Germantown Diner. Would you like a table or a booth?" The young man at the door smiled warmly at Brook.

"A booth would be great," she said. She returned his smile and wondered if she would see him in one of her classes.

"Follow me, Ma'am," he said. He grabbed a menu from the stack on a near-by table.

"Mrs. Jennings...Mrs. Jennings, would you like to sit with me?" Brook turned to see Trudy Brinkmeyer sitting alone in one of the booths along the wall. She nodded her head and Doug escorted her to Trudy's table.

"I'm so glad to run into you," Trudy said. "My son is at his girlfriend's house for dinner and I was feeling kind of lonely--I used to eat dinner with Esther a lot--so I came down here just to be around people."

"Thanks for asking me to sit with you, Trudy. I was feeling kind of lonely tonight, too." Brook slid into the seat and smiled at the friendly woman.

"I'm sure it was a shock for you to drive all that way from Baltimore and get hit with the news about Esther," Trudy began. "I hope you understand that Hillside is really a nice town and safe, too. It's usually very peaceful, and the people are friendly."

"I believe that," Brook said. In her mind's eye she saw the smiling face of Kayla Bradley.

After the two women ordered beers and decided to split a sausage and mushroom pizza, Trudy folded her hands on the table and leaned forward.

"Esther spent a lot of time in the last few weeks telling me all about Brook Jennings, the English teacher," Trudy began. "Why don't you tell me about Brook Jennings, the woman?"

Brook smiled. She wasn't sure if Trudy was being friendly or nosey. She looked at the woman with curly blond hair, big blue eyes and a pleasant smile and decided that she was a genuinely kind person.

"Do you want the 'I was born at an early age' version or just the highlights?" Brook asked. It felt so good to talk to another woman close to her own age. She couldn't help but smile.

"The highlights will do for now," Trudy laughed. "I know you've had a long day."

"I used to work in communications--that's how I met my husband," Brook began. "He owned a real estate firm in Baltimore and I went to work for him. We dated for about a year before we got married. He encouraged me to go back to school to earn a teaching certificate.

"A few years after I started teaching, Mike--my husband-- was killed in a head-on collision coming home one night from a business meeting. That was three years ago. I've been rattling around in our big old dream home ever since."

Brook took a long draw from her beer mug and continued her story.

"I decided I needed a change, so on a whim I got on the computer and found Hillside High's website. I started corresponding with Esther Gaines and...here I am!"

"I'm so sorry to hear about your husband," Trudy said. She reached over to pat Brook's hand. "My husband Bud died almost eight years ago. But I was so lucky to have my son, Brian. He was and is a great source of comfort to me. You'll probably have him in one of your English classes."

"I'll look forward to meeting him," Brook said. "Ahhh, here comes the pizza."

The two women spent the rest of their dinner getting better acquainted. Brook found out that Trudy and her husband Bud--whose given name was Elmer--were Hillside natives, high school sweethearts, former 4-H Club members and MIZZOU grads.

"I majored in home economics because Bud wanted a wife who could cook and sew," Trudy explained. "Bud majored in agriculture so he could work his family's farm. After he died I sold the property and bought a house in town. I had trouble sleeping alone in that big farm house out in the middle of nowhere."

"Speaking of sleeping, I think I'm about ready for bed," Brook said. She glanced at her watch and was surprised to see that it was after eight.

The women split their bill, gave Doug a sizeable tip and headed for the door.

"Are you going to be able to sleep in your house tonight?" Trudy asked as they stepped onto the sidewalk.

"No, my furniture isn't arriving until tomorrow so I'm going to stay at the Cliffside Inn."

"There's no need for you to do that," Trudy said. "I have a big house with a guest room and private bath on the first floor. I would love to have you stay with us. Our rooms are upstairs so you would have plenty of privacy."

"If you're sure I wouldn't be imposing, I'd love to stay with you," Brook said. She had taken an instant liking to Trudy Brinkmeyer.

The minute Brook walked into Trudy's house she could see that the woman's home economics training had paid off. Her home was warm and inviting with just the right touches of vivid and subtle color. It smelled fresh and clean and Brook loved the family pictures that were placed strategically throughout the lower level of the house.

Trudy's kitchen was painted in a cheerful yellow with yellow and white gingham curtains and a tablecloth to match. It was clear that Trudy had reached the good housekeeping pinnacle of success: a place for everything and everything in its place.

"Nobody in Hillside goes to bed without a little glass of wine," Trudy said. "Would you like one? I have a nice Riesling from one of our wineries in town. We can sit in the TV room for a while. I thought maybe the St. Louis news stations would carry something about Esther's death."

The women settled down on Trudy's couch. Trudy grabbed the remote and channel surfed until she found a station that was broadcasting the news of the day. It didn't take long until the station aired the story about Esther.

"Law enforcement officials in Hillside said in a statement today that they have brought in crime scene investigators from St Louis to help them in their efforts to find the person or persons who strangled Esther Gaines.

"Mrs. Gaines, sixty-eight, was the head of the Hillside High School English Department, a position she held for the last twenty-five years. A native of Hillside, she taught English at the school since her graduation from the University of Missouri-Columbia. It was her only teaching job.

"Hillside Police Chief Bill Tom Bradley said that Mrs. Gaines' death was a tremendous loss to her family, friends, the students at Hillside High and the entire community. He said that every effort was being made to bring her killer to swift justice."

As the anchor spoke, the station ran aerial footage of Hillside, the high school and Esther's home with the crime scene tape.

Trudy shut off the TV and shook her head.

"I still can't believe it," she said. "It's like a nightmare."

The women heard the back door open and in walked a tall young man with his mother's blond hair and blue eyes.

"Hi Mom," he said. He looked at Brook and smiled.

"You don't have to tell me. I'll bet you're Mrs. Jennings, aren't you? He walked over and extended his hand to Brook.

Brook laughed and stood up to shake hands with the boy.

"Now how did you know that?" she asked. "Have I turned into a stereotypical English teacher?"

"No, not at all." Brian smiled at Brook as she resumed her place on the couch. He pulled up the ottoman and sat next to her. "I just spent the whole evening hearing all about you from my girlfriend, Kayla."

"Kayla Bradley is your girlfriend?" Brook asked. She almost choked on her wine.

"We've been friends all our lives," Brian said. "We started dating last summer. She was so excited that she got to meet you today. It really cheered her up. We've all been pretty bummed about Mrs. Gaines."

"What did Kayla fix you guys for dinner?" Trudy asked. Her eyes were brimming over with pride and love for her son.

"Well, when Chief Bradley got home he was really grumpy," Brian explained. "I know he has a lot on his mind. So, since he was in such a bad mood, Kayla and I grilled hamburgers outside and she encouraged him to take a quick nap. When he woke up he was in a better mood. After dinner we took Moonshine for a walk and then we played a game of badminton. The chief took off in his truck. I guess he was headed back to his office.

"Who's Moonshine?" Brook asked. She had been listening to Brian's story with great interest.

"She's the biggest, friendliest Yellow Lab you've ever seen," Trudy said.

"She's very spoiled, too," Brian added. "Even though Kayla tells him not to, the chief always feeds Moonshine table scraps. Sometimes the results are not very pretty-- especially when the chief makes his homemade chili."

"None of us can survive Bill Tom's chili," Trudy laughed. "We eat a lot of TUMS after that meal."

"It's really nice to meet you, Mrs. Jennings," Brian said as he stood up. "I have to get off to bed. We have football practice in the morning at six a.m. It's almost eleven now."

"Wow, we should all go to bed," Trudy added. "I know you've had a very long day, Brook. Let me show you to your room."

Trudy's guest bedroom was as welcoming as the rest of her home. Pale blue walls with blue print curtains and bedspread, a very comfortable mattress and a spotless bathroom that surgeons could operate in combined to make any guest feel right at home.

As she curled up under the fresh, crisp sheets, Brook thanked God for Trudy and Brian…and the chance to finally meet her daughter.

Chapter 12

The next few days in Hillside were surreal. Bill Tom and Randy wasted no time interviewing Esther's neighbors and the people whose fingerprints had been found inside her home. Mary Ann served as a fortress, shielding the two of them against the steady stream of phone calls and pop-in visitors who wanted to know what was being done to solve the murder.

Through it all, Bill Tom's stomach was tied up in a knot as he constantly switched hats from Amos and Aggie's caring friend to a shrewd and relentless detective trying to solve a murder.

Esther's visitation and funeral were both painful reminders of what a great person she was and how much she would be missed by so many people. Meyer's Funeral Home in Hillside was packed as the hundreds of people who knew Esther came to bid a final farewell to their well-respected friend and teacher.

Once again Bill Tom's heart ached as he and Kayla walked hand-in-hand up to the coffin that held the body of a woman who had been such a main-stay in their lives. He was surprised and impressed with Kayla's ability to keep her composure.

Bill Tom hadn't talked to Brook since the night he sent her off to the Cliffside Hotel, but when he had the opportunity he always kept an eye out for her. During Esther's visitation at the funeral home on the Friday night before the funeral, Brook, in a tasteful navy blue suit, greeted Esther's family warmly and then took a seat at the back of the room. He noticed that Kayla took some of her friends over to meet Brook and she stood up to shake hands with them--a nice thing for a teacher to do.

Amos and Aggie decided to hold Esther's funeral on Saturday because so many of her former students who had moved away wanted to attend. The funeral procession stretched over a mile long--more than a third of the distance of the highway that traveled through the main drag in Hillside.

After the burial, about 200 people gathered at the high school where Trudy Brinkmeyer had organized a special luncheon in Esther's honor.

Bill Tom sat in a metal folding chair close to the door and watched everyone as they talked and hugged and helped themselves to the vast array of potluck dishes that filled eight long tables.

But mostly he watched Brook Jennings.

She was busy in the kitchen helping Trudy and the other ladies heat up the countless casserole dishes and prepare beverages for everyone. He caught himself staring at her several times and forced himself to look away. But she was a cool and calm vision among all the chaos. It had to be over eighty-five degrees in the high school cafeteria with all the people crammed in there, and yet Brook, looking great in a green crepe dress, looked cool and fresh amidst the steamy chaos. She smiled pleasantly, placed a caring hand on Amos's back when she served him his iced tea, and nodded politely to Bill Tom when she happened to meet his stare. In short, she was friendly, but not too familiar; caring but not overbearing--a total class act. Bill Tom couldn't stop thinking about her.

So, between his genuine sorrow over losing Esther, his concern about his daughter's reaction to such a big loss in her life, the sudden arrival of Brook Jennings, and the daunting task of finding Esther's killer, his nerves were a wreck. He alternated between taking *Pepto Bismol* and *Imodium* every few hours, neither of which was doing him much good under the circumstances.

When everyone cleared out of the school cafeteria, Bill Tom sent Kayla off with Trudy and Brian, said a polite good-bye to Brook as she helped clear the tables, and headed off to his office to do some work.

As he sat at his oversized desk, which was now cluttered with personal notes from interviews with Esther's neighbors, telephone messages from people who thought they had clues about the murder, and faxed lab reports from Beach, Bill Tom studied two things in particular--a cryptic message from Ernie Tucker, the organist at the Lutheran church, and a rap sheet on Hillside's most seedy resident.

"What should I tackle first?" he asked himself. As he leaned forward in his chair, Randy walked into his office.

"I told Chris and the kids that you'd be here, BT," he said, smiling. "I sent them off for pizza and headed on over. What can I do to help?"

"Are you sure you don't want to spend some time with Chris and the kids?" he asked. "Children grow up fast, you know. We think they're constant fixtures in our lives, but really, they're just passing through."

"I'll spend time with them tomorrow, BT," Randy said. "Right now I want to help as much as I can."

"Well, in that case, why don't you go over and see if Clifford Dunbar is home. I've been trying to talk to him since the day we found Esther, but he doesn't have a phone and he doesn't answer the door. Every time I've been there this week his car has been nowhere in sight. Maybe he went on one of his fishing trips to Springfield, or maybe he fled a crime scene. We've got to check it out."

"Okay, boss, I'm on my way," Randy said, and walked out the door.

Bill Tom picked up the phone message from Ernie Tucker to make sure he had read Mary Ann's handwriting correctly. The guy had called late Friday afternoon as she was preparing to leave for the day. The note read:

"Bill Tom--Ernie Tucker wants you to meet him at the city park by the pool tomorrow after Esther's funeral, about 6

p.m. He has information he thinks may be linked to Esther's death. Please don't call his home."

He looked at his watch: five minutes to six. It was time to go.

He parked by the pool and looked around. No sign of Ernie or his red Chevy Malibu. After waiting fifteen minutes he tried to reach Ernie on his cell phone, but the guy didn't answer.

He knew he wasn't supposed to call Ernie's home, but he thought he could get by with it if he made up a little white lie. He had to call Trudy's house first to get someone to look up the phone number.

"Hello, Brinkmeyer's," a familiar voice answered.

"Hey, Kayla, is that you, Honey? It's Dad," he said, loving the sound of her voice.

"Actually, it's Brook, Bill Tom," Brook said. "Trudy and I just got here and we're carrying in Trudy's casserole dishes--she must have made seven. I'm the only one in here right now. The kids are outside with Trudy."

"Oh, hi Brook," he said, trying to sound calm. He hadn't noticed before that Kayla and Brook even sounded alike when they talked. "I called because I need a phone number. Would you mind looking it up for me?"

"Of course not. Let me see if I can find their phone book. Ahh, here it is. What number do you need?

"Tucker. Ernest and Wanda Tucker. Trudy's probably got it handwritten on the inside cover of her phone book. He's the new organist at our church."

Bill Tom could hear Brook flipping through the pages.

"Here it is…555-7887. Got that?"

"Yeah, I got it," he said, scribbling the number on the back of a sales slip he found on the seat of his truck. "Thanks."

Bill Tom decided to drive over to the Tucker's home to see if Ernie was still there. He parked a few blocks away, but he could see that Ernie's car was not in the driveway. He decided to make the call.

"Hello."

"Hello, Wanda?"

"Yes, this is Wanda."

"This is Bill Tom Bradley, Wanda, is Ernie there?"

"Why, no, Bill Tom," Wanda answered. "He had to go to Jefferson City this afternoon to participate in a church organists' workshop at Grace Community Church. He forgot all about it until we were in the middle of Esther's funeral service. He didn't even go to the cemetery with us. Lester and I rode to the cemetery with Trudy and Brian so Ernie could come home, pack and leave. His memory is getting really bad.

"He did tell me that you might call about some choir picnic thing. He said he'd have to talk to you tomorrow. He plans to spend the night in Jeff City and make it back in time for church in the morning."

Something wasn't right. Why would Ernie leave town so suddenly without giving him the information regarding Esther's murder? If the news was so important, Ernie could have called him on his way to the workshop.

"That's okay, Wanda. I'll just call him on his cell phone. There's just a couple of things I need to ask him before church tomorrow."

"In all the rush he forgot to grab his phone," Wanda said. "It's sitting on the dresser in our bedroom. But he's probably staying at the Ramada Inn; he likes the restaurant there. Maybe you can catch him there or leave a message. The 800 number is 555-1111."

"Thanks a lot, Wanda, I appreciate your help."

He called the Ramada Inn but Ernie had not checked in yet. He left a message stressing that it was urgent that Ernie contact him immediately. Then he rubbed his eyes, turned the key in the ignition and took off slowly, looking carefully at the Tuckers' home as he drove by. He jumped when his cell phone rang.

Chapter 13

"Hey, BT, I'm at Dunbar's trailer, can you get over here right away? You won't believe what I found," Randy said.

"I'm on my way." Bill Tom jammed his phone in his pocket, turned his truck down an alley and headed for Cliff Dunbar's trailer located just outside of town, at the end of Glosterheim Road.

Randy was waiting for Bill Tom in the squad car.

"What'd you find?" Bill Tom asked, hopping out of his truck.

"He's not here, BT, and his trailer's locked," Randy began. "So I just started looking around, underneath the trailer and around back by that old shed and those two junk cars. Then I saw the trash bags out by the dumpster. I opened the first one and guess what I found. An old pair of green draperies--the kind that get tied back-- and the tie backs are missing."

"The trash bag is by the dumpster so it's on public property. I'm gonna put it in my truck," Bill Tom said. "When we get back to the office let's put out an all-points bulletin on Cliff Dunbar. Then

I'm driving those draperies in to St. Louis so Beach can check the fibers first thing Monday morning. Let's go."

Back at the office, Randy ordered the all-points bulletin using the license plate number they had on file for Cliff Dunbar. Bill Tom made another call to Trudy's house.

"Hello." This time it was the unmistakable voice of Trudy Brinkmeyer.

"Hey, Trudy, it's Bill Tom. May I speak to Kayla, please?"

"She left about an hour ago, Bill," Trudy said. "She went home with Brook. We're just getting ready to go visit Esther's family in Jeff City."

"Thanks, Trudy, I'll get a hold of her at Brook's place."

"Dammit," he thought, "what's she doing with Brook again?"

He grabbed the keys to his truck and got up to leave, taking time to look at his reflection in the frosted glass window of his office door.

"I look like hell," he thought. He frowned as he noticed the bags under his eyes and the condition of the now rumpled white dress shirt he'd worn to the funeral.

"Randy, I'm on my way. Call me if you get any leads on Dunbar, okay?"

"I will, BT."

Bill Tom drove down to Market Street and turned left toward Maple Drive. He hoped that Brook and Kayla would be at Brook's house.

"Hi," he said as Brook answered the door. She was still wearing the green dress she'd had on at the funeral. He couldn't believe she still looked so fresh, like she hadn't lifted a finger all day.

"Is Kayla still here?"

"Yes, she…"

"Hi, Dad," Kayla said, walking into the foyer from Brook's kitchen. "Mrs. Jennings volunteered to take me home with her so I wouldn't have to bother you. Brian and Trudy were invited over to Miss Esther's family's house in Jeff City. They're not coming back until Monday morning."

"Thanks, Brook, that was thoughtful of you," Bill Tom nodded politely.

"Honey," he said, turning his attention back to Kayla, "something's come up and I've got to run in to St. Louis to see Beach. I don't want to leave you alone, so you're gonna have to come with me."

"Oh, Dad, can't I stay here with Mrs. Jennings? The movers delivered all of her stuff and I want to help her organize her kitchen."

"Kayla, we don't want to impose on Mrs. Jennings, she prob…"

"It's okay, Bill Tom," Brook interrupted, gently touching his arm. "Kayla told me she loves to organize kitchens and she offered to help. I really would enjoy the company and I do need the help. She can stay here until you get back, if you don't want her to be alone."

"It might be late," Bill Tom protested. "And I hate to inconvenience you like that."

"If it gets too late I'll just sack out on the floor, Dad," Kayla laughed. "Remember, I'm a big girl now--I've stayed up past midnight."

"Okay," Bill Tom said. "It's almost eight o'clock now. I'll try to be back as soon as possible."

Chapter 14

He left the two women waving from Brook's doorway and headed for St. Louis.

That woman was going to try to steal his daughter from him, he just knew it. Organize a kitchen. What a load of crap!

Usually, the hour-long trip to St. Louis went by quickly for Bill Tom. He had his CD collection of country and western tunes and in the privacy of his truck he'd sing along--very loudly--with the familiar melodies.

But on this trip he wasn't in the mood to sing, and even though his truck moved swiftly along Highway 24 toward I-70, Bill Tom felt like the whole world was moving in slow motion. Suddenly he remembered that he hadn't called Beach to tell him he was coming. He reached for his cell phone and punched Beach's speed dial number.

"Walter Beacham," a deep voice said after the second ring.

"Beach! Put down that beer and cigar and listen to me. I'm on my way to see you with something that may be evidence. Are you gonna be home?"

"I'm already in my jammies. It's too hot to go out. You'll get to see the 'real' me."

Bill Tom laughed for the first time that day. "I'll see you in an hour, Beach."

By the time Bill Tom arrived at Beach's house, the late August sun had set behind the horizon and he could see several stars twinkling in the sky.

Beach lived in St. Charles, a bedroom community just across the Missouri river from St. Louis. When Beach answered the door of his brick and frame ranch-style home, Bill Tom couldn't believe his eyes. His friend was wearing a white tee shirt and the biggest red boxer shorts he'd ever seen. The shorts had little white hearts on them.

"Like 'em?" Beach asked with a big grin. "The girls at the office gave them to me for Valentine's Day. I think that's sexual harassment, don't you?"

The big man stepped aside to let Bill Tom through the door.

"Only if you wear them in public," Bill Tom said, shaking his head.

"So let me guess, this is the new evidence?" Beach asked as Bill Tom set the plastic bag on the living room floor.

"There's a pair of green drapes in there. We found them in the trash near the home of one of Hillside's most unsavory characters--an ex-con named Clifford Dunbar from Kansas City. He has a rap sheet a mile long. Mostly petty theft. But on two occasions he beat up his victims. One almost died. He's been out of prison for over a year. I've never had any trouble with him. He mostly keeps to himself. But now he's disappeared and Randy found these drapes this afternoon."

Beach nodded, listening to Bill Tom's explanation.

"Wanna beer?" he asked, motioning for Bill Tom to take a seat in the living room.

"Hell, yes, I want a beer. Please!" he said. Bill Tom slumped down into one of Beach's worn-out matching easy chairs. Grateful for the opportunity, he leaned back and closed his eyes. He couldn't remember when he'd been so tired.

"You look worse than you did the other day, buddy," Beach said, handing Bill Tom his beer. "I didn't think that was possible. You been gettin' any sleep?"

"Not a lot. We've been interviewing people and taking all kinds of phone calls. Today was Esther's funeral. It was sad."

Bill Tom looked at his friend and let out a sigh.

"Our local news covered the story," Beach said. "Channel seven had an aerial view of the procession to the cemetery. That was something. They said that 'law enforcement officials were working non-stop to find whoever did it.' I thought of you. You look like you've been working non-stop."

"It's just Randy and me," Bill Tom said. "We're doing our best. Bob Adermann, our mayor, is being a real pest. He calls me every hour for updates. I'd like to shove this beer bottle up his ass." Bill Tom lifted the half-empty Michelob.

Beach laughed.

"I'll bet that now he understands why he pays you so much money, huh?"

"Yep. That's why I get the big bucks."

The two men talked for a while as Bill Tom finished his beer. Then he got up to leave.

"Gotta go, my friend," he said, rubbing his burning eyes again. "Duty calls."

Beach stood up with him and walked him to the door.

"Be careful, buddy," he said, patting the tired police chief on the back. "I don't like the looks of this whole case. I think the killer is someone you all know. Someone who walks among you every day. Someone with a secret grudge against Esther Gaines and maybe other people, too. Something's happened to make that person crack."

Bill Tom nodded his head, shook hands with Beach and headed back to Hillside.

Chapter 15

When he stopped in front of Brook's house at 11 p.m. he could see that the living room lights were on.

"That was a pretty quick trip," Brook said when she answered the door. "Come on in."

"It's really late, we should get home," he said, walking past her into the foyer. He could see that her furniture had arrived and she was in the middle of unpacking boxes.

"It'll look better in a couple of weeks," Brook said, noticing his stare.

"The Monroes must have painted before they moved," he said. He was trying not to focus on how good she looked in blue jeans and a yellow tee shirt. "The walls used to be blue."

Brook nodded, smiling. "In a couple of weeks, there'll be color on the walls again."

"Hi, Dad," Kayla said, walking into the foyer from the kitchen. "Come on back and see what we've done. Things are really looking good."

Reluctantly, Bill Tom followed the two women back to the kitchen. "We really need to go, Kayla," he said, trying to get out of there as quickly as possible. "Isn't the choir singing in the morning? You're gonna have to get to church early."

"I'll survive, Dad," she said, smiling at him. "Come look at Mrs. Jennings' kitchen."

Bill Tom walked into the room and looked around in amazement. The Monroes had totally redone the kitchen and Brook and Kayla had done a great job making the room look warm and inviting.

"What's that smell?" he asked, taking in a deep whiff of chocolate.

"We made brownies," Kayla said. "Have one."

"They're just from a box mix," Brook added, handing him the plate of brownies. "Please, sit down at the table and have some. Would you like some milk or coffee?"

"You got whole milk?" he asked, shoving a huge brownie into his mouth. He hadn't eaten since the funeral luncheon and he was pretty hungry.

"Two percent," Brook answered. "But I have real cream if you want some coffee. It'll just take a few minutes to brew."

"Brew away," he answered, helping himself to a second brownie. He was thoroughly enjoying the special attention from the two women. After the week he'd had, it was nice to get some tender feminine care, even if it was at the hand of Brook Jennings.

Brook made the coffee and the three of them sat at her kitchen table making small talk about Brook's new house and the previous owners.

"School starts on Thursday," Brook said, changing the subject. "Are you ready for that, Kayla?"

"I'll be a senior," Kayla said proudly. "And next year it's off to MIZZOU! I want to go to their 'J' school."

"Journalism is a very interesting career choice," Brook said. "You'll never be bored."

"I want to be an investigative reporter," Kayla beamed. "I'd like to crack a big case--like Woodward and Bernstein did. Maybe I'll even get my own "Deep Throat" informant. Wouldn't that be great?"

Brook looked at the girl and smiled warmly. "I hope all your dreams come true, Kayla," she said.

"Speaking of dreams, it's time we get to bed," Bill Tom said, looking at his watch. "It's after midnight and church starts at 10 a.m. You're singing in the choir. If you don't get some sleep you'll sound like a frog," he teased.

"We go to Trinity Lutheran, Mrs. Jennings," Kayla said, clearing Brook's kitchen table. "Would you like to join us? You can sit with my dad since I have to sit in the balcony."

Bill Tom nearly fell off his chair.

"Thanks, Kayla, I'd love to come hear you sing," Brook answered. "It's kind of you to invite me."

"Well, we'd better be going," Bill Tom said, trying to keep Kayla from inviting Brook to come over for Sunday dinner. He put his hand on the girl's back and gently shoved her toward the door.

"Thanks for letting Kayla stay with you, Brook," he said. He risked a quick look into her eyes. "And thanks for the brownies. They were great."

"Any time, Bill Tom, I enjoyed the company." She stayed in the doorway waving until they backed out of her driveway.

"I really like her," Kayla said as they drove the short distance up to their house. "I bet she's a great teacher."

"I'm sure she is," Bill Tom agreed, frustrated with himself for starting to like the woman he hated.

Later, as he tossed and turned in his bed--he was too tired to go to sleep--his mind bounced back and forth between the clues surrounding Esther's murder and the beautiful face of Brook Jennings.

After he finally drifted off to sleep, morning came too soon. He and Kayla had to rush to get to church in time for choir practice.

Chapter 16

The church's parking lot was still half-empty when Bill Tom and Kayla arrived. As they entered the church, some members were already seated in the pews and Kayla went to join the other choir members who were getting ready to go to the balcony. From the corner of his eye he could see that Ernie Tucker was seated at the organ, leaning back against the organ bench.

"I wonder what's going on with…?" Bill Tom's thoughts were suddenly interrupted by an ear-piercing scream. He looked up to the balcony again and saw Wanda Tucker standing by the organ looking at her husband. Her hands were clasped over her mouth.

He ran upstairs pushing past the group of choir members and bolted through the door to the balcony. As he approached the organ he couldn't believe his eyes. There was Ernie Tucker, seated at the organ in his blue suit, staring straight ahead. He was dead. Bill Tom pulled at the collar of Ernie's blue shirt; sure enough, the rope burns on his neck were easily visible.

For an instant, he froze in stunned silence. Then his police training took over.

"Stay back," he shouted as he heard the choir members rushing up the steps behind him. "Don't come in here. Call an ambulance."

He heard himself barking orders as he bent over Wanda Tucker. The woman had fainted and was lying on the floor by the organ.

Pastor Harold Riebold ignored Bill Tom's order and rushed over when he saw Wanda Tucker lying on the floor.

"What's wrong with her?" he asked Bill Tom, looking down at the woman.

"She responded to that," Bill Tom said, jerking his head toward Ernie's body.

"Oh, no!" the pastor exclaimed. "What's happened here?"

"He's been strangled, Pastor," Bill Tom said. "Would you please make sure someone calls an ambulance? And please try to get everyone out of the church."

The shocked parishioners gathered at the front of the sanctuary, trying to figure out what was going on.

"Wanda," Bill Tom whispered. The lump in his throat made it difficult to get any words out. "Wanda, can you hear me?" The woman was out cold. In the distance he could hear the ambulance siren.

He reached into his pocket, pulled out his cell phone and punched Randy's speed dial number. After four rings Randy answered.

"What's up, BT?" he asked.

"Randy, I'm here at church and we've got another murder. Ernie Tucker has been strangled and the killer sat him up on the organ bench. Whoever did this is one sick son of a bitch.

"Wanda discovered his body. The whole place has gone nuts over here, can you come over?"

"Sure," Randy said. "I'm at church myself. Mary Ann is here, too. I'll tell Chris what's going on and then I'll be there in about ten minutes." The Baptist church Randy and Mary Ann attended was on the other side of town.

Bill Tom turned his attention back to Wanda Tucker and tried to calm himself down.

"God help us all," he prayed.

Chapter 17

Brook looked carefully at the young girl sitting on her living room couch. Red hair. Red face. Red eyes. She appeared to be in shock.

"Kayla, let me fix you some warm milk," Brook suggested. She sat down next to the girl and reached out to hold her hand.

"I don't think I can swallow, Mrs. Jennings," Kayla said. She held a death grip on Brook's hand. "I'm afraid if I try to drink it, I'll just throw up."

"Then why don't you lie down here and I'll get a wet washcloth for your forehead, okay?"

Kayla nodded in silent agreement, kicked off her shoes, and stretched out on the tan-colored sofa.

"What in the world is going on in this town?" Brook wondered as she walked to her hall bathroom.

She shivered as she relived the events of the morning. She had arrived at the church as members were rushing out the two main doors, many of them in tears.

"I'm sorry, Ma'am," the pastor had said, grabbing her hands, "we have to cancel services this morning. Something terrible has happened. We've had a death here at the church."

Brook looked at the frazzled pastor, his eyes wide with shock. She looked up to see Bill Tom walking out of the church, holding Kayla close to him. She was crying.

"Brook, we've had another murder here," he said. His face was white and he looked disheveled. "It looks like somebody strangled our organist.

"Would you mind taking Kayla home with you? Trudy and Brian are in Jeff City and I'm going to have my hands full for a while."

"Of course not," Brook said as Kayla reached out for a hug.

"Daddy, I'm so scared," she sobbed. She stretched one hand back for Bill Tom to hold. "Please be careful."

"I will, Sweetheart," he said. He leaned in to give the girl a kiss on the cheek. "You stay with Mrs. Jennings till I come to get you, okay?"

Kayla nodded her head and Brook started to guide her to the car.

"I'll take good care of her," she whispered to Bill Tom.

Brook turned off the water faucet in her bathroom and walked back into the living room with the cold, damp washcloth.

"Put this on your forehead and over your eyes, Kayla," she said. "I'll sit here with you while you rest. See if you can get some sleep."

Brook opened her entertainment center and turned on some soft, mellow jazz music. Then she sat in one of her two olive green wing chairs, leaned her head back and closed her eyes.

What a week it had been so far…a long drive to Hillside…a murder…a chance meeting with Bill Tom and Kayla. When her furniture had arrived on Wednesday, she was so happy to see some familiar surroundings and thought that maybe her new life in Hillside would start to settle down. The movers were true to their word and all of her belongings were in good shape. She was pleased that her stuff fit so well in the new house--just like it actually belonged there.

Roger Landry, the high school principal, dropped by to welcome her to Hillside. He gave her a set of keys to the school and told her to go over any time to check out her classroom.

"There'll be a teachers' meeting Tuesday morning at 9 a.m. in our conference room," he called to her on his way to his car. "I'll introduce you to everyone then. Because Esther is no longer with us we have to reassign the kids' English classes."

Through her correspondence with Esther, Brook had learned that she would teach Senior English, a familiar curriculum that she had taught many times before. She had already submitted her first month of class outlines.

Brook sighed deeply and opened her eyes to look at Kayla. The girl had fallen sound asleep on her sofa. She looked like an angel, a peaceful expression on her face and her long red hair gracefully covering the pillow Brook had given her.

Brook longed to reach out and hold her daughter. She wanted to smother her with kisses and tell her how sorry she was for not being able to be the mother she deserved.

"I love you, Kayla," she whispered softly from across the room. Her eyes welled up with tears--tears of sadness because of the pain her daughter was feeling and tears of joy because she was so happy just to be around the girl. She leaned back in the chair again, kicked off her black pumps and tried to relax.

"Mrs. Jennings, wake up."

Brook jumped at the sound of Kayla's voice.

"You fell asleep, too," Kayla said. She was leaning over Brook. "I'm feeling a little better now. How 'bout you?"

"I'm okay, Kayla," Brook said. She sat up in the chair and looked at the clock on her fireplace mantle. 4 p.m.

"You must be really hungry by now. Would you like something to eat?" Brook looked up at Kayla.

"I'm feeling a little weak. I don't know if it's from shock or hunger."

"Probably a little of both," Brook said. She reached down to put on her shoes. "I think some chicken soup would make us both feel better."

She stood up to go to the kitchen and to her delight, Kayla put her arm around Brook's waist and walked with her.

"My dad loves chicken soup," Kayla said, watching Brook retrieve the soup container from the fridge.

"I use my mother's recipe," Brook said. "It was a family staple when I was growing up in New York."

"Did you have brothers and sisters?" Kayla asked. "I'm an only child. My parents adopted me when I was just a day old. They couldn't have children of their own."

"I was an only child, too," Brook said. She stirred the soup and tried hard not to say the wrong thing. "So were each of my parents. I really don't have an extended family.

"I was born in Brooklyn, New York--that's how I got my name. We moved to St. Louis when I was twelve, and I always missed New York."

"The soup smells great," Kayla said. She smiled as Brook set a steaming bowl in front of her.

"If you live in Brooklyn, you have to know how to make great chicken noodle soup--it's a pre-requisite. Dig in."

Brook watched in amusement as Kayla crumpled up about a dozen crackers and added them to her soup. It was the same thing Brook's dad had always done.

"My dad would love this soup," Kayla said. She looked at Brook with concern. "Do you think he's okay?"

"He's really got his hands full. We may not hear from him for a while. Would you like me to run you home for a few minutes so you can change clothes?" Both of them were still wearing their Sunday best.

"Would you mind? I'd love to get into some shorts and--oh no--I just remembered. I need to feed Moonshine and let her go outside. That poor dog has really been neglected this week!"

Brook set the dirty dishes in the sink, ran upstairs to change into jeans and the two of them drove up to Bill Tom's house to feed Moonshine.

"Wow, you're a big one!" Brook exclaimed as she and Kayla walked into the Bradley's foyer. Moonshine jumped up to put her paws on Brook's shoulders and gave her a kiss on the cheek."

"Shiner, get down!" Kayla yelled at the dog in surprise. "I've never seen her do that before, Mrs. Jennings. She must really like you. I'm sorry. Did she hurt you?"

"No. I love big friendly dogs. Take it easy there, Moonshine." With some effort, Brook pried the big dog's paws off her shoulders.

"Come on back to the kitchen," Kayla called to Brook as she made her way down the hall. "Don't mind the mess. We haven't had much time to clean up around here."

Everything appeared to be in pretty good order, Brook thought, until she got into the kitchen. The kitchen table and the adjoining TV room were cluttered with pieces of yellow notebook paper, recent newspaper articles about Esther's murder and several open boxes of snack crackers.

"I try to clean up after him," Kayla said, "but he asked me not to touch any of this stuff. I'll bet his office is an even bigger mess."

Brook nodded her head and smiled at Kayla.

"He certainly has a lot on his shoulders right now," Brook said, watching as Kayla poured a huge amount of dog food into Moonshine's over-sized food dish.

"That's why I worry about him so much, Mrs. Jennings," Kayla said. "I mean he's really getting old and I wonder how much longer he can take this kind of stress. I don't think it's good for an old person."

Brook laughed to herself. Bill Tom was only a couple months older than she was. They were both fifty.

"He looks pretty sturdy to me, Kayla," Brook said, assessing the tall, muscular image of Bill Tom in her mind's eye.

"I hope so. Without Miss Esther, if anything happened to him I wouldn't know what to do."

All of a sudden Kayla looked like she might cry again.

"Kayla, don't borrow trouble," Brook said. She walked over to the girl and put her arm around her shoulders.

"Try to live your life one day at a time. Things have a way of working out. Most of the things we worry about never happen."

Kayla smiled at Brook while she opened the back door to let Moonshine go outside. The sudden ring of the telephone made both of them jump.

"Maybe it's Dad," Kayla said, darting for the phone. "Bradley residence. This is Kayla.

"Oh, hi, Mindy. I'm glad you called. Are you okay? I didn't see you at church this morning. Were you there?"

There was silence as Kayla listened to her friend.

Brook thought the girl might like some privacy so she walked into the living room to look around. She could see Sarah's touch in everything…dainty white lace curtains…a rose-colored couch with matching flowered pillows. Everywhere she looked there were pictures of Bill Tom, Sarah and Kayla, always smiling, always hugging, a perfect family unit.

She stared at a picture of Kayla when she must have been about three years old, a sweet little cherub with red hair, freckles and a smile that could light up the night.

"Sorry we got interrupted," Kayla said, walking into the living room. "That was my friend, Mindy. She and her boyfriend, Todd, are leaving for MIZZOU tomorrow. She's really upset about Mr. Tucker. Actually, I think she was supposed to sing a solo this morning and she seemed to be more upset about not getting to do that than she did about what happened to Mr. Tucker. She can be kind of shallow sometimes."

"It certainly sounds that way," Brook agreed.

"I see you've found the family archives," Kayla said. She nodded at the room full of photographs.

"They're great pictures," Brook said. "You look like a very happy family."

"We were," Kayla said, "until Mom died." She gave Brook a wistful smile. "It was a shock. I was only ten. I didn't realize how sick she was. Dad tried his best to take care of me. I don't know what we would have done without Miss Esther."

"It's great that she was able to help," Brook said.

"Dad was a wreck for a long time. He tried his best though, and he made sure I knew how much he loved me. The worst time we had was when I needed to start wearing bras. Dad took me to the store and when the clerk asked what size I needed he made a fist and told the clerk, 'Each one is about an eighth of the size of my hand.' He embarrassed me so much I ran to the bathroom and wouldn't come out for an hour. After that, he sent me shopping with Miss Esther."

Brook giggled at the thought of Bill Tom trying to buy lingerie for his pubescent daughter.

"I'm sorry, Kayla," she said with a grin, "but the thought of your dad trying to buy women's underwear is just too funny."

"It's funny now, but it wasn't funny then."

The two women looked at each other and started laughing.

"Oops, Moonshine wants in," Kayla said. The dog was whining as the door. "She's gonna hate to see us leave."

"Why don't you bring her along?" Brook suggested. "I love dogs and she can keep us company."

Chapter 18

Across town, at the police department, the mood was dark and somber. Bill Tom sat in his chair, staring across his cluttered desk at Beach, who had pulled an investigation team together and drove out to Hillside the minute Bill Tom had called him.

One more dead body. One more stunned family. More fingerprints. More crime scene tape. More reporters. Bill Tom couldn't believe it. The morbid aspect of the crime had triggered the attention of network news and he had actually taken a call from a producer at the Today Show.

"Bill Tom, you've got a big problem on your hands," Beach said. "An honest-to-goodness wack-o is on the loose. I gotta tell you, my friend, you're dealing with a seriously screwed up individual."

"Tell me something I don't know." Bill Tom's patience was totally worn out.

"Well, you don't know that after you called me today I called my boss and requested a leave of absence," Beach said. His cigar filled the room with foul-smelling smoke. "I have the time coming to me and when I explained the situation to him he agreed that I ought to be here. He also said to tell you that our department resources are at your disposal. That means more crime scene people and some pretty doggoned sophisticated equipment, buddy. Does that make you feel a little better?"

"Yes, it does," Bill Tom said, leaning back in his chair. He threw his pencil on his desk and closed his eyes. "Why can't I get a handle on this, Beach? Two strangled people in less than a week. What kind of a lame-ass law enforcement officer am I?"

"Billy-boy, you've got a healthy mind. And you're dealing with someone who's really gone 'round the bend. It's hard to get into that mindset. It could take weeks of collecting evidence and sorting out that evidence before you can get a line on this jerk's thinking. Maybe then you can start identifying suspects. You've got to be patient, though, and give yourself some time. If you go about this the wrong way you're gonna miss clues. And, Bill Tom, lying right here on this messy desk of yours, there are clues. The crime scenes have clues; it's up to us to discover them." Beach leaned forward and tapped his finger on Bill Tom's desk.

"And in the meantime, what do I do for the citizens of Hillside who are afraid they--or one of their loved ones--might be next?"

"Tell 'em to lock their doors. Tell 'em not to go out alone at night and to report anything that looks suspicious. How many people live in Hillside? Two thousand? You can't personally watch over each one of 'em. They're gonna have to put aside their 'I'm safe in a small town' attitudes and take some assertive action on their own."

Beach was interrupted by the unmistakable shrill voice of Mayor Adermann coming from the outer office.

"What do you mean he's in a meeting? I demand to see him right now," the feisty little man was shaking his finger in Mary Ann's face when Bill Tom opened his office door.

"Get that finger out of her face or I'll shove it up your nose," Bill Tom shouted, storming out of his office. "What do you think you're doin', comin' in here yelling orders at her? This is Sunday, Bob, Mary Ann's day off, and she came in here because she knew I needed the help, so leave her alone and leave me alone. When I've got news to share I'll come to you!"

It took all of Bill Tom's self-control to keep from punching the annoying little man.

"You can't talk to me like that," Mayor Adermann retorted. He looked defiantly into Bill Tom's face. He took a deep breath and pulled himself up to his full height of five feet, six inches. "I'm your boss and I demand to know what's going on!"

"What's going on is that I'm trying to solve two murder cases and if you keep interrupting me I'm gonna quit, and then you can go after the guy who's doing this and I'll interrupt you every five minutes.

"Now get out of here," Bill Tom opened the door with such fury that it hit the wall with a loud bang, "and stay outta my way."

The shocked little man hurried out the door and didn't look back.

Bill Tom turned around to look at Beach and Mary Ann. "I can't stand that little jerk," Bill Tom said.

"Well, thanks for clearing that up for us, Billy," Beach said with a big grin. "I was thinking maybe you guys might be lovers."

At that, the three of them started laughing and the tension in the office was broken.

"Mary Ann, see if you can get Randy on the phone for me, will you?" Bill Tom asked calmly. "He's either still at the church or over at Cliff Dunbar's trailer. And then, will you order a pizza or something? I haven't eaten all day, have you?"

"Food is already on the way, Chief," Mary Ann said. "In fact, here it is." She looked at the door as her husband, George, walked in with some deli sandwiches and two six-packs of ice cold Coke."

"I think I'm in love with her," Beach said to Bill Tom. Mary Ann blushed and giggled.

"You guys start eating," Bill Tom said. "I'm gonna check up on Kayla." He reached for his cell phone and then stopped.

"Damn," he said. "I don't know that woman's phone number."

"What woman are you looking for, Chief?" Mary Ann asked, her mouth full of ham, cheese and bread.

"Brook Jennings. Kayla went home with her this morning. I asked Brook to keep an eye on her for me."

Mary Ann flipped open her Rolodex and wrote a number on a piece of paper.

"Here's her number," she said. "She gave it to me yesterday after Esther's funeral."

"You're an amazing woman, Mary Ann," Bill Tom said, giving her a hug. "George, you married a winner."

"She reminds me of that every day, Chief," the good natured man said with a laugh.

Bill Tom left the three people eating their sandwiches and walked into his office to call his daughter.

"Hey, Brook, it's Bill Tom," he said when she answered the phone. "Is Kayla okay? I'm sorry I couldn't call sooner but I've been really busy."

"Under the circumstances she's doing very well," Brook said. "Just a second, I'll get her for you."

"Hi Dad, what's going on? Are you okay? I've been worried about you."

Bill Tom smiled into the phone.

"I've been worried about you, too, Sweetheart. I'm sorry I had to send you home with Mrs. Jennings this morning but I had my hands full."

"Oh, Dad, it's no problem. I understand," Kayla said. "Mrs. Jennings has been great to me. She makes the best home-made chicken soup and now we're making a chocolate pie. She even let me bring Shiner down to her house so she wouldn't be alone."

"Well, that's real nice, honey," Bill Tom said. He wondered about Brook's real motive. "Would you put her back on the phone so I can talk to her for a minute?"

"Okay, Dad. And I'll see ya later, okay?

"Yeah, honey, I'll see ya later.

Bill Tom waited for Brook to come back to the phone.

"Hello."

"Brook, thanks for taking such good care of Kayla," he said. "I want you to know that I really appreciate it."

"I'm happy to do it, Bill Tom," she said. "Is there anything else that we can do? Have you had any supper?"

"We're eating now," he said, "as you can probably tell." He was chewing on a big bite of his sandwich while he was talking to her. "I'll try to wrap things up around here in a little while and come to get her. I hear you have Moonshine, too."

"Yes, we didn't want her to be alone, so we brought her back with us when I took Kayla home to change clothes."

"Well, I'll see you guys in a little while then," he said, trying to remember just how big of a mess his house was in when he left it that morning.

"See you later," Brook said, and hung up the phone.

Bill Tom walked back to the outer office where Beach, Mary Ann and George were eating their sandwiches.

"Did you ever get in touch with Randy?" Bill Tom asked Mary Ann.

"The Chief is all work and no play," Mary Ann said to Beach and George.

"Actually, he did call back and he's on his way in," she said. "Still no sign of Cliff Dunbar. And we haven't received any faxes regarding the all-points bulletin, either."

Bill Tom sighed and shook his head.

"I think it's time for all of us to get some rest," he said. "Doc Schrader asked me not to question Wanda about Ernie until tomorrow. He has her so heavily sedated she probably wouldn't be able to tell us much anyway. Let's call it a day."

He called Randy and told him to go home, too. "We'll all start fresh in the morning," he said.

After George and Mary Ann left, Bill Tom helped Beach gather up his notes and the two men headed to the parking lot.

"You can stay in our guest room, Beach," he said. "I don't think I told you this before, but I'm really glad to have your help on this case."

"Thanks, Billy," Beach said. "I'm happy to help. But I don't need a place to stay tonight. I already checked into the Cliffside Inn. The last thing you need is a house guest."

"We'll reimburse you for your expenses," Bill Tom said, patting his friend on the back.

"Thanks, Billy," Beach smiled. "I was real worried about that."

Bill Tom waved to his friend and headed toward home. He looked at his watch. Seven p.m. The day had seemed twice as long.

Chapter 19

When he pulled into Brook's driveway he saw a silver Camaro sitting in front of the house. He knew it belonged to Mindy Arnold, one of Kayla's best friends and Esther Gaines' great niece.

"I'm glad you're here, I was just about to call you," Brook said when she answered the door. "One of Kayla's friends dropped by and…"

"Hi, Dad," Kayla said, walking into the foyer. "Are you okay? I know you had a terrible day, didn't you? Do you have any leads yet on the killer?"

"Yes, yes and no," Bill Tom said, answering all her questions at once. "What's going on here?" He motioned to the living room where Mindy was slouched in a chair, making herself right at home.

"Oh, Mindy came over to see if I could spend the night at her house," Kayla said. "Her mom and dad are having a small farewell party for her and Todd. "They're going off to MIZZOU in the morning, ya know? It was gonna be a bigger deal, but then Miss Esther got killed and her family didn't feel like having anything too big."

Mindy stood up and walked into the foyer.

"Hi, Chief," she said, tossing her long blond hair away from her face. "It's okay if Kayla comes over, isn't it? She can stay all night and I'll bring her home on my way out of town."

Bill Tom looked at the girl and, as always, he tried to mask his genuine dislike for her. She wore too much make-up. Her clothes were way too seductive, and he hated the way she tried to play him.

"You're not going anywhere else but your house?" he asked, looking her straight in the eye.

"Scout's honor!" she said, meeting his stare. "I'll even cross my heart," she said, running her hand slowly over her left breast.

Bill Tom looked at Kayla.

"You stay at the Arnold's house," he said. "And if the plans change, call me, okay?"

"Okay, Dad," Kayla said giving him a hug.

Then she turned to Brook.

"Thanks for everything, Mrs. Jennings," she said, giving Brook a hug, too. "I really enjoyed spending time with you."

Brook and Bill Tom watched the two girls as they climbed into Mindy's car and drove off.

"I think it's a good thing that Mindy's going off to college tomorrow," Brook said. "Would you agree?"

"As far as I'm concerned, she couldn't get far enough away," Bill Tom said.

The two looked at each other in silence.

"How about some fresh chocolate pie?" Brook asked, as she turned and walked toward the kitchen.

"Sounds good to me. Do you have any more of that coffee you served last night?"

"No. But I have a freshly brewed pot," Brook said without turning around.

"That'll have to do," Bill Tom responded, following her into the kitchen.

He sat down in one of her comfortable chairs, watching her as she sliced up a generous portion of pie.

"Well, you make great brownies and chocolate pie," Bill Tom said as he finished the last bite. "Kayla told me your home-made chicken soup is delicious. When did you get so domestic, Brook?"

"I've always been domestic, you just never knew it," she said, watching him scrape up every last bit of chocolate with his fork. "Would you like another slice of pie, or are you just going to lick the plate?"

Instantly he lifted his plate toward her. "May I please have another slice, Ma'am?

"You can have another slice now and take the rest of it home," Brook said. "It's better that you and Kayla should have it. I sure don't need the extra calories."

"From where I sit, it doesn't look like you've got much of a problem in that department," Bill Tom said, unable to hide his admiration of Brook's great body.

"Ha," she laughed. "You've never seen me naked!" she said. As soon as she said it he could tell she was embarrassed.

"Oops," she said, her face growing red, "I shouldn't have said that. I'm sorry."

Bill Tom's face turned crimson. "That's okay, Brook," he gave her a wink, "just remember that all men have an imagination, and I'm no different.

"I really should be going," he said, quickly changing the subject. His expression became very serious.

"There's just one thing I need to ask you," he looked into her eyes.

"What is that?" she asked, sitting down across the table from him.

"Please don't try to take my daughter away from me. Losing Sarah was hell for me, but I honestly don't know what I'd do without Kayla. Life wouldn't be worth living. Please let me keep her.

"I know you're her biological mother, and that you have rights that I don't have as her adoptive parent, but I beg you, please don't take her away from me. I promise, you can see her as much as you want. I'm just not ready to tell her that you're her mother. I can't do that right now with everything else that's going on in my life. I know she deserves to know and I know it's the right thing to do, but can you just give me a little time?"

"Do you really think I'd try to take her away from you? You're her father. I wouldn't dream of hurting you or her that way. Do you really believe that I would be that hateful?"

"I'm sorry, Brook. It's just that she's my whole life…" His voice trailed off as he shook his head.

"Bill Tom, all I want to do is know this wonderful young lady who shared my body for nine months," Brook said. "You can't possibly know how much I loved her then and how much it hurt to give her up. In the last seventeen years not a day has gone by that I haven't thought about her.

"It's obvious that you and Sarah did a wonderful job raising her. I'd never do anything to ruin that.

"If you decide that you want her to know, it will be up to you to choose the right time," she said. She patted his hand. "You'll get no pressure from me. I'm thrilled just to be a part of her life as her teacher and friend."

They walked slowly to the front door and Bill Tom reached for her hand.

"Thank you, Brook, for everything...the food, the help with Kayla, and for your patience. I promise that I will tell her the truth, as soon as I can." He kissed her hand, smiled, and sprinted down the porch steps to his car.

He walked into his kitchen and the sudden ring of the phone startled him.

"You forgot Moonshine," Brook said as he picked up the receiver.

Chapter 20

Mindy Arnold lived in one of the nicest houses in town. Located on Grand Mountain Skyway, the 100-year-old brick two-story had a second-level balcony on the back that allowed its occupants to take in the town of Hillside, the Missouri River and the rolling hills beyond. Since the balcony faced the northeast, it was a great place to sit on a summer evening without squinting at the sunset.

Kayla and Mindy sat on the balcony, stretched out on two chaise lounges with over-stuffed yellow cushions. The table between them held a portable CD player, two icy glasses of Coke and a bag of pretzels.

"I can't believe that no one showed up for your party," Kayla said, absent-mindedly dipping a pretzel into her Coke. "I know everyone is very upset about Mr. Tucker, but I thought at least Jessica and Breanna might come over for a little while."

She was quiet for a moment as she pictured the two girls from Mindy's class who were always at her side.

"Yeah, it's a shocker, isn't it?" Mindy asked, leaning back in the lounge with her eyes closed.

"Well, you don't seem very upset," Kayla said. "Doesn't it bother you that tomorrow you're leaving and you guys won't see one another until Christmas?" Jessica and Breanna were headed off to the University of Miami.

"They decided to leave after Aunt Esther's funeral yesterday--slight change of plans! Anyway, they were high school," Mindy said, dismissing the girls with a wave of her hand. "I'm a college girl now. It's time to move on."

"Mindy, I know you better than that," Kayla objected. "You guys have been friends since grade school. You wouldn't just cut them off like that."

"You're right, Little Red," she said, raising her glass in Kayla's direction. "Any minute now you'll figure out the truth."

"What are you talking about?" Kayla asked, confused. "You're not making any sense."

"You are so *gullible*," Mindy said as she sat up and turned around to face Kayla. "You haven't caught on yet, have you?"

"Caught on to what?"

"Think about it, Kayla," Mindy said. "I invite you to my house for a farewell party hosted by my parents, and my parents are nowhere in sight. What do you think is going on?"

"I really have no idea, Mindy," Kayla said. Her friend's condescending attitude was beginning to irritate her.

"There is no party, Kayla," Mindy said, shaking her head. "My parents may be having a party at the lake--I'm sure they're glad to be getting rid of me! They're both so brokenhearted that I'm leaving that they decided to go down to their condo right after Aunt Esther's funeral. They're not coming back for at least a week, maybe longer."

Mindy stopped talking for a moment, looked away from Kayla as she bit her bottom lip.

"My dad said since I spend all my time with Todd anyway, he could just hall all my stuff up to MIZZOU. Dad won't let me take my car to school." She glanced up at Kayla and shrugged her shoulders.

"Guess they're sick of me, huh?" Mindy asked, looking at Kayla with tears in her eyes.

"I'm so sorry, Mindy," Kayla whispered, thinking about how her own father would handle it when she was ready to leave for college. She knew he would carry her up there on his back if he had to.

"You know, people handle grief in different ways," Kayla said, searching for something to say that would comfort Mindy. "Your dad just lost his Aunt Esther--she was his aunt, right? Maybe he just couldn't stand losing you, too."

"My dad was Aunt Esther's nephew by marriage," Mindy said, disputing Kayla's reasoning. "They weren't that close. I wasn't close to her, either, for that matter. She invited us over to her house a lot, but my dad always found an excuse not to go. And in school she treated me just like she treated all the other kids. She was nice, but I was nothing special. She didn't care about me the way she cared about you!"

"She was my Godmother," Kayla said, suddenly feeling very sad. "I'm really gonna miss her. I can't believe that she's gone--and in such a horrible way.

"For that matter, I can't believe Mr. Tucker is gone either," she continued looking out over Mindy's balcony to the Lutheran church on the far hill.

"Who do you think could have done such a horrible thing?"

Kayla turned to Mindy who shrugged her shoulders and grimaced.

"Haven't a clue," she said in a carefree tone. "At least I'll be outta this crime-infested town tomorrow!"

"Do you think we're safe here?" Kayla asked, suddenly remembering they were alone in the big old house.

"I think we will be," Mindy said, in a sing-song style. She looked at her watch. "As soon as Todd finishes his last night of work at the Pizza Kitchen he's going to get Brian and the two of them are coming over here for an all-night party!"

"Brian went to Jeff City with his mom last night to be with Miss Esther's relatives," Kayla said. "They drove over there with Mr. and Mrs. Pruitt. I think they were going to take some of Miss Esther's clothes to a nursing home there. Brian said they were all going to spend a couple of nights at the Holiday Inn, just to get away from everything for a little while."

"Oh, that's too bad," Mindy said. "I guess it'll just be the three of us, then. Todd said he'd bring us a pizza. I hope pepperoni is okay."

"Fine with me," Kayla said, smiling weakly at her friend. She felt uncomfortable with the whole set up. And if her dad knew, he'd hit the roof.

"Mindy, maybe I should just call my dad and have him pick me up," Kayla suggested, looking out at the cloudy sky. It was after nine o'clock. She could see lightening in the distance. "You know, three's a crowd."

"Nonsense," Mindy said. "Besides, I'll tell you when Todd and I want to be alone. Or you'll probably get the hint when I start taking my clothes off."

Mindy laughed and jumped up suddenly.

"Come on," she said grabbing Kayla's hand. "Let's go figure out how we're gonna wear our hair for Homecoming. You know, I'm coming back to crown this year's queen--and I'm pretty sure that's gonna be you!"

Kayla laughed as her friend pulled her off the chair and dragged her by the arm into her bedroom.

They spent the next couple of hours working on each other's hair, doing their nails and looking at party dresses online.

"What kind of earrings would you wear with a dress like that?" Kayla asked, pointing at a black strapless crepe dress with a matching stole.

"Diamonds, of course. Nothing fancy, just plain and simple two-caret studs," Mindy said, opening her jewelry box and holding up some earrings.

"Are those real?" Kayla asked, looking curiously at her friend. She knew the Arnolds were wealthy, but those earrings looked really expensive.

"They're real and they're my mother's," Mindy said with a smirk. "I'm taking them to school. She'll never miss them."

"If they were mine, I'd miss them," Kayla said.

"My mother has tons of expensive jewelry," Mindy said. "Every time she and my dad get into a fight, she pouts for days and then he buys her jewelry to make up. Someday I'll inherit all this stuff and I'll be livin' on easy street because my parents couldn't stand each other."

Kayla shook her head and silently thanked God for her own parents and the life they lived on Maple Drive. Suddenly the girls heard a loud crack of thunder and the rain started to pour down.

Shortly after midnight the front door opened and a drenched Todd Mack walked in, carrying a delicious smelling pizza.

Kayla stood several feet away as she watched Todd grab Mindy into a tight hug and kiss her. She returned the kiss with equal vigor and their hands roamed up and down each other's bodies.

"I don't need this," Kayla thought, and ran upstairs to get her PJs and toothbrush.

When she came back downstairs she found them in the kitchen, Mindy sitting on Todd's lap, feeding him a slice of pizza.

"Will one of you please drive me home?" Kayla asked. "You said I'd know when it was time to disappear, and I think now's the time," she added, looking at Mindy.

"Are you kidding?" Mindy asked, looking at Kayla in surprise. "Aren't you hungry? Have a slice of pizza."

"Yeah," Todd said, laughing. "Have a slice of pizza. We'll disappear before things go too far."

"No, I'm gonna call my dad so he can come get me," Kayla said, walking toward the kitchen phone.

"Oh, no you're not," Mindy said. She jumped off Todd's lap and grabbed the receiver out of Kayla's hand. "That's just what we need--your goody two-shoes dad coming up here and seeing that my parents are gone."

"Well, I'm not gonna be a part of this," Kayla insisted, walking toward the front door. "Do you have an umbrella I can borrow?"

"Get wet," Mindy said, throwing her friend an angry stare. "It's about a half mile to your house and it's pouring down."

"I'd rather be wet than humiliated," Kayla said, returning Mindy's angry stare. "Of course, you could keep me from being either if you'd just be a friend and take a minute to drive me home."

"I want you to stay all night," Mindy said in a stubborn whisper. "I'm not gonna drive you home."

"Then I'll get wet!" Kayla said, as she opened the door. "Have fun at college."

Chapter 21

As soon as she jumped off the porch and ran onto the Arnold's sidewalk Kayla realized that it wasn't just raining. Hillside was getting pounded with a violent Midwest thunderstorm. Lightning flashed every few seconds and the trees waved wildly back and forth in the wind.

Kayla bent her head to her chest, raced down Mindy's driveway and turned onto the street. She knew the town of Hillside like the back of her hand, but the rain made it hard to see, so it was difficult to tell one street from another.

There were no cars on the road. On Sunday nights everyone in Hillside went to bed after the ten o'clock news so they'd be ready for work on Monday morning.

The wind made a howling sound as it roared through the trees and every ten seconds or so she'd get a glimpse of her surroundings when lightening lit up the sky. It seemed like forever before she reached the bottom of Grand Mountain Skyway and was able to turn onto Hickory, the street that ran into Maple Drive.

Lighting flashed, thunder clapped loudly, and hard pellets of ice began to hit her body.

"Oh, no, that's hail stones," she thought. She looked around and during the next lightning bolt she saw an old wooden shed with an overhanging wooden roof.

"That'll have to do," she thought as she ran to it, almost slipping in the huge puddles of water and mud. She tried to open the shed, but it was locked. All she could do was stand close to it with her back toward the rain.

The rain and hail increased in intensity and the wind was blowing so hard it was difficult to keep standing. Finally she risked a quick look out to the street, which now looked like a fast flowing river. The ground was white with hail stones. She looked up and, to her relief, she saw headlights.

"Ah, thank God," she thought. "They changed their minds."

Kayla ran out into the street in front of the car, hoping Todd and Mindy wouldn't miss her in all the rain.

The car stopped and she ran to hop in the passenger side.

She reached down to open the door and when she did, she froze. It wasn't Todd and Mindy. She was looking squarely into the face of Clifford Dunbar. She knew from her dad that he was an ex-con from Kansas City.

She stared at him in shock. From the car's dome light she could see his burly face, heavy with whiskers. He was wearing a filthy sleeveless tee shirt and his arms were loaded with tattoos. He reeked with the smell of sweat and beer. She was ready to turn around and run for her life when he grabbed her arm.

"Get in here, will ya," he said roughly. "What in the world are you doing out on a night like this?"

Kayla slid into the dirty car seat and couldn't keep from shaking. She was cold and scared out of her wits.

"I thought you were some friends of mine," she said, her voice shaking. "My house is just several blocks down the street."

She thought about telling him that she was Chief Bradley's daughter but her instincts told her to keep quiet.

Clifford Dunbar smashed his cigarette butt in the car's already overflowing ashtray and pushed his foot on the accelerator.

"Show me the house," he said, shaking his head. "Your parents are gonna be furious with you for bein' out on a night like this."

"You have no idea, sir," she said, hardly able to believe the predicament she was in. "I'll be grounded for the rest of my life."

He stopped the car at the corner by Kayla's house and, as she tried to get out he grabbed her arm again.

"You know, it's not safe for a pretty young thing like you to be out alone so late at night," he said, his bloodshot eyes meeting hers. "That's how ya end up dead." He let go of her arm and punched her gently on the shoulder.

"Now go on, and get inside. I'll stay here 'til somebody answers the door."

"Oh, that's okay, sir," she said, opening the door. "I have a key, and besides, my parents are really sound sleepers!

"Thanks for the ride," she said as she jumped out and slammed the door.

Kayla tried to be as quiet as possible as she ran up the back steps to the house. Her hands were shaking so badly she had trouble getting the key into the lock. But finally the door opened and she hurried inside the screened-in back porch and locked the door behind her.

She turned around and saw that Cliff Dunbar was true to his word. He waited until she was inside before he drove off.

When the reality of the situation hit her and she thought about what she had just been through she sank to her feet, put her head in her hands and started to cry.

"Don't move!" someone yelled and all of a sudden the back porch was flooded with light.

Kayla screamed as she looked up to see her dad. He was wearing his gray sweat pants and a white tee shirt. And he was pointing a gun at her. Moonshine quickly ran to her side.

"Don't shoot," she screamed, foolishly throwing her hands into the air.

Bill Tom put down his gun and ran to his daughter.

"Kayla," he yelled in surprise, "what happened to you? Why aren't you at Mindy's? Why in the world are you out in this storm?"

Not waiting for an answer, he gently picked her up, carried her into the kitchen and sat her down on one of the chairs by the table.

"Let me get a blanket," he said with a shaky voice and disappeared into the laundry room which was next to the kitchen. He quickly reappeared with an old quilt.

"Here, Honey," he said, "let me get you dried off. Are you sure you're okay? What in the world happened to you?"

"It was just a bad night, Dad," she said, being careful not to be too specific about her argument with Mindy. She knew he'd head on up there and make a scene.

"I thought I could make it home before the rain started," she lied. "Mindy's parents weren't home yet—turns out they went to the lake--and Todd came over. I felt like a third wheel so I said I wanted to come home. They wanted to drive me, but I told them not to bother. It's just a ten-minute walk. I knew you'd be asleep."

Kayla watched her dad's expression carefully. She could almost read his thoughts. He was getting ready to yell at her, but at least Todd and Mindy were in the clear. She wasn't sure why she was worried about them, but she was.

"Kayla Grace Bradley, what in the world were you thinking?" he asked, kneeling in front of her and rubbing her arms vigorously with the quilt. "There's a killer loose in this town, and you decide to take a midnight stroll--in a thunderstorm? You're more responsible than that. Why didn't you call me?"

She looked into her dad's face, trying to sum up just how much trouble she was in. He didn't look really mad, just worried about her. Nevertheless, he had started his speech using her whole name. A speech that started with just her first name never really had a bad outcome. But a whole-name speech usually included serious consequences. She figured she'd be house-bound until school started on Thursday. She reached down to pet Moonshine who was licking the rain off her legs.

"I'm sorry, Dad," she said, reaching out to touch his face. "I made the decision to do this in a hurry. I should have thought it through. Will you forgive me?" She looked into his eyes for mercy.

"Forgive you? Honey, this is not about forgiveness. This is about you putting yourself in such danger. I can't believe you'd do such a thing. It's totally out of character. Are you getting dumber as you get older? Do you have any working brain cells up there?"

He poked his finger on her forehead several times.

Once again Kayla made a quick assessment of his actions. He was going from alarmed to angry. She was really in for it.

"I'm sorry, Dad," she said, trying to come up with a plausible explanation for her actions. "I knew how tired you were and I didn't think…"

"Didn't think," Bill Tom interrupted. "That's right! You didn't think! Kayla, I don't think you know how serious this is or how angry I am at you. In fact, I don't think I can talk to you about it anymore tonight. I'll probably say something I'll regret. Now I want you to go upstairs and get to bed. We'll talk about this in the morning. And then you're gonna go get that cell phone of yours fixed." He stood up, opened the fridge and grabbed a Bud Light.

"I'm sorry, Daddy," she said, starting to cry. Between Mindy's rudeness and her dad's anger, she'd had enough. She looked at him through blurry eyes, hoping he'd ease up a bit.

"Tears aren't gonna cut it this time, Kayla, so get upstairs," he said, looking her straight in the eye. "If something had happened to you, I'd be doin' more than cryin'. I'd just go outta my mind, do you understand that? You've got to be more careful. You are the whole world to me!" he said, looking down at her and gently stroking her arm with his free hand.

She nodded her head and ran up the stairs to the bedroom, leaving a wet trail behind her. Moonshine followed her to her room.

After she took a shower she crawled into bed with Moonshine at her side. She hugged the big loveable dog and tried to sort out the events of the day.

She hadn't really gotten a good look at Mr. Tucker's body. She was really thankful for that. But just the thought of him sitting up there on the organ bench, dead, was enough to give her goose bumps. Nobody knew the Tuckers very well. They had moved to Hillside at the end of May. So, although she was sorry for his family, she didn't feel the same level of loss that she felt for Miss Esther.

She was really happy that she had been able to go home with Mrs. Jennings and get away from that whole scene. The new teacher had been great. She knew exactly what to do to make her feel better. And she was really easy to talk to. Kayla wondered if they might become close friends, the way she had been with Miss Esther.

"She's younger than Miss Esther," Kayla thought. "Maybe she can help me with all my problems with Brian."

Kayla's thoughts turned to the tall blond-haired, blue-eyed football player she was dating. She and Brian had always been friends. But during the summer between their sophomore and junior years of school their platonic friendship turned into a romantic one.

It happened simply enough. They had gone horseback riding and stopped for lunch by a creek on Grand Mountain. She was lying on a blanket watching Brian eat his ham sandwich. His last bite left a crumb of bread on his cheek. Kayla reached up to brush it off. Brian gently touched her hand and bent down to kiss her.

Since they were already friends, the new attraction between them took their relationship to a deeper level and they became even closer. But lately, Brian had been bugging her about sex. Whenever they made out she always stopped him before things went too far. But by that time they were both in such a heated frenzy it was agonizing to stop. And Brian usually ended up sulking. She wasn't sure if it was painful for a guy, or if he was just frustrated like she was.

Not long after her humiliating bra-buying experience with her dad—she must have been about eleven—he'd escorted her into their living room, handed her a Coke, took a big gulp of his beer, and explained the facts of life to her—the what goes where of it all. Until that time, she'd never even heard him use the words "penis" and "vagina." Surprisingly, he didn't seem at all embarrassed or uncomfortable.

"Kayla," he'd said, "sex is a gift from God, a precious gift. A lot of guys are going to try to have sex with you. They'll say they love you when all they really want is sex. You have to decide what you're going to do about it, because you're gonna want it, too. Sexual desire is a powerful force. Just remember that someday you're gonna fall in love and a man is gonna want to marry you. If you're smart, you'll save yourself for that man."

Kayla believed that sex was meant to be shared in marriage, and she often prayed for the strength to hold things at bay with Brian. But some of their friends at school--a few who knew they were not sexually active, like Mindy and Todd--were making fun of them. It was embarrassing and humiliating, especially for seniors. Kayla knew some freshman girls who were having sex on a regular basis.

"Maybe when I get to know her better, I could talk to Mrs. Jennings about it," Kayla thought. She knew her dad would have a cow if she ever broached the subject with him. And he'd have Brian castrated. Mrs. Jennings seemed to be more open-minded and not so uptight.

"I wonder if she dyes her hair," Kayla thought as she drifted off to sleep. "It's the exact same color as mine."

Chapter 22

Bill Tom woke up feeling like a two-ton boulder had landed on his body. His alarm clock hadn't gone off yet, but he knew by the light streaming into his bedroom window that it must be close to seven a.m.

With some effort he pulled himself out of bed, took a shower, shaved and dressed for work. He wanted to catch the early morning news on as many stations as possible. He knew the recent murders in Hillside would probably get some kind of coverage.

He sat on the side of the bed, grabbed the remote off his bedside table and turned on the TV. As he leaned down to put on his socks and shoes, his thoughts turned to Kayla and her uncharacteristic stupid behavior the night before.

"What could have made her do that?" he wondered. "She's not telling me the whole story."

He felt guilty that he'd come down on her so hard, but she had scared him so badly. He'd have to find a way to apologize without letting her off the hook. She had to understand the dangerous aspect of her actions.

"And now we have the latest news about the murders in Hillside."

He looked up instantly as he heard the St. Louis Channel Seven newscaster announce the next story.

"Members of Trinity Lutheran Church in Hillside were stunned yesterday when they arrived for Sunday worship services and found their organist sitting on the organ bench--dead. The man, forty-five-year-old Ernest Tucker, had been strangled. This latest murder follows on the heels of another strangulation last week when Esther Gaines, a sixty-eight-year-old English teacher at Hillside High, was discovered dead in her home."

The TV footage showed pictures of the church and shots of Esther's house with the crime scene tape.

"Although law enforcement officials in Hillside were not available for comment, Police Chief Bill Tom Bradley released a statement reassuring the residents of Hillside that he and his deputy, Randy James, were doing everything possible to find the killer as quickly as possible. The statement said crime scene investigators from St. Louis had been called upon to help solve the murders. And now for a look at our weather, here's…"

Bill Tom clicked the TV off with his remote and headed downstairs for breakfast. He was surprised to see that Kayla was already awake and eating her cereal.

"Mornin' Sweetie," he mumbled, keeping his eyes focused on the refrigerator.

"Good morning, Daddy."

"I'm sorry I got so upset last night, Kayla, but you really scared me," he said, shaking his head as he poured a big glass of orange juice.

"It was my fault, Daddy," Kayla said. "I used poor judgment."

Bill Tom sat down at the table across from Kayla and reached over to hold her hand.

"I won't deny that," he said with a slight smile, "and I hope you never, ever do anything like that again. But I am sorry that I yelled at you. I know you were scared and I didn't do anything to comfort you."

"Its okay, Dad. Just tell me what my punishment is so I can tell Brian how long you're going to ground me. We had plans for every day before school starts. He quit his summer job last Friday so we could spend some time together."

"Ground you? Honey, I'm not going to ground you. I'm just so thankful you're safe. All I want is your word that you'll never put yourself in harm's way like that again."

"I promise, Daddy," she said, giving him a relieved smile.

"And I'm getting you a new cell phone. You can turn the old one in," he added, letting go of her hand. "We should have done that right after it broke." He didn't know why, but he was pretty sure that Mindy had prevented Kayla from calling him last night.

"Thanks, Daddy, I'll be more careful with the new…"

"Bill Tom, are you awake?" Randy called from the back door. "Let me in, I need to see you. It's urgent"

Kayla and Bill Tom exchanged a smile that put their relationship back on track and he got up to answer the door.

"He's back, BT," Randy said as Bill Tom unlocked the screen door and held it open. "I drove by his trailer this morning on a hunch and his old Buick Electra was sitting right there in front of his door."

"Hi, Kayla," he said as he walked into the kitchen.

"Who's back?" she asked.

"Clifford Dunbar," Randy said. "He's our number one suspect in the Hillside murders."

Bill Tom glanced at Kayla and wondered why she suddenly looked so pale.

"The Hillside murders? You've been watching too much TV, Randy," Bill Tom said, grabbing his keys off the counter.

"Kayla, I have to go. Remember what we talked about? After you talk to Brian let me know what you guys are gonna do. I'd rather you stay in town, okay? No riding. No hiking or biking. Why don't you go to the pool where there's lots of people around?"

"Okay, Dad, I promise."

She blew him a kiss. He snatched it out of the air and patted it on his cheek.

Chapter 23

"I'll meet you over there," Bill Tom called to Randy as he headed for his truck. The two men drove off to confront Clifford Dunbar.

"Stay back here until he answers the door," Bill Tom said when they arrived at the guy's old beat up trailer. "You can stop him in case he tries to run."

"Okay, BT," Randy said, drawing his gun. "I'm ready for him."

Bill Tom drew his own gun and rapped on the dirty trailer door.

"Cliff Dunbar, are you in there? Open up."

Nothing.

"Open up, Dunbar. It's Chief Bradley." Bill Tom pounded on the door once again.

"Hold it down, will ya? I'm comin'."

Bill Tom waited for Dunbar to open the door.

"What the hell's goin' on, Chief? Why you botherin' me so early in the mornin'?"

As soon as Cliff opened the door for Bill Tom, Randy ran up the steps and the two officers walked into the house. They put their guns away immediately. It was obvious he was unarmed. He was wearing very dirty white boxer shorts and an old black sleeveless Harley Davidson tee-shirt with holes in it.

"Where've you been?" Bill Tom asked as he looked around the guy's filthy house. The door had opened up into the trailer's small living room. The kitchen was off to the right and the bedroom was down the hall to the left.

The brown carpet was old and worn and there was a pile of dirty dishes in the sink that looked like it had been there for weeks. Bill Tom swatted at the gnats that were flying everywhere. The whole place smelled liked a sewer plant.

"None a your damn business, where I been, Chief. I ain't done nothin' wrong so you just get outta here and leave me alone!"

"First we're gonna have a talk," Bill Tom said, grabbing Cliff's arm as he tried to walk back to his bedroom.

Cliff Dunbar yanked his arm free, shot Bill Tom a dirty look and sat down on an old orange leather couch that was loaded with tobacco stains.

"I'll ask you again, Cliff. Where have you been for the last week?" Bill Tom's patience was wearing thin.

"I was fishin' down at the lake," Cliff said. "I got me a friend who lives down there. He has an old boat. We went out every day til it started to rain. That's when I came home. I was afraid I'd get stuck down there in the mud. I got here a little after midnight."

Bill Tom cringed at the thought of him being out on the streets at the same time Kayla was walking home from Mindy's house.

"Cliff, I'm gonna give you about five minutes to take a shower and get dressed. Then we're gonna take a ride over to my office. I have a lot of questions to ask you."

"Can't take a shower, Chief. It's broken. Sorry I can't get all dressed up for ya. What do you want to talk to me about?"

"Since last Monday, two people have been strangled here in Hillside, and I have reason to believe you might have been involved."

"That's crazy. I told you I been fishin' at the lake."

"If that should happen to be true, we'll find out soon enough. Just go get some clothes on, so we can go to my office. And leave the door open. I don't want you tryin' to slip out your back door."

"The handle's broke on it, Chief. I couldn't use that door if I wanted to," Cliff said as he walked down the hall to change his clothes. Randy followed him to make sure he didn't have a gun hidden somewhere.

Seconds later he emerged from his bedroom wearing a pair of brown plaid pants and dirty sneakers with no socks. He hadn't bothered to change his shirt.

"Cuff him, Randy," Bill Tom said, as he continued to look around the disgustingly dirty trailer.

Randy and Bill Tom escorted Cliff Dunbar to the squad car and Randy drove him to the police department office with Bill Tom following close behind.

Mary Ann was already at work when the men arrived. If she was shocked at Cliff Dunbar's appearance she did not show it.

"Take him into my office, Randy," Bill Tom said as he stopped at Mary Ann's desk.

"Have you heard from Beach yet?" he asked.

"He called in about fifteen minutes ago," Mary Ann said, spraying her room freshener around the office. "He's got some people from his office working on some drape fibers you asked him to look at. He said he'd be tied up most of the morning."

"Did we ever get any responses from our all-points bulletin on Dunbar?"

"Not a one," Mary Ann said, shrugging her shoulders.

"Thanks, Mary Ann. Happy Monday." He patted her on the shoulder and walked into his office to join Randy and Cliff Dunbar.

"Cliff, when you say you were 'down at the lake,' what lake are you referring to?" Bill Tom asked as he sat behind his desk. Randy and Cliff had already taken their seats facing him.

"The Lake of the Ozarks. Where else?" Cliff answered in a nasty tone. "Take these hand cuffs off me. I ain't done nothin' wrong, I tell ya."

"That's a lie, and you know it," Bill Tom said loudly, leaning forward in his chair and pointing his index finger at the man. "We had an all-points bulletin out on your car and if you'd been at the lake a patrol car would have spotted you there, or on your way back. Now, where were you?"

"I'm tellin' you, I was at the lake. I got me a friend down…"

"What friend? What's his name? I'll have Randy call the police department down there so they can pick him up and verify your story."

"I don't exactly remember his name now, Chief," Dunbar said, squirming in his chair. "We just met up this week and I…"

"Stop lyin' to me, dammit," Bill Tom said. "I want you to tell me where you've been every day for the last week."

"If you want me to cooperate with you, you're gonna have to take off these damn handcuffs. They're cuttin' into my wrists and they hurt! I can't think with all this pain."

"You're gonna have more pain than you can stand," Bill Tom said, jumping out of his chair so fast it fell over backwards. He stormed around his desk and leaned down to look at Dunbar face-to-face.

"Now, tell me where you've been."

"Okay, okay. You don't have to get so riled up about it. Soon as I heard about that Gaines woman gettin' strangled I headed for the hills. I knew you'd come lookin' for me. But I tell you, I ain't done nothin' wrong. I wasn't near that woman. She was too uppity for me, always usin' big words and stuff. I couldn't understand a thing she said."

"Where were you last Monday when Esther was strangled?" Bill Tom asked, returning to his chair.

"I was at my trailer all day and night mindin' my business. Some guys walked by Tuesday afternoon and asked me did I hear that folks were saying that Gaines woman was murdered. I figured you'd come after me so I drove up on Grand Mountain, found an old dirt road and followed it til it ended at a creek. There's nothin' and nobody up there. I just stayed there all week, 'til I thought it was safe to come home. I thought you'd have caught whoever done it by now."

Bill Tom shook his head and rubbed his eyes with both hands.

"What did you do for food, Cliff?"

"I ain't no dummy, Chief," Cliff said, looking insulted. "I took me some chips and some peanut butter and bread and some canned soup. I got by."

Bill Tom leaned back in his chair and sighed. He looked at Randy and raised his eyebrows.

"You expect us to believe that?" Randy said, turning in his seat to face Cliff. "It's a pretty convenient story, isn't it? Two people in town are murdered and you're nowhere around. Nobody else had to run and hide. What are you hidin', Cliff?"

"Nobody else in town is an ex-con," Cliff said, gesturing with his hand-cuffed hands. "I knew you guys would automatically think I was guilty. And I don't know nothin' about a second murder. I wouldn't a known about that Gaines' woman if it hadn't been for those two guys who walked by when I was workin' on my car. You know me, I stick to my business. I don't want no trouble. I don't want no part a goin' back to prison."

"Cliff, we found some old green drapes in a trash bag by your trailer," Bill Tom said. "Where'd they come from?"

"You was lookin' in my stuff?" Cliff asked, turning his attention back to Bill Tom. "You got no call to go snoopin' through my stuff."

"Answer my question or I'll get a search warrant and tear that place apart. God knows what I'll find. What else are you hidin' in there?"

"Them old drapes were there when I rented the place," Cliff said, suddenly becoming very cooperative. "I got tired of lookin' at 'em so I decided to pitch 'em.

A knock on Bill Tom's door interrupted Cliff's explanation. It was Mary Ann.

"Chief, may I speak to you out here for a second, please?" she asked, barely poking her head in the door.

"How can you stand that smell?" she whispered when Bill Tom came out of his office.

"It's really bad, isn't it? What's goin' on?"

"Mr. Beacham just called. He's been on the phone with his people in St. Louis all morning. They tested fibers from some drapes you asked about and he said to tell you they're not a match. I thought you might like to know.

"He's finishing up over at the hotel, then he's going over to the church again to look around. He said he'd check in later."

"Okay. Thanks, Mary Ann," Bill Tom said. "Has Kayla called in yet?"

"She called a little while ago and said she was waiting for Brian to pick her up. He and Trudy got back from Jeff City early this morning. The kids are going to spend the day at the pool."

"Good," he said nodding his head. "Wish I could spend my day at the pool."

"Me, too," Mary Ann said, with a wistful sigh. "Right now, though, we've got work to do. That news director guy from the Today Show called again. They'd like to do an interview with you. Seems like a dead organist sitting on his organ bench is worthy of national news."

"Oh, damn!" Bill Tom said. "That's all I need. If I don't do it, they'll go after Adermann. God only knows what he'd say on national TV. See if you can get that New York guy on the phone for me, will ya?"

Bill Tom walked back in his office where Randy was continuing their interrogation of Cliff Dunbar.

"I think we've got everything we need for right now," Bill Tom said, interrupting Cliff's diatribe about looking through his stuff and putting him in handcuffs.

Randy gave his boss a surprised look.

"You sure, BT? I'm still not convinced…"

"It's okay, Randy," Bill Tom reassured his deputy. "Just take him back to his trailer for now.

"Cliff, I want you to stay in town and stay close to home. If you leave, I'll come after you and lock you up. And there'll be no peanut butter and no soup from a can. You understand me?" Bill Tom looked Cliff squarely in the face.

"Take him home, Randy. Take off his handcuffs and come on back to the office. The drape fibers weren't a match."

Randy took Cliff by the elbow and escorted him out of the room.

Just then Bill Tom's intercom rang.

"I have Mr. Lauer on the line for you," Mary Ann said. She used her very business-like manner to announce the call.

"MATT Lauer?"

"Matt Lauer."

Bill Tom couldn't believe it.

Chapter 24

"Well, he's a nice guy for a reporter," Bill Tom said to Mary Ann, walking out of his office after his short conversation with the well-known news anchor. "They're sending a TV news crew out from St. Louis to set up a satellite link from our office tomorrow morning. We have to be here at 5 a.m. They want to do a live interview with Randy and me. I hate the thought of doing this, but if we don't, Adermann will. And that would be a catastrophe."

"I'm gonna have to get your autograph, Chief," Mary Ann smiled. Then, in an instant, she frowned.

"I just hate it that Hillside is getting all this attention because of something so bad," she continued. "It's such a wonderful place to live."

"I'm gonna say that in the interview," Bill Tom said, pointing his finger at her. "Right now I've got to call Woody Schrader and see when I can go talk to Wanda Tucker. I need to ask her some questions about Ernie."

"I called him while you were in there with Cliff Dunbar," Mary Ann said, sitting down at her well-organized desk. "He said she was much calmer today and that she wants to talk to you. She and Lester are waiting for you to come over."

Bill Tom drove over to the Tucker's white frame house and sat in the driveway for a moment. He didn't know the family well, they'd only lived in Hillside since May. They moved to the town when Ernie accepted the job as organist and music director at Trinity Lutheran.

He knew from Kayla who, along with her mother, had always been involved in the music ministry, that Ernie had a good sense of humor and got along well with the choir members and the pastor. So everybody grew to like him in a short amount of time.

Ernie's wife, Wanda, took a job at the Midwest Bank as a teller, and soon became a favorite among all the customers. She was very quiet, but also courteous and competent.

The only mystery about the family was Ernie and Wanda's son, Lester. He was a tall, skinny seventeen-year-old kid with sad brown eyes and pale skin. Whenever Bill Tom spoke to him at church the guy couldn't make eye contact. And he hardly ever smiled.

Bill Tom jumped out of his truck and walked up the sidewalk to the Tucker's porch.

"Come on in, Chief," Wanda Tucker said as she opened the door. A tall, thin lady with short blond hair, she looked sad and tired in her blue seer-sucker bath robe.

"Pastor Riebold was here just a little while ago. He's been helping us make the funeral arrangements" she said, pointing to a big easy chair by the door. "Please sit down."

She sat in a matching chair on the other side of a skirted table with a lamp on it, and stared at Bill Tom.

"Wanda, I'm so sorry for your loss," he began. "I want you to know that we're doing everything we can to find out who did this to Ernie. You have our deepest sympathy."

"Thank you, Chief. Everybody's been real nice to us." She dabbed at her eyes with a worn out tissue.

Bill Tom waited for her to continue, but she stopped talking and stared straight ahead, looking past him.

He decided to come right to the point.

"Wanda, Ernie called my office late Friday night and told Mary Ann he had some information about Esther Gaines' murder. He said he wanted to meet with me on Saturday. Do you know anything about that?"

She looked at him blankly.

"He didn't say anything to me about it. I don't know what he was talking about."

Bill Tom leaned forward, put his elbows on his knees and folded his hands under his chin.

"I think that Ernie must have come across some information about Esther's murder. He may have suspected someone. Maybe the murderer knew about Ernie's suspicions and that's how he ended up dead. I need you to think real hard about what happened the day of Esther's funeral. Did Ernie have an argument or some kind of disagreement with someone recently?"

"Not that I know of. He never said anything about it, if he did," she said, again zoning out on him. He wondered just what Doc Schrader had given her to calm her down. He realized he wasn't getting anywhere with the highly medicated woman.

"Is Lester around?" he asked. It was strange that the boy had not come into the room when he arrived.

"He's in his room. Lester," she raised her voice slightly as she called to the boy, "come on out here. Chief Bradley wants to talk to you."

Bill Tom looked toward the door that led from the living room into the hallway. Soon the boy appeared, wearing black cargo shorts and a red St. Louis Cardinals tee shirt. He was barefooted.

"Hi Lester," Bill Tom said as the boy leaned against the doorframe.

Lester looked up briefly and nodded. His eyes were bloodshot and his face was white.

"I'm so sorry about your dad, Lester" Bill Tom said, walking over to the boy to shake his hand.

Lester looked up briefly then looked down at the floor. He raised a limp hand for Bill Tom to shake.

"You want to come in here for a minute and sit down with us?" Bill Tom suggested. "I know this is a difficult time for you, but

I really need to get some information about the events leading up to your dad's death."

"I was sick yesterday, Chief," Lester said, still looking at the floor. "I was throwing up all morning and I didn't feel like going to church."

"I'm sorry you were sick, Lester," Bill Tom continued, fascinated by the kid's catatonic demeanor. "But I'm not necessarily talking about yesterday morning. Did you observe anything unusual about your dad's behavior before his death? Did anything strange happen?"

"I don't think so. Everything seemed normal."

Bill Tom wondered how they defined normal in the Tucker household. He focused his attention back to Wanda.

"Would you mind if I send my deputy over here to have a look around your house, Wanda? Maybe he can find something that will help us figure out what was going on with Ernie."

"He can come over any time, Chief," Wanda said. Now she was also looking at the floor. "Pastor Riebold's comin' to get us in a little while to take us to the funeral home. We don't have close family members to help us, just distant cousins in Nebraska."

Bill Tom nodded his head and stood up to leave.

"I'll have Deputy James call you before he comes over," Bill Tom said, reaching for Wanda's hand.

"We're all so sorry about this," he said. "Please let me know if there is anything we can do to help you."

Wanda nodded her head and opened the door for Bill Tom. He said good-bye to Lester, but the kid didn't respond.

Bill Tom climbed back into his truck and called Mary Ann. The noonday sun was really bright and the temperature had to be over ninety. He hoped Kayla had remembered to take her sunscreen to the pool.

"What's up?" he asked when Mary Ann answered the phone.

"Randy took Cliff Dunbar back to his trailer and then went home to take a shower," Mary Ann reported. "He's over at the church now going through all of Ernie's stuff with Mr. Beacham. Doc Schrader released Ernie's body to the funeral home a little while ago and I found out that Grace Community Church in Jeff City hosted a church musician seminar this weekend. Ernest Tucker was scheduled to be one of the speakers, but he never showed up."

"That's interesting," Bill Tom sighed. "Okay, I'm gonna grab some lunch. Call me if you need me." Bill Tom said as he headed his truck toward Hillside's business district.

Chapter 25

He thought about going to the Germantown Diner for lunch. They made great sandwiches and he was starving. As he approached the diner he realized that it would be full of people wanting to know what was going on with the investigation. He decided that the best place to eat lunch was in the privacy of his own kitchen. He passed the diner and headed for home.

As he turned onto Maple Drive his eyes, like magnets, were drawn up the tree-lined street to Brook's house on the left. He nearly ran off the road when he caught a glimpse of her. She was standing in her front yard in her swimming suit, a royal blue one-piece that showed off her slender body and great tan.

As he drove closer he realized she was planting a tree. She had already dug the hole and was struggling to place the tree in it. He pulled into her driveway and hopped out of his truck.

"Well," he said, trying to be clever, "a tree grows in Brooklyn's yard." He was very pleased with himself for thinking of the literary reference.

She peeked around the branches and smiled at him.

"Yeah, and I hope the good earth will nurture it."

He laughed at her quick-witted response.

"Let me help you with that," he said getting a grip on the tree.

Together they lifted the tree into the hole and Brook held it in place while Bill Tom reached for the shovel.

"Did you dig this hole all by yourself?" he asked, wondering how anyone could look so good doing such hard work in the stifling heat.

"It took me three hours. I started this project at nine this morning," she said, laughing. "I'm not as young as I think I am. I had to stop and rest every ten minutes or so. I forgot how hot and muggy it is in the Midwest in the summer. It really saps a person's strength."

He looked at her and smiled. "You're lucky you didn't pass out," he said, painfully aware that he was beginning to sweat as he shoveled the dirt around the tree.

"It's really nice of you to help me out here, Bill Tom," Brook said, "but isn't this the middle of a work day for you? I don't want to keep you from your work. I know you must be swamped with things to do."

"I am," he said, patting the last bit of dirt around the tree. "I was just coming home to get some lunch."

"Well, why don't you come in and let me fix you a sandwich?" she suggested. "That's the least I can do to thank you for your help. I was wondering how I was going to hold that tree and shovel the dirt back into place at the same time. You came along at just the right moment."

"Brook, you've got a deal," he said, feeling foolish because he couldn't seem to stop smiling.

He poured a bucket of water around the tree, picked up the shovel and the two of them walked around her house to the back door.

Her kitchen was dark and cool as they came in from the heat and the bright sun.

"There's beer and soda in the fridge," Brook said. "Help yourself. I'm going to run upstairs and put some clothes on. I'll just be a minute."

Bill Tom wanted to tell her not to change on his account, but kept his mouth shut. He grabbed a Coke out of the fridge and sat down in one of her comfortable kitchen chairs. The blue plaid cloth-covered cushions matched her kitchen curtains.

"How'd she manage that so fast?" he thought to himself.

When she re-emerged some minutes later she was wearing khaki shorts and a matching knit top. He noticed that she had taken the time to take a shower. Her curly hair was wet and she wasn't wearing any makeup.

"How can she look so good?" he asked himself. "I know she can't be much younger than me."

"I have ham or chicken salad," she said, giving him a warm smile. "I'm sorry I only have wheat bread."

"Wheat bread's fine," he said, enjoying the company and the ice cold soda. "I'll have the ham."

Brook got busy making the sandwiches and filling matching blue plates with potato salad and fresh tomato slices. When she placed the sandwiches on the plates she carried them to the table and sat down opposite Bill Tom.

He grabbed his sandwich and took a big bite. How could she make something as simple as a ham sandwich taste so good?

"How is the investigation going?" she asked.

"Slow. Beach and Randy are over at the church now, looking through all of Ernie's stuff. Hopefully they will find some kind of clue or evidence that will help us identify his killer."

He ate his food quickly and looked up to smile at her.

"Best ham sandwich and potato salad I've ever had," he said, swiping his mouth with a napkin. "Sorry I had to gulp it down but I really do need to get back to work." He stuffed the last bite of sandwich in his mouth.

"Sounds like a plan to me," Brook said. She stood up to walk Bill Tom to the door. "This afternoon I have to prepare myself for a meeting at the school tomorrow morning. I need to think about how I'm going to dazzle them with my brilliance."

"Oh, no," Bill Tom said suddenly. "I almost forgot. Guess what I get to do in the morning?" He looked at Brook sheepishly.

"I have no idea. What?"

"The Today Show is doing a satellite link-up at my office and Randy and I are doing a live interview with Matt Lauer."

"National media attention, huh? Good luck."

"Brook, you used to work a lot with the press," Bill Tom said, suddenly thinking she might be able to give him some advice. "Could you clue me in on how to prepare for this thing?"

"Sure, I can give you pointers--and I'd be happy to do that-- but I need to leave in a few minutes to go to the beauty shop. These curls are not doing well in this humidity," she said grabbing a hand full of red hair.

"Why don't you and Kayla come over for dinner? Maybe we can grill hamburgers or something and I'll grill you on the ups and downs of TV interviews."

"We'll see you around six," he said, walking to the front door. "Is that a good time for you?"

"See you then," she said.

Chapter 26

When Bill Tom got back to his office, Randy and Beach were sitting by Mary Ann's desk eating corned beef sandwiches from the Germantown Diner.

"Randy just went to pick up these sandwiches, Chief," Mary Ann said. "If I'd known you were on your way back I'd have ordered one for you."

"That's okay, Mary Ann," he said with a foolish grin. "I just had a sandwich."

"Did you take happy pills with that sandwich, Billy?" Beach asked.

"No," Bill Tom said, quickly becoming serious and averting his eyes from Beach's questioning gaze. "It was just a really good ham sandwich – had Swiss cheese and mayo on it."

"Where'd you go, BT, Daily Bread? I hear they have great sandwiches." Randy was referring to the new deli on the south side of town.

"Ah, no, I was going to go home for lunch and…"

Suddenly, the door opened, to Bill Tom's immense relief, and Amos and Aggie Pruitt walked in.

"Are we disturbing your lunch, Chief?" Amos asked, looking at the group.

"Not at all," Bill Tom walked over to the couple and shook hands.

Bill Tom escorted the elderly couple into his office and motioned for them to sit at the conference table. He sat next to Aggie.

"I've been meanin' to call you," he said, looking at their sad faces, "but with Ernie's murder yesterday we've really had our hands full over here. We're doing everything we can to find out who's behind all this. I want you to know that."

"We know that, Chief," Aggie said, reaching out to touch Bill Tom's hand. "That's why we wanted to come over here. You said that if we found something suspicious we should let you know and we were just at Esther's house--we're going through all of her things--and we discovered that a piece of jewelry is missing."

"What piece of jewelry?" Bill Tom asked.

"A family heirloom ring," Amos said. "Our mother gave it to Esther on her 21st birthday. It's a diamond-shaped ruby ring with tiny diamonds all around it. It belonged to our great grandmother."

"Esther wanted Trudy to have it since she was such a good friend and neighbor," Aggie added. "So when we got back from Jeff

City this morning and dropped Trudy and Brian off at their house I said I'd go get the ring. But it wasn't in her jewelry box."

"Was anything else missing?" Bill Tom asked.

"No. Everything was in perfect order, just no ring."

"Could she have put it in a safe deposit box at the bank?"

"We checked there before we came here," Amos said, reaching for his wife's hand. "It wasn't there, just the deed to her house and the title to her car. Trudy said that she remembered Esther wearing the ring on that Saturday when they were all baking cookies at Esther's house. We looked all around the kitchen to see if maybe she left it there, but we couldn't find it."

"And you're sure nothing else is missing?"

"Everything else is neat as a pin," Aggie said. "With Esther, everything was always neat. And her house always smelled so fresh."

"Well, except for that one day," Amos said, looking at Aggie and wrinkling his nose.

"What do you mean, Amos?" Bill Tom asked.

"About two weeks ago I dropped by Esther's for a minute to give her some tomatoes and cucumbers from our garden," Amos said. "When I walked into the kitchen I smelled a real foul odor--like a backed up sewer. It was very faint, but I did smell it. When I asked Esther about it, she said she hadn't noticed it. I looked in the bathroom and the basement and nothing was out of order. By the time I got back up to the kitchen she had used an air freshener and the smell was almost gone.

Bill Tom nodded his head, thinking that his own office had smelled the same way earlier that morning--right after Cliff Dunbar had been there.

"Do you know who Cliff Dunbar is?" he asked?

"Yeah, he's that ex-con who lives out by the end of town," Amos said. "Why do you ask?"

"He smells like a backed up sewer," Bill Tom said. "Do you think Esther knew him?"

"I don't know how well she knew him, but I know she felt sorry for him," Amos said, looking at Aggie with a concerned expression. "She felt like nobody in town gave him a chance to fit in. I think she may have hired him to do some odd jobs around the yard and the garage earlier this summer. Do you think he may have strangled her?"

"He denies it, Amos," Bill Tom said. "Randy and I brought him in here this morning. He says he was hiding out all week because he knew when he heard about Esther that we'd come looking for him."

"But do you think he did it? Why would he want to kill my sister when she was the only one who was nice to him?" Amos asked. "Can you lock him up or something 'til you find out for sure?"

"I have nothing to hold him on," Bill Tom said. "At this point there's no evidence to hold him. If I did lock him up, a lawyer would have him out within an hour."

"I want to go talk to him," Amos said with growing anger in his voice. "If he hurt my sister I want to…"

"Amos, that's the worst thing you could do," Bill Tom said, leaning forward in his chair. "Do you want to put yourself and Aggie in danger? You can't go around accusin' people of murder. You need to just calm down and let us do our job here. I promise you I'll keep you up to speed on the investigation, okay?"

"I'm sorry, Chief," Amos said, looking first at Aggie and then at Bill Tom. "I'd never do anything like that, I just feel so damn helpless!" The man's voice was filled with frustration.

"I understand that, Amos, and I thank you for coming in here and telling me about the ring. If you think of anything else, no matter how trivial it may seem, I want to know about it, okay?

"Okay, Chief, we'll let you know," Amos said, nudging Aggie to stand up with him. "We'll go now so you can get to work. I'm sorry I lost my temper."

"It's understandable, Amos. I know how you feel, I loved Esther, too. We'll get to the bottom of this, but it's gonna take some time."

Bill Tom escorted the couple to his office door.

"Before I forget," he asked, turning around to face them, "did Esther know Ernie Tucker very well, outside of church on Sunday?"

"I don't think so," Amos said, "she never mentioned it."

"Okay, thanks," he said, nodding his head. "And thanks for coming in." He escorted them through the outer office to the front door and turned to talk to his colleagues. He pulled up a chair and joined them sitting around Mary Ann's desk.

"What did you guys find at the church?" he asked, looking at Randy and Beach.

"Piles and piles of sheet music for the organ," Beach said, "and one hand-written note that said, 'I love you, Ernie.' It had a heart on it with an arrow drawn through it. Naturally, we're studying it for fingerprints. Who knows how many people may have touched it, though. He didn't have it hidden. That place was like Grand Central Station--just like Esther's kitchen."

"Did you go visit the Tuckers, BT?" Randy asked. "What'd they have to say?"

"Not much," Bill Tom said as he shrugged his shoulders. "Wanda's all doped up and Lester acts like he's in another world. I did tell them you'd come over later to look around. They were going to the funeral home to make the arrangements. I'd give them an hour or so before you call them," he added, looking at his watch.

"It's okay with them if I search the house?" Randy asked.

"Yes. Wanda said it was okay. Beach, please go with Randy and have your crew check out the fingerprints inside Ernie's car. There's something strange going on there. Ernie left his keys in the ignition and parked the car on the street rather than his reserved parking space. I wonder if somebody else was with him."

"We'll get on it right away," Beach said.

"Okay, we've got a game plan going here, guys," Bill Tom said. "Let's get crackin'." Bill Tom slapped his knees and started to stand up.

"Oh, damn," he groaned, slumping back in the chair. "I forgot to tell you guys--we're gonna be on TV in the morning. The *Today Show* called and we need to prepare…"

"Mary Ann told us all about it," Randy said. "You talked to the man himself? Matt Lauer? I'm gonna have to take the afternoon off to get my hair cut," he added, running his hand through his hair.

"That's not the kind of prep work I'm referring to," Bill Tom said. "We've never been interviewed on TV. We need to know what to expect. That new English teacher--Brook Jennings--used to work in public relations. She knows how to talk to the press. I asked her to give us some help. Are you guys busy tonight? For supper?"

"A home-cooked meal?" Beach's face lit up. "Just tell me where and when."

"I have to check with Chris to make sure I don't have to run the kids somewhere," Randy said. "I'm pretty sure I can work it out. Actually, I will make it work out."

"Mary Ann, what about you? I'd like you to come, too."

"Sure. I've got some leftover stew that George can heat up for supper," Mary Ann said. "Can I bring something, Chief?"

"Nope. Just yourself. You guys just show up at my house at 6 p.m. sharp," he said. "You have your game plans for this afternoon, right? I'll be in my office if you need me. Let me know if anything interesting turns up during your investigations."

He patted both guys on the back, winked at Mary Ann and walked into his office. He had to call Brook to let her know that dinner would be at his house since he invited so many people.

He sat down behind his desk and punched Brook's number into the phone. Amazing how he already knew it by heart.

"I've invited Kayla and Brian and Trudy to come over for barbecue," Brook said when Bill Tom explained what he had done. "The kids dropped by on the way home from the pool for a visit. Kayla mentioned that she was going to fix you a nice supper since you've been working so hard. I told her about our plans and invited them and Trudy to join us.

"Just tell the others that dinner will be at my place. You've got enough to do; you shouldn't have to worry about fixing dinner. When you get here you can flip the hamburgers if you want to help."

"I'll make this up to you, Brook," Bill Tom said, smiling like a fool into the phone.

"No need. Tell your staff they should include their spouses and…Randy has kids, doesn't he? They should all come. We'll have a party. I think everybody needs one."

Chapter 27

God couldn't have made a more perfect evening for Brook's barbecue. The rain storm from the night before made all the flowers look brighter, and the grass and the trees looked green and lush. The mid-day heat and humidity was gone and, as the late August sun sank behind one of the Hillside hills around six p.m., a cool breeze drifted across Brook's back yard.

Bill Tom stood at the barbecue grill, dutifully flipping hamburgers and turning hot dogs with the long-handled tongs Brook had given him. A couple of Bud Lights and the sheer pleasure of just being around that woman had put him in the best mood he'd been in since the day before Esther was killed.

From his vantage point at the side of Brook's covered patio, he surveyed the scene and found himself wondering how she could pull off such a nice dinner on such short notice.

Her patio furniture chairs had very comfortable cushions with tiny brown, blue and white stripes and she had set her table with blue placemats and brown linen napkins. A blue candle was burning in the middle of the table.

As soon as everyone arrived Brook offered them a drink and encouraged them to sample some hors d'oeuvres while they waited for Bill Tom to barbecue the burgers and hot dogs.

Bill Tom watched Brook in amazement as she tended to her guests. Wearing rust-colored Capris with a matching rust and white striped knit shirt, Brook mingled comfortably with her guests, refilling their drinks, asking questions about their lives and, in general, making everyone feel welcome.

She had set up a volleyball net and Brian and Kayla were playing a game with Randy's two young sons, Logan and Christopher. The boys had enlisted their father to join the game.

Mary Ann and Randy's wife, Chris, sat in lawn chairs under the big oak shade tree watching the volleyball game and, wonder of wonders, Trudy and Beach had struck up a conversation at one of Brook's card tables.

Bill Tom couldn't help smiling as he watched the unlikely pair talking and laughing together. It was certainly different than their first meeting, when Trudy had attacked Beach for eating the roast beef sandwich.

"What's so funny," he yelled to them, hoping to be heard above the screams and giggles coming from the volleyball players.

"Oh, Mr. Beacham and I were just talking about the day we met," Trudy yelled back as she turned around to face Bill Tom. "He just told me it was the most interesting sandwich he ever ate!"

Bill Tom smiled, decided the burgers and hot dogs would be okay for a few minutes and walked over to join Trudy and Beach.

"I wondered when you two would figure out that you're both pretty nice people," he said, taking a seat at their table. "I've known Trudy a long time, Beach, and believe me, I've never seen her so worked up."

"I promise I'll never do anything like that to you again, Mr. Beacham," Trudy said, still laughing.

"I'm kinda sorry to hear that, Trudy, and why don't you call me 'Beach?' Everyone else does."

"Don't you have a first name?" Trudy asked, her blue eyes twinkling.

"Walter," he said, smiling back at her. "Walter Fredrick Beacham the third, at your service," he added, bowing his head. "I'm available for potholder beatings and other kinds of abuse."

"Oh, Mr. Beacham, you really are a funny man," Trudy said, waving her hand toward him.

"What's going on over here?" Brook asked, walking up behind Bill Tom. "I think I'm missing out on all the jokes." She put her hand on Bill Tom's right shoulder and his whole right side began to tingle.

"Trudy and Beach were just talking about the day they met, Brook," Bill Tom said, resisting the urge to reach up and grab her hand.

"It's a funny story, Brook, I'll tell you inside while we get the food ready," Trudy said, standing up. "I think these two men need to talk business."

Both men watched the women as they walked into Brook's kitchen.

"Did you have business on your mind, Beach?" Bill Tom asked, grinning at his friend.

"A little monkey business, maybe," Beach answered with a smile. "Want another beer?"

"Why, yes, Mr. Beacham, that would be lovely," Bill Tom said in a high-pitched voice, batting his eyes at his friend.

Beach wrinkled his face and stood up to get to ice cold brews. Bill Tom followed him so he could check the meat on the grill.

"Hey, Brook, I think everything's ready out here," he yelled after a while.

"We'll be out in a minute," she called back.

By that time, Mary Ann and Chris had joined Trudy and Brook in the kitchen and each of the ladies walked out carrying a dish of food--potato salad, baked beans, a huge lettuce salad, and deviled eggs--the perfect barbecue dinner.

Brook surprised Bill Tom by suggesting that they begin the meal with a prayer. He never knew what religion she was or if she was even religious. He had thought that the only reason she came to church on Sunday was because Kayla had invited her. She surprised him even more when she offered an original prayer--not a simple table prayer she had memorized. She was so comfortable praying in front of people, and the prayer was so genuine, he realized that this was a woman who prayed pretty often. Somehow he hadn't thought she was the type.

Until he met Sarah, he hadn't attended church regularly. He was raised in a non-denominational church and attended public schools. As an adult he went to church only when it was absolutely necessary--weddings and funerals. Sarah changed all that for him.

After her prayer, Brook invited everyone to find a seat and help themselves. She helped Chris fix plates for Logan and Christopher and got them settled at a card table with Kayla and Brian. Then she sat at the empty seat next to Bill Tom at the big table with the rest of the group.

"So Brook, I hear you're going to give us some pointers about working with the press," Mary Ann said as Brook sat down. "Were you a reporter before you became a teacher?"

"No. I worked in communications for a steel manufacturing company," Brook said, passing the potato salad to Bill Tom.

"That's why you look so familiar to me," Beach said, pointing his fork at her. "You worked with Billy at Cramer Steel, didn't you?"

"We worked at the same company, but we didn't know each other that well," Brook said quickly. "A couple of times we worked on the same business problems, but beyond that we…"

"Yeah, I remember that one fire at the plant and Billy-boy here called us in to do some investigative work," Beach interrupted. "I think I actually talked to you a few times about it. Of course, I was thinner and cuter then." Beach gave Brook a big grin.

"I remember you, Beach," Brook said, smiling. "It's just that I don't think much about my life in St. Louis; it wasn't the best time for me."

"Oh my gosh, did you know my mom?" All of a sudden Kayla chimed in the conversation from her seat at the card table on the other side of the patio.

"Yes, I did," Brook said, "but it was all so long ago and I..."

"I can't believe you never said anything," Kayla said in an excited voice. "Dad, I can't believe you didn't mention it."

"Well," Bill Tom swallowed hard, trying to get the lump out of his throat. "Like Brook said, it was a long time ago. Over the years you end up working with so many people, it's hard to keep track of everyone.

"Anyway, the important thing is that Brook is with us now and she's willing to help us deal with the *Today Show* in the morning."

He looked around the room and felt like every eye in the place was burning a hole in his skin. Every eye except for Brook's-- she was busy looking at her plate and scooping up potato salad.

"I think you're right, Bill Tom," Trudy said suddenly, nudging Beach, who was sitting beside her. "Tomorrow morning he has to face the national press. Brook, if you've got advice for handling that then I say you're a God-send."

"Indeed," Mary Ann added, holding up her Bud Lite Lime. "I'm just not sure why you want me to be there tomorrow, Chief. You and Randy are the only ones who are going to be interviewed, right?"

"He needs you for 'B' tape supervision, Mary Ann," Brook explained. "There will be lots of media people coming out from the St. Louis NBC affiliate in the morning…maybe more than one reporter and the cameramen and crew who will set up the satellite link.

"While the reporters keep Bill Tom and Randy busy preparing for the interview and the crew sets up the link, the cameramen may be free to walk around and tape anything they see. And that's tape they can use later if they continue to cover the story.

"Your job is to keep their 'B' tape at a minimum while they're with Bill Tom and Randy. The only tape of those guys should be their TV interview. Don't let them get footage of Bill Tom scratching his head or Randy laughing. That's material they could use in a follow-up story that might not be so flattering. Just keep those guys busy eating doughnuts and drinking coffee. Give them a specific place where they can set their cameras down and make sure that no taping lights are on."

"Oh, my goodness," Mary Ann said with a smile. "Now I feel very important!"

"What's your advice for the actual interview, Brook?" Bill Tom asked. He was beginning to feel uneasy about the whole idea.

"No matter what his first question is, the first thing you do is express sorrow and sympathy to the family and friends of Esther Gaines and Ernie Tucker," Brook said. "Then answer his questions. Keep your answers short and to the point. Don't speculate. Don't speak for someone else. If he asks you about the feelings and opinions of people around here you can tell him honestly that many have expressed concern, and that the focus of your office is on finding the person or persons who committed these crimes.

"Don't accept the premise of the question if it's wrong or unflattering," Brook continued. "In other words, if he says *'Since you and your deputy have little experience in solving murder cases, do you think you will be able to catch the person who committed these crimes?'* tell him that between the two of you, you have what?--at least thirty-plus years of hard-duty law enforcement experience--and you're moving ahead rapidly with the investigation.

"If he continues to hound you about it remind him politely that it's an on-going activity and you're limited in the amount of information you can give him because you don't want to impede the investigation. You should tell him that you've enlisted the help of crime scene investigators from the St. Louis Police Department Major Case Squad."

"What should we wear, Brook?" Randy asked, putting down his pen. He'd been taking notes while she talked.

"Wear what you'd normally wear," she answered. "Light colored shirts and blue jeans would be fine. Stay away from white, bold colors or busy designs and you'll look fine. They may ask you if you want make up, tell them yes. It's just cake powder and since the lights will be hot your skin may become moist."

"You mean we may sweat?" Bill Tom asked with a smile, amused by the delicate way she put it.

"Like a celibate rabbit!" Brook laughed, winking at him. "Keep your eyes on the reporter--don't let them wander around the room and don't look at the camera. The interview will take place in your office, Bill Tom, so insist on chairs with arm rests. Sit up straight in the chairs and lean slightly forward. During the interview let your elbows rest on the arm rests of your chair and let your hands fall where they may. Don't fold them in your lap and by all means, don't cross your arms. And don't fidget.

"Also, when Matt Lauer says good morning to you, say good morning, but don't ask him how he is. It's an unnecessary question and it wastes air time. It's just a habit and many people who are inexperienced doing interviews tend to ask it."

"How long do you think they'll be on the air?" Chris asked, looking at her husband.

"Probably two or three minutes at the most," Brook estimated. "However it will seem like a lot longer and remember this--you can get into a lot of trouble in two or three minutes if you don't think about what you're saying.

"When we're done with dinner we can sit down and make a list of possible questions he may ask. Then you can put together some draft answers."

"Dad, can Brian and I come to watch you?" Kayla asked. She had been following the conversation closely since she found out Brook had known her mom in St. Louis.

"Sure, Kayla," he answered with a smile. "We have to be dressed and in my office at 5 a.m., okay?"

Kayla wrinkled her face.

"I'll watch you on TV, Dad," she said. "We've only got two more days to sleep in before school starts. I want to take advantage of them."

"I have football practice in the morning anyway, Kayla," Brian said. "I wouldn't have been able to go. Coach Chapman has been making us practice early in the morning--from six to nine a.m.-- because of the heat. I'll be glad when it cools off and we can practice in the afternoon."

"Speaking of Coach Chapman, I hear that Lester Tucker tried out for the team," Randy said to Brian. "Did Chap put him on the roster?"

"No way," Brian frowned at Randy. "Lester was really bad. He couldn't keep up with the exercises. He couldn't even run two laps around the field. I don't think he understood any of the plays. I think all the guys were willing to give him a shot at it. So was Coach.

But he was so bad. Coach pulled him aside at the end of practice and told him that he'd help him find another sport."

"Was he okay with that?" Bill Tom asked. He tried to imagine Lester Tucker playing football.

"He seemed to be," Brian said. "He just shook hands with Coach and left the field. When we got back to the locker room he wasn't there."

"Well, I hate to interrupt this nice gathering," Mary Ann said, standing up and looking at her watch, "but I need to go pick up George from Pastor Daniels' house. I dropped him off on my way over here. He was so sorry he couldn't come tonight, Brook, but the elders had an emergency meeting with the pastor about security at our church after what happened to poor Ernie."

"I understand, Mary Ann," Brook said, standing up. "Tell George we missed him. I hope there will be many more times when you'll come over for a visit. Would you like to take some food home for him? How about a couple extra pieces of peach pie?"

Bill Tom watched the two women as Brook opened the back door for Mary Ann and they both disappeared into Brook's kitchen.

"Dad, Brian and I are going to take Chris and the kids home so Randy can stay here and talk about tomorrow," Kayla said.

"Dad," she whispered, sitting down in Brook's empty seat. "Maybe you could invite Mrs. Jennings to come with us on Saturday to hear Brian and me give that presentation at Lincoln University."

"Is it a secret that you're doing that?" he whispered back, grinning at her.

"No," she said smiling and talking in a normal voice, "but I didn't want you to say 'no' and have her hear it."

"So you're gonna give a presentation at Lincoln University on Saturday?" Beach asked in a loud voice, with a big grin.

"Yes," she said loudly, smiling back at him. "Brian and I wrote a story about the history of Hillside and we get to read it in front of a group of English professors from all over the country on Saturday. We'd love to have you come too, if you'd like."

"It really is an honor," Trudy added, unable to contain her pride in her son and Kayla. "Esther encouraged them to enter this state-wide, university-sponsored essay contest called 'The History of Our Town,' and the authors of the three best-written stories were invited to read them at the annual professors' symposium. Kayla and Brian's essay won first prize out of five thousand entries."

"One thousand entries, Mom," Brian looked at Beach with a grin. "She really likes to brag about this to people."

"Well, it is quite an honor," Bill Tom said. "I think we should all go hear you guys give your presentation.

"Are you free on Saturday?" Bill Tom asked Brook when she returned to the patio.

"I think so. What's going on?"

"Brian and Kayla have invited us to attend a meeting of teachers at Lincoln University where they will read their winning essay on the history of Hillside."

"I'd love to go," Brook said. "Esther--Mrs. Gaines--explained the whole contest to me in one of her letters. She said that two of her students had entered and that their essay was very well written."

"Great! It's a date," Bill Tom said, slapping his thighs as he stood up. "Now I think it's time we clean up out here and get to work on that interview."

"We'd better go too, Brian," Kayla said. "Where did Chris and the kids go?"

"She and Randy wanted to wash them up before they ride in Brian's car," Brook said. "I sent them all to the bathroom with washcloths and a bar of soap."

"Mom, we'll come back to get you in a few minutes," Brian said, as he watched Trudy clearing off Brook's table.

"Don't worry about your mom, Brian," Beach said, "I'll give her a ride home later."

"Oh, Walter, that's so nice of you to offer," Trudy said, smiling at him.

"I know," he said grinning back at her. Then he turned to Bill Tom. "She likes to call me Walter."

"I see," Bill Tom said. He raised his eyebrows and smiled at Beach.

Bill Tom collected the rest of the stuff lying on the tables, made sure the barbecue fire was out and walked inside.

They said their good-byes to Kayla, Brian, Chris and the kids, and Brook and Trudy quickly cleaned up the dishes.

Chapter 28

"That was a great supper, Brook," Bill Tom said as he walked over to the sink. He took the scouring pad from her hand and motioned for her to sit down while he cleaned the grill.

"Did you like it better than the ham sandwich you had for lunch?" she asked.

"Are you the one who made him that ham sandwich?" Beach asked.

"Yes, I am," Brook said. "It didn't make him sick, did it?"

"No, on the contrary, it made him very happy," Beach said, smiling at Bill Tom.

"Yeah, I like ham the way you like roast beef," Bill Tom said, and both men cracked up as Trudy walked back into the room.

"What'd I miss?" she asked.

"I'm not sure, Trudy," Brook said. "It's something about ham and roast beef sandwiches. Let's go into the dining room. I think we'll be more comfortable in there."

"Oh, Brook, I have the best recipe for crock pot roast beef," Trudy said as the two walked out of the kitchen.

Beach and Bill Tom cracked up all over again.

Randy was sitting at the kitchen table next to Beach, quietly taking in the whole scene.

"Something tells me there are things going on here that I don't know about," he said. He looked at Bill Tom and Beach with raised eyebrows.

"Whoever said you couldn't pick up on a clue?" Bill Tom asked him as he gave him a pat on the back. "Let's go get to work."

The three men sat down at Brook's dining room table and the rest of the evening they all focused on the interview that was less than twelve hours away.

Chapter 29

Brook stared at the piece of paper in her hand and leaned against her chair with a sigh. Sitting at her dining room table in jeans, an over-sized white tee shirt and bare feet, she decided she'd need a drink before continuing her project. She was reviewing the results of the first writing assignment she gave to her Senior English Composition class.

Standing up slowly--she was stiff after sitting so long--she stretched, yawned and strolled to the kitchen to find her bottle of Scotch.

It had been a challenging and exciting week. Bill Tom and Randy represented themselves and Hillside very well during their brief *Today Show* interview on Tuesday. Later that morning Brook attended a school planning session, finally getting to meet the rest of the teachers.

On Tuesday evening the entire staff of Hillside High surprised her with a housewarming party, bringing food and paint brushes. They had heard from Ike Spader, the owner of the local hardware store, that she had bought a lot of paint for her house.

Someone had called Trudy and she came over with refreshments and decorating books. By Thursday morning--the first day of school-- Brook was totally settled into her new home.

Walking back into the dining room with a tall glass of Scotch and water in one hand and a bag of pretzels in the other, Brook thought about the first two days of school. Her head was a blur as she tried to remember the names and faces of all her students. She had four classes--one Senior English Composition class, two Freshman English classes, and a Senior Creative Writing Honors class. She was also assigned to monitor one study hall right after the noon lunch hour. To Brook's delight, Kayla was in both the Senior English Comp class and the Senior Honors Writing class.

Brook was especially pleased to see how well Kayla handled herself at school. She seemed very comfortable and confident in her surroundings and genuinely fond of her fellow students. It was quite apparent that they were fond of her, too.

As she sat down at her dining room table again, Brook sipped her drink and picked up the piece of paper she had been looking at earlier. She closed her eyes and leaned against the chair's tall padded back.

During the action-packed week that just ended, the thing that weighed on her mind most heavily was Ernest Tucker's memorial service on Wednesday. Although no family members were there to support Wanda and Lester, many people from Hillside came to pay their respects. Ernie's choir members sang *"Amazing Grace"* and

"I'm But a Stranger Here, Heaven is My Home." It was a touching moment.

Wanda opted to have Ernie cremated so there was no viewing prior to the service. People who walked up to offer their sympathy to Wanda and Lester were greeted with a hug or a handshake from Wanda and a sullen stare from the pale-faced boy. When the service was over, Pastor Riebold escorted Wanda and Lester out of the chapel and directly into his car. She had requested that no reception be held after the service. The next day people were surprised to see Wanda back at work at the bank and Lester attending his first day of school.

"And now this," Brook thought, opening her eyes and again staring at the piece of paper in her hand.

That morning she had asked her Senior English Comp class to participate in a short writing project. Each student was supposed to complete a sentence beginning with, "I am…." The papers scattered across her dining room table were filled with the usual responses: "I am…already tired of school." "I am…glad it's Friday." "I am…going to be a doctor." One student chose brevity: "I am…seventeen."

Brook was reviewing all these pieces of information about her students, reading each one, looking at the name and then checking the school's most current year book to put the name with a face. She had smiled when she read Kayla's sentence: "I am…going to be an investigative reporter."

This type of writing exercise had always given her valuable insight into the minds and personalities of her students.

And now she was staring at Lester Tucker's sentence, scratched out with the worst handwriting she had ever seen from a student. "I am…a puppet with clean gloves." He was the only student in the class who had written metaphorically.

During their next class time together, Brook intended to talk to the students about their sentences. She wasn't sure what to say to Lester. She and the other teachers at Hillside High had watched him carefully during the first two days of school. They could not believe that the kid was even there the day after his father's funeral. In addition, they all agreed that they had never seen a kid who appeared so lost and so alone. He didn't speak unless someone asked him a direct question. Even then, he struggled to make eye contact and his answers were soft, muffled and brief. At lunch, he grabbed a bag of potato chips and disappeared.

There wasn't a teacher at the school who didn't sympathize with any new student, especially a senior. But most new students made a visible effort to carve out a place to fit in. With the exception of his feeble attempt to join the football team several weeks before school started, Lester showed no social ability or personal desire to fit into his new academic surroundings.

"I think I understand the puppet part," Brook thought as she gathered up all the papers on her table and placed them in her briefcase. "It seems like Wanda controls his every move. But what's with the clean gloves? Does she keep a totally immaculate house? Is she the kind of mother who won't allow her child to sit on the good furniture or eat snacks in his room? And isn't it usually the puppeteer who wears the gloves?"

She wasn't sure about Lester's home life; she was sure he'd have a tough time at school if he didn't change his behavior.

"Time for bed," she thought as she straightened the dining room tablecloth and carried her briefcase into the hallway. She glanced into the living room where the clock on the mantle indicated in was ten-thirty. "Tomorrow my daughter is going to read an essay before a group of college English professors," she thought with a smile.

On impulse she poured herself another scotch and water and walked out onto the screened-in porch that was adjacent to her dining room. In the short time she had lived in Hillside, she had learned that hot, humid days were sometimes followed by cool, comfortable evenings--if the barometric pressure was just right. This was one of those evenings.

She lit the huge round three-wick candle that sat on the wrought iron table next to the hunter green lounge chair that Jim had bought her for her birthday, just a month before he died. He had bought an identical chair for himself and as she curled up in the over-stuffed piece of furniture, she looked across the table to the empty chair and felt the familiar bittersweet pain of love, regret and loneliness.

Jim Jennings had changed Brook's life. They had worked together for about a month when one day he knocked on her office door and invited her to lunch.

Over turkey club sandwiches and two bottles of beer, they had chatted easily about their lives, their jobs and their hopes for the future. She couldn't help but notice his prematurely gray hair that glistened in the sunlight and his electric blue eyes that sparkled whenever he smiled--which was pretty often.

During dinner several weeks later, he told her about his first marriage--just five years before--to a woman named Tabitha who had cheated on him at every opportunity. The union lasted a full ten months before she ran off with the tattoo-laden auto mechanic who worked on her car.

Of course, Jim admitted to Brook, he had been pretty gullible to marry a very immature twenty-year-old girl when he was thirty-five. He had thought that she'd keep him young and in retrospect he realized that he was thinking with his hormones instead of his brain cells. Next time around, he promised himself he'd find a woman who knew who Neal Diamond was.

Jim's description of his ill-fated marriage had sent her into peals of laughter and at the end of their date, on impulse she gave him a quick peck on the lips. When she backed away he gently grabbed her arms, pulled her close and they enjoyed their first real kiss.

In the weeks that followed they spent most evenings and every weekend together.

Soon their friendship blossomed into romance and during one Friday night dinner date, she found the courage to tell him about the daughter she'd given up for adoption.

Typical of Jim, he'd gently grabbed her hands, kissed them and told her he loved her with all his heart. He said he wished he could have spared her the pain of giving up a child. Then he took her breath away when he got down on one knee, opened a small red velvet box containing a gold one-caret diamond ring and asked her to marry him. Three months later she became Mrs. James Jennings.

As she relaxed in the lounge chair she thought about the new people in her life who had made her feel so welcome in her new home and--although they weren't aware of it--were also helping her heal from the loss of her husband.

Faced with two horrible murders and the possibility that they might have a serial killer on the loose in their community, these people had still taken the time to make her feel welcome and were trying hard to keep up their daily routines without interruption.

She learned that if some family had an illness or some other misfortune, friends and neighbors quickly rallied around with kind words, thoughtful deeds and a never-ending array of food.

People of different religious backgrounds talked freely about their faith, attended each other's church fund-raising dinners and were never shy about praying in public when the family went out for dinner at a local restaurant. Nowhere was the Midwestern Bible Belt buckled more securely than in the very charming town of Hillside.

Brook finished her drink, took the glass to the kitchen and walked up to her bedroom with a smile. She was looking forward to waking up in the morning.

Chapter 30

Everyone in the large assembly hall at Lincoln University was quiet as the university president introduced Kayla Bradley and Brian Brinkmeyer--first-place winners of the "History of Our Town" writing contest.

Brook, sitting between Bill Tom and Beach, was barely able to breathe as the kids approached the podium. Brian, who looked very handsome in a Navy blue pin-striped suit with a white shirt and red tie, offered his arm to Kayla as the two of them walked up the steps that led to the podium.

Kayla looked beautiful. She was wearing a simple red column dress with navy heels. Her long, straight hair was tied back with a red, white and blue scarf.

Brook leaned forward, looked past Beach, smiled at Trudy and gave her a "thumbs up" signal. As she sat back in her seat, Bill Tom surprised her by reaching over to grab her hand. His own hand was shaking.

The entire essay took less than ten minutes to read and when the kids finished, she joined everyone else in the hall in a standing ovation. The palms of her hands were stinging because she was clapping so hard.

She glanced up at Bill Tom who had an enormous grin and over at Trudy who was, to Brook's surprise, giving Beach a big hug.

Brian and Kayla nodded to their audience and graciously accepted the two-thousand-dollar first place prize on behalf of their high school's English department.

"Our school plans to use the money to start a scholarship program in honor of our late teacher and friend, Esther Gaines," Brian said, holding up the check for all to see.

Again, the kids received thunderous applause. Apparently everyone at the symposium was aware of Esther's recent murder.

Trudy and Bill Tom had told the kids that they would treat them to lunch after they read their essay. Brian and Kayla chose "Thai One On," a local Asian restaurant that featured a huge buffet and a relaxing ambiance.

"I can't eat another bite," Bill Tom said, pushing his plate away and leaning back in the huge rounded booth that accommodated six people very comfortably.

"If everybody's done eating can we get going?" Kayla asked. "I was hoping that maybe we could go up to Columbia and walk around the MIZZOU campus for a while," she said, smiling.

"Honey, I have to get back to the office," Bill Tom said, apologetically. "I have a lot of phone calls to return and some leads to follow up on. Ever since we were on TV we've been overwhelmed with people wanting to give us help or thinking they have clues about the murders. Randy and I have to check out every one of them."

"I could take them to Columbia," Beach offered. He had driven to Jefferson City separately since he had spent Friday afternoon and night back at his house in St. Louis. "Trudy, would you like to come along to see where the kids are gonna hang out next year?"

"That sounds like fun," Trudy said. "Maybe we could go to a show later. I think that new movie with Nicole Kidman sounds great. She's such a gifted thespian."

"I always thought she was straight," Beach said, scratching his head. Everyone at the table laughed.

"Oh, Walter, you are so funny," Trudy said. She gave him a gentle punch on the arm.

They said their good-byes on the parking lot and Brook and Bill Tom watched Trudy and Beach drive off with the kids. They strolled back to Brook's Camry.

Chapter 31

"Would you like me to drive?" Bill Tom asked

"That would be great," Brook said, yawning. "I'd like to kick off my shoes and lean my head back."

Bill Tom smiled at her and nodded his head. He climbed into the car and leaned forward to turn on the radio.

"I thought I might be able to catch the Cardinal's game, if you don't mind," he said to Brook. "They're playing the Cubs this afternoon in Chicago."

"You listen to the game. I'll take a nap," Brook said, leaning back against the seat and closing her eyes.

She fell sound asleep listening to the radio announcers describe the progress of the Cardinal baseball game.

Somewhere deep within her mind she could hear music playing…it was the Righteous Brothers singing "Unchained Melody." She was swaying back and forth, matching the song's slow rhythm. Her head was resting against someone's chest. She felt strong warm arms around her waist and tingled when the dark stranger nuzzled her neck with light kisses. All of a sudden the mysterious man picked her up and laid her on a bed. She looked into his face and raised her head slightly to meet his kiss. His hands created trails of sizzling pleasure as they explored her body.

"Brook, wake up!"

She jumped and woke with a start. She opened her eyes to see Bill Tom hovering over her.

"I didn't mean to startle you," he said with a smile, "but we're home and I thought you'd rather sleep in your bed than in your car."

She sat up rubbing her eyes, hoping that she looked okay after such a sound sleep and vivid dream.

"I can't believe I slept all the way home," she said, yawning as she looked into his eyes. "I must have really been tired."

"Come on," he said, "I'll escort you to your door."

She climbed out of her car and realized they were in front of her house.

"Why didn't you go to your house?" she asked. "Now you have to walk home."

"I didn't want you driving after such a sound sleep," he said, walking her to her front door. "Besides, I could use the exercise. I ate a huge lunch."

"Well, I wasn't going to mention it," Brook said with a smile, "but I was glad you and Beach didn't have to pay by the pound."

"Yeah, the restaurant owner's probably glad we don't live in Jeff City," Bill Tom laughed as he unlocked the door for Brook.

"When you get inside, remember to lock the door, okay?"

"Okay," she said looking up at him with a smile. He grabbed her hand and gave it a quick kiss.

"I don't want anything to happen to you," he said, quickly stepping off the porch.

"Oh, by the way," he called back to her as he headed up the street. "Did I tell you that you make a cute little snoring sound when you sleep?"

With that he turned around and began to sprint up the street.

She laughed as she closed her door and locked it.

Chapter 32

Bill Tom wasted no time changing out of his black "church" suit and into his jeans and his favorite red Polo shirt. After he fed Moonshine and gave her a potty break, he hopped in his truck and headed toward his office. He called Randy from his cell phone.

"I've been returning phone calls all day, BT," Randy said. "I can't believe it. We were on TV Tuesday morning and every nut in the country must have seen us. I've gotten calls from psychics claiming to know who the killer is. I've gotten six confessions from people who said they were sorry they shot those people. One guy claimed that he poisoned them. I'm telling you, BT, I've got a giant headache."

"I'll be there in a few minutes to relieve you," Bill Tom said as he turned left onto Market Street.

Once he was back in his office, he sat down with Randy and reviewed the events of the day.

"First thing this morning I went over to the Tucker's house to see how they're doin'," Randy said, leaning back in his chair.

"There was no answer so I peeked in the garage window and their car was gone. Old Mrs. Frasier from next door told me they left early this morning with suitcases. I guess, since this is Labor Day weekend, Wanda decided to get away from it all for a few days. I checked with the bank; she wasn't scheduled to work this morning."

Bill Tom nodded, wondering where two grieving people with no apparent close family members or friends would go to "get away from it all."

"Randy, you sound really tired," Bill Tom said. "Why don't you go home to Chris and the kids and relax. It's Labor Day weekend so take them to the pool on Monday and get your mind off all this. It helped me to get away for a little while today. You deserve some R and R, too."

"How did Kayla and Brian's presentation go?" Randy asked.

"They were great," Bill Tom said. "I was very proud of both of them, as always."

"And I guess you enjoyed the company of Mrs. Jennings?"

"Now why would you ask me something like that?"

"Because she's one hot mama," Randy said. "And I know you well enough to know that you've noticed that."

"I enjoy her company," Bill Tom said, "and that's all I'm going to say about it, okay? Now go home to your wife and family."

"On my way, BT. Thanks for the time off."

Bill Tom walked into his office and looked at all the messages scattered across his desk. He leaned back in his chair and closed his eyes.

Two murders in one week and he was nowhere close to solving them. He didn't even have any significant leads.

With some effort he sat up in his chair and sifted through all the messages Randy had left for him.

Randy was right. It looked like every nut-case in the country had seen their TV interview. Mary Ann had been inundated with phone calls all week, but Bill Tom didn't think there would be so many on a Saturday, especially over a three-day weekend when lots of people planned special end-of-summer activities.

But there were messages from all over the country from people who wanted to help, even one guy who wanted to write a TV movie about the "Hillside Murders."

"You can't have a story without an ending," Bill Tom thought. "And we're not even close to wrapping this up."

He returned some phone calls, reread some notes and decided to call it a day around 8 p.m. He didn't know what time Kayla would be home. Beach would probably take the whole gang to dinner after they went to the movie.

He closed up the office, stopped at the Pizza Kitchen to pick up a large mega-meat pizza and headed home. As he passed Brook's house, he noticed that her living room light was on and decided to stop.

"Pizza delivery," he said as she opened the door.

She laughed, shook her head, and gestured for him to come inside.

"Look at what I've got on my coffee table in the living room."

He walked past her and peered into the brightly lit room. There on the coffee table was a half-eaten pizza from the Pizza Kitchen, and a can of Bud Light.

"Great minds think alike," he said. "I was going to invite you to share this with me, but since you already have your own I guess I'll just go on home and eat this by myself."

"Oh, please stay," Brook said. "I'd really enjoy the company. I was just doing some reading to pass the time. For some reason I feel really restless."

"Me, too," he said, walking into the living room. "Mind if I go get a beer?"

"I'm already after it," she called from the hallway.

He sat on the couch, put his pizza on the coffee table next to Brook's and leaned back against a pillow.

When she came back into the room he thought about Randy's remark and agreed with him; she was one hot mama, even in old jeans and a tee shirt.

"What are you reading?" he asked as she handed him a beer.

"The Road Not Taken, " she said. "It's a collection of Robert Frost poems. He's my favorite American poet. I'm thinking of putting this book in my American Literature class for next semester."

"You got any whodunits around?" he asked, taking a big gulp of his beer. "Or maybe a crime-solving textbook?"

"I wish I could help you, Bill Tom," she said, sitting next to him on the couch. "Unfortunately, I think you've got yourself a really unique situation here. It may be because I'm inexperienced at solving crimes, but I can't seem to fit these two murders together. It doesn't seem to me that there is anything that links them except for the fact that the victims were both strangled. And yet, what are the chances that two separate killers are out there when there hasn't been a murder in Hillside in--what did you say--over a hundred years?"

"I'm just as confused as you are, Brook," Bill Tom said. "I thought that today would do me some good. I'd get away for a while, clear my head and come back with a fresh perspective. Instead, I just looked at my desk, read my messages and developed a giant-sized headache. I feel like I've hit a brick wall and the whole time I'm worried about who might be next."

"If I can help in any way, please let me know. That sounds really lame coming from an English teacher who deals with syntax rather than strangulation, but I do wish there was something else I could do to help."

Brook closed the lid on her pizza box, swallowed her last bite of pizza and looked at him.

He stood up, rubbed his hand through his hair and began pacing around the room.

"Brook, I'd really appreciate any help or input you may have to give me, but right now I think we need to have another discussion. We've been tiptoeing around it now ever since the barbecue and I think it's time we get it out in the open."

He sat back down on the couch and looked at her. "I can't get the crime monkey off my back, but I'd like to get the elephant out of the room," he said. "I know you feel its presence too."

She nodded her head and her eyes remained riveted to his.

"I didn't know which one of us should bring it up," she said. "We never talked about it. In fact, after that memorable night, we hardly ever talked again."

He closed his eyes and bowed his head.

"It was a horrible night for me, Brook, and also the most wonderful night I'd ever spent with a woman. You brought out emotions in me that I didn't know existed. The next morning I hated both of us for what we did. I was angry with you and angry with myself. I kept asking myself how I could cheat on the most wonderful wife in the world…and then I took the easy way out and blamed you for what happened."

Bill Tom shifted in his seat, leaned back against the couch and closed his eyes.

"We were on a business trip together," Brook said. "We both had too much to drink and…"

"I knew exactly what I was doing, Brook. I wasn't drunk. From the first time I met you and shook your hand I felt a strong attraction to you. I felt so guilty, loving Sarah and wanting you. And then fate stepped in and our paths crossed on a two-day business trip. That night in the hotel lounge when I asked you to dance I knew I couldn't resist you. I knew what that dance would lead to. The next morning I was so ashamed I could hardly look at myself in the mirror while I was shaving. So I took the easy way out and blamed you for everything. I'd like to just say now that I'm sorry for that."

"I felt guilty, too, Bill Tom. Sarah was my best friend." Brook shifted in her seat and shook her head. "I knew what I was doing. You didn't lead an innocent young thing down the path of promiscuity. I think we just need to go on with our lives and forgive ourselves and each other for what happened. Can we do that?"

Bill Tom opened his eyes, leaned forward and grabbed one of Brook's hands.

"I think we need to give it a try," he said. "I am sorry for what we did, and extremely sorry for the way I treated you after that night. I just couldn't continue seeing you all the time now and not get this thing out in the open."

Brook swallowed hard and nodded her head in agreement. "I'm glad you had the courage to bring it up."

"Please don't take this the wrong way, Brook," Bill Tom said, tightening his grip on her hand. "You are a very different woman than the one I thought I knew in St. Louis. It occurs to me now that I may not have known you at all. I just want to say that I'd like to get to know you better. I'd like for us to be friends without our past hanging over our heads."

"I'd like that, too," she said, squeezing the hand that held hers so tightly. "Let's consider it a closed subject. It happened. We're sorry. It's over."

"I guess I'd better be getting home," he said, suddenly releasing her hand and standing up. "I want to be there when Beach brings Kayla home. And Brook, I'm not sure when or how, but soon I think we need to tell Kayla that you are her birth mother."

"That's something I never thought would happen, Bill Tom. I was prepared to keep silent about that forever. I promised that to you and Sarah the day we signed the adoption papers. So now, circumstances being what they are, I'd say it is entirely your call. And I'll support whatever you decide."

He picked up the empty pizza boxes and the beer cans and started to walk to the kitchen.

Just then, Brook's phone rang. It was Beach.

"Brook," he said, his voice shaking, "is Bill Tom there? He's not answering his cell phone and I need to speak to him quickly. There's been an accident. Kayla and Brian were hit by a car."

Chapter 33

Bill Tom stopped Brook's car with a screech in a parking space at the University Hospital Trauma Center in Columbia. Hand-in-hand, he and Brook ran across the parking lot to the Emergency Room entrance.

During their harrowing ninety-mile-an-hour trip from Hillside, they had learned, through cell phone calls from Beach, that the kids had been hit on the Breakfast Barn parking lot by a hit-and-run driver who apparently aimed for them. Brian, who was walking right behind Kayla, saw the car coming and pushed her forward, out of the way. The car grazed Brian's leg and the impact sent both of the kids flying into the grill work of a parked car. They sustained cuts and bruises to their faces and right sides. Kayla had a concussion and a possible broken right leg. As far as Brook and Bill Tom knew, she had not regained consciousness.

"How is she?" Bill Tom called out as they ran through the Emergency Room doors. Beach was waiting for them at the admitting desk.

"They've taken her up to get a CAT scan of her head," Beach said, walking toward them. "Bill Tom, we have witnesses who say that car was deliberately aiming for Kayla. If Brian hadn't acted as quickly as he did, I think the driver may have killed her."

"What have the doctors said about her condition? Is it critical? Do they think she has brain damage? Did any of them say anything specific?"

"They told us she's stable and that she's a very strong young lady," Beach said. "They're doing the CAT scan so they can rule out any serious head trauma.

"As soon as I see one of the doctors who worked on her I'll let you know."

"Where's Brian?" Bill Tom asked with a sigh, still holding tightly to Brook's hand.

"He's down in one of the treatment rooms," Beach said, gesturing toward the brightly lit hallway. "Trudy's with him. His right leg is bruised and he needed fifteen stitches on his forehead. He has no broken bones. The doctor said the kid is built like a tank.

Bill Tom nodded and rubbed his eyes, silently thanking God for Brian's heroic gesture. He realized how hard he was squeezing Brook's hand, so he let go and put his arm around her shoulders instead.

"When do you think I can see him?" he asked. "I'd like to thank him for saving Kayla's life. I also want to talk to those witnesses who saw what happened. Do you know what kind of car hit them?"

Beach nodded his head. "It was an older model red Ford Mustang."

"Why don't you guys sit down over there in the waiting room and I'll go check on Brian to find out when you can see him," Beach suggested. "The policemen who responded to the scene said that they would send a detective to the hospital as soon as they finished taking in all the witness statements. Apparently there were three people who saw the whole thing. Trudy and I were still inside. She saw one of her former college roommates and we were talking to her and her husband.

"I'm sorry, Bill Tom, I should have taken better care of Kayla," Beach added in a shaky voice.

"There's no way you could have known anything like this would happen," Bill Tom said, patting his friend on the back. "If Brook and I had been with you, we would have been inside talking, too. Don't even think about feeling guilty. Just help me find out what happened. I want to talk to that detective as soon as possible."

Beach nodded and walked off to check on Brian.

Bill Tom looked down at Brook's tear-stained face and tightened his squeeze on her shoulder.

"Let's go sit down for a minute," he said, patting her on the arm.

He gently guided her to a couch in the waiting room and sat down next to her.

"It's gonna be alright," he whispered. "Everything's gonna be alright. God was watching over the kids. And I'm gonna get the maniac who did this to them."

"Somebody did this on purpose," Brook said, burying her head against Bill Tom's chest. "Who would do something like this and why?"

"I'll get to the bottom of this, I promise you, Brook," Bill Tom said, his head pounding.

Brook sat up to put some distance between herself and Bill Tom.

"I need to talk to you about something," she began. "I was going to bring it up back at my house but then we got the phone call…" Her voice trailed off.

"What is it, Brook?"

"I kept thinking that you knew the truth, that you finally figured it out, and maybe you did, I just have to know for sure."

"What do you need to make sure of?"

Brook looked at him, took a deep breath and grabbed both of his hands.

"Bill Tom, before the night we made love in that hotel room I hadn't had sex in at least three months. And the next time I had sex was when I met my husband, Mike."

"That doesn't make any sense, Brook. If that was the case, then how did you get…" Bill Tom stopped short when he realized what she was telling him.

"You mean you think I am Kayla's biological father?"

"That's exactly what I mean. You are Kayla's father," Brook whispered.

"You knew all this time and you never told me?" Bill Tom pulled his hands out of Brook's grip and stood up. "How could you keep such a thing from me, Brook?"

"I thought maybe you suspected it and besides, I didn't want to hurt Sarah and ruin your relationship with her. That's why I wanted you to adopt her. And if people at work had found out about it the gossip would have been horrible for both of you.

"After that night you avoided me. I don't think I spoke to you again until the day we all signed the adoption papers. Come to think of it, you didn't say a word to me then, either. Sarah did all the talking. I just hope you can understand my…"

"Bill Tom!"

He turned around to see Trudy and Beach walking into the waiting room.

"Trudy! He jumped up, grabbed the little blond woman and gave her a big hug.

"I'm so sorry about Brian, Trudy," he said. "How is he doing?"

"He'll be okay," Trudy said. "The doctors gave him some pain medication and he's resting now. They want to keep him overnight for observation."

Trudy let go of Bill Tom and wrapped her arms around Brook who had also stood up to greet her. The two women sat down on the couch to cry on each other's shoulders.

"Beach, will you stay with them for a while?" he asked. "There's something I've got to do."

Beach nodded, patted his friend on the back and sat down next to the sobbing women.

Chapter 34

The University Hospital Chapel was cool, dark and deserted as Bill Tom entered through the heavy wooden doors. Candles on the altar and in lamps mounted on the side walls provided just enough light to help people find places to sit.

Bill Tom sank down onto a teal-colored padded pew in the back of the chapel.

He leaned forward to rest his elbows on the back of the pew in front of him and buried his face in his hands.

"Oh, God, thank you for saving my daughter's life. MY daughter!"

That was all he could get out before he started to cry, big gut-wrenching sobs that he would never let anyone but God see or hear from him. From the moment Brook had answered the phone and he watched the blood drain from her face, he had tried to remain strong and brave for her sake. But it was all a farce; inside he was falling to pieces.

"Thank you for saving my Kayla," he whispered again, trying to gain control over the sobs.

It was crazy. His mind was filled with so many conflicting emotions. He was thankful Kayla and Brian were alive; he was angry with Brook for keeping such a big secret from him; he was filled with anger toward the person who tried to kill the kids; and…he was overwhelmed with the knowledge that Kayla was his biological daughter.

It really didn't make any difference. There was no way he could love her more than he already did, but he felt a lot differently about himself. In the midst of this terrible tragedy his self-esteem had just shot up about a thousand notches and--it felt ridiculous--but he wanted to give himself a pat on the back and offer cigars to all his friends. He wanted to crow like a rooster. He felt like a fool. After numerous fertility tests, the doctors always told them that Sarah was unable to conceive a child…but secretly he had always suspected that it was his problem.

He tried to pull himself together so he could have a much-needed talk with God.

"I committed a great sin against you and Sarah," he began praying silently, "and still you blessed me with this precious gift. I don't deserve it, but I beg of you, please don't punish me now by taking her away from me. Take me, instead. It was my sin; you can strike me dead right now, just please keep my Kayla safe."

"Stop it, Bill Tom!"

The firm, but gentle voice and the hand on his shoulder made him jump.

He raised his head and turned around.

"Trudy, how did you know I'd be in here?" he whispered. He noticed that her eyes were dry and she looked very calm and composed.

"Bill Tom, we've known each other a long time," she began, as she slid into the pew next to him and grabbed his hand. "You pray all the time, especially in a crisis. So I knew you would be here in the hospital chapel. And...I always knew that someday this moment might come and I've prayed that I'd have the strength to help you through it."

"What did you always know, Trudy? That my daughter would almost get killed and that your son would almost get killed trying to save her?"

"No," she said, shaking her head and looking him straight in the eye. "Since Sarah died I've known that someday you'd have to confront your guilt about Kayla and that I'd be the only one who could help you."

"Trudy," he said with a sigh. "What are you talking about?"

"I'm talking about the fact that you cheated on Sarah and that Kayla is your biological daughter," she said, squeezing his hand tighter. "I know it and--this may come as a shock to you because you guys always think we women are not too bright--Sarah knew it, too, almost from the beginning."

All Bill Tom could do was stare at her.

"Bill Tom, Kayla doesn't look like you--thank God for small favors--but she has your personality, your physical movements," Trudy continued, smiling weakly into his shocked face.

"Sarah noticed the similarities right away and pointed them out to me when the kids were just a year old. She also knew about the strong attraction between you and Brook. Wives have special radar about that kind of thing, you know?

"When Brook asked you guys to adopt her baby, Sarah was already suspicious; but her suspicions were confirmed as Kayla got older."

"Sarah knew and she never said anything?" Bill Tom asked, his eyes and throat suddenly very dry. "She must have hated me.

"Trudy," he added, looking directly into her eyes. "I didn't know Kayla was my biological daughter until a few minutes ago. Brook just told me. We had sex once, on a business trip--it was a spontaneous thing--it wasn't planned. I never dreamed that Kayla was mine."

Now it was Trudy's turn to be surprised.

"Bill Tom," she began, shaking her head, "don't take this wrong, but sometimes you're not the sharpest knife in the drawer."

"I think that's what Brook thought just now when she told me," Bill Tom said. "Why didn't Sarah ever say anything to me about it?"

"She didn't want to hurt your relationship, and she thought it would make both of you feel awkward," Trudy said. "And, of course, she didn't know how she would explain it to Kayla that you were her biological father and she wasn't her biological mother. Can you understand that?"

"I understand that," Bill Tom said, nodding his head and closing his eyes.

"I came in here looking for you to tell you that you need to forgive yourself for whatever happened. This accident is not God trying to punish you. You need to forgive Brook, too, if you haven't done so already. Sarah forgave you a long time ago. And if I know you, you've asked for God's forgiveness a thousand times. The only one who can't get past it is you."

"I feel like such a jerk, Trudy," Bill Tom said with a heavy sigh.

"Well, you'll get no argument from me on that point," Trudy said, smiling at him and patting his hand. "But at one time or another, we all make mistakes. The best thing we can do is forgive ourselves and get on with life. That's what you need to do now. Besides, you've got to get ready to take the next step."

"What's that?" Bill Tom asked, stretching out to lean his pounding head against the back of the pew.

"You have to tell your daughter who her biological parents are."

"I know," he said squeezing his eyes shut. "And that's going to be tough.

"You haven't said anything to her, have you?" he asked, suddenly sitting up to look at her.

"Of course not," Trudy answered. "But, I can tell you, Brian told me she plans to make the announcement during her eighteenth birthday party in a couple of weeks that she's going to search for her birth parents. He said that Kayla has this fantasy about Brook being her birth mom since they look so much alike. And then at the barbecue the other night she found out that Brook knew you and Sarah in St. Louis. Kayla's going to make the announcement to try to get Brook to admit she's her birth mom. She won't be surprised about that, but when she finds out that you're her biological father, it's anybody's guess how she'll react. I know she's not expecting to hear that news."

Bill Tom nodded in silent agreement.

Suddenly the big wooden chapel doors opened and Beach peaked in.

"Brook said you guys might be in here," he whispered. "They just brought Kayla back from those tests."

Bill Tom jumped off the pew and the three of them rushed back to the emergency room.

Chapter 35

Trudy and Beach stood back as the nurse ushered Bill Tom through the door.

"Your wife is already in there," the nurse whispered. "The doctor will be in to see you in a minute."

Bill Tom took one look at Kayla and froze. The right side of her head had been partially shaved, her beautiful red hair replaced with a long row of black stitches. The rest of her hair looked like it was matted with blood. Her whole face was swollen and red, but the right side also had tones of black and blue and her right eye was swollen shut. Her right arm was wrapped in bandages. The bright neon light above the bed made the rest of her exposed skin look like white plastic.

For a moment he thought he might faint, but Brook came to his rescue. She was standing on the right side of the bed holding Kayla's hand.

"Bill Tom, come on over here," she said, extending her free hand toward him.

Fighting back tears he walked over to Brook who quickly squeezed his hand and then gently placed Kayla's hand in his.

"Your little girl has been asking for you," Brook said, looking up at him with a smile.

He couldn't believe how well Brook had pulled it together for Kayla's sake. All of a sudden she was a confident tower of strength.

"I'll just wait outside," she said.

"No, stay," Kayla whispered weakly. "I want you to stay."

"Okay, Kayla, I'll stay," Brook leaned down and whispered to her.

"Daddy, I'm sorry," Kayla continued speaking in a weak voice. "I must have stepped out in front of that car, but I didn't see it." She looked at him through her half-open left eye and a tear rolled down her cheek.

"Brian grabbed me. Where is he? Is he okay? I don't remember anything."

Bill Tom swallowed hard as he struggled to fight back his own tears. Brook stood behind him, patting his back gently with her hand and he took all his courage and strength from her.

"Brian's fine. And you don't have a thing to be sorry about, Sweetie. None of this is your fault. You just have to concentrate on getting better."

He bent down to kiss her gently on her forehead.

"Daddy, don't leave me. I want you and Mrs. Jennings to stay with…"

The treatment room door opened and a tall young man with blond hair and a white lab coat walked in.

"Mr. and Mrs. Bradley, I'm Dr. Ralston," he said, extending his hand to Brook and then Bill Tom. "We've just completed some x-rays and a CAT scan on Kayla. We won't know the results for a few hours but I can give you an overview of what we do know about her condition."

Dr. Ralston walked around to the right side of Kayla's bed and leaned down to talk to her.

"Kayla, one of our nurses just gave you a sedative to help ease your pain and give you a chance to sleep," he said, reaching over to pat her left hand.

"We're going to take good care of you so I want you to relax. When you wake up you'll probably be in a different room, but I promise you your parents will be close by, okay?"

"Okay," Kayla whispered, already drifting off.

"Why don't we go talk in the waiting room," Dr. Ralston suggested, gesturing toward the door.

Bill Tom and Brook each bent down to kiss Kayla before they followed the doctor to the waiting room. Trudy and Beach were sitting on one of the couches, talking.

"These are our friends," Bill Tom said motioning to them. "I'd like for them to hear what you have to say. Trudy is Brian's mother; he's the boy who saved Kayla's life."

Dr. Ralston shook hands with Trudy and Beach and they all sit down at the end of the waiting room where there was another couch and two chairs. He grabbed a chair from a near-by table and sat to face them.

"We're going to keep Brian overnight," Dr. Ralston began, looking at Trudy. "He was alert when he came in and he shows no signs of a concussion. He has a bruise on his right thigh. We just want to observe him for a while before letting him go. Once he's home, he's going to have to take it easy for several weeks. No football."

"Did he tell you he was a football player?" Trudy smiled at the doctor.

"You don't get muscles like that without playing football, Ma'am," the doctor smiled back at her.

Then he turned to face Brook and Bill Tom.

"I know Kayla's face looks really bad to you now with all the bruises and contusions, but those will heal," Dr. Ralston said. "I'm sorry we had to shave off some of her hair, but we had to get those stitches in.

"My main concern with Kayla is that she was unconscious for a long time and we had trouble rousing her. That could indicate that there is some brain trauma."

Bill Tom felt Brook tighten her grip on his arm.

"I really don't think she has any broken bones," Dr. Ralston continued, "but we need the x-rays to confirm that. We're going to put her in a room and keep her here for a couple of days. At the very least she's going to be stiff and sore and we can help her deal with that pain.

"Do you have any questions for me?" The doctor looked at all four of them with raised eyebrows.

Brook gingerly lifted her hand.

"I was just wondering," she began, "when you say 'brain trauma,' what exactly do you mean, Dr. Ralston?"

The doctor nodded his head, glanced at his chart and then looked directly at Brook.

"We're looking specifically for any swelling of the brain, any bleeding or maybe a bump that's growing inward instead of outward," Dr. Ralston said. "When Kayla did regain consciousness she was alert, knew her name, remembered that she was hit by a car and asked if Brian was okay. That's a very good sign that everything is okay. Still, I wouldn't be doing my job if I didn't make sure."

Dr. Ralston stood up and looked down at the group.

"If you don't have any more questions for the moment, I'm going to go check on Brian and Kayla and then follow up on the results of those tests."

"Thanks for taking such good care of our kids, doctor," Bill Tom said. He stood to shake the doctor's hand. "We're very grateful."

Bill Tom waited until the doctor left the room and then sat down to face Beach.

"What did you say about a detective being assigned to this case? Is he supposed to come over here or something?"

"He's on his way," Beach said. "I called the police department while you guys were in the room with Kayla."

As on cue, a man in his mid-thirties, with dark curly hair, knocked on the waiting room door.

"Excuse me," he said, "I'm looking for a man named Walter Beacham. Would one of you…?"

"I'm Walter Beacham," Beach said, walking toward the man. "Are you the detective from the police department?"

"Yeah," he said. He extended his arm to shake hands with Beach. "Doug Williams. I've been assigned to your case."

"This is Bill Tom Bradley," Beach said, motioning to Bill Tom who walked over to join them. "He's Kayla Bradley's dad."

"And the police chief of Hillside," Detective Williams said. "I'm pleased to meet you, sir. I'm so sorry this had to happen to you on top of all the problems you have in Hillside right now. I recognize you from the *Today Show*."

Bill Tom nodded his head, shook hands with the detective and suggested that they all sit down with Brook and Trudy.

After he introduced Detective Williams to the ladies, Bill Tom wasted no time getting to the point of their conversation.

"What can you tell us about the person who hit our kids, detective?" he asked, sitting on the edge of the couch with his hands on his knees. He looked like he was ready to pounce on Detective Williams.

"I took a lot of notes from our three witnesses and I want to go over them with you first and, please, call me Doug," the detective said as he flipped through his note pad.

"Let me start by telling you that there were three different witnesses–an elderly couple in their mid-seventies and a college co-ed who was just arriving to work the night shift. Their stories vary slightly, but they all agree on one thing: the car was definitely aiming for your daughter.

"The elderly couple--Herb and Molly Zimmer--had just finished eating. As they were returning to their car they noticed a man and a woman sitting in the front seat of a red car, with the motor running. The car was parked three spaces down from their own car. They said they only noticed it because the motor was so loud and the driver had backed into the space just like they had done, so the front of the car was facing the parking lot driveway. They didn't get a good look at the people who were in the car, although they both agreed that the driver was a man and the passenger was a woman.

"They climbed into their own car," Detective Williams continued as he flipped the page of his notebook, "fastened their seatbelts and were about to leave. Just then Mr. Zimmer saw Kayla step off the sidewalk and onto the parking lot. The young man who was with her--Brian Brinkmeyer--turned back to pick up something from the sidewalk. They couldn't tell what it was.

"About that time, they heard a loud screech and saw the red car take off, without lights, heading straight for Kayla. They said the young man who was with Kayla saw the car, ran after her and pushed her forward out of the way. The next thing they knew the kids were lying on the ground in front of a parked car. Mr. and Mrs. Zimmer tried to get the license plate of the car that hit them, but it was too dark and they couldn't read it. They drove up to the spot where the kids were lying on the ground. Mr. Zimmer rushed inside to get help and Mrs. Zimmer stayed behind to see if she could help Kayla and Brian."

Bill Tom shook his head, grabbed Brook's hand to keep his own from shaking so hard and asked the detective to continue.

"What about the co-ed? What did she see?"

"Her name is Christine Carter," Detective Williams began. "She was walking up the sidewalk toward the entrance to the Breakfast Barn. She saw Brian go back to pick something up from the sidewalk--she thought it looked like a scarf--and then she heard the revved up motor of the car. By the time she turned to look she only got a glimpse of the people inside, but she says that a man was driving and a woman with long blond hair was in the passenger seat. She also said the car was a red Mustang with a license plate that ended with a 'Y' and that the car was definitely aiming for Kayla."

Detective Williams stopped for a moment and looked at the group.

"That's about all I have from the witnesses for now, although we'll get in touch with them again in the morning," he said. "Right now I do have some questions for you guys.

"Do you know of any reason why someone would want to hurt your daughter, Chief Bradley?"

"I can't think of a one," Bill Tom said, shaking his head, "unless it was somebody trying to get back at me for something."

"Off hand, do you know anybody who has a red Mustang with a license plate ending in 'Y'?"

"I know some people with red cars. I don't know their license plate numbers."

"Do you think that someone may have tried to hurt your daughter in an effort to hurt you?"

"I think that's possible but right now I can't think of anyone specific." Bill Tom stood up to pace back and forth.

"We've had these murders in Hillside and I've been grilling a lot of people," he said, running his hand through his hair as he paced. "Maybe I offended someone."

"Maybe you offended the killer," Beach said.

They all looked at each other in silence.

Chapter 36

Bill Tom leaned over the bathroom sink, threw cold water on his face and rubbed his eyes. Drying off with a bunch of paper towels, he glanced at his watch. Four a.m. In a couple of hours he'd call Randy and Mary Ann and let them know what happened. Maybe one of them would go to his house, feed Moonshine and let her go outside.

Beach had gone back to the police station with Detective Williams to see if they could get a list of red Mustangs with license plates ending in "Y." Brook and Trudy curled up on the couches in the hospital waiting room to get some rest. They tried to get Bill Tom to do the same thing but he was too tense.

Not long after Beach and the detective had left, Dr. Ralston came back with the good news that all of Kayla's tests were negative--no damage to the brain and no broken bones. Miraculously, all of her injuries appeared to be on the outside. Bill Tom said a silent prayer of thanks and made a vow to thank Brian as soon as the kid woke up.

He walked back into the waiting room expecting to find Brook and Trudy sound asleep. Instead, they were sitting side-by-side on one of the couches, holding hands. Their eyes were red--the result of too many tears and too little sleep--but otherwise they both looked pretty good for what they'd been through.

They looked up at him as he walked into the room.

"We're talking motherhood," Trudy said, raising her hand that held Brook's, "and all the joys and challenges that come with it."

"I guess that means you told Brook that you know the truth about us," Bill Tom asked as he sat next to Brook.

"I did," she answered with a smile. "We mothers have to stick together at a time like this."

"She told me that Sarah knew, too," Brook said, looking at him with a sad expression. "I'm sorry, Bill Tom, I never meant to hurt her."

"Me neither," he said. He put his arm around her shoulders. "But there's nothing we can do about that now, Brook, except be thankful that Sarah was such a wonderful person and that, in some way, she must have understood what happened between us."

"Remember what I told you," Trudy said, "you two just have to find a way to forgive yourselves--and let your daughter know who you are."

"Neither one of those things is going to be easy," Brook said, leaning back against Bill Tom's arm.

"Excuse me, Mrs. Brinkmeyer?"

They looked up to see a young nurse standing at the doorway.

"I'm Trudy Brinkmeyer," Trudy said, sitting forward on the couch.

"Your son is awake and asking to see you," she said.

Trudy let go of Brook's hand and hopped to her feet.

"You guys come with me," she said, turning to look at Brook and Bill Tom.

The nurses had put Brian into a quiet room at the end of the hallway where there was usually less action during the night.

As Trudy, Brook and Bill Tom walked into his room they were surprised to see Brian sitting up in bed. He had two pillows propped up in back of him and he was examining his stitches with a mirror that a nurse had given him.

"Hi, Mom," he said. He gave them a big smile. "Hi, Chief and Mrs. Jennings. How's Kayla and when can I see her?"

"She's okay, but they want to keep her for a couple of days," Bill Tom said as Trudy bent down to kiss and hug her son. "There are no internal injuries or broken bones."

Bill Tom and Brook walked over to his bedside and Bill Tom grabbed his hand.

"Good," Brian said with a bright smile. Even with his black and blue face and that awful long line of stitches, he was still a very handsome young man. "When can I see her?"

"She's in a room upstairs," Bill Tom said. "I think as soon as she wakes up she'll ask for you. It could be a few hours, though.

"Brian," he continued, now holding the boy's hand with both of his own, "we owe you a great debt of gratitude. She probably would have been killed if you hadn't risked your life for her. How can I ever thank you, son?"

"Chief, I love Kayla," Brian said, looking straight at Bill Tom. "I'd do anything to keep her safe. It was a life worth saving."

Bill Tom squeezed the kid's hands tighter and nodded his head.

"She's very lucky to have you, and so am I. We're just glad that you're okay, that you're both okay."

"Did anybody see who did this?" Brian asked as Bill Tom released his grip on the boy. "I can't believe that anybody with any sense would be going that fast in a restaurant parking lot."

Bill Tom looked at Trudy for guidance on just how much to tell the boy.

"Brian," she said, gently stroking the left side of his face while she held his hand. "There are three witnesses and they all say that the car headed for Kayla deliberately."

"Can you tell us what happened, Brian?" Bill Tom asked. "What do you remember about the accident?"

Brain leaned back against the pillows and closed his eyes for a second and then opened them again.

"We were just walking out of the restaurant and talking about MIZZOU," Brian said. "We were talking about the dorm we want to stay in next year--I forget the name but it's that co-ed dorm close to the book store. As we stepped onto the street, the scarf Kayla had in her hair blew off and I ran back to pick it up. I don't think she even noticed.

"That's when I heard the revved up motor and the screeching tires. I looked up to see the car speeding up the parking lot with no lights and I ran to push Kayla out of the way. The next thing I knew some little old lady was spittin' on a handkerchief and tryin' to wipe blood off my forehead. Then I must have blacked out, or something."

"Did you get a look at the car or the people inside?" Bill Tom asked.

"I just saw the front of the car--the grillwork mainly-- that's what I focused on. I think it was some darker color. I mean it definitely wasn't white or a light color. I didn't look inside at all. I'm sorry, Chief. It all happened so fast."

Bill Tom shook his head and let out an amused little laugh.

"You have nothing to be sorry for, young man," Bill Tom said, again grabbing Brian's hand. "You're a hero. You did good."

"Brian, we're all very proud of you and very grateful for what you did to save Kayla," Brook said. Standing right next to Bill Tom, she leaned forward to pat the boy's arm. "I'm so thankful you're okay."

"Thanks, Mrs. Jennings," Brian said with a big smile for his teacher. "Hey, we thought about you while we were on campus. We were in the book store for over an hour and we each bought a copy of *Hamlet* so we'll be ready to start reading next week."

"That's great, Brian," she said. "What else did you guys do before you went to the movie?"

"We had a great time walking around the campus," Brian said. "We saw some friends from Hillside...we ran into Mindy Arnold and Todd Mack as we were leaving the student union. That turned out to be a bummer."

"What happened with them?" Bill Tom asked, suddenly becoming very interested in their afternoon activities on the MIZZOU campus.

"Well, it started out okay," Brian said. "They seemed happy enough to see us. Kayla told them we were going to a five p.m. movie and then to dinner at the Breakfast Barn. Actually, she invited them to come along. They said they were tired and still had to study.

"We kept talking--about MIZZOU mostly--and they were telling us how neat it was to be really independent, with no parents around--sorry, Chief, sorry Mom--and then Mindy pushed her hair out of her eyes and that's when Kayla noticed the ring."

"What ring?" Trudy and Bill Tom asked in unison.

"I don't know, just some ring. It was red and it had little diamond-looking stones around it. Kayla said it was a ruby ring. Anyway, she asked Mindy, 'What are you doing with Miss Esther's ring?' and Mindy said, 'What do you mean, Miss Esther's ring? It's my ring. I got it for my birthday.'

"I guess things would have been okay if Kayla had just accepted that, but she kept insisting that the ring belonged to Miss

Esther. Actually, I think I've seen Miss Esther wear a ring something like that, but I couldn't swear to it. I'm not real good at details about women's jewelry."

Bill Tom could feel his heart beating faster.

"What happened after that?" he asked Brian.

"Mindy said they needed to get going," Brian continued. "Todd and I shook hands real quick because Mindy started to pull him away. She yelled back at us that she'd see us at Homecoming. And that was it. Then we walked back to the Columns, met Mom and Mr. Beacham and we went to the movie."

"And then you went to supper at the Breakfast Barn?" Bill Tom asked.

"Yeah, that's what happened."

"Brian, Todd Mack has a red Mustang, doesn't he?" Bill Tom asked, his eyes narrowing.

"Yeah, it's an *old* Mustang. I think it's about ten years old. He bought it for three hundred dollars from some guy in New Haven. He worked on it for a long time. I helped him paint it and we finally got the motor working pretty good."

"I don't suppose that you happen to know Todd's license plate number?" Bill Tom asked, looking at the boy with raised eyebrows.

"Oh, sure. All the guys know it. It's 'Feisty.' He thought that old car was feisty."

Bill Tom looked at Trudy and Brook and then back at Brian.

"Brian, you've been a big help," he said. "I'm going to go to the police station to work with Beach now. Your mom and Mrs. Jennings will stay here with you and Kayla."

"Chief, you don't think Todd and Mindy tried to hit Kayla, do you?" Brian asked. He look confused. "I can't believe that they would try anything like that. I know Kayla and Mindy have had their differences, but they've always managed to stay friends. I wouldn't want…"

"Brian, don't worry about it," Bill Tom said, once again patting the boy's arm. "Just try to get some rest. We have witnesses who saw a red Mustang with a license plate ending in "Y." They say a man and a woman with blond hair were in the car. That describes Todd and Mindy. I have to check it out. I promise you, I won't accuse them prematurely. But I've got to do my job, okay?"

"Okay, Chief," Brian said, still looking stunned, "I understand. I just can't believe…"

"Brian, none of us wants to believe it," Bill Tom said. "But I've got to go check it out."

He patted the boy on the arm and turned to Brook.

"Will you come with me for a minute," he asked, looking into her shocked face.

Once they were out in the hall, he grabbed her and gave her a tight hug.

"I swear to you, Brook," he said, through gritted teeth, "if those spoiled brat kids did this to Kayla and Brian I'll take them apart piece by piece."

"Bill Tom, get a hold of your temper," she said, pulling away from him and grabbing his face with both her hands. "You can't accuse those kids before you have more proof, and you sure can't go get them and beat them up. Remember, you're supposed to uphold the law, not break it.

"I know." he said, his voice cracking. "It's just so damn senseless."

He shook his head, trying to clear his mind. He knew that the combination of fear, heartache and exhaustion was impairing his judgment.

"Brook, I'm going over to the police station. I'll tell Beach and Doug the detective what we learned from Brian and, if we decide to pay a visit to Mindy and Todd, I'll let them do most of the talking, okay?"

"That sounds like a good idea," she whispered.

"Walk with me to the door, okay? There's something I need you to do for me," he asked as he looked at his watch.

"It's five fifteen," he said. "I'm going to leave my cell phone with you, Brook. In about an hour will you call Randy and Mary Ann and let them know what happened. And ask one of them to check on Moonshine for me. Their numbers are programmed into my phone under their first names."

"Okay," she said hugging him goodbye. "Why don't you take my cell phone so you can call me?

"I'll keep in touch," he said. "And Brook, I just want to say that I'm sorry if I sounded angry when you…"

"Don't even think about it," she said. "Just put it out of your mind and go find the people who tried to hurt Brian and Kayla."

Chapter 37

The Columbia, Missouri police station was bustling with activity as Bill Tom walked inside. People in street clothes and uniformed police officers were either rushing around with paper in their hands or answering what seemed to be a constant barrage of phone calls. He walked up to the reception desk and greeted the officer on duty.

"My name is Bill Tom Bradley," he said. "I'm looking for Detective Williams and my friend, Walter Beacham. Is it always this busy here this early in the morning?"

"On a Saturday night," the young cop said, "it's often busier than this. Columbia is a college town, Mr. Bradley. That means Saturday night parties. This is the first week the kids are back at school, so there's lots of celebrating, which leads to lots of problems. If you follow me, I'll take you back to Detective Williams' desk."

Bill Tom followed the young man through a maze of desks, chairs, filing cabinets and people, finally spotting Beach and the detective. They were standing at the detective's desk, looking at a computer print-out.

"Detective Williams, someone's here to see you," the cop yelled out, pointing at Bill Tom.

"Thanks, Larry," Doug Williams called back, motioning for Bill Tom to come over to his desk.

"We just got a list of red Mustangs and license plates," Beach said as Bill Tom walked up to them. "How are the kids doin'?"

Beach and Detective Williams both looked up to hear Bill Tom's response.

"Kayla's tests came back negative," he said. "She has no broken bones and no head trauma. It looks like both kids escaped with just superficial cuts and bruises. They're very lucky. We're very lucky."

"That's great. Were they able to tell you anything?" Detective Williams asked.

"When Brian woke up a little while ago he gave us some interesting information," Bill Tom began. "He told us that he and Kayla ran into two kids from Hillside yesterday while they were on campus and that Kayla and the girl--Mindy Arnold--had a minor disagreement about a ring that Mindy was wearing. Kayla said it belonged to Esther Gaines, one of our murder victims.

"Then Brian told us that Todd Mack's Mustang is red and that his license plate is 'Feisty.' Since Mindy Arnold has long blond hair, I thought…"

"Do you know where they live on campus?" Detective Williams asked. "We need to pay them a visit. How bad was that disagreement about the ring?"

"Brian said it just lasted a few seconds. Mindy ended it by saying she and Todd needed to get going. I should have asked Brian if he knew where Todd and Mindy live on campus," Bill Tom said, rubbing his eyes.

"We can get that information from the campus security office," Detective Williams said, grabbing his car keys. "Let's go."

The campus security office directed them to an apartment building about three blocks from the main entrance to the MIZZOU campus. Bill Tom was mildly surprised that Todd and Mindy were living together.

As Detective Williams parked his car and the three guys headed toward the door of the building, he turned to Beach and Bill Tom.

"Look," he began, "I mean no disrespect to you guys, but I need you to let me do most of the talking here, okay? This is personal to you and I don't want any emotional outbursts to get in the way of a conviction if these two kids are guilty of attempted murder, okay?"

"We're with ya'," Beach said, patting Bill Tom on the back. "We don't want that either."

The three men walked up the main stairway of the brightly lit hallway to Apartment 201 on the second floor.

"Open up," the detective commanded as he knocked loudly on the door. "This is Detective Williams from the Columbia Police Department." He motioned for Bill Tom and Beach to stand behind him.

After the third loud knock, they heard a faint voice on the other side of the door.

"Who are you and what do you want?"

Bill Tom recognized the irritated voice of Mindy Arnold.

"This is the Columbia Police Department, Ma'am," Detective Williams answered. "We need to ask you a few questions."

"About what?" Mindy asked, her voice getting louder.

"Just open the door, Ma'am. We need to talk to you now."

Mindy opened the door and gave the detective a defiant look. She hadn't bothered to put on a bath robe. She was wearing a thin white tee shirt that barely covered her red nylon thong.

"What the hell do you mean by waking us up at…?"

Mindy suddenly noticed Bill Tom standing behind the detective and stopped in shock.

"Chief Bradley, what are you doing here in the middle of the night?"

"It's not the middle of the night, Mindy," he said, walking around Detective Freeman and past Mindy, into the tiny apartment. "It's six o'clock in the morning. Time to get up and go to church," he added, as he turned around to look at her.

Beach and Detective Williams followed Bill Tom into the small living room.

"Ask her your questions, detective," Bill Tom said, looking at Doug Williams.

"Miss Arnold, I need to know where you and Todd Mack were between seven-thirty and nine p.m. last night," the detective began. "You are both suspects in a hit and run accident at the Breakfast Barn restaurant."

"What? Are you out of your mind?" Mindy asked. "We wouldn't hit someone with our car and run away. Besides, I hate the Breakfast Barn and…"

"What the hell is going on?" Todd interrupted Mindy as he walked into the room. He had at least taken the time to put on a pair of navy sweat pants before greeting their visitors.

"They think we hit somebody with your car and ran away from…"

"I'll explain it, Miss Arnold," Detective Williams said. "Just sit down here on the couch and answer some questions for me."

"Go get some clothes on first," Todd said to Mindy. "It's okay if she does that, isn't it? Or are you guys enjoying the view?"

"Get a bathrobe, Miss Arnold," the detective said.

The four men waited until Mindy returned in a white terrycloth bathrobe and sat next to Todd on the couch.

"Last night Kayla Bradley and Brian Brinkmeyer were hit by a car on the Breakfast Barn parking lot," Doug Williams began. "Witnesses say..."

"Oh, no! Are they okay?" Mindy asked, clasping her hand over her mouth.

"We just saw them yesterday afternoon," Todd said, instantly sitting forward. His look had changed from one of irritation to one of concern.

"We have witnesses who told us that the Mustang was red and the license plate ended with a 'Y.' That would fit you, wouldn't it?" Detective Williams asked.

Without waiting for a response the detective added, "The witnesses also say that a guy was driving and that his passenger was a woman with long blond hair."

"I swear to you, sir, we were nowhere near the Breakfast Barn last night," Todd said. "We ordered a pizza and watched a movie. I fell asleep; the movie wasn't that good."

"Brian told us you had an argument with Kayla about a ring," Bill Tom said to Mindy. "What was that all about?"

"Nothing, really," Mindy said. "She thought a ring I was wearing belonged to someone else, that's all. It was a case of mistaken identity. Look, you haven't told us how Kayla and Brian are. Are they okay, or what?"

"They'll live," Bill Tom said to her with an icy stare.

"We're going to need someone to verify your story," Detective Williams said. "Did anyone else see you here last night?"

"We were *alone*," Mindy said, clearly annoyed that she had to keep repeating herself. "We got home about five, ordered a pizza and watched movies, just like Todd said."

"Who delivered the pizza?" Detective Williams asked. "I mean, what restaurant?

"I always order from Marco's Pizza King, it's about six blocks away," Todd answered. "The pizza's always hot when it gets here."

"Where do you park your car?" Bill Tom asked, anxious to get on with the investigation. "Mind if we go check it out? If you hit somebody, you might have some body damage."

"Sure. Go check it out," Todd said, looking at the chief. "It's parked on the back side of the building. Just take the stairs down to the first floor and go out the back entrance. My car's sitting in the first space."

"Beach, why don't you come with me?" Bill Tom asked. "We'll let Detective Williams talk to the kids alone."

Once they were outside Mindy and Todd's apartment, Beach turned to Bill Tom.

"You know, buddy, I don't know these kids at all, but either they are innocent, or have absolutely no conscience. They were way too relaxed to be guilty. And they seemed to be genuinely shocked about Kayla and Brian."

"I don't know Todd Mack too well, but I wouldn't put anything past Mindy Arnold," Bill Tom said as they reached the bottom of the stairs. He pushed the apartment door open and there, in the first space on the right, was Todd Mack's car.

The two men examined every inch of the car very carefully, trying to find any dents or traces of blood. The overcast, early morning sky made it difficult to see anything specific.

Suddenly a light came on and the two men turned to see an elderly woman with gray hair and a pink bathrobe looking out the sliding glass doors of her apartment. She looked concerned until Bill Tom quickly flashed his police chief badge at her. Then she opened her door.

"Is something wrong, officer?" she asked Bill Tom.

"Ma'am, I'm Police Chief Bill Tom Bradley and this is Walter Beacham," he said. "We're investigating a hit and run accident that occurred last night. We have reason to believe that this car may have been involved. May we come in and ask you a few questions?"

"Of course," the lady said. "You can step over my flower bed there and come in through these patio doors. I just made some coffee. Would you gentlemen like a cup?"

"That sounds real nice, Ma'am," Bill Tom said looking around the lady's tidy living room. "You have a nice place here, Mrs.--I'm sorry I don't know your name."

"Audrey. Audrey Brenner," the lady said. "My husband died two years ago and my children thought I'd be more comfortable in a smaller place. At least one of them comes to visit me every day. I'm very blessed."

"Yes, you are, Ma'am," Bill Tom said, reaching out to take the coffee from Mrs. Brenner.

"Why don't you gentlemen sit down?" she suggested, gesturing toward her living room couch. "I'm sorry I don't have any baked goods to offer you. I gave my last frozen coffee cake to my daughter last night."

"That's quite alright," Beach said, "this coffee really hits the spot."

"We'd like to ask you a few questions about your neighbors upstairs, Mrs. Brenner," Bill Tom began. "It's the young couple in 201. Do you know them?"

"I know the young man," Mrs. Brenner said. "He's lived here for three years. This is his last year, he told me. He's a senior now. His name is Mr. Mack. I think his first name is Todd, but since he calls me Mrs. Brenner, I call him Mr. Mack."

"Do you know the girl who lives with him now," Bill Tom asked, sipping the steaming hot dose of caffeine.

Mrs. Brenner wrinkled her nose.

"She's not very neighborly," Mrs. Brenner said. "Never says 'hi' or 'how are you?' She just flits in and out of here in some very suggestive clothing. I would have thought that Mr. Mack would have better taste in young lady friends."

Bill Tom and Beach nodded in silent agreement.

"Mrs. Brenner, Mr. Mack and the girl--Mindy Arnold-- have told us that they were home last night by five p.m. and that they were in their apartment for the rest of the night," Bill Tom said. "We need someone to confirm that the red car outside did not move, specifically between the hours of six and nine p.m. Can you do that for us? I mean, can you be certain about it?"

"Why yes, I can," Mrs. Brenner said. "My daughter and my two grandsons were over for a visit. They came about four-thirty, not long before Mr. Mack and the girl got home. I know because the kids were playing in the empty parking space while my daughter and I talked on the patio.

"When they drove in, we said 'hi' to them and as usual, Mr. Mack said 'hello' but the girl just walked inside like we weren't even there. After they went upstairs, I came inside, got our supper out of the oven and we ate at my table on the patio. There was a nice breeze so we stayed out there until almost ten o'clock talking and watching the kids play on the sidewalk. Mr. Mack's car did not move from that spot the whole time."

Bill Tom finished the last of his coffee in three big gulps and stood up.

"Mrs. Brenner, you've been a big help to us," he said reaching out to shake her hand. "Thank you for your information and for your hospitality. You're a very kind lady. Your husband was a lucky man."

"Why, thank you, Mr. Bradley," Mrs. Brenner said with a smile. His comment made her blush.

"You have a nice day now, Ma'am," Beach added, also shaking her hand.

As the two men walked back upstairs, Bill Tom shook his head.

"I think they have a reliable alibi, Beach. What do you think?"

"I think I just had coffee with Aunt Bea."

Once they were back inside Todd and Mindy's apartment, Bill Tom looked at Detective Williams and shook his head.

"I think we have all we need for now," the detective said. "We should get going. "What's your phone number in case I need to get back in touch with you?"

After he jotted the number down in his notebook the three men left the apartment and headed back to the police station.

Back at Detective Williams' desk, they began reviewing the computer-generated listing of all red Mustangs in Columbia, Missouri with license plates ending in "Y."

Detective Williams' phone rang and he handed it to Beach. "It's someone named Trudy for you," he said, handing the phone to Beach.

"We need to get back to the hospital," Beach said as he hung up the phone. "Kayla's condition has gotten worse."

Chapter 38

Dr. Ralston pushed open the glass door of the hospital waiting room and gave a quick thumbs up sign to the four people who had stood up to greet him.

"She's fine, now" he said. "She gave us a scare earlier this morning. When she woke up she was very weak…couldn't keep her eyes open or squeeze my hand. She couldn't remember what happened to her. Her blood count was so low we did some further lab work. Turns out, she's anemic. It's not uncommon in young girls her age. I'm recommending a vitamin with extra iron. That ought to do the trick."

"When can we see her?" Bill Tom asked, holding his arm tightly around Brook's shoulders.

"She's on the third floor now, Room 316. When I left her she was sitting up in bed asking for her boyfriend, Brian. I'm sure she'd be happy to see you, too."

Dr. Ralston shook hands with Brook and Bill Tom and turned to Trudy and Beach.

"Mrs. Brinkmeyer, if you want to come with me I'm going to look in on Brian. I'd like to admit him for a day, just so he can get some supervised rest. I think I'll be able to discharge him in the morning."

"I'll go with Trudy," Beach said, patting Bill Tom on the back. "We'll come up to see Kayla as soon as Brian is settled into a room."

"We'll be waiting for you," Bill Tom said, as they headed to the door.

"Let's go see our daughter," he added, turning to Brook.

"We need to talk first," she said, motioning toward one of the couches. "Can we sit down a minute?"

"Yeah, sure, what's the matter?" he asked, as he sat next to her.

"When the nurses came in to get Kayla this morning they thought she may need a blood transfusion," Brook said. "All along they've just assumed that I was Kayla's mother, so when they asked me if I would be willing to give blood if she needed it, I said I would do anything to save my daughter's life. I thought Kayla was asleep, but when I looked at her she had her eyes open. I was talking softly to the nurses, but I think she may have heard me."

Bill Tom grabbed her hand and gave it a tight squeeze.

"If she's strong enough and clear-headed enough, we'll tell her today," Bill Tom whispered to Brook. "It's time she knows the truth--about both of us. Trudy told me last night in the chapel that

Kayla already suspects that you're her birth mom. I don't think that'll come as a shock. When she hears about me, though, I can't imagine what she'll do or say."

"Maybe we shouldn't upset her." Brook shook her head. "After all, she's just been through a horrible ordeal. It might be too much for her right now."

"Kayla's an intuitive young lady, Brook, relentless and stubborn, too. Once she gets something in her head she's like a dog with a bone. She won't stop picking at it until she gets what she wants. And in this case, it's information. If we tell her about you, her first questions will be about her biological father. If she's gonna have a fit about it, she may as well have it in a hospital where she can be sedated, if it goes that far. I think we need to take the chance."

"Okay," Brook nodded. "I'm with you! Oh, by the way, I called Randy and Mary Ann while you were gone. They were shocked to hear the news. Randy's going to take care of Moonshine and Mary Ann said she and George would drive up right after church. I wouldn't be surprised if she brought the whole town with her!"

Hand-in-hand they left the waiting room and found their way to the third floor, Room 316.

"Kayla, may we come in?" Bill Tom knocked lightly on the door to her room.

"Come in, Daddy," Kayla said in a muffled voice. It sounded like she had been crying.

Bill Tom opened the door and stepped aside to let Brook go in ahead of him.

"Kayla, what's wrong?" Brook asked, rushing to the girl's bedside. Bill Tom walked to the other side of the bed to grab the girl's hand.

"One of the nurses was just in here to give me some kind of vitamin shot and I asked her if she'd help me get to the bathroom," Kayla said, between sobs. "That's when I got a good look at myself in the mirror. I look terrible! Like some kind of monster."

"Sweetheart, it would be impossible for you to look bad," Bill Tom said, bending to kiss his daughter on the forehead. "You were hit by a car last night. These bumps and bruises are only temporary. Before you know it, they'll be gone!"

"They shaved my hair off," Kayla continued, still upset. "I wanted to wear my hair up for Homecoming. Now I'll have this big bald spot."

"Kayla, Homecoming is six weeks away," Brook said, patting the inconsolable girl on the hand. "I'll bet there are some beauticians out there who will be able to make your hair look just perfect for Homecoming.

"If we can't find someone in Hillside, I'll take you into St. Louis. I remember a salon that…"

Brook's comments were interrupted by a knock at the door.

"Is anybody home? May we come in?" Trudy peaked into the room and smiled at the group.

"Kayla, I have a guy here who is really anxious to see you."

"Brian?" Kayla asked, suddenly forgetting her hair dilemma.

Trudy opened the door and Beach pushed Brian into the room in a wheelchair.

"I'm fine, Mr. Beacham, I can walk," he said, climbing out of the chair with some effort.

He walked slowly over to Kayla and bent down to get a hug from her outstretched arms.

"I was so worried about you, Kayla," Brian said, kissing her gently on her left cheek.

"I was worried about you, too, Brian," Kayla said, now beaming from ear-to-ear. "Daddy told me you saved my life."

"It's a life worth saving," Brian said as he smiled back at her.

"Maybe the kids would like some time alone," Brook suggested, looking up at Bill Tom with a grin. "I saw a waiting room down the hall. Why don't we go down there for a little while?"

"That's a good idea," Trudy said, nodding her head. "I think in this case, two's company and six is a crowd!"

The four adults excused themselves and walked down to the empty visitor's lounge at the end of the hall. The room was painted in a soft blue with peach and blue couches and chairs. Several tables held countless magazines and books and there was a TV in the corner.

"Why don't I go get us something to eat?" Bill Tom suggested as they all found a place to sit.

"I'll go with you, Billy," Beach said. "You ladies try to catch a nap while we men forage for food."

The two guys climbed into Brook's Camry and headed for Campus Blvd., where fast food restaurants were lined up on either side of the street. Once they had put their order in at the McDonald's drive-thru and were waiting in line for their food, Bill Tom turned to Beach with a sigh.

"I've got a couple things I need to talk to you about, buddy," he said, glancing over at Beach.

"I think I may have a line or two on one of those things," Beach said. "Are you gonna tell me you have a crush on Brook? I hope not, 'cause that would be an insult to my intelligence."

"It's more than a crush," Bill Tom said with an amused smile. "Beach, Brook is Kayla's birth mother."

"Wow! That is big news, although nobody could miss the fact that they really look alike. Did she ever tell you guys why she wanted to give up her baby?"

Bill Tom took a deep breath and gently eased his foot onto the gas pedal to move up in line.

"She wasn't married at the time," Bill Tom said, once again looking at his friend. "And the father was."

Beach was quiet for a moment before he spoke. "And I'm guessin' that you were the father?" he asked, sitting up straighter in his seat.

"We had sex once, Beach, on a business trip. We both had too much to drink. We both had--have--a strong attraction to one another. It was just one of those things that happens. Brook was a party girl. She had lots of boyfriends. When she asked us to take her baby I had no idea I was the father. I didn't know until she told me, just last night, actually.

"I'm telling you this because today we're gonna tell Kayla," Bill Tom continued as he dug into his pocket for money.

"Let me get this," Beach said, handing money past Bill Tom to the clerk at the window. "Does Trudy know all this?"

"Turns out Trudy knew all along because Sarah guessed it and confided in her when Kayla was about a year old. I was too stupid to put two and two together."

Bill Tom took the bag of food and the tray of coffee and handed it to Beach.

"Trudy told me last night that Kayla suspects that Brook is her mother," Bill Tom continued, easing the car onto Campus Blvd. "But today, when she finds out I'm her biological father, I don't know what she might do. She'll realize that I cheated on Sarah."

"She might surprise you, Billy," Beach said. "She's a great kid, very mature for her age. She may be shocked at first. I think that would be a natural reaction. But in the long run, she's gone from being a kid with no biological roots to a kid who has both natural parents in her life. And the father she's always loved is really her biological father! In the end she'll still love you."

"I hope you're right," Bill Tom said, guiding the Camry into a parking space in the hospital parking lot. The guys hopped out of the car and wasted no time getting the hot food up to Brook and Trudy.

"Egg McMuffins, hash browns, coffee and orange juice" Bill Tom called out, as he pushed his way through the glass doors of the third floor waiting room. "Get 'em while they're hot!"

The smell of the food made the four of them realize just how hungry they were and in no time the food was gone and they were relaxing over their steaming coffee cups.

"I think I saw a coffee bar down the hall," Brook said. "We can probably get refills if we want them."

"Speaking of 'down the hall' I think it's about time I go pry Brian away from Kayla," Trudy said, looking at her watch. "The doctor told me not to let him stay up for more than an hour. They put him in room 312, just down the hall from her room.

"Walter, would you like to go with me?" Trudy asked as she stood up.

"Why, yes, Gertrude, I'd be happy to accompany you to your son's room."

Trudy wrinkled her nose.

"Please don't call me 'Gertrude'," she said, shaking her head. "It sounds like a little old lady."

"And please don't call me Walter," Beach said with a smile. "That was my dad. I'm Beach."

"Glad to make your acquaintance, Beach," Trudy said, extending her hand with a slight curtsey.

"The pleasure is all mine," Beach said, gallantly bending to hold and kiss Trudy's hand.

The two disappeared down the hall as Brook and Bill Tom smiled at one another and leaned back against one of the peach-colored couches. Bill Tom put his arm around Brook and she leaned against him, with her head on his shoulder.

They were asleep for what seemed like only seconds before Bill Tom felt a cool hand patting his cheek.

"Is it time to wake up?" he asked, not wanting to open his eyes. He gave the hand a quick kiss.

As he opened his eyes, he saw his secretary, Mary Ann, leaning over him, and he sat up quickly in his seat.

"I'm sorry, Mary Ann," he said, with a sheepish grin. He could feel his face getting hot. "I thought it was…I didn't realize it was you!"

He couldn't tell if she was shocked to see him and Brook curled up together on that couch.

"I called your name, but you didn't answer," she said with a gentle smile. "I know you must be tired."

"Thanks for coming," Brook said, sitting up straight on the couch and rubbing her eyes. Bill Tom's sudden jerk had jolted her out of a sound sleep.

"Would you guys like some coffee?" Mary Ann asked, holding up some cups with the steaming hot brew. "We passed a coffee bar just down the hall."

She pulled up a chair and sat down directly across from Brook and Bill Tom, and grabbed their hands as she looked at them.

"We were all just shocked to hear this terrible news," Mary Ann began, "and we're so happy that the kids are going to be okay. George and I came up to see if there is anything we can do to help."

"She brought enough food to feed an army," George said, patting his wife on the back as he pulled up a chair and sat next to her. "We have chicken salad sandwiches, potato salad, and her special home-made apple pie."

No one could miss the pride the man felt about his wife's ability to pull a meal together on short notice.

"Thanks for the food, Mary Ann," Bill Tom said, this time leaning forward to kiss the kind woman on the cheek. "We appreciate it for sure, but just having you here is the best comfort."

"Well, Chief, I have to warn you," Mary Ann said, grabbing his hand, "this news swept through town like a tornado. I think a lot of people will come up today to see you and the kids. Are they up for visitors?"

"I think so. Kayla's pretty upset about the way she looks-- they had to shave some hair off to put stitches in the right side of her head--but I think she'd like to see some friends."

For the next several hours, Brook, Bill Tom, Trudy and Beach were busy greeting friends from Hillside and monitoring the amount of time each well-wisher stayed to visit.

Bill Tom was shocked to see that even Mayor Adermann and his wife made the hour-long trip to express his "dismay over the unfortunate incident."

One of the English professors who had heard Kayla and Brian's essay showed up at the hospital with flowers for Kayla and a cookie bouquet for Brian.

Half way through the afternoon, Trudy and Beach decided to make a trip back to Hillside to get clean clothes for another night's stay in Columbia.

Randy and his family came with carefully hand-crafted get well cards that the boys made after church. Randy assured Bill Tom that Moonshine was okay and he was staying on top of things at the office, having deputized Cletus Morgan and Harry Jackson. Cletus and Harry were members of Hillside's emergency response team. As ex-Marines who served in Desert Storm, they each had keen ears and sharp minds.

Chapter 39

About four p.m., all the visitors left for home. Brook and Bill Tom once again found themselves alone in the waiting room.

"Kayla seems to be in a pretty good mood," Bill Tom said, thinking about her room, which was now filled with flowers, cards, stuffed animals, fashion magazines and a huge box of chocolate-covered strawberries. "Should we go introduce ourselves?"

"Let's go see how she is," Brook said. "I think we'll be able to tell if she's up for conversation."

As they entered Kayla's room there was no doubt between them that the girl was alert and feeling okay. Her bed was cranked up to the sitting position and she had her knees propped up. She was reading the latest issue of *Seventeen* magazine.

"Hi," she said, greeting them with a grin. "I think I found a hair style that will work with my shaved head."

"That's great, honey," Bill Tom said, looking at Brook for the go-ahead signal.

Brook nodded slightly and they walked to Kayla's bedside, standing next to each other.

"How do you feel, Kayla?" Bill Tom asked. He could see that the swelling on her face was already subsiding--she was able to open her right eye--and the bruises were starting to fade.

"I'm really sore all over and the stitches feel funny, but besides that I think I'm pretty good. It helped to see Brian. Miss Trudy made him go back to his room for a nap."

"Honey, Brook and I need to talk to you," Bill Tom said, turning to let Brook stand in front of him. "We have some really serious stuff to talk about."

"Did you find out who did this to us?" Kayla asked, dropping the magazine in her lap.

"No, Honey, it's not about the accident," Bill Tom said, gently taking hold of her hand. "I know that you've always said you wanted to find your birth mother and I always told you that I'd help you find her when the time was right.

"The truth is, Kayla, your mom and I always knew her identity. We planned to tell you on your eighteenth birthday, when we thought you'd be old enough to understand.

"Kayla," he said, feeling his heart beating fast and his mouth getting dry, "your birth mother is Mrs. Jennings--Brook." He looked at Brook, who was white as a ghost, and he put his hand on her shoulder. "She came to Hillside so that she could meet you."

Kayla looked at Brook and her eyes welled up with tears.

"I knew it," she whispered, wiping the tears from her face. "I knew it the first day we met, when we shook hands. I saw your red hair and your eyes and I knew it. I...I...don't know what to say," Kayla said, sniffling. "I can't believe it! I wanted it to be you and it is you."

Brook hesitated a moment and then moved in toward the girl, in front of Bill Tom.

"Kayla, may I give you a hug?" Brook asked. Tears were streaming down her face, too.

Instantly the girl raised her arms and the two of them shared a mother-daughter hug for the first time.

Bill Tom let go of Kayla's hand and backed away to give the two of them more room.

"How did you find me?" Kayla asked, gently rubbing her hand across Brook's face.

"I've always known where you were, Kayla," Brook whispered. "Not a day went by that I didn't think about you or pray for you. I've always loved you, Sweetie, from the moment you were born. You've got to *believe* that. I couldn't take care of you, so I gave you to two wonderful people I knew would be great parents."

Bill Tom pulled up a chair so Brook could sit down. Her whole body was shaking.

"Why did you have to give me up?" Kayla asked, holding Brook's hand in a death grip.

"I wasn't married. My parents were dead. I was all alone, Kayla. I wasn't strong enough to raise a child on my own. I wanted the best for you and I knew I couldn't give it to you."

"Well, what about my father?" Kayla asked, her eyes now wide with curiosity. "Didn't he want me? Didn't he love you enough to marry you? Oh my gosh, you weren't raped, were you?"

Brook shook her head.

"No, Kayla, I wasn't." Brook said with a deep sigh, "Your father was married. I never told him about you."

"Did you know he was married?"

Brook lowered her head and closed her eyes before looking again into her daughter's eyes.

"Yes, Kayla, I knew," she whispered and took a deep breath. "But I loved that man, and in a moment of weakness I let things go too far. I'll always be ashamed of myself for that and sorry that it happened, but, Kayla, you were the wonderful result of that weak moment. I can't imagine a world without you in it, Sweetie. I look at you now and I know that God has forgiven me for what I did. I hope that you can, too."

Kayla once again lifted her arms and the two of them shared a long embrace.

"I guess since he didn't know about me I can't think of him as a jerk," Kayla said, letting go of Brook and leaning back against her pillow. "Did he love you?" Brook glanced at Bill Tom quickly and then back at their daughter.

"I think he cared about me," Brook said carefully.

"Do you have a picture of him? Could you at least tell me who he was so I know? Aren't you curious about him, Dad?"

Kayla looked at her dad with raised eyebrows.

Now it was Bill Tom's turn to come clean. His stomach was tied up in knots and he was breaking out in a cold sweat.

"Why don't you sit down here?" Brook suggested, getting up from her chair.

Bill Tom sat down and looked at his daughter's bewildered face. His heart was aching for her. He grabbed her hand and tried to speak but at first words wouldn't come out.

"Kayla…Sweetheart…" he was struggling to speak. "I'm your dad. I mean, not just your dad, but your biological father. Brook and I knew each other from work and there was a strong attraction between us. We didn't mean for…

"What?" Kayla asked, raising her voice as the reality of what he was saying sunk in.

"You cheated on Mom? And even though you knew how much I wanted to know, you never told me that you were my real father? How could you do that, Daddy? How could you betray us like that?"

Her eyes were wide open now and her expression was a mixture of anger, disappointment and accusation.

"I feel so humiliated," she said, looking away from them. She buried her head in her hands.

Bill Tom stood up and put his hands on her shoulders.

Kayla shook her shoulders so he would take his hands away and turned to look Bill Tom straight in the eye.

"All these years you've treated me like a fool. I feel so stupid. I…"

"Kayla, your dad didn't know that he was your biological father until last night," Brook said, putting her hands on Bill Tom's shoulders as she tried to defend him. "I never told him.

"Your mother was my best friend. She and your dad really wanted children and couldn't have them. That's why I gave you to them."

"Some friend you turned out to be!" Kayla said.

"Kayla!" Bill Tom raised his voice to her. "She did the best she could under the circumstances. I know that you're upset, but this isn't exactly easy for us, either!

"We thought you were old enough and mature enough to know the truth and that you'd be able to handle it in an understanding and forgiving way. Were we wrong about that?" Bill Tom asked, his own temper rising.

Kayla's eyes met his with an angry glare.

"You just told me that you cheated on my mother. I look at the two of you and now all I see are two irresponsible, sex-crazed people who hurt the best person in the world--my mom! I want you to leave now. I want my real mom. I want Sarah."

Kayla turned over on her side and began to sob loudly.

Bill Tom felt like she had jabbed a knife into his heart. He stood up slowing, looked into Brook's red, blood-shot eyes, and the two of them walked out of the room in silence.

As they stepped into the hallway and closed the door to Kayla's room Brook called to a nurse who was standing nearby.

"We just had to give our daughter some very serious news," she explained, fighting back tears. "I'm afraid that we've upset her quite a bit. Is there something you could give her that might calm her down and let her sleep?"

"I just saw Dr. Ralston," the nurse said. "I'll ask him to look in on her and prescribe something. Is there anything I can do for the two of you?"

"We'll be okay," Bill Tom said, rubbing his forehead. "Please just make sure that she gets something to calm her down, okay? She doesn't want us in there right now and I don't like leaving her alone when she's so upset."

"We'll take care of her," the nurse said. "In the meantime, you might want to consider getting some rest yourselves. You two look pretty tired."

"We're gonna do that," Bill Tom said, putting his arm around Brook. "We'll be in the…"

"Hey, you guys, we're back," Trudy called out to Brook and Bill Tom. She stopped abruptly when she got a look at their faces.

"Oh, no. What's happened?" she asked, instantly grabbing Brook's hand. "Is Kayla okay?"

"Let's go into the waiting room for a minute," Bill Tom said, looking at Beach.

"We told Kayla that we're her biological parents," Bill Tom said after the four of them settled into their seats. "She hit the roof. Brook asked the nurse to give her a sedative."

"Bill Tom, it's a knee-jerk reaction," Trudy said, leaning forward to pat him on the arm. "She's just a kid. You guys gave her some shocking news. She's going to need some time to sort it out."

"She looked at us like she hated us," Brook said. Bill Tom grabbed her hand.

"You know, what we all need is a good dinner and good night's sleep," Trudy said, trying to smile. "Things will look better in the morning.

"Wal...Beach and I rented a couple of rooms at the Holiday Inn across the street. We stopped by your houses and picked up some clean clothes for you. Randy and Chris took Moonshine to their house so she's in good hands.

"I'll go check on Brian to make sure that he's settled in for the night and then we can go."

Trudy looked at the group with a weak smile.

After a leisurely dinner at a steakhouse near the highway, the foursome settled into their respective rooms at the Holiday Inn. They wasted no time getting a good night's sleep...all except for Bill Tom, who had to listen to Beach snore.

Chapter 40

Kayla stirred slightly and immediately gasped as she felt the pain in her right arm. Her whole body felt like it was made of lead. She tried to pull herself into full consciousness, but the drugs the nurse had given her were too strong. She could barely manage to open her eyes.

It didn't matter. She knew that her room was dark. She could feel the needles in her arms and she could tell that someone was sitting in the chair by her bed. She thought it must be Brian. Her internal clock told her that it was very early—too early for visitors. Brian must have sneaked out of his room to come and sit with her. From the sound of his steady breathing she decided he must be asleep.

"I wonder when we'll get out of here," she thought. "Maybe Daddy knows…"

At the thought of her father, Kayla suddenly remembered their conversation from the night before and the shocking revelation that Bill Tom and Brook were her biological parents.

She let out a long, slow groan, this time from the pain of heartache and the feeling of betrayal and humiliation. At the sound, the person in the chair quickly got up and hustled out the door.

"Brian…" She tried to call to him but her lips were unable to form the words. "Why did he leave?" she wondered, very carefully trying to sit up without causing herself more pain. "I need to tell him what happened last night."

When all her efforts to sit up proved pointless, she turned carefully onto her side and began to cry silently into her pillow.

She had never been so miserable. First she got hit by a car, then she got hit with the news that Brook was her mother, and then, unbelievably, her adopted dad told her he was her biological father.

"I feel like such a fool," she thought. "They must have had such a grand time, laughing at me behind my back. I wish that car would have killed me."

Kayla's sobs grew louder and she pressed her head hard into the pillow, openly wailing in a fit of self-pity.

"What's going on in here?" a nurse asked, letting in a blast of bright light from the hallway as she entered the room.

"Are you in pain, Kayla?" she asked, quickly checking all of Kayla's vital signs, the saline drip and a myriad of monitors that were hooked up to the girl.

"Yes," Kayla answered weakly. She tried to explain that it was more emotional pain than physical pain, but she was too weak to get the words out.

"Is it your arm, Kayla," the nurse asked, bending over the girl. "You need to let me know where you feel the pain."

"All over," Kayla whispered, weakly. "Everything hurts."

"Kayla, before I can give you more pain medicine I'll have to get permission from your doctor, do you understand?" The nurse gently rubbed Kayla's forehead. "You're not scheduled to receive another dose for several hours, yet."

"It's okay," Kayla said, "I don't want the medicine. Just have Brian come back in and sit with me. I don't want to be alone."

"Kayla, Brian's asleep," the nurse said, now stroking her cheek. "He's been out like a light since about ten o'clock last night."

"No," Kayla said, shaking her head, "he was just in here, sitting in the chair next to my bed. I could hear him breathing."

"Kayla, I think you might have been dreaming," the nurse insisted. "It wasn't Brian who was in here. He's asleep, as I said, and visitors--unless they're your parents or siblings-- won't come until much later--at least ten a.m."

"I don't want to see my parents," Kayla said sharply, wrinkling her nose. "If they come, tell them to go away."

The nurse shook her head and patted Kayla's hand.

"Kayla, I know you've been through a lot and I know your whole body hurts right now, so why don't you try to get some more sleep? The next time you wake up the pain medicine will have kicked in and you should feel much better, okay?"

"Okay," Kayla said in a barely audible voice.

When she woke up again at ten a.m. Trudy and Brian were standing next to her bed.

"Hi there, sleepy head," Trudy said with a big smile. She reached out and gently patted Kayla's hand.

"Did you have a good night's sleep?"

Kayla managed a weak smile.

"I think I slept okay, but it was only because Brian sat in the chair by my bed all night," Kayla said, looking past Trudy to the young man she loved.

"I wasn't in here at all, Kayla," Brian said. "I've only been up for about an hour."

"Someone was in my room," Kayla insisted, trying to focus her eyes on her visitors. She reached up to grab Brian's hand. "It wasn't my Dad, was it?" she asked, her voice getting louder. "Because I don't want him in here. I don't ever want to see him again."

"Kayla, take it easy," Trudy said. She leaned down and gently stroked the girl's forehead. "Don't let yourself get upset. You need all your strength to get well."

"I'll never be well again, Miss Trudy," Kayla answered pathetically. "Do you know what happened in here last night? Does Brian know?

"Mrs. Jennings told me she's my biological mother," Kayla continued, looking at Brian. "Just like I told you I thought she was. And I was so happy to hear it. And then my Dad…" She could hardly talk as she began to cry. "My Dad told me he was my biological father," she ended in a barely audible whisper.

"What did you say?" Brian asked, leaning forward to hear her better.

"She just told you that Mrs. Jennings and the Chief are her biological parents," Trudy said, sparing the girl from having to repeat the disturbing news.

"Wow," Brian exclaimed, as he pulled up a chair to sit down next to her bed. "Your dad is your biological father? But that means that he and Mrs. Jennings…"

"Had an affair," Kayla sobbed, tears running down her cheeks. "They cheated on my mom, and I was the unfortunate result!"

"Wow!" Brian said again, his eyes wide with surprise.

"Mom, did you know about this? "Why didn't you tell me?"

"I thought Kayla should be the one to tell you, Brian," Trudy said, smiling weakly at her son. She walked around the room to stand next to the boy.

"I want to talk to you guys about this," Trudy continued, putting her left arm around Brian and gently placing her right hand on Kayla's forearm.

"Mrs. Jennings and the chief--and Miss Sarah, too--all knew each other because they worked together," Trudy began. "Sarah and Brook were good friends. When Sarah introduced Brook to the chief, there was an instant attraction. It happens, sometimes. One night they consummated their feelings for one another--while they were away on a business trip, they told me. It wasn't something that they planned--and Brook got pregnant. She never told the chief that the child was his. Instead she asked Sarah to adopt the baby and raise the child as her own. Until Brook came to Hillside, the chief had no idea Kayla was his biological daughter."

"How stupid can a guy be, Mom?" Brian asked. "They have sex. She gets pregnant. Did he need a calculator to put two and two together?"

Trudy took a deep breath.

"Brook said she was kind of a party-girl at that stage in her life, Brian. I'm not trying to defend their actions. But I hope you two can maybe understand. I hope you will also keep this information to yourself and not share it with your friends. That would certainly be embarrassing for Brook. At the time, she was very lonely because she was in love with a man who was married. It was a very sad time for her. She protected the chief--and Sarah--from scandal and she gave up the baby she loved deeply, so that the three of them could have a normal, happy life. She made a mistake, but she tried to make it right. I think she acted heroically."

Just then a nurse came into the room.

"Good morning to all of you," she said, with a pleasant smile. "Would you mind if I interrupt you for just a minute to check up on Kayla?"

Trudy and Brian stepped aside to make way for the nurse.

"Did you figure out who spent the night in here with you?" the nurse asked Kayla. "When you told me someone was in your room and I knew it wasn't Brian I checked with the other nurses on duty and one of them remembered a young man going into your room. She thought it must have been your brother. That's why she didn't question him."

"I don't have a brother," Kayla said, in a dull voice. "At least I don't think I do. But who knows? That could be another surprise."

"Kayla, you don't have a brother," Trudy said, shaking her head.

"Then what young man was in here with her all night?" Brian asked, raising his eyebrows at Trudy.

"You're sure it wasn't Chief Bradley, her dad?" Brian looked inquisitively at the nurse.

"No, it wasn't him," she said. "This was a young guy, probably about your age...very tall, pale and skinny. He was here for a long time, and then all of a sudden he was gone."

"From his description, I'd say it might have been Lester Tucker," Brian said, "but what would he be doing here all night? I can't even imagine him getting up enough courage to come in for a short visit."

"Well, maybe that's why he would come in the middle of the night--so he wouldn't have to talk to anyone," Trudy said, trying to make sense of it.

The nurse finished her check-up, pulled the side railing up on the bed and stared at something on the white sheet.

She pulled a long piece of thread off of the bed and turned to throw it into the trash can.

"What is that?" Trudy asked, noticing the green color.

"It's just a piece of fuzzy green thread, probably from a visitor's clothing," the nurse said. "I was just going to toss it away."

"Could I have a look at it, please?" Trudy asked.

The nurse handed the thread to Trudy and walked toward the door. "I'm going to order you some breakfast, Kayla. It should be here in a few minutes."

"Mom, why did you ask for that piece of thread?" Brian asked when the nurse left the room.

"Just wanted to get a better look at the color," Trudy said with a smile. "I'm fond of this color green.

"Would you guys excuse me for a minute, I need to go get some coffee. I'll be back soon. Brian, you stay here with Kayla, okay?"

"I hadn't planned on leaving her side, Mom."

"Good!" Trudy said as she hurried out the door.

"What got into her all of a sudden?" Kayla asked, looking at Brian.

"I don't know," he said. "You know how old people are. Sometimes they get the urge to go to the bathroom and they can't wait. She probably just didn't want to say anything."

For the first time that morning, the two of them laughed.

"I'd love to give you a big hug, Brian, but I just don't have the strength," Kayla said, gently touching the boy's hand.

"It's something I'll look forward to," he whispered, as he leaned down to kiss her gently on the lips.

Chapter 41

Trudy ran down the hospital corridor as fast as she could, weaving in and out of pedestrian traffic. It seemed like every doctor, nurse and visitor with flowers was in her way and felt like an eternity before she reached the waiting room where Brook was pacing nervously.

"We've got to call Bill Tom and Beach," Trudy yelled to Brook in between gulps of air. She wasn't used to running so fast.

"What happened?" Brook asked. "Did something happen to Kayla or Brian?"

"Someone spent the night in Kayla's room," Trudy said, trying to catch her breath. "She thought it was Brian or Bill Tom. But it wasn't. The person the nurse described matches the description of Lester Tucker. And guess what the nurse found on the side of the bed! A piece of green thread! That's what the guys found around Esther and Ernie's necks! Fuzzy green thread!"

"Oh, no, Trudy! Do you think the killer was in Kayla's room last night? We can't let those kids alone!" Brook said, running her hand through her hair. "Do you think Lester Tucker could be the killer?"

"I don't know, but we've got to get this piece of thread to the crime lab."

Trudy quickly punched Beach's number into her cell phone. Her hands were trembling.

"Beach!" Trudy yelled at the sound of his voice. "You've got to get back over here. Someone was in Kayla's room last night. From the nurse's description, I think it might have been Lester Tucker. And the nurse found green thread on the side of the bed. You've been looking for green fibers, right? What if he was there to strangle her and got interrupted by something or somebody? I'm so scared, Beach, please come now."

Trudy clicked off her phone and looked at Brook.

"He's going to get Bill Tom out of Detective Williams' office and come on over. He said not to let the kids alone. We've got to get back to their room."

"I can't go in there," Brook said, shaking her head. "I know my presence will just upset Kayla. I'm the last person she wants to see right now."

Trudy put her arms around Brook and tried to console her.

"Give her some time to get used to this news, Brook. She's a sweet and kind-hearted young lady. And she's pretty smart. She's just trying to deal with a huge piece of news, and, after all, she did just get hit by a car. She's got an awful lot on her plate. Just give her a chance to come to terms with this. I know the three of you will get past this and become a happy family. I *know* it!"

"I wish I could share your confidence," Brook said, patting Trudy on the back and pulling her way out of the hug. She sat down on the couch and put her head in her hands.

"Brook, I'm going to go back to Kayla's room," Trudy said. "I don't want them to be alone right now. Can I get you something before I go? Coffee, soda?"

"Thanks, Trudy, but I don't want anything," Brook said sadly. "Just send Bill Tom down when he gets here. Kayla probably doesn't want to see him, either."

Trudy walked slowly towards Kayla's room, thinking about everything that had happened since she woke up that morning. The four of them--Bill Tom, Brook, Beach and Trudy--were enjoying coffee and juice while they waited for their eggs and bacon at the Holiday Inn where they had spent the night.

They were in the middle of discussing Kayla's reaction to the news about her parents when Bill Tom's cell phone rang. It was Detective Williams from the Columbia police department. He wanted Bill Tom and Beach to know that Jefferson City police had just arrived at a crime scene where the victim was strangled. He thought they might want to check out any similarities from that scene and the murders in Hillside.

The men ate a hasty breakfast and headed off to Jeff City. That left her alone to face Kayla and Brian.

Trudy finally made it down the hall and pushed the door to room 316 open. She was surprised to see Todd Mack and Mindy Arnold visiting with Kayla and Brian.

"Hi, Mrs. Brinkmeyer," Todd said, extending his arm. "We just dropped by to see Kayla and Brian for a minute. We were shocked to hear the news."

Trudy shook his hand and smiled weakly at the pair. Of all her son's friends, Todd Mack was her least favorite. He was three years older than Brian and he had an Eddie Haskell air about him, she thought, like he could hood-wink parents into thinking he was a great guy when all the time he was really a trouble-maker.

"Actually, we were just leaving," Mindy said, grabbing Todd by the arm. "We've already got plenty of homework to do for school tomorrow."

"Why aren't you in school today?" Trudy asked, absentmindedly.

"It's Labor Day," Mindy said, "No school!

"We'll see you guys later," she said, turning around to wave to Brian and Kayla as she walked out the door.

"How long were they here?" Trudy asked, walking over to Kayla's bed.

"About five minutes," Brian said, glancing at his watch. "Mindy came in all gushy. She gave us each a big hug and said she hadn't been able to think about anything but the accident since she heard the news."

"I wonder how they found out about it," Kayla said. "I guess it was one of the kids from school who came by yesterday."

"Actually, your dad paid them a visit yesterday morning, Kayla," Trudy said, trying to measure her next words.

"The car that hit you was a red Mustang, just like Todd's car and the license plate ended in "Y", just like Todd's. There was a blond woman in the passenger seat."

"I told your dad about the argument you and Mindy had over that ring thing," Brian added, "and he and Beach went over to Todd and Mindy's to check it out."

"Oh no!" Kayla exclaimed. "Like what? Like just because we disagreed about the ring, she and Todd would try to kill us? What was he thinking? I'm so embarrassed. That man has absolutely no judgment. I can't believe that…"

"Okay, that's enough!" Trudy said, raising her voice and putting the palm of her hand out in front of her.

"Kayla, I'm sorry, but I can't stand to hear you bad-mouthing your parents any longer," Trudy began. "I know they hurt you. I know you're in physical pain with your injuries. But that's reality and you're just going to have to face it."

"Mom!" Brian exclaimed. He was shocked at her harsh words to Kayla.

"Just be quiet a minute and let me finish," she said, giving Brian a look that told him to shut up or else.

"Sometimes life isn't pretty and this is one of those times," she turned her attention back to Kayla. "But will you stop and think about how lucky you are? You barely escaped being killed by a hit and run driver. You're alive! No broken bones; no long-term problems.

"And besides that, you're a kid with two parents who love you, love you enough that they changed the course of their lives just for your happiness. So they made a mistake. They're not perfect. No one is perfect. Not even you. They made a mistake and they tried to correct it with your best interest in mind.

"This hospital is filled with people who are dealing with real tragedies. People facing incurable diseases, agonizing pain, life-altering situations. And look at what you're facing, a few bruises that will heal and two people who love you more than life itself. You poor little girl! It's time you get your self-righteous big head out of your arrogant little butt."

"Miss Trudy!" Kayla whispered, her eyes filled with tears. "You've never, ever talked to me like that before. I can't believe…"

"We were never in circumstances like this before," Trudy sighed. She grabbed the girl's hand.

"And do you know what? I couldn't ever love you more than I do right this minute. You are a constant joy in my life, Sweetie, and I thank God for you every day, just like I thank Him for my wonderful son." Trudy looked at Brian and smiled.

"And I'm not going to stand by and let your misguided feelings get in the way of your happiness. I know that in time you'd sort this out on your own. But Kayla, we don't have the luxury of time. Your mom is down the hall in the waiting room, just praying that at some point you'll forgive her and let her come back in here. And any minute now your dad is going to come bounding in here to see if you're alright...he's not going to wait for an invitation. How are you going to treat him? Like the enemy? Think about it, Kayla. Are these people really that bad? Can't you see them for the wonderful parents they are?"

Kayla tried to pull away from the death-grip Trudy had on her hands.

"I'm sorry Miss Trudy," she whispered, tears streaming down her face. "But they made a fool out of me and they hurt my mom-- Sarah--and I loved her so much."

"We all did, Kayla," Trudy said, now patting the girl on the head, "especially your dad. He went through such agony when she died. But you're old enough to know--and you've experienced it first-hand--in our imperfect world we sometimes hurt the people we love, though we don't intend to, it just happens."

"I don't want to see them. I don't want to talk to them. When I get out of here I want to go live with Miss Es...oh, no, she's dead! I can't go live with Miss Esther. I don't know what I'll do. This is just terrible. The only thing I know for sure is that I'll never speak to them again. I'm sorry, Miss Trudy, but I feel so humiliated. I'd never, ever do something so awful. I just can't talk about it anymore. I'm sorry."

With some effort, Kayla rolled over on her side so she wouldn't have to look at Trudy. She reached up for Brian's hand.

There was a light knock at the door and Beach walked in, smiling at the group.

"Good morning, boys and girls," he said, walking over to the side of the bed where Trudy was standing.

"How are you guys feeling this morning?" He looked at Trudy and Brian and raised his eyebrows.

"The doctor's going to release me this morning," Brian said, extending his arm across Kayla's bed so he could shake hands with Beach.

Beach looked down at Kayla and glanced at Trudy, who quickly shook her head, warning him not to talk to her.

"Looks like Kayla's asleep and you guys have things under control in here. I think I'll go find some coffee and wander down to the waiting room" he said, motioning for Trudy to join him.

Chapter 42

"Brook is in the waiting room," Trudy said, as soon as they were outside of Kayla's room. "Where's Bill Tom?"

"He went straight to the waiting room to sit with her," Beach said. "I know they're both hoping that Kayla will have a change of heart and want to see them."

"It's still too early," Trudy said with a sigh. "It's going to take her a while to sort through all of this."

Brook and Bill Tom looked anxiously at Trudy and Beach as they entered the crowded waiting room. Trudy gave them a thumbs' down sign as they settled into the seats Brook had saved for them.

"You guys are going to have to give her some time," Trudy said, grabbing Brook's hand. "You've got to remember her body's had quite a shock and now her mind is dealing with some shocking news, too. That's a lot for a kid to handle, even for a mature kid like Kayla."

Trudy looked into their sad faces and tried to force a weak smile.

"She loves you guys, I know she does," Trudy said. "Just let her take the time she needs to sort this out."

"What if she sorts it all out and decides that she still hates us?" Bill Tom asked, shaking his head. Trudy had never seen him look so sad.

"I think that's highly unlikely, Bill Tom," Trudy said, again forcing a weak smile. "Think back to when you were a kid. Weren't you shocked and disappointed the first time you realized your parents were real people who made real mistakes? How long did it take you to get a grip on your feelings about that?"

"Why don't you guys go on back to Hillside," Beach suggested. "I'll arrange for hospital security to place someone outside Kayla's room when we leave for the night. That way we know she'll be safe.

"I'm going to take a quick ride to the police station so I can give the piece of green fibers Trudy found to their crime lab people.

"Billy, don't you guys worry about Kayla," Beach continued, patting them on their backs. "She'll think this through and everything will be okay."

Bill Tom nodded his head and put his arm around Brook's shoulders. "Thanks, Beach. We appreciate you guys more than you'll ever know. I am anxious to get over to the Tuckers and find out if Lester was in Kayla's room last night."

Chapter 43

Bill Tom stared straight ahead as he maneuvered Brook's Camry around the frequent curves of State Highway N, the longer but less traveled route back to Hillside. He knew there would be a lot of people taking the interstate on this last day of the Labor Day weekend and he was in no mood to deal with a lot traffic.

As he drove through the countryside, he was barely aware of the beautiful rolling foothills of the Ozark Mountains and the lush green heavily wooded areas that would soon be ablaze with the colors of autumn. Instead, his mind switched rapidly from his daughter lying in her hospital bed hating him and the green fibers that were found in her room.

After a good cry, Brook had fallen asleep and now he was alone to confront the memories he did not want to face. Once again he felt a headache forming at the base of his neck as he remembered Trudy's innocent question to him: "Weren't you shocked and disappointed the first time you realized your parents were real people who made real mistakes?"

Her words had sent a chill down his spine as he remembered his parents and the way he had treated his mother.

Bill Tom was born and raised in the west Texas town of Braxton, a dusty little hole in the road every kid yearned to leave as soon as they sobered up from their high school graduation party.

His dad made a decent living as the only dentist in town and his mother worked as a checker in the local grocery store.

As a kid, he never thought much about their marriage, if they were happy or if they made each other miserable. They barely spoke to one another and when they did it was all business: "Gene, did you remember to take the lawn mower in to be fixed?" "They'll have it ready sometime this weekend, Irene."

That was pretty much it. He never heard them speak words of endearment to one another--or to him for that matter--and he only saw them touch once, when his mom lost her balance on the stairs and his dad reached out to steady her.

Bill Tom had vague memories of sitting on his mom's lap when he was a small child; but once he was eight or nine she no longer hugged him or showed any displays of affection. When he tried to hug her, she told him that he was a big boy and she didn't want him to be a 'momma's baby.' She was all business, stressing the importance of school work and duty to society.

Gene Bradley was not much better, but on weekends he did take the time to show Bill Tom a thing or two about carpentry and working with cars. As they spent their Saturday afternoons together in the garage, Gene showed him how to make minor repairs on the family car and taught him how to build bird houses, dog houses and small pieces of furniture.

Bill Tom enlisted in the Marine Corps a week after his high school graduation. When he came back for a visit on furlough after basic training his home life fell apart. His dad suffered a fatal heart attack and after the funeral, his mother admitted to him that she'd been having an affair with a man in another town about thirty miles away for over ten years and, now that she was free, he was going to get a divorce and they were going to move to Florida to start a new life.

Bill Tom looked her straight in the eye and said, "This is the last time you'll ever see me." He had found out his mother was human, and he never forgave her.

"Would you mind if I turn off the air for a while and open the windows?"   Bill Tom nearly ran the car off the road as Brook's question startled him back into the present.

"No, you go right ahead," he said with a small laugh. "You surprised me; I thought you were asleep!"

Brook leaned forward to turn off the air conditioning and shot a look at Bill Tom.

"Were you thinking about Kayla?" she asked. "You looked very unhappy."

"Partly," he said, not mentioning his parents. "I'm just curious about those green fibers, you know?

"I know that you're concerned that Lester Tucker may have spent the night in Kayla's room," Brook said yawning as she stretched out her legs. "I'm curious about that, too, but I also want to know what happened at that crime scene you looked at this morning."

Bill Tom shot a quick look at the woman beside him. Head back. Eyes closed. Her blue-jean-clad legs stretched out so that he could barely see her feet below the dash board.

"Brook, the crime scene we went to look at was a music store. The store clerk was strangled alright, but there were no traces of green fibers and all the money was taken from the cash register. It looked like he was counting it, getting ready to make a night deposit at the bank. Beach and I--and the Jeff City police--think it was a random act of burglary. We don't think it's remotely related to our murders.

"Naturally we're going to look for matching finger prints from the crime scene, and anything else that may link the crimes together. Beach's crew is working with the Jeff City crime scene people."

"The minute we get to Hillside I have to go over to the Tuckers' house," Bill Tom said, keeping his eyes on the highway's sharp curves. "I need to see if Lester was in Kayla's room last night.

"Would you reach for my cell phone and make sure it's on?" Bill Tom asked Brook. "Beach said he'd call us the minute he finds out about those green fibers."

Brook reached for the phone that was attached to his belt and checked the signal.

"It's on," she said. "Do you really think we'll get an answer anytime soon? I mean, it's Labor Day and how many people do you think are working in a crime lab today?"

"Beach will pull out all the stops to get the tests done today," Bill Tom said. "He's a very influential man, and well-respected throughout the state. We're lucky to have him on our side."

Brook nodded her head, still looking at Bill Tom's phone in her hand.

"Did you know that Wanda and Esther Gaines had become good friends?" she asked, unable to get the Tuckers out of her mind.

"How do you mean?" he asked, carefully braking the car at a four-way stop along the county highway. "I know they sat in church together most every Sunday. I usually sit a few pews back from them. Kayla's always up in the balcony with the choir."

"Trudy told me that all through the summer, Esther, Wanda and Lester went for an early morning walk every day," Brook said. "They'd meet at the corner of Market and North Second about six a.m. and walk down Main Street and back. Trudy said that Esther told her that Wanda had become a good friend. She said Esther wanted to help Lester break out of his shell and that the two of them had spent some time reading Shakespeare together this summer."

"If they went for a walk every morning, where were they on that Tuesday morning when we found Esther's body?" Bill Tom asked. He looked at her and raised his eyebrows. "I don't remember either one of them in the crowd at the crime scene."

"I don't know," Brook said, shaking her head. "You'd think that when she didn't show up down at the corner, they would have walked up to her house; she only lived a few blocks away from their meeting spot. I can't believe that they wouldn't have at least tried to check on her."

"Maybe they did and when she didn't answer they thought she was sleeping in, or not feeling well," Bill Tom tried to reason, suddenly wrinkling his forehead. "Or maybe they didn't come by because they knew she wasn't going to be able to meet them."

He looked at Brook and grimaced as the throbbing in his head suddenly became stronger.

"I've really got to get over to their house," he added, noting that around the next curve they would come into Hillside.

"We've got work to do, Brook," he said as he aimed the car up Market, toward Maple Drive. "You've got classes tomorrow and I've got to prepare a presentation on personal safety. Did you know I was going to be the star at a Hillside High student assembly in the morning?"

"It was the talk of the school on Friday," Brook said, giving him a big smile.

Bill Tom pulled into Brook's driveway, stopped the car, jumped out and walked around to her side of the car.

"Why don't you just drive up to your house so you don't have to walk," Brook asked as he opened her door. "I can manage to drive back down to my house without an escort," she said, smiling at him.

"A gentleman always takes his lady to the door," Bill Tom answered, grabbing her bag of clothes and helping her out of the car. He took her hand and led her up the sidewalk to her front door.

"Do you want me to come in with you to check things out?" he asked as she opened the door.

"No, thanks. You go do what you have to do. I'll be okay."

He watched her as she unlocked her front door and stepped inside.

"Brook, I'm so sorry for everything," he said as she turned to say good-bye. "I'm sorry for the way I treated you so long ago and also when you first came to Hillside. I was so afraid that you wanted to take Kayla away from me. And now I look into your face and I see a woman who's given me the greatest gift in the world...my daughter.

"I hope you can forgive me, Brook, and that maybe you and I can..."

"No forgiveness necessary, Bill Tom." Brook reached for him and gently placed her fingers on his lips. "I think you and I are friends now. That's the best place for any relationship to start. Right now you have to concentrate of finding a killer. Once that's done we can think about the future."

He grabbed her hand, kissed her fingertips, and gave her a wink. "And that's even more incentive for finding the killer," he said.

He hopped off the porch, turned to blow her a kiss and began sprinting his way up Maple Drive toward his house.

Chapter 44

He stayed home long enough to take a quick shower, change clothes and call Randy to check in. Within twenty minutes he was in his truck, headed up Market Street. He felt edgy, almost nervous, as he thought about what he would say to the Tuckers. But he needed to know if Lester had been in Kayla's room during the night.

"Why doesn't Beach call about those green fibers that nurse found?" he asked out loud. If the fiber matched, that would mean that the killer had been in Kayla's hospital room. Just the thought of it made his stomach churn.

It was three-fifteen p.m. when Bill Tom arrived at the Tuckers' house.

He rang the doorbell and waited for someone to answer. After several rings, the door opened slowly and Bill Tom looked into the sullen face of Wanda Tucker.

"Wanda, I'm so sorry to drop in on you unannounced," he began. "I know this is a really difficult time for you. But I have to talk to you about a couple of things…could I come in for a minute?"

Wanda shook her head and opened the screen door so Bill Tom could enter.

The house was dark, cool and quiet; Wanda turned on a lamp that brought only dim light into the room.

"Please have a seat, Chief Bradley," she said, pointing to one of the chairs by the front window. The drapes were pulled shut. She sat in the facing chair, and stared at him, her hands folded in her lap.

"Is Lester around," he asked. "I'd like to talk to both of you."

"No, he went for a walk about ten minutes ago."

"Wanda, I know you and Lester went away for the weekend," he began, leaning forward in his chair. "Would you mind telling me where you went?"

"We went to Jefferson City," she answered, showing no emotion. "I thought a change of scenery would be helpful."

"Was Lester with you the whole time you were in Jefferson City?"

"Most of the time," she answered, pushing her hair out of her eyes. "Sometimes he likes to go off by himself, on long walks. Long, long walks. He's very quiet, you know, he keeps all his thoughts to himself. I wish he would tell me what he's thinking, but when I ask him questions he just looks at me and turns away. He's always been a strange boy, but ever since Esther was killed he's been different."

"How so?" Bill Tom asked.

"He goes off by himself more and stays gone for longer periods of time. He locks his bedroom door and the other night…" She put her head in her hands and started to cry.

"The other night what?" Bill Tom asked, folding and unfolding his hands.

"The other night I woke up with a start. I could tell someone was in the room. I rolled over and there he was, just staring down at me. I have a digital clock with big green numbers. The light cast a green shadow on his face and he looked so scary. He had this blank, almost lifeless look in his eyes. I screamed and he ran out of the room. When I asked him about it the next morning, he told me I must have been dreaming because he was never in my room. But Chief," she said, now looking straight into Bill Tom's eyes, "it wasn't a dream. I know he was in there."

"Wanda, has Lester ever mentioned my daughter, Kayla? I mean, does he know her, have an opinion about her?

"He told me when we first moved here that Kayla was the only one of the church youth group members who talked to him, her and that Brinkmeyer boy. I think Lester's always kind of liked her because of that, but I don't think he feels like he really knows her, or any of the kids in Hillside."

"Did he have friends in––where did you move from? Nebraska?"

"When he was a little boy he played with some of the neighbor kids and he did okay when there was only one other child, but when he tried to play with a group of kids, he always got left out. I don't know why, but it just got worse as he got older. Ernie and I thought that our move here would help him get a fresh start, but I guess it didn't.

"The person here that he really got close to was Esther. She had a way with kids, an easy, friendly manner that just made them trust her. Lester was no exception; he spent hours at her house, doing odd jobs for her, reading Shakespeare with her. I didn't even know he liked Shakespeare. He was devastated when she was killed."

"Trudy Brinkmeyer tells me you guys went walking every morning," Bill Tom said. "Did you go for a walk the morning Trudy found Esther?"

"I got up and got dressed," Wanda said, swiping a hand through her hair, "but when I tried to wake Lester, he said he wasn't feeling well and didn't want to go out. I walked over to his bed to feel his forehead and he was burning up with a fever. I decided to stay home with him."

"Did you try to call Esther, to let her know you wouldn't be walking that morning?"

"No. We had an agreement; if one of us was more than ten minutes late, the other one would go on alone. I didn't know anything happened to her until mid-morning when I went to the grocery store. I was off work that day because I had worked the Saturday before."

Bill Tom shifted in his seat and once again leaned forward toward Wanda.

"I'm sorry for all these questions, Wanda," he said, "but Kayla and Brian were involved in a hit and run accident in Columbia on Saturday night and last night a boy fitting Lester's description spent the night in her hospital room. "Can you tell me, does Lester drive? And could he have been the one who was in Kayla's room?"

"A hit and run accident? I had no idea! What happened?"

"They were walking across the parking lot of the Breakfast Barn in Columbia and a car deliberately aimed for Kayla; Brian pushed her out of the way. They were both injured but they'll be okay. Do you know where Lester was last night?"

"Chief Bradley, surely you don't think that Lester would have tried to hurt Kayla and Brian? He was with me all the time on Saturday; we slept in the same hotel room, it was a double. He did ask to go out Sunday night. He said he wanted to go to a show in Columbia. He's a real careful driver so I told him to go and get his mind off of things."

"What time did he get back to the hotel?"

"I don't know. I took one of the sleeping pills Dr. Schrader gave me and I slept all through the night. When I got up this morning Lester's bed had been slept in. He left me a note saying he would be in the lobby."

Bill Tom nodded his head, stood up and walked around the small but tidy living room. No family pictures with smiling faces. No dust. No clutter. It was very pristine. He turned around, sat back down in the chair and once again faced Wanda.

"I'm sorry to keep asking you all these questions, Wanda," he said, giving her a slight smile. "Can I get you a glass of water or something?" he asked. "I know my questions are difficult for you, but I wouldn't be doing my job if I didn't investigate every lead. Is there someone I can call to come over and stay with you for a while?" he asked, not knowing what else to do.

"Trudy Brinkmeyer is still in Columbia with the kids. How about Brook Jennings? You know her, don't you? Maybe she would come over for a while, if you'd like some company."

"I'd like that, Chief," Wanda said, looking at him with red-rimmed eyes. "I really don't want to be alone right now. I feel so lost without Ernie, and Lester is so…" She shook her head and reached for a tissue from the box on the table next to her chair.

Bill Tom excused himself, stepped out on the porch and called Brook on his cell phone. When he told her how sad Wanda was, Brook offered to drive over immediately. He walked back inside to tell Wanda and then waited anxiously for Brook's Camry to pull up to the house. He was lousy at small talk and the whole situation made him very uncomfortable.

When Brook showed up a few minutes later, it was apparent that she knew exactly what to do.

"Oh Wanda," she said, reaching out to hug the woman, "I'm so sorry you and Lester are going through such a trying time. Would you like me to make you some hot tea?"

Wanda nodded her head and the two women walked arm-in-arm to the kitchen.

"We'll be okay, Bill Tom," Brook said, throwing him a glance and a quick smile. "If you need to go, that's okay, we'll be fine."

"I do need to get to the office," he said, glancing at his watch. It was five-thirty. "I'll see you ladies later."

Bill Tom wasted no time getting out of there.

"Thank God for Brook," he thought as he backed out of Wanda's driveway.

Chapter 45

He headed his truck toward Market Street, reached for his cell phone and punched in Beach's number.

"Walter Beacham."

Bill Tom smiled at the sound of Beach's voice; at the moment he was in great need of a friend.

"Beach, what have you found out about the green fibers?" Bill Tom asked.

"The initial tests were inconclusive, Billy," Beach said. "They want to run them again to make a final determination. They won't know until sometime tomorrow."

Bill Tom let out a heavy sigh.

"Beach, I want those test results," he said, feeling tired and frustrated. "And I want to know if Lester Tucker was in Kayla's room last night. I'm tired of…wait a minute, I have an idea. I think Lester's picture was in the paper about a month ago, before Esther was killed. It was a story about a volunteer project that our church youth group participated in over at the park. I kept it because Kayla was in the picture. When I get to my office I'll try to find the clipping and I'll take a picture with my phone and send it to you. Maybe the nurse who saw him can make a positive identification.

Bill Tom spent the next hour rummaging through all his papers at the office. He finally found the clipping and sent a picture of it to Beach.

He was surprised when Mary Ann walked in, bringing him a sandwich and a coke.

"I was thinking about your speech tomorrow and thought you might need some help with editing it," she said. "It's on your desk along with that video on personal safety. If you want to make changes I can stay until we get it the way you want it."

"What would I do without you?" he asked, as he walked into his office.

"You'd have to retire," she said with a slight giggle.

Bill Tom looked at the video to make sure it was the one he had wanted and then started to review his speech to the kids. He was almost through making the minor corrections when his cell phone rang. The sudden noise made him jump.

"Mary Ann, I have the changes completed," he called out to her as he answered the phone.

"Hi Billy, it's Beach," the caller said. "I got the picture but the nurse who was on duty last night will not be on duty tonight. I got her home phone number, but she doesn't answer. She switches to mornings tomorrow, so if I can't get in touch with her before, I know she'll be here around seven a.m. tomorrow. She is apparently the only person in America under fifty who doesn't have a cell phone."

Bill Tom leaned back in his chair and ran his free hand over his face. "Why was everything taking so long?" he wondered.

"Okay, thanks for all your help, Beach. How's my daughter doing?"

"She's been really quiet and she's just picking at the pizza we brought in," Beach said. "Do you want to try to talk to her?"

"No, I'll just leave her alone for now. Just make sure there's a policeman outside her door all night, okay?"

"Will do. Talk to you later."

Bill Tom placed the phone back in the cradle, leaned back in his chair and yawned.

"Mary Ann, it's time for us to go home," he said, looking at his watch. It was seven-fifteen. "I've got to go get Moonshine from Randy's house and then I'm going to crash."

Chapter 46

When his alarm clock rang at six the next morning, Bill Tom could have sworn his eyes were glued shut. After short cat naps on Saturday night, listening to Beach snoring away at the hotel on Sunday night, sleeping in his own bed had felt like heaven on earth.

Moonshine must have felt the same way. She was still curled up on the bed, her head resting comfortably on Bill Tom's pillow.

"You were just waiting for me to give that up, weren't you?" he asked her.

After a quick, steamy shower, he felt better. He stared into his bedroom mirror to assess his appearance. He carefully studied his third wardrobe change of the morning and decided that he'd found just the right outfit. At first he thought he should wear a suit, so he pulled out his Sunday best and delivered the first three sentences of his speech into the mirror.

"I look like a mortician," he thought, and went back to the closet to see what else he could find.

Once, when they were at a J.C. Penney store in St. Louis, Kayla had made him buy some tan dress slacks and a cream-colored polo shirt with thin tan lines running through it. But when he put those clothes on he looked like he was going to a singles bar.

"This is the best choice," he said confidently, carefully eyeing the blue button-down shirt and some well-worn jeans. "I look like…me!

"Good morning, ladies and gentleman, I'm Chief Bill Tom Bradley and I'm here to talk to you about personal safety," he said to the mirror.

"Yep! This is me," he said, clapping his hands together.

He was about to leave the room when his phone rang.

"Bill Tom Bradley," he said, half expecting to hear Beach on the other end of the line.

"Good morning! Are you ready to give your speech?" It was Brook.

"I'm in such good shape I could sing it," he said, smiling into the phone. "How are you this morning?"

"I'm fine, but I'm calling to ask a favor. I was just leaving to go to school and my car has a flat tire. Would you mind picking me up?"

"I'd be delighted," he said, "and after I give my speech I'll come back and fix that tire."

Brook laughed into the phone.

"I'll be out front waiting for you," she said.

He hung up the phone, took another quick look in the mirror to make sure his nose hairs weren't too long and headed for the door.

"Come on, Shiner," he said, "let's go get 'em."

Brook was standing on her porch as he pulled up to the curb.

"How in the world does she manage it?" he thought to himself as he looked at her. The woman had to be approaching fifty and she looked like she was thirty, a vision of loveliness in a bright blue dress.

He jumped out of the truck and ran around to open the door for her and help her into her seat.

"You wouldn't have to do that, you know," she said, smiling at him. "I can open a door by myself."

"You deserve to be treated like the great lady you are, Brook." He closed her door and walked around to the driver's side of his truck. "It's seven-fifteen. We've got a whole forty-five minutes before we have to show up at school. Do you want to go get something for breakfast?"

"Umm," she said, "That sounds great but I really need to get to my homeroom. The kids are supposed to go directly to the gym for the assembly, and I want to get some work done before class.

"I do need to talk to you about something, though," she said, turning to face him as he made the right turn onto Market Street. "The strangest thing happened to me last night at Wanda's. I made her some hot tea and we talked for hours, about Ernie and Lester. I just let her talk and when she seemed like she'd pulled it together I told her I needed to go home to finish grading some papers and get ready for school today. I gave her my phone number so she could call me if she needed to talk. Lester never showed up and she didn't seem at all concerned about it. We said our good-byes and I walked out to my car. It was about nine o'clock so it was dark and the moon was shining.

"I walked around to get in the driver's side and there was Lester, sitting on the street, leaning against my car. He startled me and I gasped for breath. When I did he jumped up and walked toward me. He said, 'What are you doing here, Mrs. Jennings, am I in some kind of trouble?'" He just kept walking closer and closer to me so I backed away.

"I said, 'No, Lester, you're not in trouble, I was just visiting your mother.' He kept pressing the point, asking me again and again if he'd done something wrong. He said he knew that you had been at his house earlier.

"He looked so creepy, Bill Tom. He was wearing a black hoodie and the moon was shining on that pale face of his and with those dark eyes! He looked like a creature from a monster movie."

"What happened then?" Bill Tom asked, shooting a quick glance her way. He didn't want her story to distract him from his driving.

"His hands were at his side but he kept drawing them into fists and then letting them relax," she said. "For a minute there I thought he was going to hit me, just because I was visiting his mother. Then he just took off and ran around the back of the house.

"It was just such a weird encounter I felt really uncomfortable all night," she said with a shiver. "I locked my bedroom door and pushed my dresser in front of it."

"Why didn't you call me if you were scared?" Bill Tom asked as he pulled his truck onto the school parking lot. "I'd have spent the night on your couch."

He jumped out of the cab and walked around the truck to help her down.

"I didn't want to bother you," she said, holding out her arms so he could grab her. "And besides, it was the first time in forty-eight hours you got to sleep in your own bed. I thought you needed it before facing the kids this morning."

"The next time you're scared, you call me," he said sliding his arm around her waist. "I'll come chase the boogie man away."

They both laughed as they headed down the sidewalk toward the school.

Chapter 47

Built in the mid-sixties, Hillside High School was a two-story tan brick building with big windows, tan tiled walls and no air-conditioning. Since the Columbine tragedy in 1998, a security camera had been added to a strategic location in the main corridors by the entrance, but no one had been hired to keep constant surveillance on the TV monitor. So the camera was there mainly for show, to comfort the minds of concerned parents.

The school had an enrollment of three hundred sixty students and so it also had its share of typical teenage problems, including some vandalism and drinking on--and off--the campus. On several occasions drug paraphernalia had been found by the dumpsters next to the cafeteria.

Even with those problems, Principal Roger Landry--a tall and muscular guy--seemed to be able to keep discipline in the school without too much effort. He'd never had to call Bill Tom's office for help.

Bill Tom walked Brook to her classroom on the first floor and then walked down the long hallway in the other direction toward the school gym. He couldn't help but smile as he passed classroom doors, lockers and bulletin boards announcing upcoming events. Everything reminded him of his own high school days in a rural west Texas ranching community.

"The more things change, the more they stay the same," he thought as he read about the upcoming school elections, the first pep rally that was sure to catapult the state champion Hillside Tigers into another victorious football season, and the first announcements about one of the school's biggest social events--Homecoming. Bill Tom noted that it was going to be held the second weekend in October.

"I wonder what Kayla's hair will look like by then," he thought, having heard from various sources that she was certain to get elected to the homecoming court.

Students were starting to arrive at school and Bill Tom greeted many of them as he made his way down the corridor.

The Hillside High gymnasium was huge. When the forward-thinking school board of 1966 approved the building plan for the school, members decided that the gym should also be large enough to use as an auditorium, where band concerts, school plays and musicals, and large student body assemblies could be held. So the space was big enough to play regulation basketball, with bleachers climbing up the sides of opposite walls. A big stage, complete with a red velvet curtain with white trim--the school's colors--took up most of the front wall, and doors to the locker rooms and storage areas were located on the back wall. A unique feature about the gym was that the gym teachers' offices were located right behind the back wall, with picture windows made of shatterproof glass so the coaches could always see what was going on in the gym. Each office was accessible from either an outside hallway or through the gym door that led to the locker rooms.

Bill Tom knocked briefly on Coach Dan Chapman's hallway door and entered as the coach beckoned him.

"Hey, Bill Tom, good to see ya," Coach Chapman said, standing to shake hands with the chief. "We were all so sorry to hear about Kayla and Brian. I'd have come to the hospital, but I just heard the news last night when we got home from the lake. I hear they're doing okay, is that true?"

"It's true, Chap," Bill Tom said, smiling at his friend as he settled into a chair. "Those two kids are lucky to be alive and to have survived the ordeal with only minor injuries."

"I heard it was a hit and run," Chap continued. "Have they found out who did it?" Chap sat in his desk chair and turned to face Bill Tom.

"Not yet, but we're working on it. I was just wondering…"

Bill Tom was interrupted by the sharp ring of Chap's phone.

"Hold that thought," Chap said, raising his finger.

"Good morning, this is Coach Chapman," Chap said cheerily into the phone.

Bill Tom looked around Chap's office and tried to take it all in. The room contained a plethora of items pertaining to sports:

trophies, basketballs, bats, a catcher's mitt, and a pile of clothing in the corner that looked like a bunch of sweaty jock straps.

"That's where the smell is coming from," Bill Tom thought, noting that Chap could use one of Mary Ann's scented candles.

Numerous family pictures and official photos of the teams Chap had coached hung haphazardly on the barely visible light blue walls. Bill Tom took a special interest in one of the pictures. Chap had cut out a photo of the Hillside High Drill Team from the newspaper and taped it to the bottom of a picture frame right above his desk.

As a man with a healthy sex drive, Bill Tom couldn't help but look at the girls in the picture, posing coyly in their Dallas Cowboy Cheerleader-type "uniforms." But as a father, he wasn't particularly impressed with most of the girls in the photo; their gymnastic ability made him wonder just what the girls' gym teacher was teaching them.

All the girls wore so much make-up that he had at one time, in a conversation with Kayla, referred to them as the "Hillside Hookers."

"Daddy, most of those girls are my friends," Kayla had said in protest. From that moment on, he kept silent about them, but he made sure Kayla understood that, if she ever wore that much make-up, he'd take her to the power car wash to get it off.

One of the girls in the picture was Mindy Arnold. She was standing at the end of the first row and she had written a note on the side of her picture. Bill Tom reached into his pocket, pulled out his cheaters, stood up from his chair and leaned in close to the wall to study the note she had written.

"You've been a great 'coach.' Love, Mindy," the note read.

"Like that picture of our drill team?" Chap asked as he hung up the phone. "I should probably throw that away," he added, pulling it off the wall as Bill Tom stared at it. "I've got too much clutter in here."

"The dirty jock straps in the corner are a nice touch," Bill Tom said, smiling at the coach as he returned to his seat. He watched as Coach Chapman tore the newspaper article into little pieces and threw them into the trash can.

"That was an interesting note from Mindy Arnold," he added, looking at his friend carefully.

"I think she was just suffering from senior sentimentality, ya know? Lots of kids start to feel it right after they graduate. Suddenly all of us old and familiar teachers seem like a safe haven before the kids move on to college, or whatever."

"Or whatever," Bill Tom said, looking at his friend. "Hey," he exclaimed, hitting the palms of his hands on his knees. "I've got to get set up for my speech." He was anxious to change the subject. And judging from the look on Chap's face, he was eager to change it, too.

"Yeah, it looks like the kids are starting to arrive," Chap said, glancing out of his window. "You were going to ask me something before my phone rang. Do you remember what it was?"

"Oh, yeah," Bill Tom said. "I was just wondering if you have an opinion about Lester Tucker. I mean, I hear that he tried out for football and you told him he didn't make the team. How'd he react to that?"

"He just stared at me, nodded his head, shook my hand and walked away," Coach Chapman said, shrugging his shoulders. "I told him I'd be happy to help him in gym class and he seemed like he was okay with that. He's just a quiet, introverted kid."

"That's my assessment, too, Chap," Bill Tom said, watching the kids file into the gym. "Guess I'd better get out there and get this over with.

"Good to see you, Chap." He extended his arm to the coach. "We need to get together one of these days."

"Hey, I'm ready for it," Chap smiled, slapping Bill Tom on the back. "Beer and football. Sounds good to me."

Chapter 48

Bill Tom walked out of Chap's office by way of the locker room door, made a left turn and opened the door into the gym. As he walked toward the stage, he noticed that his palms were getting sweaty. How was he ever going to have any credibility with these kids when he hadn't been able to catch the psycho who was killing people in Hillside?

Once all the students had assembled in the gym, Principal Landry approached the podium and the low din of chatter in the room stopped instantly.

"Good morning ladies and gentlemen," he began. "Thank you for coming here today for this important assembly on personal safety.

"You all know Police Chief Bill Tom Bradley and in a minute I'll call him up here to the microphone. But before I do, I want to express to him for myself, our staff, and on behalf of the entire student body, our deep sorrow over the incident this past weekend that injured Kayla Bradley and Brian Brinkmeyer.

"Chief Bradley," Principal Landry said, turning to face Bill Tom, "please know that our thoughts and prayers are with you and your family. We are all thankful to God that those two young people will recover from this horrible tragedy."

With that, the entire student body stood and joined in a long round of applause.

When the students sat down again, Principal Landry continued.

"Having said that, I'd like to welcome you to Hillside High and invite you to come up here and share your thoughts on safety with us."

As Bill Tom approached the podium, the student body once again joined in an enthusiastic round of applause.

Bill Tom scanned the audience quickly to see if he could find Brook. He smiled and felt slightly more relaxed when he saw her sitting at the back of the room on one of the bleachers near the floor, surrounded by students. Beyond the bleachers, Bill Tom could see Chap working in his office.

"Thank you," he said, now smiling broadly at the group of kids assembled in front of him. "I appreciate your kind words, Principal Landry," he said, turning slightly to face the man, "and I appreciate your kind welcome," he said, looking again at the students. "Kayla and Brian are very fortunate to have friends like you. I know they are very anxious to recover and get back into the swing of things here at school.

"Now I'd like to turn your attention to the critical matter at hand. As you all know, we've had a tragic turn of events here in Hillside, with the brutal and thoughtless murders of two of our friends and neighbors. Although a lot of you didn't know Ernie Tucker, his son is a senior at Hillside High this year and I'm sure that all of you feel a great deal of sympathy for him.

"Of course, you all knew Mrs. Gaines," he continued, "and I know you have a great sense of loss. One of the reasons that I am here today is to make sure that you take the steps necessary to keep yourselves safe.

"There are some simple rules I want you to follow: when you go out, go out in groups, never go out alone, keep your doors and windows locked, and always let your parents know where you are, or where you're going. When you have to stay after school for sports or other activities, make sure you're with other students or faculty members.

"I'm going to show you a video now. It's called 'Safe Keeping' and it's about twenty minutes long. It will give you some valuable insights on ways to keep yourselves, your friends and your families out of harm's way."

Bill Tom sat down as the student working the technical board dimmed the lights, pressed a button to lower the big screen and started the video.

As the video played, he hoped the kids would listen to its valuable advice, although he secretly wondered how anybody could keep themselves safe with such an unpredictable maniac running around.

He looked out across the group gathered in the huge darkened gym and noticed that Chap had turned off the light in his office so he wouldn't distract the students.

Once the video was over, Bill Tom returned to the podium and looked at the group.

"What I'm going to tell you now is difficult to say and it's going to be difficult for you to hear," he said looking at the students. "Since the person who committed the two murders here in Hillside did so by strangulation, I've arranged for a Marshall Arts specialist to work with you in gym classes this week to give you some specific pointers about what to do if someone tries to strangle you.

"Looking at the clock I think I have about five minutes to answer questions and I'll be happy to do that now. Also, remember that my office is always open to you. Please feel free to call me anytime if you have questions or concerns, or if you think you have information that may lead to the arrest of this killer."

Bill Tom answered questions from a number of students and noted during the process that Chap had turned his office light on and seemed to be particularly interested in what was going on. He had stopped working altogether and was listening intently to the kids' concerns.

"That's just like him," Bill Tom thought, "to be interested in the kids' safety."

Finally, Principal Landry came to the podium, called for the last question and the assembly was over.

"Ladies and gentlemen, let's give Chief Bradley a hand for coming here today to share this valuable information with us," the principal said, reaching out to shake hands with Bill Tom.

Once again all the students stood and applauded.

When the applause subsided, Principal Landry asked the students to take their seats.

"I'd like for you to stay for a few minutes so I can talk to you about some last-minute schedule changes today."

Bill Tom walked down the steps from the stage and was going to go out the side door. He looked up to give Brook a smile, but something in Chap's office drew his attention.

Chap was still staring straight out at the crowd; he hadn't moved from his position and his expression was…

Suddenly Bill Tom's heart began to beat wildly and he broke out in a cold sweat as he walked quickly to the exit door by the stage entrance. He ran down the hallway to Chap's office and didn't bother to knock. Once he got inside his worst fears were confirmed: Chap had been strangled! It must have happened while the video was playing. He was just sitting there, his head resting on the back of his chair and his blank eyes staring straight ahead.

"Oh My God," Bill Tom prayed, "what am I going to do?"

He knew that in a few minutes, students in Chap's first class would come into the locker rooms and maybe want to talk to him in his office.

Bill Tom quickly pulled the blinds down over the big window and closed them tightly so the kids couldn't see into the room. He grabbed his cell phone and called Randy. He could barely breathe.

"What's up, BT," Randy said in a cheerful voice.

"Get over to the school gym right now, Randy. We've had another murder. It's Chap. Somebody strangled him while I was giving my speech. Don't use the sirens; whoever did this might still be in the building. But hurry!"

As he heard the kids starting to leave the gym, he ran over to the locker room entrance to Chap's office and locked the door; then he ran back to the hallway door, turned out the light in Chap's office, locked the door and stood outside waiting for Brook to come out of the gym.

He tried to act normal, smiling and nodding at the kids as they walked past him. But when he finally saw Brook and their eyes met, he knew by the expression on her face that he was not doing a good job at acting normal.

"What's wrong?" she asked, hurrying over to him. "You're white as a sheet."

"Brook, while I was giving my speech someone came in and strangled Chap," he whispered. "The killer could still be in the building. I need you to go get Landry for me and get him over here, pronto! We've got to find a way to get the kids out of this building."

Brook gasped and put her hand over her mouth.

"Strangled Chap? While you were…?"

"Brook, I'm sorry, you don't have time to take this all in. You can be shocked later, just go get Landry. *Now*!"

He gently pushed her toward the gym door and she took off running.

Bill Tom could hear kids knocking at Chap's other door, calling out his name.

Principal Landry rushed through the gym doors with Brook close behind him.

"Are you sure he's dead?" he asked, the color totally gone from his usually tan face.

"Yes," Bill Tom said. "Roger, I need you to get everyone out of this building now. Create some story about a safety hazard or something and then tell them you have to cancel classes and all other activities for the day."

"I'll do it right now, Bill," Principal Landry said. "But are you *sure* he's…"

"Yes! I'm sure. Now go and…wait a minute, I'm going to need keys to get back into his office. I locked the doors so no one could get in. Do you have a set of…?

"Right here in my pocket."

Principal Landry handed Bill Tom the keys and walked swiftly toward his office, three doors down from the gym.

"Brook, get to your class and try to act as though everything is normal," he said, grabbing her hand. "But be careful. Don't let yourself be alone. As soon as everyone is dismissed come right back here to me, okay?"

"Okay," she nodded, taking a deep breath. "I'm on my way."

Bill Tom watched her as she walked quickly down the long hallway to her classroom.

He grabbed for his cell phone and called Beach.

"It's happened again," he said when he heard his friend's voice on the other end of the line. "Another murder!"

"You're kidding me!" Beach exclaimed. "Who is it this time?"

"Coach Chapman. You're not gonna to believe this, Beach, but it happened while I was giving my speech on safety to the kids. Chap's office has a big window that allows him to see out into the gym. It was open the whole time. The killer must have done it while I was showing the video. Chap had turned out his lights so I couldn't see what was going on inside his office.

"Beach, the killer did this right in front of me!"

"I'm on my way," Beach said, without needing to be asked. "I'll tell Trudy what happened and she can decide what to tell the kids. I'll let my crime scene people know they need to get back to Hillside."

"Thanks, Beach.

He leaned his head against Chap's office doors and closed his eyes for a second, trying to get a grip on the moment. Then he heard Principal Landry's voice over the loud speaker.

"Ladies and gentlemen, may I have your attention. We have detected an electrical problem in our wiring system and need to shut off power to get it corrected. Since the repair work could take some time I am dismissing classes today and I ask that everyone--students, faculty--everyone leave the building immediately. We will follow the same procedure we use when school is closed early for bad weather. Thank you for your cooperation."

Within seconds the doors to the classrooms began to open and the entire student body spilled out into the long, wide corridors. At first, Bill Tom could hear only a small din of chatter but the decibel level rose quickly as more students entered the hallway and everyone began to realize they had just been handed a free day. They stormed out of the building like inmates during a prison raid.

"Poor kids," Bill Tom thought. "Wait until they find out what really happened."

"BT! BT!"

Bill Tom could barely hear Randy calling to him above all the shouts of jubilation.

"I got here as fast as I could," Randy said. "How'd you get all the kids to leave?"

"Landry faked an electrical problem," Bill Tom said, looking down the hallway for Brook.

"Randy, I need you to go through the building and see what you can find. Whoever did this didn't just vanish into thin air. He or she might still be around here somewhere."

"Or else they just walked out with the kids," Randy said, looking out into the parking lot.

Bill Tom nodded his head in agreement. They had absolutely no description of the killer.

"Do me a favor and go to Brook's room first," Bill Tom said, rubbing the back of his neck. "She was supposed to come out with her students, but I don't see her."

"I'm on my way," Randy said.

"And Randy," Bill Tom looked at him and pointed his finger. "Watch your back."

Randy gave him a quick salute and ran down the hallway.

Bill Tom looked out into the parking lot again, feeling about as helpless as he had ever felt in his life.

"I think most of the kids are gone now," Principal Landry said, walking up to Bill Tom. "The cooks, my clerical staff, Melvin, our janitor, everybody's out of the building."

"Then we need to get an ambulance over here right away," Bill Tom said. "Also, we have to let Jennifer Chapman know that her husband has been murdered!"

The sound of his own words brought tears to Bill Tom's eyes. How could he have let this happen? The man was literally sitting in plain sight. However was he going to explain to Jennifer that someone killed her husband while the police chief was watching?

"Bill Tom, Chap was on my staff for seventeen years, I'm the one who has to call Jennifer," Principal Landry said, putting his hand on Bill Tom's shoulder. "I'll tell her that there's been an accident and I'll bring her to the hospital.

"Let's get into Chap's office and call an ambulance."

Principal Landry was about to turn the key in the lock when Randy's excited voice stopped them.

"BT! BT! Come quick. Someone has attacked Brook in her classroom."

Bill Tom took off running down the hallway.

"Get into Chap's office and call that ambulance!" he yelled, looking back at the principal.

Bill Tom ran into Brook's classroom with Randy several steps behind. She was lying at the front of the room next to her desk. There was a bruise on the side of her head, but Bill Tom could tell she was still breathing.

"Brook! Brook!" he called, trying to get her to respond. He knelt down beside her, pulled her into his arms and brushed her hair out of her eyes.

"Brook," he whispered, very tenderly this time, "what happened to you?"

Slowly Brook responded. She opened her eyes, squinted and grimaced in pain, raising her hand to her forehead where a bruise was forming.

"I'm okay, Bill Tom," she said, trying to sit up, but then she groaned and collapsed back into his arms.

"Randy, go find out where that ambulance is and have the attendants come in here first," Bill Tom commanded.

"I'm okay," she said, patting his hand. "I just tried to sit up too quickly. I think he hit me in the head with the dictionary that was on my desk."

Bill Tom looked up and, sure enough, the thick dictionary was lying on the floor next to Brook.

"Who did this to you?" he asked.

"He was hiding under my desk," Brook said. "I stood in front of the desk and was talking to the kids when the announcement came over the public address system. Of course I dismissed the kids immediately and came around my desk to grab my purse. That's when I saw him."

"Saw *who*, Brook? *Who* attacked you?"

"It was Lester Tucker," she said. "He was hiding under my desk, holding some kind of green rope. When I asked him what he was doing there he crawled out, said he didn't mean to hurt anybody and then he grabbed the dictionary. That's the last I remember."

"You're sure it was Lester Tucker?" Bill Tom asked, trying to get all the facts straight.

"Yes, I'm sure. I said, 'Lester, what are you doing under there?' and he climbed out, grabbed the book and everything went blank."

"What's going on in here?"

Brook and Bill Tom turned toward the door at the sound of Doc Schrader's voice.

"Lester Tucker hit Brook over the head with a dictionary," Bill Tom said.

"BT! Mary Ann just called me," Randy said, rushing into the room. "Clyde Voss called the office and said somebody has climbed the winery lookout tower and is threatening to jump. One of his sample room employees thinks it's Lester Tucker!"

"Oh, damn!" Bill Tom exclaimed, shaking his head.

"Brook, I've got to go check this out. Will you be okay with Doc Schrader?"

"Of course," she said, trying to sit up. "I'll be fine. It's just a bump on the head."

"I'll be back," he said, helping her into her desk chair. He tapped Randy on the shoulder.

"Let's go get this guy," he said.

Chapter 49

Hillside High School was just a few blocks from winery hill, home of the Grand Mountain Winery. On their short trip up the hill, Bill Tom and Randy decided that Randy would keep Lester's attention on the ground while Bill Tom climbed up the outer wall of the lookout tower to get the kid.

Randy stopped the squad car at the lower end of the winery, out of Lester's view, to let Bill Tom out. Then, as Bill Tom instructed, he drove around to the front, making sure that Lester saw him.

Bill Tom waited until he could hear Randy talking to the boy.

"Lester, what in the world are you doing up there?" Randy asked.

"I didn't mean to hurt those people," the boy yelled, sobbing. "You go away! You go away or I'll jump. I didn't mean to hurt those people!"

"And I don't want to hurt you, Lester! That's why I'm here, to help you get down from there. That's a dangerous place, sir!"

While Randy held the boy's attention, Bill Tom carefully climbed up the old, rickety winding staircase that had been built on the outside of the tower. He guessed that's how Lester had made it up there. The staircase had been roped off with chains and locked for over a decade because the tower was so old and unstable. He was trying to be quiet, but the steps were very creaky.

"You tell Chief Bradley I didn't mean to hurt those people," Lester repeated. "They just, they just…did some wrong things!"

"If you come down here, I'll get Chief Bradley and you can tell him yourself, Lester," Randy yelled back at the kid. "He's a reasonable man; he'll listen to your side of the story."

After a long, arduous climb, Bill Tom finally reached the top of the stairs that led to the open-air tower. He slowly lifted his right leg over the ledge and tried to hop over without Lester hearing him. But as his foot landed on the concrete floor, his boot slid on some loose gravel and Lester turned around to face him.

"No!" he exclaimed, running toward Bill Tom. "You can't take me! I didn't mean to hurt those people!" The boy started hitting Bill Tom with the green rope he held in his hands.

"Lester, I'm not here to hurt you," Bill Tom said, raising his arms to protect himself from the sting of the rope. "Now calm down and let's go back downstairs and talk about this."

"You don't want to talk about anything," Lester yelled, getting closer and closer to Bill Tom. "You just want to take me away. Just like all those other people tried to do. But I'll keep running from people like you who want to put me away when I didn't mean to hurt those people!"

Bill Tom knew he could reach out, grab that ridiculous rope, and overpower the kid in an instant, but he wanted the boy to keep talking.

What was he really saying? Was he admitting that he killed Esther, Ernie and Chap? And that there had been others in other places where the Tuckers had lived? Were Wanda and Ernie really aware that their kid was capable of murder?

Bill Tom's head was spinning as he kept backing up, circling around the lookout tower.

"Lester, I don't want to hurt you," he said in a low, calm voice. "I just want to get out of this damn lookout tower before it collapses from our weight. It's dangerous up here! Why don't you let me call my deputy and have him come and help us down? Then we can talk about this thing like two grown men."

"I didn't mean to hurt those people!" Lester screamed. He had one hand on each end of the rope now and was holding it in front of him like a weapon.

"Lester, I…"

Without warning, Lester lunged toward Bill Tom, trying to get the rope around his neck. Bill Tom grabbed for the rope; Lester pulled it back, lost his balance and fell over the ledge of the lookout tower. The boy's body slid right down the old steps, doing several summersaults until it landed on the parking lot with a thud.

"Randy, get around to the steps. Lester *fell*!" Bill Tom yelled to his deputy. He jumped over the ledge and ran down the steps as fast as he could to get to the kid.

They reached Lester about the same time and Bill Tom knelt down to see if he was still alive. Amazingly, there was only a small cut on his right arm. His skin was scratched from the old, rotten wood, but other than that there was no external damage.

"He's still breathing," Bill Tom said to Randy. "We need another ambulance!"

"Lester!" He looked down at the boy again and patted him on the check.

"Lester, can you hear me?"

Slowly the boy turned his head and moaned. He opened his eyes slightly and looked at Bill Tom.

"I didn't mean to hurt those…" he whispered, sinking immediately back into an unconscious state.

Winery employees had heard the commotion and were gathering near the side of the building to see what was going on. Bill Tom could hear Clyde Voss trying to get them to move to another part of the winery grounds.

"It's okay, everyone," Clyde was saying, "just a minor little accident. Someone tripped on the stairs and our police chief is trying to help him."

Bill Tom could hear an ambulance siren in the distance. Just then, his cell phone rang. It was Beach.

"Hey, Bill," Beach said. "Just thought you'd like to know, the green fibers from Kayla's room matched the ones found on Esther and Ernie. And I got in touch with the nurse on duty Sunday night. She identified Lester Tucker as the boy who was in Kayla's room."

Chapter 50

After sending Randy back to the high school to wait for Beach and the crime scene team, Bill Tom followed the ambulance to Hillside Community Hospital.

"Has Brook Jennings come in yet?" he asked, as he sprinted up to the Emergency Room check-in desk.

"She's in Exam Room Three," the receptionist said, pointing down the hall to her right. Her name tag indicated that she was Sally Gorman.

"Doctor Schrader rode in the ambulance with her and he's in the room with her now," Sally said. "You can go in if you like. She was asking for you."

"I want to check in on her, but I need to know Lester Tucker's condition as soon as possible. He's the boy they just wheeled in."

"I'll let you know as soon as I know something," Sally assured him.

Bill Tom knocked lightly on the door of Exam Room Three and entered without waiting for an invitation. Brook was sitting up on the side of the exam table and Doc Schrader was checking her eyes.

"Come here and hold my hand," Brook said, extending her arm to him.

"Is she okay, Doc?" Bill Tom asked as he grabbed her hand and kissed it.

"She seems to be," Doc answered. "Her eyes look fine; she's not dizzy or nauseated. She doesn't seem to be groggy. I'm just going to keep her in here for a few hours so we can keep an eye on her."

"Is that really necessary, Doctor Schrader?" Brook asked. "I feel fine. My head is just kind of sore, you know?"

"Just do what he says, Brook," Bill Tom said, wrapping his arm around her shoulders. "He just wants to make sure you're okay. Besides, school's been cancelled for the day. What else do you have to do?"

"Nothing. But I don't want to be a bother when the doctor has other things he has to do."

"You're no bother, Brook," Doc Schrader assured her. "I'm going to put you in one of the ER rooms with a comfortable bed, give you some magazines and let you rest. I just don't want you to fall asleep. If you feel groggy, you've got to call a nurse, okay?"

"You're the doctor," Brook said.

They all turned at the sound of a knock on the door.

"Lester Tucker is in Exam Room One," Sally said. "The attending physician would like to talk to you about him."

Bill Tom squeezed Brook's shoulders and walked down the hall to Exam Room One.

"Hi Bill Tom. Can you tell me what happened to this boy?" The attending physician, Dr. Winston Reed, was examining Lester for broken bones.

"He fell down a flight of stairs at Grand Mountain Winery while I was trying to talk him out of jumping from the lookout tower," Bill Tom said. He watched as two nurses hooked up IVs and vital sign monitors.

"Is he going to be okay?" Bill Tom asked.

"I need to do an MRI," Dr. Reed said. "I can't do that without his parents' permission."

"His mother is Wanda Tucker," Bill Tom said. "She works at the bank. I'll have my deputy go get her. But before I do, I have to know, is he going to be okay?"

"I'll know more after I see the MRI," Dr. Reed answered. "Right now he's breathing on his own. I don't think he has any broken bones and he doesn't seem to be bleeding internally. He's definitely stable for the time-being."

"If he comes to, please have someone come get me as soon as possible. Okay?"

"I'll do that, Chief," Dr. Reed said as he continued his examination.

Bill Tom turned around, walked out of the room, and reached for his cell phone.

"Randy, can you go get Wanda Tucker at the bank and bring her to the hospital?" he asked when he heard his deputy's voice. "Try not to alarm her. Just tell her that Lester had an accident and the doctors are examining him."

Bill Tom found the room where Brook was resting, made sure she was okay and then went to the ER lobby to wait for Wanda and Randy. The area was pretty busy for a small town hospital. People in lab coats were rushing about, carrying trays, pushing carts, and checking the status boards. One old couple and a young mother with a crying child were sitting in the waiting area. He didn't feel like joining them so he just paced back and forth in front of the glass doors of the ER.

Finally he saw Randy's squad car pull up with Wanda inside and he braced himself for a difficult confrontation.

Chapter 51

"He won't tell me anything." The usually soft-spoken Wanda Tucker yelled to Bill Tom as she ran through the doors. Her eyes were wide with fear.

"What happened to Lester? Is he okay? Can I see him? He was fine this…"

"Wanda! Wanda!" Bill Tom whispered. He put his hands on the distraught woman's shoulders. He could feel her shaking.

"He's okay," he said. "I'm going to take you in to him. He's unconscious, but the doctor thinks he's going to be okay. Once you see him, we'll go somewhere private and I'll tell you what happened."

"Randy," Bill Tom looked back at his deputy as he led Wanda down the hall to Lester's exam room, "ask Roger to initiate his emergency high school communications line. He should ask all the kids and the staff if they saw anything or anyone suspicious at the school this morning and, if so, they need to let you know immediately."

Bill Tom reached Lester's ER room and stayed outside while Wanda looked in on her son and gave permission for the MRI.

After they wheeled Lester down the hallway, Bill Tom found a small conference room near the ER, sat Wanda down at a table with a pot of coffee and two cups and told her the whole story. When he finished she stared at him in shock.

"My son is not a murderer," she said in a low voice, her stare daring Bill Tom to disagree with her.

"Wanda, he told me he didn't mean to hurt those people and he was holding a green rope with fibers like the ones found on the victims," he said, trying to reason with the woman. "He hit Brook over the head with a dictionary and knocked her out!"

Wanda stared at him in disbelief as tears started to form in her eyes.

"He's never done anything like this before. We thought the worst was over," she whispered. "He just has such a temper! He keeps all his anger inside until it just explodes."

"What do you mean when you say you thought the worst was over?" Bill Tom asked as he handed the woman a cup of steaming black coffee.

"When he was five years old we had a cat named Perky," Wanda said. "One day Perky jumped up on Lester. He was wearing a sleeveless shirt and her claws accidentally scratched him. Before I could stop him, he grabbed her, threw her to the ground and kicked her, hard. He broke her back and we had to put her to sleep.

"I scolded him, of course, and when Ernie found out about it he spanked Lester and told him he'd never have another pet. All Lester said was, 'That was a bad cat, and she needed to die.' We told our pediatrician about it and she recommended that Lester see a counselor. After a couple of sessions he seemed remorseful for what he had done and we thought that everything was back to normal. A couple years later when he was about seven years old he was playing on the swings with a little girl from his class. She was teasing him because she could swing higher that he could. So he jumped off his swing, grabbed the rope of her swing to make it stop and he knocked her to the ground. Their teacher saw the whole thing and called me.

"We took him back to the counselor, but this time he showed no remorse for what he had done and didn't even seem to understand that his actions were wrong."

Wanda stopped talking long enough to sip some of the hot coffee and dab her eyes with a tissue.

"After that, most people avoided us and none of the kids would play with Lester. So Ernie and I decided to move, to a town about a hundred miles away. We were scared, you know? We hadn't ever thought that he might try to hurt another person."

She stopped talking and looked at Bill Tom.

"What happened then?"

"We kept telling him that what he did was wrong, but he just stared at us and walked away. He never said he was sorry. We found another counselor who told us he needed psychiatric care. Ernie and I

have never had a lot of money, but we managed to take Lester in for
several meetings with a child psychiatrist in Omaha. He told us that
Lester did those things because he had a violent temper. He said he
would need to work with Lester to discover the source of his pent-up
anger."

"How long did the psychiatrist work with him?"

"They met for three more sessions, but Lester never said a
word. The doctor suggested that we send him to a psychiatric
hospital for more in-depth treatment, but we couldn't afford it.

"I knew our insurance would not pay for it. So, after a few
more temper flare-ups, we moved again, to Norfolk, Nebraska."

"Did he ever try to hurt any other children?" Bill Tom asked.

"Mostly he just yelled at people and waved his arms in the
air," Wanda continued. "But last year, when some boys were teasing
him as he walked by the baseball diamond at school, he picked up a
bat and tried to hit one of them on the head. They overpowered him
and beat him up pretty badly. They all got suspended for their
actions, including Lester.

"When Ernie found out about it he hit the roof. He told Lester
that, because of him, we'd have to move and that if he ever did
anything like that again, he'd have him committed to a mental
institution and he'd never see the light of day for the rest of his life.
I'd never seen Ernie so angry."

"How did Lester respond to that?" Bill Tom asked.

"He didn't say a word. He just went to his room and shut the door very quietly."

"And then you moved here?"

"Yes."

Bill Tom sat back in his chair and closed his eyes.

"Wanda," he said with a cough to clear his dry throat, "Lester told me he didn't mean to hurt those people. What could they have done that would have made him angry enough to strangle them?"

"I don't know," Wanda said in a barely audible voice, her eyes once again filling with tears. "I don't believe he did those terrible things. I don't want to believe it."

"It doesn't make sense to me, either," Bill Tom said, shaking his head. "None of it makes any sense, Wanda. We're just going to have to wait until Lester regains consciousness and then ask him to explain his actions. I'm going to put him in protective custody because, once word gets out about…"

Bill Tom was interrupted by the sound of Mayor Adermann's voice booming in the hallway.

"You tell me where Chief Bradley is right now!" he was yelling, no doubt at that nice receptionist, Sally Gorman. "I want to see him right now."

Bill Tom jumped up, excused himself and left Wanda in the conference room while he went out to face the mayor.

"This is a hospital, Mayor. Keep it down," he commanded in a stern, low voice.

"Chief Bradley, I demand to know what's going on!" the little man said, shaking his finger and looking up at Bill Tom. "I hear that Coach Chapman was strangled at the school, while you were there! What kind of protection are you giving this town anyway? I demand a full explanation of your actions, sir! And I want to know right *now*!"

Totally fed up with the guy's pompous attitude, Bill Tom grabbed the mayor by his tie and pulled him down the hall, away from the hospital entrance.

"Let go of me! You let go of me right now!" Adermann's voice shook with indignation. "How dare you! I'll have you fired, sir. And I can do it in a…"

"Split second! I know, Mayor, you've been threatening me with that for a long time," Bill Tom said as he let go of the guy's tie. "You want to fire me, go ahead. Who are you gonna get to clean up this mess?

"We have a person of interest in custody right now and if you'll shut up, go back to your office and let me do what's gotta be done, I'll make a full report to you as soon as I can. But right now you're just in the way and you're slowing things down."

"I want these killings to stop!" Mayor Adermann said, in a calmer, quieter voice.

"Good! That's what I want, too. Finally we agree on something!

"I promise, as soon as I can give you a full report on what's going on I'll call you or drop by your office."

"I'm holding you to that," the mayor said, once again pointing a threatening finger at the chief.

Bill Tom watched the guy walk down the hallway and then he grabbed his cell phone to call Beach.

"Things are going to hell in a hand basket," Bill Tom said when he heard his friend's voice. "Please tell me you and your team are on the way to the high school."

"My team should be at the high school within the hour," Beach said with a sigh. "I'm still in Columbia with Trudy and the kids. Bill, something's come up with your insurance and it looks like the hospital is going to have to release Kayla this morning. It's something about no broken bones, no head trauma, so no hangin' out in a hospital room trying to recover. Apparently recovery happens at home these days.

"Trudy's talking with the doctors, trying to see if there isn't some way they can keep her another night, but right now it looks like we might be bringin' your little girl home today."

Bill Tom sighed heavily into the phone.

"That's just great," he said, running his left hand through his hair. "Do the kids know about Chap?"

"Trudy told them right away. She thought that would be best, with the way kids communicate through social media today. She didn't want them to get the news in a text message from one of their friends.

"Kayla looked stunned, but she held it together," Beach continued. "Brian turned white and ran to the bathroom to puke his guts out. But, that was an hour ago. Right now we're dealing with our latest crisis--how to get a very sore little girl home in a truck.

"I'm talking to you from outside Kayla's room. When I left them they were okay--at least okay for what they've been through."

"Beach, I don't know how to thank you for what you're doing for me," Bill Tom said. He noticed some kids from the high school standing near the entrance of the ER waiting room. Word must have gotten out about Chap and Lester. "Obviously, I'd love to have Kayla home again, but I think it's too soon. If it ends up that they have to release her, you can rent a car so she can stretch out in the back seat? I'll reimburse you when I see you."

All of a sudden Bill Tom heard the noise in the waiting room get louder.

"Something's going on here, Beach, I've got to go," Bill Tom said. "Keep me posted, okay?"

"Up to the minute, pal. You go get 'em!"

Bill Tom walked out into the waiting room. The hospital administrator was trying to get a small group of high school students out of the building.

"Let's keep it down in here," Bill Tom said, approaching the group. "Please do what the man asks and get back outside." He motioned for the kids to follow him.

He waited to speak until the group was assembled outside next to the ER entrance.

"What are you guys doing here?" he asked.

"We heard that Coach Chapman was strangled during your speech at school," one of the boys said, "and that you have a suspect in custody. Is that true?"

"Yes, I'm sorry to say that the Coach was strangled," Bill Tom said. "We have a person of interest in custody right now. It's too early to call that person a suspect. As soon as we have substantive information we can share with you we will do it.

"Did any of you see anything or anybody out of the ordinary this morning when you first got to school?" he asked the four boys and two girls in the group. They all looked like they had been punched in the stomach.

The kids shook their heads slowly and looked back at Bill Tom with blank faces and eyes full of fear.

He stretched out his arms and tried to pull them close to his side, but one of the boys pulled away and gave him a dirty look.

"I know you guys have gone through a horrible ordeal this morning." Bill Tom looked at the boy with pity and understanding…at the moment he didn't like himself either. "But there is something you can do to make things a little better," he said, patting their shoulders.

"You can go home, or to a friend's house and stay there. Mr. Landry is sending out an email to see if he can find some people who may have seen something suspicious. My best advice to you is to stay home. Order a pizza. Say your prayers. That's what we need now.

"I promise you, we'll share vital information as we receive it," Bill Tom said.

"Tell Kayla and Brian we're praying for them," one of the girls said as the group turned to leave.

Chapter 52

Once the kids drove off the parking lot, he walked back inside to continue his talk with Wanda.

"She's in ER Three," Sally Gorman called to him as he was about to go into the conference room. "She's waiting for her son to get back from the MRI."

Bill Tom walked briskly down to ER Three, knocked softly and entered the room.

He found another chair in the corner, pulled it up and sat next to her near the bed.

"Wanda, I'm sorry I have to keep asking you questions right now, but I've got to get to the bottom of this whole thing. Do you understand?" he asked, leaning forward to pat the woman's hand.

"I understand, Chief," she said much calmer than she had been earlier. "But I want you to know that I just can't believe that there's any way my son committed these horrible crimes, especially strangling his father. They had their disagreements, but I know they loved each other. I just can't..."

Wanda was interrupted by a knock on the door.

"Is it okay if I come in?" Brook asked, peeping in behind the door. "I was feeling a little groggy and Dr. Schrader suggested I take a walk. He told me that he thought you guys might be here. If this is a private conversation, I'll leave."

Bill Tom looked at Wanda with raised eyebrows and she nodded her head.

"Come in and join us, Brook," Wanda said, as she and Bill Tom both stood up. "You take my chair. I hear my son hit you on the head and knocked you out. I'm so sorry. I can't imagine why he would do something like that."

"Don't think about it, Wanda," Brook said, sinking into the chair Wanda offered her. "Sometimes our kids do things that even they can't explain." Brook looked up at Bill Tom, who was now sitting on the side of the bed so Wanda could have his chair.

"Wanda, I need to ask you some questions about a green rope that Lester was holding when he fell," Bill Tom said, looking down at the lady. She looked very fragile from his new vantage point.

"What green rope?" Wanda asked.

"When I tried to talk to Lester before he fell down the steps, he was holding a long piece of green rope--it looked like the kind of thing people use to tie back curtains or drapes. Do you know where he got it?"

"Not from our house," Wanda said, shaking her head slowly. "I've never used tie-backs. I don't have any idea where he got it, or what it meant to him."

"We found traces of green thread on all of our strangled victims, Wanda," Bill Tom said, as gently as he could. "Our crime scene investigators discovered that the threads from that rope match the threads on our victims.

"Wanda," he continued, leaning down to take her hand, "I need to hear what Lester has to say about the rope. I may have no choice but to arrest him, do you understand?"

Wanda quickly pulled her hand away from Bill Tom and buried her head in both her hands.

"I know he didn't do it, Chief, I just know it! And now he's in a coma and can't speak for himself. I don't even know if he's going to live or…and I just lost Ernie. I feel so alone."

Brook walked over to the distraught woman's side, sliding her arm around Wanda's shoulders.

"Maybe we could let her rest for a while, Bill Tom," Brook suggested. "She's had an awful lot to deal with here this morning."

"I don't want to rest," Wanda protested, shaking herself loose from Brook's grip. "I want to get to the bottom of this. *Now!*"

She gave Bill Tom a defiant look as she hit the chair arm with her fist.

"Wanda," he said, with a heavy sigh, "I've told you, I can't exclude him as a suspect until I get a chance to talk to him. His behavior has been so bizarre."

Bill Tom looked up at the ceiling and closed his eyes. His head was pounding.

"Brook," he said, trying a different approach to his questioning, "you had Lester in class for just a couple of days, but did you notice anything out of the ordinary about his behavior during that time? I mean, anything that would have warned you that he might lose his temper or hit you?"

Brook shook her head slowly, meeting Bill Tom's questioning stare.

"No, he was a very quiet boy, but also very polite," she said, remembering those first two days of school. "He didn't say much in class--wouldn't participate unless I asked him a direct question, but when I did, he always knew the answer. He completed his homework assignments and..."

Suddenly Brook's eyes grew wide and she looked at Bill Tom and then at Wanda.

"Wait a minute," she said, "I do remember something unusual that happened with Lester. As a get-to-know-you exercise, I asked the kids to complete a sentence starting with 'I am...' They could say whatever they wanted to say. It could be a long answer or a short answer, whatever. Lester wrote, 'I am a puppet with clean gloves.'

"Do you know what that means, Wanda?"

Brook and Bill Tom stared at Wanda expectantly.

Wanda looked at both of them as her eyes welled up with tears. She threw her hands over face and began to cry again.

"I can't believe he still remembers that," she said between sobs. "He must be in so much pain from the past."

"What does it mean, Wanda?" Bill Tom asked, leaning down toward the woman.

"When Lester was in the second grade, his teacher played a game with the children. One child played the part of a puppet and the other child was the puppeteer. She asked the puppets to put on plastic gloves and she tied string to both of their wrists. She put a sheet of paper on the table, in front of the place where each puppet was sitting. The puppets got to choose their favorite finger paint color. The puppeteers were supposed to write their names on the paper by guiding the puppets hands with the string. The winner of the game was the puppeteer whose name was written the most legibly.

"The teacher asked the students to choose partners and decide which role each would play," Wanda said, wiping her tears with her right hand. "There was an uneven number of students in the class, so when all the teams were chosen, Lester was left without a partner.

"The teacher told Lester that as soon as they finished the game, one of the students would take a turn with him. But in the end, all the students refused. The teacher used everything but physical force to persuade someone from the group to play the game with him, but no one wanted to touch him or be touched by him. She offered to play the game with him, but he just looked at her and then ran out of the room. She called me that night to tell me about the incident, but when I asked Lester about it he just shrugged his shoulders and said it was no big deal. Apparently, it was."

Bill Tom watched Brook wipe a tear from her cheek as he reached down to pat Wanda on the shoulder.

"Kids can be very cruel," he said. "I guess we all have our hurtful childhood memories, but…"

Suddenly the door to the ER room opened and two orderlies wheeled Lester in on a stretcher. Dr. Reed followed them into the room.

"We'll have the results of the MRI in a little while," he said, looking at the group. "Right now, let's just focus on the positive things we know. He has no broken bones, he has a good strong heartbeat and all his vital signs are normal."

"How soon do you think he will wake up from this coma, or whatever it is?" Bill Tom asked.

"I have no idea, Chief," the doctor said. "Could be an hour, a day, a week, or a month. Your guess is as good as mine. Unless the MRI shows that there's some serious internal damage, my guess is that he'll wake up sooner rather than later."

As soon as the orderlies lifted Lester back onto the ER bed, Wanda walked over to hold his hand.

"Are you telling us that my son will live?" she asked in a quivering voice.

"I'm telling you that his vital signs are stable and he has no external life-threatening injuries," the doctor said, walking over to her side. "He has quite a bit of bruising from the fall, but I have no reason right now to think that his condition is critical at this time unless the MRI tells us differently. He is in a coma, though, and we will have to monitor him constantly until he wakes up."

Doctor Reed nodded politely to the group and turned to leave.

"If you need me for anything, Mrs. Tucker, I'm on duty all day and the ER nurses will know how to get in touch with me."

Chapter 53

"I need to put a guard by Lester's door," Bill Tom said quietly as he followed the doctor into the hallway. "I don't know how many people may have heard about what he did, or even that he is a person of interest in the deaths of three people, but I can't take the chance that someone might decide to seek premature justice. I know tensions around here are running pretty high."

"We have four security guards on duty round the clock here. They can take a turn keeping watch," the doctor said.

"Thank you. We really need and appreciate your help!"

The doctor started down the hall toward the nurses' station, stopped and turned around to face Bill Tom.

"Chief," he said, "I don't want to try to tell you how to do your job, but do you think maybe it's time to bring in the FBI, or some law enforcement officials from the state? We've got a serious problem here and, please forgive me, but I don't see that you guys are making any progress to find and stop this killer. And now you have Kayla's hit and run driver to find. Maybe it's all just too much for you right now."

The doctor's words cut through Bill Tom like a knife...because they were true.

"We've had a former FBI profiler and some crime scene investigators on the case since we found Esther's body," Bill Tom said. "They've been working non-stop to put all our clues together. Now we have a suspect in custody. If it turns out that Lester is not our killer, I'll turn the case over to the FBI."

Dr. Reed nodded his head and turned to walk down the hall.

Bill Tom, aching from that uncomfortable encounter, escaped into the privacy of the hospital conference room to call Beach.

"Hey, buddy, any word on Kayla?" he asked as he heard the familiar voice on the other end of the phone.

"We're on our way home, Bill," Beach said. "We have her tied to the top of the truck."

"As long as she's comfortable." The chief tried to act normal.

"No, we're taking good care of her, my friend," Beach said. "Your insurance company wouldn't budge on their position, so the hospital released her about fifteen minutes ago and we're on our way to Hillside. The doctor gave her some pretty strong pain medication, plus a mile-long list of stuff you need to pick up at the drug store. She's sound asleep in the backseat of this full-size Pontiac we rented. Brian keeps turning around to check on her and Trudy's following us in my truck. She didn't want to drive the rental. The hospital admissions office gave us some old phone books for her to sit on so she could see over the steering wheel of my truck. I didn't realize she was so short. I don't know how she's reaching the pedals."

Bill Tom smiled slightly at the visual image.

"Just as long as you all arrive back here in one piece I'll be happy," Bill Tom said. "I haven't heard from Randy, so I assume your crime scene crew made it to the school?"

"Yep! They're on it. I just got a call from the crew leader. Green fibers in the neck wound, fingerprints all over the place. It's your basic Hillside forensic nightmare."

"Our principal, Roger Landry, sent out an email asking that any student who may have seen something unusual call our office. I'm hoping someone will come forward with some information we can use," Bill Tom said, peeking through the blinds of the conference room window. I'm gonna leave here now and go home to get the place ready for Kayla," Bill Tom said. "Brook and I will want to be there when you guys arrive."

"I'll see you then, buddy," Beach said.

Bill Tom started to walk out of the room and almost ran into Roger Landry and Jennifer Chapman, the coach's wife.

At first, he didn't think Landry had told her what happened. She was impeccably dressed in a blue pant suit that complemented her neatly styled shoulder-length blond hair that glisten in the light. Her make-up was in perfect condition--no tear stained cheeks, no runny mascara. She was an extremely attractive woman.

"Jen," he said, looking at Roger Landry for guidance. "I'm so …"

"I'm okay, Bill Tom," she said, looking at him with a serious expression. "I was afraid that someday something like this might happen."

"Why don't we go back into the conference room?" Principal Landry suggested.

"Could I get you some coffee or would you like one of the doctors to give you a sedative or something?" Bill Tom asked as they sat at the table.

"Really, I'm fine," the coach's wife insisted. "Let me make sure both of you understand, I'm brokenhearted but I'm not surprised. Chap has had a number of affairs with his nubile teenage cheerleaders and female athletes. I'm not surprised that some father finally decided to seek revenge. I loved him and I think he loved me…but I could never understand why he had to fool around with those girls. I kept hoping he would grow up."

With that, Jennifer Chapman broke into tears.

"I had no idea any of this was going on," Bill Tom said.

"I put up with it because I loved him and because I had twin boys to raise. I don't want them to know about their father's actions. It would break their hearts."

Bill Tom looked at the woman in shocked disbelief. He had spent many happy days with Chap, going to sporting events, watching everything from football to golf on TV, playing on the church softball league in the summer. He was totally unaware of his friend's extracurricular activities. During his frequent visits to the Chapman's home, Jennifer was always a charming hostess and everyone seemed happy.

He had pleasant memories of barbecues on the Chapman's deck, when, after a delicious meal, he and Chap would sink down onto the family room couch to watch the St. Louis Cardinals on TV while Jennifer and Sarah laughed and talked over coffee in the kitchen and Kayla and the boys played Ping-Pong in the basement. The Chapman's had seemed like the ideal family.

Now he looked at the woman sitting at the conference room table and felt like he never really knew his friend.

"Jen," he said, grabbing for the hand she had resting on the table, "I'm so sorry for what happened between you and Chap. You have to believe me, he never said a word about it to me. I talked to him this morning and…"

All of a sudden, Bill Tom remembered the picture in the newspaper of the Hillside drill team on Chap's wall and the cryptic note Mindy Arnold had written.

"And what?" Jennifer asked between sobs.

"And we talked about sports as usual," Bill Tom said, deciding not to say anything about the picture.

"Is Chap here?" she asked suddenly. "I'd like to see him, if possible."

"The ambulance hasn't brought him in yet," Roger Landry said.

"It's a crime scene investigation," Bill Tom explained. "They examine everything, from the victim's body to the fingerprints found at the site. In this case, they found green fibers on Chap's neck, which means that he was probably killed by the same person who strangled Esther Gaines and Ernie Tucker."

"What's going on, Bill Tom?" Jennifer asked. "Who in the world is doing all this killing?"

Jennifer looked at Bill Tom with pain and fear in her eyes.

"I think they were all killed by a very sick person with a grudge against each one of them. It's my job to find that person," Bill Tom said. "Do you want me to call the boys, Jen? I'll do whatever I can to help."

"Just go get whoever did this," Jen said, shaking her head. She turned her attention to Roger Landry.

"Roger would you please stay with me while I call the boys? I want to stay here until I can see Chap." The Chapman twins were sophomores at Michigan State.

Bill Tom gave the woman a tight hug as she and Roger Landry stood up to leave the room.

Once he was alone he slumped down into one of the chairs, put his elbows on the table and pressed his hands against his throbbing temples. He looked at his watch and jumped up with a start. He had momentarily forgotten that Beach was on his way home with Kayla.

He quickly walked down the hall to get Brook, told Wanda to call them if she needed them and then headed home to greet Kayla.

Chapter 54

The blinds were closed and the curtains were pulled tightly shut in Kayla's room. The bright sunlight still managed to provide enough light so Brook and Bill Tom could look at their daughter, home at last and nestled comfortably in her own bed, with Moonshine snuggled against her.

With their arms around each other, they looked down at the sleeping girl. In the soft light, the bruises on her face were almost invisible. Whatever the doctor had given her, it was enough to knock her out cold. She slept soundly through the sixty-mile trip home from the hospital and didn't even wake up when Bill Tom lifted her out of the rental car and carried her up the stairs to her bedroom.

As they stared at Kayla, Bill Tom could hear the din of chatter in his living room rising to a higher decibel level.

"We'd better get downstairs and see what's up," he whispered to Brook, gently squeezing her shoulder. "I think she'll be okay without us for a little while."

Brook smiled at him and the two happy and relieved parents made their way downstairs to join Beach, Trudy and Brian.

"Randy just called," Beach said, looking at the pair. "He's on his way back to the high school to look at some school surveillance tapes from this morning. Mary Ann asked him to tell us she needs us at the office as soon as possible. She got a call from some people in Hillside who think their daughters are missing."

"Missing daughters?" Bill Tom asked. "Did he give you any names?"

"Yeah, he told me, but I didn't write them down," Beach said. "I figured we'd just hop in our trucks and get over there now."

"You boys take these sandwiches with you," Trudy said, walking into Bill Tom's living room with a sack full of food.

"Trudy, you amaze me," Bill Tom said, reaching down to hug the tiny woman. "Only you would think about feeding us at a time like this."

"Actually, I didn't think of it," she said, looking past Bill Tom and winking at Beach who was standing behind him.

"Beach thought of it, so we stopped at The Food Pantry as soon as we got into town. Now you two guys get going before Randy calls again. He seemed pretty uptight."

The two men said their good-byes and headed in their separate trucks to Bill Tom's office, twelve blocks away.

"Oh, you're back!" Mary Ann exclaimed, clapping her hands together as the two men entered her office. She jumped up from her chair, and gave each of them a hug.

"It's just terrible about the coach, Chief," she said, grabbing Bill Tom's hands. "I know you guys were close friends. I just can't imagine that this happened while you were at the school giving a speech!"

"Neither can anyone else," Bill Tom said. "The whole town is probably wondering what kind of police chief would let a man get killed right in front of him!"

Saying the words out loud made the pain in Bill Tom's heart feel more acute, and for a moment he felt nauseated.

"Hey, Bill," Beach said, "don't even go down that road. How many people do you know who can see clearly in the dark from such a distance?"

Bill Tom gave his friend a forced smile and slapped him on the shoulder.

"You're right," he said. "Besides, there's no time for me to feel sorry for myself right now. We've got work to do. Mary Ann, have you heard anything from Randy? And what's this about some missing girls?"

"Randy drove over to the high school to look at the surveillance tape with Roger Landry," MaryAnn said, walking back to her desk. She sat down in her chair and picked up a sheet of paper with scribbled notes on it.

"The Freemans and the Steins returned from their South American mission trip early this morning," Mary Ann began her story. "You know, Dr. Freeman goes down there every year with a bunch of dentists who work on the natives' teeth. The Steins went along to conduct a Bible school for the children. They've been gone since the first of August.

'Anyway, their daughters--Jessica and Breanna--were going to leave for college--the University of Miami--on the day after Esther's funeral. The girls had already shipped most of their stuff down to Miami by UPS so all they had to take with them were two small carry-on suitcases. The plan was that the girls would drive Dr. and Mrs. Freeman's van to the St. Louis airport and leave it in the long-term parking garage until the couples returned from their trip.

"When they arrived in Houston last night, the first thing they did, of course, was try to call their girls," Mary Ann continued, reading from her notes. "While they were in the Interior--that's what they call the jungle down there--the Interior--they were unable to contact them. The girls didn't answer their cell phones. They thought the girls might be at the library or a movie or something so they weren't worried until they tried to retrieve their van, and the parking lot attendant had no record of it ever showing up."

"Where are the Freemans and the Steins right now?" Bill Tom jumped in with a question when Mary Ann stopped talking long enough to take a breath.

"They were still in St. Louis, at the Marriott Hotel across from the airport," Mary Ann said. "They were waiting for a call from the school to see if the girls ever checked in. They tried all night to contact the girls on their cell phones, but neither of them picked up.

They left them numerous messages. If the school says the girls checked in, they're going to get the first plane out to Miami. They said it's not like either one of them to ignore a cell phone message. They're confused because of the van and the fact that the girls didn't follow that part of the plan--they're very responsible girls, you know. Dr. Freeman thinks that maybe the van was malfunctioning and the girls were afraid it would break down and they'd get stuck out on the highway or something, so maybe they got a friend to take them. It's not like they could contact their parents to let them know what was going on."

"When they called here, what did they want us to do?" Bill Tom asked. "Did they want us to search their houses?"

"Absolutely!" Mary Ann said. "Dr. and Mrs. Freeman said their neighbor--Elda Applebaum--has a key to their home and the Steins gave me their garage door entrance code. Dr. Freeman wants you to see if the van is still in the garage and if you can start it. There's an extra set of keys in an old tin box on the counter by the door."

"Do you want me to check this out?" Beach asked Bill Tom as he chomped into one of the sandwiches Trudy had made for them. "I know you're anxious to talk to Randy about that school surveillance tape."

"I'd appreciate that," Bill Tom said with a sigh. "I really need to find out what was on that tape.

"Mary Ann, will you give Beach directions to those houses so he can go check things out?"

"Of course I will, Chief," she said, tearing off a clean sheet of paper from her notepad. "You go do what you have to do; I've got things covered here."

"Thanks Mary Ann," he said, giving her a thumb's up. "I'll be in my office if you need me."

"I'll be in touch," Beach said looking at the map Mary Ann drew for him. "I don't think I can get lost with these directions. Is this a building, a church or a winery?" he asked, smiling at Mary Ann.

Bill Tom shut the door to his office, leaving Mary Ann and Beach alone to decipher the map.

He sank into his oversized executive chair, put his head in his hands and tried to think clearly. He was worried now about the two missing girls, but he couldn't wrap his arms around the problem just yet. He was still agonizing over Coach Chapman and his brief conversation with Dr. Reed.

Another murder! And this time he was actually in the same building, looking into the very office where the murder was committed.

In his mind's eye he tried to recreate his actions during his speech to see if he could remember what he saw in Chap's office while he was on that stage. But it was no use. His mind was racing with all kinds of images and thoughts...Kayla coming home, Brook getting hit over the head, the confrontations with Lester Tucker and the mayor, his meeting with Wanda, his talk with Jennifer Chapman and the stinging words from Dr. Reed. The disturbing news about two girls from Hillside who were apparently missing was more than he could handle at the moment.

"I've got to get a grip," he said out loud, pounding his fist on his desk.

He picked up his cell phone and dialed his home number.

"Hey, Hon," he said, as he recognized Brook's familiar voice.

"This isn't 'Hon,' this is Trudy," he heard the voice say.

He laughed into the phone.

"Hey, Trudy, I was just calling to make sure Brook and Kayla weren't there alone. It sounds like you've got that covered."

"You're not to worry Bill, Brian and I wouldn't let them out of our sight," Trudy said. "Since Brook's not supposed to sleep, she's dusting your living room to keep active; I'm cleaning your kitchen. Brian's upstairs with Sleeping Beauty who has not budged since you left. We've got the doors locked and we're not leaving here. Nobody gets in or out—unless Moonshine has to go potty."

"Thanks for all your help, Trudy. I'll see you guys later. Call me if you need anything." He smiled into the phone as he hung up. Then he called Randy.

"Any luck with those video tapes?" he asked, hopefully.

"There's just one video—the camera is focused on the front entrance. It shows a bunch of kids entering the school, talking to each other, waving to their friends. Landry watched it over and over again and said he was pretty sure that, by the way they were dressed, everyone on the video was a student who should have been there, including, by the way, Lester Tucker. I watched that part of the video and he walked in late, right before the tardy bell, holding his books with both hands, close to his chest, head down. He looked like he'd rather be going to the dentist than going to school.

"One thing, though. I don't know how Landry could know for sure that every person coming into the building was a student who actually belonged here. Some of the girls were wearing their school jackets with the hoods over their heads. He says that's typical for girls with first hour gym. They wash their hair at home, come to school with it wet and then dry it when they take a shower after gym class."

"Okay, Randy, thanks for hanging in there. How's Beach's crew doing?"

"They're all fascinated by this killer's sense of humor," Randy said, with a sigh. "I heard them talking and one of the guys said it was like the killer is laughing at all of us behind our backs. Do you think that's true, BT? Do you think the killer's here in Hillside somewhere, just sitting back and laughing at us?"

"I do, Randy. I think the killer is toying with us for fun. Just remember, 'He who laughs last, laughs best.' Who said that? Do you know?"

"Don't have a clue, BT."

"Well, anyway, whoever is doing this will stop laughing the minute I get a hold of him. I've got to get back to work over here so I'm going to let you go. Just stay with the crew and help them get what they need to gather evidence, okay?

"Will do, BT."

He was about to sit back in his chair to read some mail stacked on his desk when he heard someone talking loudly to Mary Ann.

"Now what's going on?" he thought as he jumped up and headed toward his office door.

Chapter 55

"What's going on out here?" he asked, walking into the outer office. The man who was making all the noise was Andrew Arnold, Mindy's father.

"I was just telling Mary Ann that I must have a backed up sewer at home and our only town plumber is busy," the man said in an exasperated tone. "The wife and I got home from the lake and the house smells like an outdoor toilet."

"Andy, just exactly what do you think we can do about that?" Bill Tom asked, looking the man straight in the eye.

"Nothing, Bill Tom," Andy said. "I was just making conversation with Mary Ann. Actually, we stopped by The Food Pantry on our way home and the checker told us what happened to Kayla and Brian. I came by to say how sorry we were to hear about it. The driver was probably some half deaf, half blind ole' geezer who has no business behind the wheel of a car!"

Andy extended his arm to shake hands with Bill Tom.

Bill Tom shook hands with the guy and thanked him for his concern. He wondered what Andy would say if he knew that his own daughter and her boyfriend had been suspects in the hit and run.

"Actually, witnesses say that there were two young people in the car, Andy," Bill Tom said. "You may as well know, you're going to hear it sooner or later, we questioned Mindy and Todd Mack about the accident. The car that hit Kayla and Brian was a red Mustang and the witnesses who saw the accident said that the passenger in the car was a young woman with long blond hair."

Andy pulled his hand away from Bill Tom's and gave him a defiant look.

"You mean just because it was a car like Todd's and a long-haired blond was in the front seat you suspect that my daughter was part of a hit and run accident? What's wrong with you, Bill Tom? Talk about grasping at straws!"

"There's more to it than that," Bill Tom said, motioning for the man to move into his office. "Why don't you come in and sit down and we can talk."

Mary Ann followed the two into the room with two cups of coffee.

"Is black okay, Mr. Arnold?" she asked with a smile as she handed him the cup.

"It's fine, Mary Ann," he said, in a calmer voice. "Thanks."

"My pleasure, Mr. Arnold," she said patting the man on the back as she left the room.

After Bill Tom explained the similarities in the license plates and the tiff that Kayla and Mindy had on the MIZZOU campus about the ring, Andrew Arnold seemed to agree that Bill Tom had been right to check things out with Todd and Mindy.

"I know you have to cover all the bases, Bill Tom," he said. "I also hope you know that my Mindy would never do something so terrible to anyone. She has a rough edge to her, I know that. I also know that she has a smart mouth--she gets that from her mother--but down deep she's a good kid."

Bill Tom nodded his head and kept his mouth shut. He had his own opinions about Mindy Arnold, and they were quite different from those of her father.

"One thing I don't understand is about this ring business," Andy said, wrinkling his forehead. "I know that Esther didn't give Mindy any ring and I don't think Todd did, either. Mindy has a nice dinner ring that her mother and I gave her for her birthday last year. Maybe Kayla mistook it for Esther's ring."

"Maybe so," Bill Tom conceded. He was in no mood to get into a debate about jewelry with Andy Arnold. He didn't approve of the way the guy was raising his daughter. How could he give his kid an expensive dinner ring and then choose to go to the lake instead of taking her to college to begin her freshman year? He was willing to give her material things but not his time. Something was rotten in the Arnold household--and it wasn't just a backed up sewer.

"Andy, have you talked to Mindy since you got back from the lake?" he asked. He was actually feeling a bit sorry for the girl.

"No, you know how kids are," Andy said, shrugging his shoulders. "She's got her own life now, that's what she always wanted. She's probably happy that we're not bothering her. I guess she'll come home for the holidays, you know, Thanksgiving and Christmas."

Bill Tom really didn't want to get into a parenting debate with the guy, but he just couldn't help pursuing the subject.

"Don't you think that she would like to know that you guys miss her and love her?" he asking, raising his eyebrows.

"I don't think she's interested in our love," Andy said, tipping his cup to get the last drop of coffee. "I think she's happy to have us out of her life!"

He set the cup on Bill Tom's desk and stood up to leave. He was obviously anxious to end the conversation with such an uncomfortable subject matter.

"It seems like she has always tried to put distance between us," Andy said risking a look into Bill Tom's eyes. "I wanted a little girl who would look at me like I was the greatest man on earth—the way Kayla looks at you. Instead I got a child who rarely even makes eye contact with me and has always made it clear she'd rather be somewhere else than in my company."

Bill Tom watched as the man struggled to keep his composure.

"I'm sorry, Bill Tom," Andy continued, "I just can't talk about Mindy right now."

He reached across the desk, shook hands with Bill Tom and walked out of the office.

Bill Tom heard Mary Ann tell him goodbye, but he did not respond.

A few seconds later, she peeked in the doorway of Bill Tom's office.

"Everything alright in here?" she asked.

"It's okay," he answered, looking up at her. "We were having a heart-to-heart talk about daughters. Emotions just got a little too close to the surface."

Mary Ann nodded and disappeared behind the door as Bill Tom leaned forward to tackle the mail on his desk.

It took him about sixty seconds to realize that he'd had it. He just couldn't concentrate on any one thing. Not too far in the back of his mind he was harboring the fear of what Kayla would say to her mom and dad when she woke up at home.

He tried to call Beach and discovered that the battery in his cell phone was too low to get a signal. He hadn't recharged it since Saturday morning when they had gone to hear Kayla and Brian's presentation at Lincoln University.

Lifting his office phone off its cradle, he rifled through the papers on his desk to see if he had Beach's number written down somewhere. He finally found it in a stack of business cards and quickly made the call.

"Hey, Beach, what's going on?" he asked as he heard his friend's voice. "It's not good news, Billy," Beach said with a sigh. "The Freeman's van is still parked in their garage and it started right away. The girls' overnight bags are in the family room next to the garage door.

"There's no sign of violence. Whatever happened is anybody's guess. I called Randy and asked him to come over and help me. We're going to contact all the neighbors; I thought they would be more comfortable if they were talking to a familiar face."

"That's a good idea, Beach," Bill Tom said. "Keep me posted, okay? I'm going to call the Freemans and the Steins to let them know what's going on."

He clicked the telephone switch hook and dialed information for the St. Louis area. He knew he had the Marriot number written down somewhere, but he didn't want to take the time to look for it.

"Your van is still in the garage," he said as he heard Dr. Freeman's voice on the other end of the line. "Randy is talking to all of your neighbors to see if they saw anything."

"We've already called all our neighbors," Dr. Freeman said. "They didn't see anything out of the ordinary. They did say there were a lot of kids stopping by to see the girls on the Saturday before they were going to leave. I guess that was after Esther's funeral.

"I just can't believe what happened to her and to that organist at your church. What in the world is going on out there, Bill Tom?"

Bill Tom ran his fingers though his hair and closed his eyes. He had more bad news for the worried doctor.

"Harold, there's more bad news. This morning someone strangled Coach Chapman while he was in his office at school. It happened while I was showing a video on personal safety to the entire student body, if you can believe that. The last two weeks in Hillside have been a nightmare."

He decided not to mention the hit and run incident with Kayla and Brian. He'd given the doctor enough to digest.

"Who's doing this, Bill Tom? Do you have any leads? Nothing like this has ever happened in Hillside. That's why we felt safe leaving the girls when we left for South America. They were staying together at our house and we were comfortable with that…as long as neither of them was alone. Do you think whoever is doing this got them, too?"

Bill Tom could hear the anxiety in the doctor's voice, coupled with the hint of accusation that the police chief wasn't doing his job very well.

"Harold, let's not jump to conclusions, that's not going to do us or the girls any good. I want you to contact the University of Miami. Find out if the girls checked in and, either way, ask someone at the school to contact the local police to put out an all-points bulletin with their description.

"I'm going to call the Missouri and Florida state police departments and explain what happened so they can alert their squad cars to be on the lookout for the girls.

"I already have a former FBI agent working with me on the murders. He'll help with the girls' disappearance, too.

"In the meantime, I'm going to do whatever I can to help you find the girls."

"And what should we do, Chief?" the doctor asked. There was a crack in his voice and Bill Tom knew he was fighting back tears of concern and worry.

"Don't jump to conclusions," Bill Tom said. "Call the school; see what they say. Take one step at a time. If the girls did not show up for registration, come on home immediately. You know who their best friends are so you can give me a list of names and we'll talk to all of them. Someone has to have seen something!

"Just don't give up and don't let your mind go to places it doesn't need to go! Try to keep calm and--pray! We'll find your girls!"

"We'll try to do that, Chief."

Chapter 56

Bill Tom hung up and immediately dialed his home phone number.

"Hi Brook is Kayla still asleep or did she finally wake up?"

"Hi. Yes, she did. She doesn't want to see me but--you won't believe this--she and Brian are doing chemistry homework up in her room. They've both had something to eat and, although she's pretty weak, she seems to be alert and really ready to get back into her normal routine. At least that's what Trudy says."

"They're doing chemistry, huh," Bill Tom asked. "Are you sure it's book chemistry and not body chemistry?"

"Trudy's keeping an eye on them. Anyway, what's the harm if they steal a kiss or two? It's obvious those two kids are in love. I hardly think either one of them is up to much more than a little making out. Remember making out?"

"I remember it well and I know where it leads," Bill Tom said, laughing slightly. "By the way, how are you feeling?"

"I feel like a woman who's been hit over the head with a big book. I've got a headache and a bump on my forehead, but otherwise I'm fine."

As Bill Tom hung up the phone he said a silent prayer of thanks to God that Kayla was home safely. He also prayed that she would find it in her heart to forgive him, and not treat him like he had treated his mother. He didn't even know if the woman was still alive.

He quickly made the necessary calls to the Florida and Missouri state police departments and then he called Roger Landry.

"Roger, how's Jennifer doing?" he asked.

"About as good as can be expected," Roger answered. "I stayed with her while she called her boys—that was tough—and then I waited until one of her friends came over to the hospital to be with her. It's just such a sad situation."

"I know you've had a tough day," Bill Tom said, "but I need your help with something. Can you get me a list of all the kids in the senior class that graduated in June? Jessica Freeman and Breanna Stein were supposed to register at the University of Miami last week and they never made it. Their parents are worried and so am I. I want to contact some of their friends who may still be in town."

There was silence at the other end of the line.

"Roger? Are you there?"

"What in the world is going on in this town?" the principal asked, obviously upset. "It seems like all of a sudden everything is falling apart."

Bill Tom took a deep breath.

"Roger, there's a killer on the loose, probably a serial killer with an axe to grind. That's one big problem. The other big problem now is two missing girls, but I have no way of knowing and nothing to indicate that the one issue is related to the other. Let's deal with facts and not speculate.

"Can you get me that list of names? And I'll need phone numbers, too, okay?"

"I'll fax the list to your office as soon as possible, Bill Tom," Roger said. "I'm in the middle of an emergency school board meeting. Everyone has agreed that, under the circumstances, it will be best if we close the school for the rest of the week. I finally found Brook--at your house--and asked her if she was up to preparing a brief notice that we can send to our school families. By now almost everyone has heard what really happened this morning. She's writing the notice now. When the board approves it, my secretary will send it out as a broadcast email.

"Bill Tom, I may as well tell you, Adermann is here, too, and he's asking the board to recommend to the town council that you be relieved of your duties as police chief," Roger sighed. "Some of the board members voiced similar opinions. I want you to know that I'm not included in that group, but I can see that everyone is on edge."

"I appreciate your support, Roger. I understand their concern. I am concerned too. We're doing the best we can and I promise you that we will find this person and bring him to justice. You have my word on that."

Bill Tom hung up the phone and put his head in his hands. With a deep sigh he pushed himself away from his desk and walked out to talk to Mary Ann.

"I've got to get out of here," he said, looking at her and shaking his head. "I can't seem to concentrate in there. I'm not sure where I'm going, but I need to find a place to think."

"Before you go will you sign these checks, Chief? I need to pay these bills today," Mary Ann asked as she held up a stack of paper.

He bent down to sign the checks and suddenly looked up at her.

"Just think, Mary Ann, a couple of weeks ago there were days when this was one of the most difficult things I did!"

"I know, Chief," she said with a slight smile. "And I also know we'll get back to those days again. You're going to find this sick person and stop all this senseless killing. I have faith in you!"

"How could I get along without you, Mary Ann?"

"You couldn't," she said, grinning at him, "that's why I'm still working at 68!"

"I'll see you later," he said.

As he walked out the door he stopped abruptly and headed back inside.

"I'm going to lock the outer door since you're here alone," he said to her. "If anybody knocks, ask who it is and what they want before you let them in, okay?"

"Okay, Chief. Thanks."

Chapter 57

Bill Tom closed the door and tested it to make sure it was locked. He dug into his pocket for his keys and started to walk across the small parking lot toward his truck. All of a sudden he stopped and looked up at the sky. During the last two weeks he hadn't really noticed the subtle changes that were beginning to take place as summer was fading into fall. Although the temperature was still in the mid-eighties, the gentle breeze was fresh and the sky was a brilliant blue with just a few billowy white clouds floating around. The trees were beginning to turn and the burning bush that Mary Ann had planted in front of the building on her first day of work some seventeen years earlier was starting to get a few bright red leaves.

"I need to trim that thing back," Bill Tom thought, noticing how its branches were hanging over the sidewalk.

"It's a good day for a walk," he thought, putting his keys back into his pocket. For just a short time he needed to clear his head, get away from the office, his cell phone and his problems.

He headed east down the tree-lined street toward the old deserted mill. He loved the setting because the creek next to the mill cascaded downward over a mound of rocks, creating a small waterfall. Years ago the owners of the mill had placed park benches among the trees so people could relax, enjoy the tranquil setting and listen to the water tumbling over the rocks.

As he found his favorite spot—he had often brought Sarah and Kayla to this place for a picnic—he could feel his muscles start to loosen up. He settled back onto a bench built around a big oak tree and leaned his head against the bark. In his mind's eye he could see Sarah walking along the creek bank with a tiny little red-haired Kayla toddling along beside her.

"Oh, Sarah, there's so much I have to say to you," he thought. "I haven't been up to visit you for a long time, two weeks ago today as a matter of fact. And I miss talking to you. Somehow I know that you are aware of everything that's gone on here and I know you know about Brook.

"I think I love her, Sarah, but I want you to know that I loved you, too, and I always will. If I was twenty years younger and it was twenty degrees cooler I'd hike on up to the cemetery and tell you that, but somehow I know that you can hear my thoughts. I'm sorry we cheated on you, Sarah. You didn't deserve that kind of treatment and I'll regret it till my dying day. I pray that you can forgive us.

"Brook is really a wonderful person and she's going to be a great mother to Kayla. I don't know how all of this is going to end but…"

"Bill Tom! Bill Tom!"

Beach's loud voice and his hand shaking Bill Tom's shoulder startled him and woke him from a sound sleep.

"I must have fallen asleep," he said, looking sheepishly into the concerned face of his friend. "What time is it?"

"It's six o'clock," Beach said. "We've been looking for you all over the place. Brook is worried about you since you didn't answer your phone. Finally, we called Mary Ann at home and she suggested that you may have come down here since you didn't take your truck when you left the office."

"She knows me pretty well," Bill Tom said as he stood up to stretch. He reached for his cell phone and remembered that he'd left it at the office.

"May I use your phone to call Brook?" Bill Tom asked smiling at his friend.

"The minute I saw that you were still breathing I called them," Beach said with a grin. "My instructions are to get you home right now. By the time we get there supper will be on the table."

As they walked toward Beach's truck, Beach filled Bill Tom in on the events of the afternoon.

"The University of Miami has no record of Jessica Freeman or Breanna Stein registering for classes last week and, it took some work, but we got American Airlines to confirm that the girls did not take their scheduled flight out of St. Louis," Beach began, "so their parents came back home. Needless to say, they're worried sick.

"Randy and I walked door-to-door in each of the girls' neighborhoods, asking people if they saw anything unusual. Nobody saw anything. Aren't the people in this town even just a little bit nosey? If I so much as fart on my deck, it's the talk of the neighborhood."

"I'm surprised they don't issue an air quality warning!" Bill Tom said with a grin.

Chapter 58

The guys hopped into Beach's truck, stopped by Bill Tom's office so he could get his cell phone, the faxed list of the missing girls' friends, and his truck. Then they made their way back to Maple Drive where supper was on the table.

In the back of his mind, Bill Tom was scolding himself for falling asleep in a park with his gun in its holster. "And I did that with a serial killer on the loose. Maybe it is time for me to step down," he thought.

He took a few minutes to call Mayor Adermann and fill him in on the day's events. Then he walked into the dining room and shook his head. Trudy had outdone herself. The whole setting looked like something out of a Norman Rockwell painting.

The table was set with Sarah's best tablecloth and china. The matching cloth napkins had been folded into an interesting shape and placed on everyone's plate, and a platter of Trudy's legendary fried chicken sat between two candles held by sparkling crystal candleholders.

Beach had carried Kayla downstairs so she could enjoy the company. Although she said she did not feel like eating anything, and made it obvious that she didn't want to talk to Brook or Bill Tom, she looked comfortable and content snuggled up on the couch in the living room with Moonshine at her side. From that vantage point she could look through the small entry foyer into the dining room and listen to the dinner conversation.

"Trudy, Brook, this looks wonderful," Bill Tom said, taking his place at the head of the table. Everyone else had already found a place to sit.

After reciting a well-known table prayer--he wasn't too good at leading a group of people in a made-up prayer--he encouraged everyone to grab a bowl and dig in.

"It's been a tough day for all of us," he said as he helped himself to a heaping spoonful of mashed potatoes. "We've had some real tragedies in this town, but right now I'd like to concentrate on the fact that our two wonderful kids are safe and back home with us once again.

"Brian, Kayla, this is a toast to you," he said lifting up his wine goblet. Trudy had found a perfect white wine to serve with the chicken.

"To Brian and Kayla," Beach said, raising his glass high in the air. "We're very happy and thankful that you two are home."

"Amen!" Brook and Trudy said at the same time and everyone laughed.

Somewhere between the wine, the candlelight, the good food and the wonderful company, Bill Tom felt himself begin to relax. The heavy weight on his shoulders was somehow lifted, momentarily suspended in time. In the back of his mind, he knew that the overwhelming circumstances he was facing would have to come forward again to take their rightful place on the top of his list of concerns, but he wanted and needed to treasure this brief respite, this precious moment with good friends and his wonderful daughter.

He leaned back in his chair and watched them as they talked happily among themselves. Brian and Beach engaged in a conversation about Beach's truck; Trudy and Brook exchanging their ideas about the way Kayla could wear her hair for homecoming; and Kayla herself looking cozy, comfortable and above all, safe, as she drifted in and out of consciousness on the couch in the living room, with Moonshine, as always, right by her side.

All too soon the meal was over. Trudy and Brook cleared the table and Brian strolled into the living room to talk to Kayla and pet Moonshine. Beach waited until the boy was out of the room, then picked up his second bowl of vanilla ice cream with chocolate sauce and walked down to the other end of the table toward Bill Tom.

"I'm going to see if the ladies will make us another pot of coffee," he said, looking at Bill Tom's half-empty cup.

"We already did," Trudy said, walking into the room with the steaming brew. "We know you guys have business to discuss."

"Trudy, you're wonderful," Bill Tom said, grabbing her free hand and planting a kiss on it.

"Hey, give me some of that action," Beach said, trying to look jealous. He took the coffee pot from Trudy's hand and set it on the table. Then he grabbed both of her hands and planted a firm kiss on each one of them.

"I've been looking all over the world for a woman who could read my mind," he said, winking at her.

Trudy patted the big man's cheek tenderly and giggled.

"I'm going to get out of here before you make me blush," she said, as she turned and walked through the swinging door into the kitchen.

"Crisis situations have a way of bringing people close in a short amount of time," Bill Tom thought as he watched his two friends flirt with each other. Just two short, action-packed weeks before, Trudy had attacked Beach in Esther's kitchen over a pot roast sandwich.

Beach sat down next to Bill Tom and poured each of them a fresh cup of coffee.

"She's a keeper," he said, looking at his friend with a big smile and a gleam in his eye. "Too bad we have to discuss business tonight."

Bill Tom nodded his head and they both took a sip of the hot brew.

"I don't think we have our killer in custody," Beach said, looking at Bill Tom apologetically. "We're dealing here with a person who has suffered a life-time of humiliation, who's taken one hit after another and something that Esther, Ernie and Coach Chapman did—probably something minor—turned out to be the straws that broke the camel's back. If that's the case, the killer wouldn't say he didn't mean to hurt those people. Isn't that what Lester kept repeating to you? The killer would feel vindicated, proud that he'd finally taken action against people who hurt him. If he got caught he'd be all too willing to confess, to take credit for his actions."

Bill Tom stared into his coffee cup as he absentmindedly watched the reflection from the chandelier light shimmer in the steaming hot, black liquid. He knew that Beach was right.

"I don't want to jump to conclusions here," Beach continued. "But this business with the two missing girls really has me concerned. I think they might also be victims of this sick SOB and if so, then I think we're definitely looking for a young person between eighteen and twenty-five at the most. It's the combination of authority figures and young people that makes me want to focus on that age group.

"There's some kind of common thread between these people and the killer and we have to try to find out what it is. Once we get that information we can start to put the puzzle pieces together."

"First thing in the morning I'll try to talk to Jessica and Breanna's parents." Bill Tom said, talking softly to his friend. He didn't want Kayla and Brian to overhear the conversation. "I want to go over that list of friends that Roger faxed to me," Bill Tom said, taking another sip of coffee. "But first I want to call the girls' parents right now. They probably think I'm not even concerned about their kids!"

Bill Tom started to get up, but Beach's hand on his arm stopped him.

"Randy's with the girls' parents," he said, motioning for his friend to sit down. "Just call him with the list of names and their parents can add to it. He's really been great with those people. He said he'd stay with the girls' parents and help them contact people. He called some guys--I guess they're men you deputize once in a while--and asked them to form a search party. First thing in the morning they're going to scour the woods up on Grand Mountain Skyway.

"By the way," Beach stopped for a moment and quickly glanced into the living room, "did I tell you that the Freeman's said their dog was missing, too? A huge one hundred-forty-pound Mastiff named Tiny."

"I know Tiny," Bill Tom said with a sigh. "Jessica used to bring him over here when she came to visit Kayla. That dog slobbered all over everything. He drove Sarah nuts."

"Well, Jessica was supposed to take him to some kennel on Highway 24 near the interstate on that Sunday morning when they were scheduled to fly to Miami, but of course they never showed up. So I think that wherever the girls are, Tiny's with them!" Beach said. "Anyway, Randy's very good at his job, as I'm sure you know, and he has that situation well in hand. So I think you can try to get some rest tonight and first thing tomorrow we'll get with him and go over his notes. Whaddayathink?"

Beach stood up and looked at his watch.

"It's almost ten o'clock, buddy," he said, looking down at Bill Tom. "I don't know about you, but I've got to get my beauty sleep!"

"I think that would take an awful lot of shut-eye," Bill Tom said, laughing as he stood up to pat his friend on the back.

As Trudy, Brian and Beach prepared to leave, the group decided that Brook would spend the night with Bill Tom and Kayla. No one thought she should stay alone in her home, even though it was just down the block.

Trudy promised that she and Brian would be back over to Bill Tom's house in the morning after she took Brian in for an appointment with their family physician.

"Tomorrow night I'll make lasagna and a salad," she called to Brook as Beach ushered her out the door and down the steps.

"Thanks, Trudy," Brook said softly, waving to her as Bill Tom closed the door.

Chapter 59

The two tired people looked at each other and Bill Tom pulled her into his arms for a tight embrace.

"I'm glad you're staying here tonight," he whispered. Before he could stop himself he leaned down to kiss her and felt a rush of excitement as she slid her arms around his neck and returned his tight embrace.

"We need to get Kayla up to bed," she whispered when he finally forced himself to end the kiss.

"We need to get ourselves to bed," he wanted to say, but he carefully guarded his words and his feelings.

"I'll put fresh sheets on the bed in the guestroom as soon as we get her tucked in," he said, as he walked into the living room to get Kayla, who was sound asleep.

"Trudy already did that," Brook said, "right after she drove over to my house to get me some clean clothes. She also washed the sheets on your bed and remade it."

Bill Tom shook his head as he followed Brook up the stairs with Kayla fast asleep in his arms. Together they tucked their sleeping daughter back into bed.

"I'm going back downstairs to let Moonshine go outside," Bill Tom said, looking at Brook. He was suddenly embarrassed by the situation.

"You go on to bed and if you need anything I'm right down the hall," he said, kissing her lightly and very quickly on the lips. He couldn't bare the agony of having to pull himself away from her again.

"Good night, Bill Tom," she whispered. "I just have to say this…I think I'm falling in love with you."

"That's the best news I've heard in a long time," he said, gently touching her cheek. "Come on Moonshine, let's go outside."

After Moonshine came back inside and ran back up to Kayla's room, Bill Tom checked all the doors to make sure they were locked. He walked slowly up the stairs wondering how he would ever get any sleep with Brook Jennings curled up on a bed just down the hall.

Chapter 60

Somewhere in his subconscious mind he knew he was dreaming. Brook was sitting next to him on a couch near a huge fireplace. They were both drinking wine out of crystal goblets and laughing at Beach and Trudy, who were standing in the middle of the room playing Twister with Brian and Kayla. Coach Chapman was standing on the side, yelling instructions at them as they tried to put their hands and feet on the right colors. Bill Tom could hear a phone ringing, but he didn't want to get up to answer it.

All of a sudden he sat up in bed fully awake and instinctively reached for his gun in the night table drawer. He quickly put the gun away when he realized that it was the ringing telephone that startled him.

"Chief Bradley," he answered, clearing his voice.

"I'm sorry to bother you at four in the morning, Chief," a cheery voice said on the other end of the line. "My name is Elissa Daniels and I'm the ER charge nurse on duty at the hospital. My instructions were to call you the minute Lester Tucker regained consciousness and I wanted you to know that he is definitely coming around. He's very groggy and not making much sense, but I think it's just a matter of time before he'll start talking to us."

"Thanks for the call, Elissa," he said, rubbing his eyes with his free hand. "I'll get over there right away."

He replaced the phone on the cradle, hopped out of bed and headed for the shower. He hoped the telephone call hadn't disturbed Kayla or Brook.

When he was ready to leave, he gently knocked on Brook's door as he cracked it open. From the light in the hallway, he could see that she was sleeping on her side with her face to the door, both hands tucked under her chin. He didn't want to startle her but he wanted her to know that he was leaving, and that she and Kayla would be alone in the house.

"Brook," he whispered, as he walked over to her bed. "Brook, can you wake up a minute?"

He gently touched her shoulder and she opened her eyes and immediately smiled at him.

"I heard the phone and then I heard the shower running," she whispered softly. "I figured you'd be in here in a few minutes to tell me what's going on."

She sat up in the bed and squinted at him.

"Lester Tucker has regained consciousness and I have to get over there," he said, brushing her hair from her face. "I'll make sure all the doors are locked."

"Okay," she said, leaning toward him for a kiss. She slid her arms around his neck and he pulled her close to him. The touch of her moist eager lips and the pleasure of her warm, soft body made it difficult for him to pull away.

With every ounce of determination he could muster, he ended the kiss, told her he loved her and got up to leave. He was so dizzy he could barely make it down the stairs.

He drove several blocks from his house before his heart started beating normally. By the time he walked through the hospital emergency room doors he had fully recovered from the sensuous moment and was in complete control of all his faculties.

As he walked through the ER lobby a nurse behind the reception desk greeted him warmly.

"Chief Bradley, I'm Elissa Daniels." She extended her arm and they shook hands. "I'm pleased to meet you. I've seen you around town, of course, but we've never really met. My husband and I are very impressed with all the great programs you've started for teenagers in Hillside. Our son, Mike, goes to school with your daughter. They worked on the DARE program together last year."

"I'm pleased to meet you, too, Mrs. Daniels, and thanks for the kind words...I haven't heard many of those lately."

Nurse Daniels smiled at him. "Most of the people here in Hillside—at least the ones with any sense—know you're doing everything you can to find the person responsible for these murders. I hope you know we're all on your side."

"I appreciate that, Ma'am," Bill Tom said, smiling at her. "You can't imagine how much I needed to hear that."

"Lester Tucker and his mother are in Room 207 upstairs," she said. "You can take the elevator."

Bill Tom thanked her and headed down the hall.

Wanda! After his shocking conversation with Jennifer Chapman, and his rush to get home to see Kayla, he had forgotten all about her. Had she been at the hospital all that time? Randy had picked her up from the bank and brought her to the ER so she didn't even have a car at her disposal. He was pretty sure nobody else checked up on her. Everyone had just abandoned her at the hospital.

"She must think I'm a total jerk," he thought, as he knocked quietly on the door to Room 207.

"Come in," a tired voice called out.

He entered the room expecting to get an icy glare and a cold greeting, but instead, Wanda Tucker was beaming with happiness as she held her son's hand.

"He's coming around, Chief," she said with a big smile. "The doctor says my Lester is going to be just fine."

"That's great news, Wanda," he said, walking toward the bed. "I'm sorry I…"

"I've just been by his side every minute praying for a miracle," Wanda interrupted. "The nurses have been so kind; they brought me food and offered me a blanket so I could sleep in the chair. And then about an hour ago, Lester turned his head and opened his eyes. He called out to me and reached for me with his hand. The doctor said that is a very good sign."

Bill Tom had been about to apologize for abandoning the woman at the hospital, but he quickly realized that she hadn't even noticed that no one was around to help her and that, if someone had offered her a ride home, she wouldn't have left her son's side.

"That's great news, Wanda," he said, putting his arm around the woman's shoulder. He gave her a quick, one-arm hug.

"Can I get you some coffee, or something?" he asked.

"I was feeling pretty tired a little while ago, but when Lester called my name all that went away, you know?"

"I know," Bill Tom said, remembering how he and Brook had reacted with Kayla in the hospital. "Do you think he can hear us?" he asked, looking at the boy who was once again sleeping.

"I don't know," Wanda said, shrugging her shoulders, "but he keeps waking up and looking around."

"Wanda, you know that when he's fully awake I'm going to need to ask him some questions," Bill Tom said as gently as possible. "I've got to find out what he knows about Coach Chapman's murder."

"I understand," Wanda said, her face becoming very serious. "But I want you to know that my son is innocent, Chief. I hope you won't upset him by accusing him of such an awful crime."

"All I want to do is get to the truth, Wanda. I'll do everything in my power to keep from upsetting him."

The door to Room 207 opened and Dr. Schrader walked in.

"Woody, I didn't know you'd be on night duty," Bill Tom said, smiling at his friend.

"All the doctors take a rotation for night duty, Bill," Dr. Schrader said, extending his hand toward Bill Tom. "So do the nurses.

"I just came in to ask you to go gently with this boy when you do your questioning; he's been through a lot. I know your job is to find out what happened, but my job is to do what's best for him."

"I promise I'll be careful."

Bill Tom's phone rang and he glanced at his watch. It was five-thirty.

"Mornin' BT!" Randy's voice sounded tired and strained.

"Hold on a second, Randy." Bill Tom motioned for Doc Schrader to follow him into the hallway.

"Did you get any sleep, Randy?"

"Not much. I just keep thinking how I'd feel if my boys were missing. I'd do anything to find them."

"Is your search party already organized?"

"We're all up here on Grand Mountain Skyway getting ready to walk the woods," Randy answered. "Dr. Freeman and Ed Stein have joined the search while their wives are sitting at home by the phone. We're going to wait about fifteen minutes or so until the sun pops over the ridge."

"Well, be careful. And if you find anything at all, let me know, okay?"

"I'll call you first thing!"

Bill Tom ended the call and stared at the doctor.

"Did you hear that two teenage girls are missing?"

"Dr. Freeman's daughter and some other girl? I heard something about it yesterday, but somehow I got the idea it was just a case of crossed signals. I didn't know that they really are missing. Do you think their disappearance is related to the murders?"

"I have no idea." Bill Tom shook his head. "At this point I have no idea what's going on. But I do know that Lester Tucker knows something, and I need to get back into his room and wait for him to wake up."

"Ask the nurse to page me if you need anything, Bill," Dr. Schrader said.

"I'll do that." Bill Tom answered as he opened the door to Lester's room.

"Chief, I think he's starting to wake up!" Wanda Tucker's face was flushed with a happy glow.

Bill Tom walked over to the boy who still had his eyes closed.

"He called out to me, Chief," Wanda said with a big smile. "And he reached for my hand again. That was just a few seconds ago. He keeps opening his eyes and shutting them again and…"

"Is that Chief Bradley?"

Wanda stopped short and she and Bill Tom looked anxiously at the boy as his eyes slowly began to open. He squinted at the bright lights in the room.

"Yes, Lester, it's me," Bill Tom said, reaching down to pat the boy on the shoulder. "You're in the hospital, son, and you're going to be okay. You fell down those steps at the winery but you're going to be okay."

"I didn't mean to hurt those people," Lester said, squirming in his bed. "I didn't mean to cause any trouble."

"Take it easy, Lester," Bill Tom said, trying to reassure the boy. "Nobody is accusing you of anything. Just try to relax now. Are you in pain? Do you need us to call the nurse?"

"No...nurse...no...pain," Lester said softly, once again closing his eyes.

"The nurse told me they gave him some pretty strong pain medication," Wanda said, looking at Bill Tom with a happy glow in her eyes. "That might be why he's still so groggy."

"Could be. I'm just going to sit in this chair for a little while, and close my eyes, Wanda. When Lester wakes up again let me know."

Wanda nodded at the chief with a smile and then turned her attention back to the sleeping boy.

Chapter 61

They both jumped when Bill Tom's cell phone rang.

"Mornin', Beach," Bill Tom said, glancing at his watch. It was almost seven a.m. "Did you join the search for the…"

"Bill Tom, I found the girls!" The urgency in Beach's voice made Bill Tom's heart start to race.

"I found the girls and they're alive––barely alive––but they're alive! I've called an ambulance and I'm going to follow them to the hospital. Randy told me you're already there." Beach was breathing heavily and his voice shook while he spoke.

"I'm in Lester's room," Bill Tom said. "But how did you…?"

"I'll tell you all about it when I get there, BT. I hear the ambulance now. Meet me in the emergency room."

"Wanda, something's come up and I've got to leave for a few minutes. I'll be back as soon as I can," he called over his shoulder as he left the room.

As he entered the ER waiting room area he noticed that some reporters had begun to arrive. The press had heard about the latest "Hillside Murders" news. He was surprised that he hadn't seen any of them when he came in earlier and thankful that they all seemed to be more interested in using their lap tops or texting than getting interviews from him.

He walked over to the reception desk to talk to Elissa Daniels.

"Mrs. Daniels, I know that you're aware that two girls are on their way into the ER and right now we can't have these reporters inside the waiting room. Can you get your security people to ask them to wait outside, away from the ER entrance?"

"I'll call them right now, Chief."

Bill Tom walked down the hall away from the waiting room so he could watch without being noticed. Within seconds the security guards escorted the protesting reporters outside. Some cafeteria people followed the guards with carts of coffee, juice and Danish rolls.

"Nice touch, Nurse Daniels," Bill Tom thought. "Soften the blow."

He watched while the emergency medical team guys wheeled the girls inside and down the opposite hallway. Their parents were following close behind. As soon as he saw Beach, Bill Tom called to him.

"Come in here," he said, motioning for Beach to follow him into the hospital conference room. He couldn't wait to hear how Beach found those two girls.

Once they were inside the room with the door closed, Bill Tom turned to his friend and smiled.

"Are you the miracle worker?" he asked with a smile. His expression soon changed when he saw the strained look on Beach's face.

"It was a miracle, Billy, but I had nothing to do with it," Beach said, sitting down in one of the cushioned chairs. "I've never seen anything like this. It almost made me sick. And I have a strong stomach!"

"What happened?"

Bill Tom sat beside his distraught friend and patted him on the shoulder.

"I got up early to join the search party. I figured they could use all the help they could get. Randy said he'd just talked to you and we were beginning to divide up into groups when Andy Arnold came walking down the street. He said he saw all the commotion and wanted to see what was going on.

"When we explained what we were doing, he offered to join the group. He said he couldn't sleep anyway because there was such an awful odor in his house. He thought it was a backed up sewer in the basement. It was so bad his wife packed up some clothes and went to spend the night at some bed and breakfast in town. He was very frustrated because he couldn't get in touch with the town plumber. Do you guys really only have one plumber in town?

"Anyway, so many people had showed up to search the woods I offered to go to his house with him to check out what was going on in the basement. He can't get down those steps because of his arthritis. And his description of that horrible smell—well it just made me curious—so we walked back to his house and he was right, the smell was overpowering.

"I grabbed a towel from their hall bathroom to hold over my nose and mouth and opened the door to the basement. When I got down there, I didn't see anything at first, just your basic basement, with a furnace and a hundred years' worth of clutter sittin' around. The drain by the washer and dryer seemed to be okay and I couldn't see anything that looked suspicious.

"Then I saw the door. It looked like another room had been built and closed off near the back of the basement. I called up to Arnold and asked him what was in the room and he told me that they had built a separate room where they kept their freezer and a small wine collection.

"As I walked closer to the door I could tell that the overpowering odor was coming from inside. The door was locked so I had to force it open and when I did…"

Beach stopped for a moment and put his hand over his mouth. Bill Tom was afraid he might be sick.

"Beach, do you need…"

"I'm okay, Bill," Beach continued, swallowing hard. "I just have to tell you this. When I looked inside I found the light switch on the wall, but the light was burned out. From the basement light I could see something lying on the floor and the floor was all dark around it. I opened the door a little further and then I saw the two girls lying next to each other on the floor. I pulled them out one by one, realized they were both alive and I called for an ambulance. Then I called Randy, and he and the search party team came right away. They helped me get the girls upstairs and out into the fresh air.

"One of the search party guys came out to tell us that the smell was coming from a dead dog that looked like it had been beaten to death with something. The Freemans said it was their dog, Tiny.

"It looked like the girls managed to stay alive by thawing out some food and some bags of ice."

Beach paused for a moment and looked at his friend.

"God only knows how long those girls were in there, Billy. They had to use part of the room as a toilet."

Bill Tom was about to respond when someone knocked on the conference room door.

"The girls are going to be okay," Doc Schrader said, coming into the room. "We're putting them on oxygen and saline drips. The nurses are going to give them each a bath–they smell pretty bad. Neither of them seems to have been hurt in any other way. Have you guys gotten any kind of explanation from Andy Arnold about what might have happened?"

"I don't think he had any idea what was going on," Beach said. "He was just as shocked as the rest of us and actually broke down in tears as we brought the girls upstairs. He felt bad that he didn't check out the odor sooner. I've seen a lot of guilty suspects in my life, and believe me, he's not one of them."

"Then how did those girls end up in…"

Bill Tom's question was interrupted by another knock on the door.

"Chief Bradley, Lester Tucker is calling for you," Nurse Daniels announced in an urgent tone.

Chapter 62

Bill Tom jumped up and ran down the hall to Lester's room with Beach and Doc Schrader close behind.

As they entered the room Wanda greeted them with a look of concern.

"He just woke up and said he had to talk to you, Chief. He seems so agitated."

Bill Tom looked down at the boy who was shifting from side to side in his bed and groaning.

"Lester, it's Chief Bradley. What's wrong? What did you want to tell me?"

"She did it," he said, meeting Bill Tom's anxious stare. "That girl. That mean girl. She had that rope that night in the hospital and she used it to kill the coach. She used it to kill Coach Chapman.

"I came to see Kayla in the hospital in the middle of the night," Lester said, tears streaming down his face. "I went to the movies in Columbia and saw some kids from school who told me about Kayla and Brian. I drove over to the hospital to see them, but visiting hours were over. Finally, I just walked up to Kayla's room anyway and when I opened the door that mean girl was standing over Kayla's bed with a rope in her hand. When she saw me she said a bad word, pushed me out of the way and ran out of the room.

"And then yesterday morning I wanted to talk to Coach Chapman about the football team so I walked into his office while you were giving your speech—I'm sorry that I didn't go to the assembly, Chief—but I wanted to talk to the Coach. And that's when I saw her. Coach's office was dark, but from the light in the hallway I could see that she was sitting on his lap facing him, and I could tell she had that rope around his neck. She jumped off of him and came after me.

"I turned on the light and ran out of the room. She followed me and pushed me down. I grabbed her ankle and she fell. She jumped up, yelled at me and kicked me in the side. She must have thought someone was coming because she looked around suddenly and just took off running down the hall toward the door.

"I was so scared I didn't know what to do, so I picked up the rope, ran to Mrs. Jennings' room and hid under her desk. I didn't mean to hurt Mrs. Jennings but I wanted to get away. I didn't want anyone to think that I would hurt the coach."

"Lester," Bill Tom said, once again patting the boy on the shoulder. "Tell me who the girl is. Tell me who was in my daughter's hospital room and who attacked Coach Chapman."

Lester looked at Bill Tom with his eyes full of fear.

"It was Mindy Arnold, sir. It was Mindy Arnold."

Everyone in the room stared at Lester in shocked silence.

Bill Tom ran his hand through his hair and tried to collect his thoughts. Could Mindy Arnold have really strangled all those people? Did she have it in her to lock her friends in a wine cellar and try to run down Kayla and Brian with a car?

He was just about to speak when there was a knock on the door.

"Excuse me, may I come in for a second?" It was the voice of Deputy Randy James. "I didn't mean to interrupt," Randy said, as the group stared at him, "but I just wanted to see how Lester's feeling."

"He just told us that he saw Mindy Arnold strangle Dan Chapman," Bill Tom said, looking at Randy. "I think we're all in shock.

"Beach, what was the name of that detective we worked with in Columbia? I'm going to have him arrest Mindy Arnold and…"

"Wait a minute, BT," Randy interrupted Bill Tom, "I don't think she's in Columbia. I drove back to the office to file a report about the girls and when I came back to the hospital I took the short cut through your neighborhood. Doesn't Mindy Arnold have a silver Camaro? It was parked in front of your house."

Chapter 63

Kayla stirred in bed and groaned as she felt the pain of her stiff muscles, sore ribs and stitched up head. She opened her eyes, looked around her room and let out a long sigh of relief. It hadn't been a dream; she really was snuggled cozily in her very own bed in her very own room. She reached across her bed to pet Moonshine, but the dog was not there.

"She probably had to go potty," Kayla thought. "I hope somebody let her go outside. I wonder who's in the house with me."

Kayla could tell from the light streaming in the window that it was about seven o'clock in the morning. She looked around her room again and smiled at the familiar surroundings filled with good memories: light purple paint on the walls, purple and white flowered curtains with a matching bedspread that her dad had bought her for her sixteenth birthday; the bulletin board above her desk with all the pictures of her friends from school; and the eight-by-ten color photo of her and Brian at the junior prom.

"Lots of happy times collected in this room," she thought as she smelled the delicious aroma of frying bacon making its way upstairs from the kitchen.

Although her memory from the night before was a bit fuzzy, she thought she remembered Miss Trudy saying that she and Brian would come back early in the morning.

With some effort, she got out of bed and crept to the bathroom down the hall. She brushed her teeth and washed her face, looking carefully at the purple bruises that seemed to be fading away pretty quickly. The long line of black stitches near the hairline on her forehead was beginning to itch. "That's a sign of healing, isn't it?" she asked herself. She wanted to take a hot shower and wash her hair but knew that she was way too weak to do that on her own. She called downstairs thinking that Trudy was making her breakfast but there was no answer.

"She'll probably bring breakfast up to me," Kayla thought, mindlessly wondering who had dressed her in her favorite nightshirt.

Kayla inched her way back into her room, studying her arms and legs to see how many other bruises she had. As she looked up she gasped in surprise. Mindy Arnold was in her room sitting in the chair by her dresser.

"Surprise! Surprise!" Mindy shouted, holding her arms out. She was grinning from ear to ear. She looked terrible. Her usually shiny blond hair was dark and stringy and she was wearing old black sweat pants and a dirty white tee shirt.

"Mindy, what in the world are you doing here? Shouldn't you be at school?" Kayla asked, hobbling over to her bed. She couldn't believe that Trudy just let Mindy come upstairs unannounced.

"I came to check up on you, Kayla. Some things are just more important than school. Our friendship is one of them.

"Actually, I came back yesterday morning; I had some…unfinished business to take care of. When I heard that you came home, naturally I wanted to stop by to see you. That's what friends are for, you know?"

Kayla slowly sat down on her bed. She wanted to put her feet up and get back under the covers, but something about Mindy's surprise visit and her unusual manner made Kayla very uncomfortable. Mindy rarely did anything out of the kindness of her heart.

"Mindy, that day on the quad at MIZZOU things didn't go very well," Kayla said. "I thought you were mad at me."

"Oh, silly, it was just a misunderstanding, that's all," Mindy said as she stood up. She walked over to Kayla's side of the bed.

"Here, let me fluff up those pillows for you so you can put your feet up and lean back on them. You look uncomfortable."

Mindy smiled, but her eyes seemed cold. The look made Kayla shudder.

"I think Trudy is going to bring my breakfast up soon, or maybe my Mom. Would you like something to eat?" Kayla offered, picking at her chipped nail polish. She thought that Brook might also be in the house.

"Mom? You're calling Mrs. Jennings 'MOM' now?" Mindy asked. "Why would you do that?"

Kayla watched as Mindy wandered restlessly around her room, looking at everything.

"You know that I was adopted, Mindy," Kayla said as Mindy opened one of her dresser drawers. "As it turns out Mrs. Jennings was my birth mother and she came back to Hillside to meet me."

Kayla decided not to mention the part about Bill Tom being her biological father.

"Once again a fairytale ending for dear ole' Kayla," Mindy said as she pulled a pair of black tights out of Kayla's underwear drawer.

"What are you doing with my tights?" Kayla asked, becoming more annoyed at than wary of the situation.

"Oh, it's just a little surprise I've prepared for you, Kayla," Mindy laughed as she held up the black stockings.

"What do you mean, 'a surprise,'" Kayla asked? "What kind of surprise could possibly include my tights?" Her warning bells were going off, but they were somewhere in the distance.

"It's kind of a sad surprise, really," Mindy said, walking slowing towards Kayla. "You see, I'm going to strangle you with these tights."

Mindy stopped walking and looked down at Kayla with a broad smile.

Kayla's heartbeat flew into hyper drive as she looked at Mindy. She knew the girl, and the girl was not joking. She could see the hatred in her eyes. The warning bells were loud and clear now.

"Mi…Mindy, what are you talking about?" Kayla swallowed hard as she struggled to talk, throat dry, heart racing, the pain of her injuries intensified. "Why would you want to strangle me? We've been friends since pre-school. Be…besides my mom is right downstairs and if I call her she'll be up here in a flash and she'll call my dad and…"

Kayla screamed in pain as Mindy reached down and slapped her across the face.

"Mommy dearest won't be coming up to save little Kayla," Mindy said, with a laugh. "Didn't you hear the noise her body made as she went bouncing down your basement steps? She hit the bottom like a rock. I'd pretty much say that your birth mother is a thing of the past. Too bad, little Kayla. For once things didn't go your way!"

Kayla's eyes welled up with tears and her heart was filled with terror. If Mindy was telling the truth, the woman she just learned was her mother, was now dead and she had been so hateful to her when she found out about the affair.

Her mind was racing. She knew she was too stiff and sore to out-run Mindy and too weak to fight her off. If Moonshine was around and sensed that she was in danger the dog would…Kayla's train of through came to a screeching halt.

"Oh, no, Mindy, did you…did you do something to Moonshine, too? Did you hurt my dog?"

"I just tell you that I killed your birth mother and you're worried about the dog? What kind of daughter are you anyway?" Mindy asked, winding the tights around her hands. "Besides, I'd never hurt that dog, she's never done anything bad to me, not like the rest of you pathetic people. Do you think I'm crazy?"

"I'm beginning to," Kayla thought silently, but she kept her mouth shut. Her lips now swelling thanks to Mindy's slap on the face. Kayla's instincts told her she had to think of a way to keep Mindy talking until she could figure out how to defend herself. If she could just get over to her desk where she kept her scissors…

"Why do you keep looking at your desk?" Mindy turned around to see what had piqued Kayla's interest. She saw the scissors in a container with pencils and pens.

"Ooooooooooo," she said slowly, walking over to the desk. "Were you thinking you might defend yourself with these, Kayla dear? She picked up the scissors and walked over to Kayla, throwing the tights on the bed."

"Were you going to jab these scissors into my heart?" Mindy raised the scissors and aimed for Kayla's neck, stopping just inches away from her body.

Kayla screamed and turned her head.

"Oh, shut up, Kayla. The fun has just begun. I wouldn't let you die that easily. I made it quick for those other losers, but I've decided to take my time with you. After all, Daddy dearest is off trying to find the Hillside strangler so I have you all to myself."

Kayla swallowed hard, trying to keep her thoughts together. She knew from stories her dad had told her that she needed to keep Mindy talking. "You make a killer tell his story. They always want to tell their stories," her dad had said, describing a case he had worked on in St. Louis.

"Mindy, what did you mean when you said you 'made it quick for those other losers'?"

"Can't you guess? Do the names Esther Gaines, Ernie Tucker and Dan Chapman sound familiar to you?"

"You killed Miss Esther and Ernie Tucker? And what about Coach Chapman? How…how did you do it? And why? What did they ever do to you?"

"You want the whole story, kiddo? I'll give it to you; I love to relive it. I love to bask in the glory of my triumph over their cruelty!"

Mindy sat down on the bed, facing Kayla. She kept a strong grip on the scissors.

"Did you know that Miss Esther was my great aunt?" Mindy began her story. "And she treated me like dirt. She was always telling me that I wore too much make-up or that my clothes were too tight. She told me that I didn't apply myself in school…and then she chose your essay over mine to enter into that state contest. I just decided I'd had enough of it.

"That Saturday when we were all in her kitchen making cookies I took the spare house key that she kept under the backdoor mat. When she came back from the book fair on Monday I was waiting for her with my trusty green rope.

"Strangling that ole' crow was easy; she couldn't even put up much of a fight. I'm just glad that at the last minute, she got to see who was strangling her. It made up for all the times she hurt me.

"As a final touch I wrapped that cheap old white wool scarf she gave me for Christmas around her neck. Remember last Christmas? You got the matching skirt and sweater, and I got the scarf?"

"Oh Mindy," Kayla whispered, her voice raspy with fear, "Miss Esther didn't hate you. Whenever she talked about you her eyes were filled with pride. She…"

"Oh, don't sugar-coat it, sweet pants, the woman was a bitch," Mindy said, raising her voice in irritation. Without a lot of force, she poked the scissors into Kayla's left arm to break the skin. "Do you want to hear the rest of this story or not?"

"Yes, yes I do," Kayla said quickly, wincing from the pain. "I'm sorry I interrupted. I'll be quiet." Her arm hurt but she didn't dare touch it or try to wipe away the blood.

"Thank you," Mindy said, nodding her head at Kayla. "I thought that would get your attention. And I really want you to pay attention because this is an interesting story. I wouldn't want you to miss it, since it's had your dad all tied up in knots for a couple of weeks. You need to know how I out-smarted the stupid jerk."

Kayla opened her mouth to protest, but thought better of it. Her heart was pounding. She tried to suck in a deep breath of air but her chest was too tight.

"Ernie Tucker was a little more difficult to deal with," Mindy continued. "He deserved it because he gave the solo part in that church musical to Leah Melhern instead of me, when it was obvious that I have the better voice. Admit it, Kayla, I have the better voice, right?"

"Yes, Mindy, you have the better voice."

"I ran into Ernie at the Grab and Go. He was on his way to Jefferson City. He seemed like he was in a hurry. I begged him to give me one more chance, to let me audition for the part one more time before the Sunday morning performance.

"He hesitated a bit so I winked at him and told him I'd find a way to make it worthwhile. He seemed reluctant, but he agreed to take the time to do it.

"When we got to the church I asked him to accompany me on the organ. While I sang I walked behind him and caressed his shoulders with my hands. I stopped singing and ran my tongue along the outside of his ear. Then I leaned around and kissed him hard. By the time I pulled out my trusty old rope he was in no state to defend himself. I strangled the jackass without any trouble at all. And then I decided to just let him sit there, leaning against the back of the organ bench. He looked so funny with his eyes wide open. What a surprise, huh? Good thing that organ bench has a head rest."

Kayla stared at the girl in stunned and terrified silence.

"Let me see, that happened on a Saturday--the day of Miss Esther's funeral. That was a big day for me. I took care of three losers in one day."

"Three?" Kayla asked in surprise.

"Oh, that's right, you probably don't know about Jessica and Breanna yet, those double-crossing bitches. They're stuck down in my dad's wine cellar. We'd all planned on going to the University of Miami together. And then I didn't get accepted into the marine biology program. But they decided to go anyway, without me, when we'd been so close all our lives. Now how thoughtless is that? I couldn't let them do that to me, could I? So, after I left Ernie on the bench, I called them and invited them over for a farewell dinner. Jessica brought that stupid dog of hers along because her parents were out of town and she didn't want to leave him alone.

"I made lasagna--you know that recipe you and I got off of Pinterest that time--and they loved it. After dinner I asked them if they'd like to see my dad's wine cellar. I told them that we would celebrate going away to college with a bottle of sparkling champagne. They didn't even sound like they were sad that I was going to MIZZOU and they were off to Miami. It really hurt me, you know?"

"I understand," Kayla whispered, running her tongue across her dry lips.

"Of course, what they didn't know is that I spiked their drinks with a very heavy dose of my mom's sleeping medication. We just sat on the floor, leaned up against the wall of the wine cellar and I waited for them to fall asleep. It sure didn't take long.

"On my way out I leaned down to tell Tiny to say good-bye to Jessica. The stupid dog licked me in the face so I bashed in his head with a wine bottle. It took a few hard whacks to do the trick, but by the time I left he wasn't moving."

"You locked Jessica and Breanna in the wine cellar?" Kayla asked in shock. Chills rippled down her back and she shivered.

"I did. And they were in there the next night when you came over to my house. I think they were already dead, though. I gave them each huge doses of the sleep drug. They were so busy talking about their trip to Miami that they didn't even notice when I spiked their drinks. Self-absorbed bitches!"

Kayla was dumb-founded, but her fear momentarily succumbed to her curiosity about the hit and run incident in the Breakfast Barn parking lot.

"Mindy, did you try to kill Brian and me at the Breakfast Barn?" Kayla asked. "Was it really you and Todd in that car?"

"It was me, but it wasn't Todd," Mindy said, once again with a proud smile. "We ordered a pizza when we got home and I slipped the good old sleeping medication into Todd's beer. He was out like a light. He has a friend who has a red Mustang and the guy has well, how shall I say it, a thing for me. I promised to give him some action if he would help me even a score with one of my 'friends.'" She used her hands to put the word "friends" in quotation marks.

"I knew your dad would come looking for us and that our nosey neighbor downstairs would give us a solid alibi because Todd parks his car right in front of her patio doors. That's why I had to use someone with a red Mustang."

"Do you really hate me that much, Mindy?" Kayla asked with tears in her eyes, her heart pounding harder and harder.

"More than words can express!" Mindy said, shrugging her shoulders, once again punching the scissors into Kayla's arm. "But you're interrupting again. Do you want to hear the rest of this story, or not?"

"I do. Of course. Please go on."

"Next on my list was Coach Chapman. When I heard that your dad was giving a safety speech at the school yesterday I just thought it would be a great time to settle the score with Danny Boy-- that's what all the girls who slept with him called him--Danny Boy.

"For three years in a row I was his special girl; he liked me best. Then he dumped me for Crystal Sinclair, can you believe that? Crystal Sinclair, with the tiny boobs and the big butt? I couldn't let him get away with that, could I? I mean, how would it look? I couldn't let him humiliate me that way.

"So yesterday morning while your dad was showing his safety video, I sneaked into Dan's office and slid onto his lap. I kissed him and made him put his hands on my body. Then, at just the right moment I jammed my knee into his groin. Guys are so helpless when they're really turned-on! Anyway, after that, strangling him was a piece of cake!"

Mindy looked at Kayla with a triumphant grin. Then, suddenly, her face became very serious.

"Things would have been perfect if it hadn't been for that idiot, Lester Tucker. He walked into Dan's office just as I was done strangling him.

"Lester ran out of the room and I ran after him. I tackled him and he fell to the floor. But he grabbed my ankle and then took my rope.

"I heard the video ending so I got up and ran out the back entrance of the school by the dumpsters. I'm so mad at myself for letting him get my rope and messing up my plans a second time."

"A second time?" Kayla ventured the question in a weak voice, sweat now pouring down her back.

"I tried to strangle you in the hospital, Kayla, in the middle of the night, but that crazy guy walked in on me and I ran out. What was he doing there so early in the morning? Does he have a crush on you, or something?

"You tried to strangle me in the hospital?" Kayla asked, feeling herself sinking into a daze. She felt like she was living in a scene from a horror movie.

"Oh, Kayla, keep up with the story and don't be so dramatic," Mindy said, delivering two more jabs with the scissors. "I've thought about strangling you for so long that actually doing it is going to be like an anti-climax. And you know what? Those tights just aren't going to do the trick. If I can't use my trusty rope I'll just have to use these scissors." She ran the pointed edge of the scissors across Kayla's neck.

"Wha what's so special about the rope?" Kayla stuttered. "Keep her talking. Keep her talking," she thought.

"It's my concentration rope…the rope I used to stare at every night in bed," Mindy explained. "Do you remember how ugly my room used to be with those old heavy green brocade drapes and that awful wallpaper? My mother always said it was a room fit for a queen--but I was a ten-year-old kid!"

Mindy looked away from Kayla for a moment, gazing at the windows and walls of Kayla's bedroom. When she looked back, her eyes were filled with tears.

"Every night after I went to bed I waited for it to happen. The door would open, the warning to be quiet would be whispered and the abuse would begin. Night after night. Year after year. The things that were done to me…and the things I was made to do! When it was over, I would just lie there like I was dead, staring at the rope that tied the curtains back. I wanted to scream, but I was told that I'd get into big trouble because I was a bad girl. I must have liked it because I let it happen. I was told that they'd come and take me away and put me in an asylum for the mentally ill if I ever told anyone what happened."

"Oh Mindy," Kayla was shocked. "Your dad abused you all those years and no one knew?"

"It wasn't my dad, Kayla," Mindy said with tears now streaming down her face, "it was my *mom*. She kept it up until I got too old. Once I turned thirteen it stopped and she just treated me like dirt after that."

"I'm so sorry Mindy," Kayla whispered.

"Don't feel sorry for me, you little wimp!" Mindy snapped at her. "Can't you see that I'm evil? I must be. As humiliating as it was, I let it go on for years. I pretended that everything was okay. And now, I'm just so sick of people taking advantage of me and living such happy lives while my life is such a mess. Why couldn't I have had just one moment of happiness? Just one? I swear I'd treasure it forever!"

Mindy was sobbing now, but still in full control of the situation.

She stared at Kayla and suddenly smiled.

"My mom and dad are the last two people on my get-even list and you can't even imagine the special treats I have in store for them! But I'm going to thoroughly enjoy these last few minutes with you." She lifted the scissors toward Kayla's face.

"That's an interesting hairstyle you've got going, Kayla. I think the shaved head suits you. I think I'll just cut your hair to make you even more beautiful. A whack, whack here, and a whack, whack there."

Kayla cringed as she watched the locks of hair falling on her bed. She was too frightened to move or to say anything. Then she saw an unbelievable sight--the reflection of her dad in the mirror on her dresser. He was standing right outside her door. He quickly backed away so Mindy couldn't see him.

She tried to gather all her wits to gain some control of the situation. She knew Mindy was in an intense emotional state--which could work in her favor or against it, depending on how she played it.

With desperate determination, she willed herself to get a grip on her emotions. The sight of her dad in the mirror gave her some hope and much needed courage. She began talking very carefully, measuring every word. Her mind was racing. "Don't screw this up, Kayla," she thought. "It's your only chance."

"Mindy, you're right," Kayla began, trying to muster up a matter-of-fact tone, "people have treated you in a terrible way. You've led a tragic life and I don't blame you at all for trying to even the score."

"Damn straight!" Mindy said, nodding her head in agreement as she continued to cut huge hunks of Kayla's hair. "It's about time somebody acknowledged it!"

"You know, Miss Esther gave me a white lace shawl that she wanted me to wear to Homecoming this year," Kayla said, encouraged by Mindy's positive response to her last statement. "But I'd like for you to have it. It's in the bottom drawer of my dresser if you'd like to get it. I'd really like to see how you look in it. I bet you'll look beautiful. I think Miss Esther might have been jealous of you because you're so pretty."

Mindy was quiet for a few agonizing seconds. "I think you might be right," Mindy said, considering Kayla's remarks. "And yes, I would like that shawl. Where did you say you have it?"

"It's in the bottom drawer of my dresser."

Kayla knew that Mindy would have to turn her back to the door to get the shawl; she also knew the bottom drawer stuck and it would take two hands to open it.

Mindy walked backwards to the dresser, keeping a close eye on Kayla. She knelt down on one knee and tried to open the drawer with her free hand. Just as Kayla had expected, Mindy couldn't get the drawer open with one hand.

She gave Kayla a quick glance, turned around, laid the scissors on the floor and started to pull the drawer open with both hands.

Just that quick Bill Tom ran into the room, kicked the scissors out of the way and grabbed Mindy by the arms. Randy ran into the room behind him and both men wrestled her to the floor and put handcuffs on her.

"You double-crossing little bitch," Mindy screamed at Kayla as Bill Tom and Randy pulled her to her feet.

"Don't talk to my daughter like that," Bill Tom said sternly. "You go on downstairs with Deputy James, Miss Arnold. You've got a lot of explaining to do."

Bill Tom wasted no time rushing to his daughter's bedside. Kayla hurled herself into his arms and began to sob uncontrollably.

"Oh, Daddy, I was so scared," she said. "Mindy told me she killed all those people and she was going to kill me, too and, oh, Daddy, she told me she pushed Mrs. Jen…Mom down the basement steps and…"

Bill Tom shook his head and held the girl tightly in his arms.

"Brook--your mom--is okay, Honey. Mindy just hit her with a beer bottle. She's got another bump on her head, but she's okay. Beach is downstairs with her now. Come on, I'll take you downstairs with me."

"Daddy I'm sorry I was so hateful to you and Bro--Mom-- in the hospital. I was just shocked, you know, and I felt betrayed."

"Don't worry about it, Sweetheart. Don't worry about that now. Everything will be okay."

Bill Tom gently lifted his daughter off the bed and carried her down to the living room where Beach was helping Brook hold a zip-lock bag full of ice on her head.

"Mindy told me you were dead," Kayla sobbed, as she wiggled out of Bill Tom's arms to get to Brook.

"I'm fine, Sweetheart. Really, I'm okay. Just a bump on the head. See?" Brook and Kayla held each other in a tight embrace.

"Looks like this nightmare is over," Bill Tom said.

At that moment they heard Trudy and Brian coming in the back door. Moonshine came in with them and made a beeline for the living room.

"What's going on in here?" Trudy asked, as she and Brian came into the room. "We just saw Randy drive off with Mindy Arnold in his car."

Trudy walked over to the couch where Brook and Kayla were sitting. She saw the blood running down Kayla's arm. "Brian, go get a washcloth--quickly! What in the world happened to you, sweet girl?"

"We found our strangler, Trudy," Bill Tom said, saving Kayla the trouble of an explanation. "It was Mindy Arnold. She paid us a visit this morning. She tried to kill Brook and Kayla. I don't know how she got in but…"

"She knows where we keep the spare key, Dad, remember? She watched Moonshine for us that weekend we went to Branson."

Bill Tom stared at his daughter and shook his head. "That was two years ago," he said. "The girl has a good memory. You'd think that somebody that smart would have parked their car where no one could see it if they intended to do harm to somebody. That's how we found out Mindy was here. Randy drove by and recognized her car."

"You mean that silver Camaro parked in front of your house?" Brian asked as he came back into the room with the washcloth. "That's not Mindy's car. It belongs to my friend, Greg Johnson. He's been having trouble with the motor and I told him I'd take a look at it today, but that he'd have to leave it here because I was going to stay by Kayla all day."

Everyone was silent for a moment and then Bill Tom shook his head and smiled. "Well, son," he said, "it looks like you saved my daughter's life for a second time."

Brian gave Bill Tom a broad smile. "Like I said before, Chief, it's a life worth saving."

Epilogue

She looked at the letter in her hand and placed it carefully on her desk by the window. Through the white lace curtains she could see the vast, perfectly tended hospital grounds and every day she watched the white-uniformed doctors and nurses come and go. From this vantage point in a chair by her desk, Mindy Arnold had watched the winter snows melt into spring flowers and summer shade trees turn into brilliant splashes of fall foliage. For five long years she had witnessed this perpetual process of nature.

At first the letters she received from her father were filled with remorse; mindless, rambling rhetoric saying that if he'd only known what was going on he would have stopped the abuse. He would have tried to give his little girl a better life. He would have divorced her mother sooner. During his visits with her he expressed the same sentiments and she willed herself to stare at him and muster up some tears to stream down her face for effect. He, and the "best minds to work with the criminally insane" that were supposedly assembled at Coffman-Whittier Sanitarium thought it was sadness that kept her from speaking; she knew it was hatred.

By the end of her first year of incarceration, her father's letters began to take on a different tone, filled with hometown news instead of heartfelt confessions. He'd given up seeking her forgiveness. So, although it turned her stomach to do it, she forced herself to read about the way everybody else was going ahead with their lives while she sat, day after day, in a white, starched hospital gown, which hid her awesome figure. Her only jewelry was a hospital band that listed her name, blood type and a warning not to leave her unguarded at any time.

She read about weddings and babies, graduations, anniversary celebrations, all the happy stuff that happens in normal lives. She forced herself to read all about it while she sat in her pristine room in her antiseptic prison and spent long hours talking to different psychiatrists about mindless issues.

She thought back to the day she was arrested and that dirty double crossing little bitch, Kayla Bradley, who tricked her into looking for a white shawl in a dresser drawer. The ultimate savvy player got played big-time by a spineless little wimp. She thought about the nightmare of a trial that followed, where her "friend" Kayla had shared in annoying detail, every confession that Mindy had made to her on that day in Kayla's bedroom. And mostly she thought about the thunderous applause from the crowded courtroom on the day the jury announced its final determination that Mindy Arnold was criminally insane and would be sent to the Coffman-Whittier

Sanitarium near Bloomington, Indiana, where she would live out the remainder of her life under lock and key.

But Mindy was a smart girl. She watched and waited. She learned the ropes and she kept her mouth shut. During the five years she had been at the sanitarium, she had seen people come and go-- other patients who had killed someone or were about to; some who were dangerous to others and some who were only dangerous to themselves. Her goal was to convince the "minds" that she was neither. That she was, after all, just a young, innocent victim of severe and ongoing child abuse, who had no other way to express her fear and anger than by hurting the people who had treated her so poorly.

Once in high school, which seemed like a hundred years ago, she had won a Drama Club award for her leading role in *The Diary of Anne Frank*. She was a good actor and she needed to use that ability to her advantage in this glistening white hell-hole where she lived.

This latest letter from her father was particularly annoying. Over the past five years she had read about the weddings of Chief Bradley and Brook Jennings, Mrs. Brinkmeyer and that huge, horse of a man, Walter Beacham. She'd read about Lester Tucker and the way he changed, from an insecure, mousy kind of a guy into a confident young man who enlisted in the United States Navy and was stationed near Washington, D.C. She read about Todd Mack and how he became a model student at MIZZOU, graduated with high honors and finished law school at Columbia University in New York. And her father even shared with her the happy news that both Breanna Stein and Jessica Freeman had graduated from the University of Miami and were pursuing their chosen professions as marine biologists somewhere north of Ft. Lauderdale.

She had taken all this news in stride. After reading the first letter with hometown news, she had torn it up in little shreds of paper. But when she saw how one of her "team associates" had looked at the pile of shredded paper, she decided she'd better spruce up her act. From that point on she read the letters, sometimes threw up in the bathroom, and then folded them neatly and kept them stacked in her desk drawer.

The only letter she read that made her happy was the one her father wrote stating that her mother had committed suicide with an overdose of sleeping pills at some motel in Kansas City. Mindy forced herself to cry over that one for the sake of the "minds;" but inside her heart was dancing.

But the letter that came today was the hardest one ever. As Mindy looked out over the hospital grounds she could see how the lush green trees of summer were once again gradually turning into vibrant splashes of autumn golds and reds. It had been a long time since that memorable autumn when she tried to even the score with all the people who had been mean to her.

She picked up the letter again and stared at her dad's handwriting. How could he think that news like this would make her happy? He even included the newspaper clipping! "Kayla Grace Bradley marries Brian Douglas Brinkmeyer."

The story was filled with accolades about those two goodie-goodies, how they both graduated from the University of Missouri with high honors; how Brian was going to work at Hillside High as a math teacher and a football coach; and how Kayla—with her fancy journalism degree—had landed a job as a reporter at the Hillside Herald.

Mindy was green with envy. She wanted to tear up the letter, stomp on it, spit on it, pee on it, and throw up on it, but from the corner of her eye she saw Dr. Lyons looking through the observation window into her room. She knew he was trying to assess her reaction.

She slowly picked up the letter and made herself read it again. Then, against every natural instinct in her body, she held the letter close to her heart and leaned her head back like she was sending a prayer of thanks to God. She kissed the letter, folded it and placed it, ever so gently, in her desk drawer with the others.

She waited until Dr. Lyons walked away from the observation window. Then she quickly made her way to the bathroom to throw up. The thought of their happiness made her sick with envy and filled her with a firm resolve.

Her brilliant plan was almost in place…just a few loose ends to tie up and she'd be ready to go. She'd had five long years to think about it, to go over every detail and finally it was time for action.

"I swear by all the saints in heaven that I will get out of here," Mindy whispered, as she once again sat in her chair by the window. "I'll get out of here and I'll get my revenge. But I'll have to make sure that I protect myself against the cruel people who may try to hurt me. There's a lot of sick people in this world!"

About the Author

Margie Lee Schlinker is a retired corporate public relations and communications manager living in St. Peters, Missouri. Today she is a freelance writer who spends the bulk of her time creating greeting cards with special verses for her clients.

Following her love for mysteries and her addiction to TV crime drama, Margie decided to create a mystery of her own. *Stranglehold* is the result of that decision.

She's already planning the story line for a sequel.

In her spare time, Margie teaches piano and guitar, volunteers in her church's card stamping ministry to raise money for the benevolence fund, loves to travel and enjoys entertaining friends and family in her home.

She loves animals, especially dogs and cats. At the end of the day, she enjoys relaxing with her cat, Oliver.

58446087R00280

Made in the USA
San Bernardino, CA
28 November 2017